I0762311

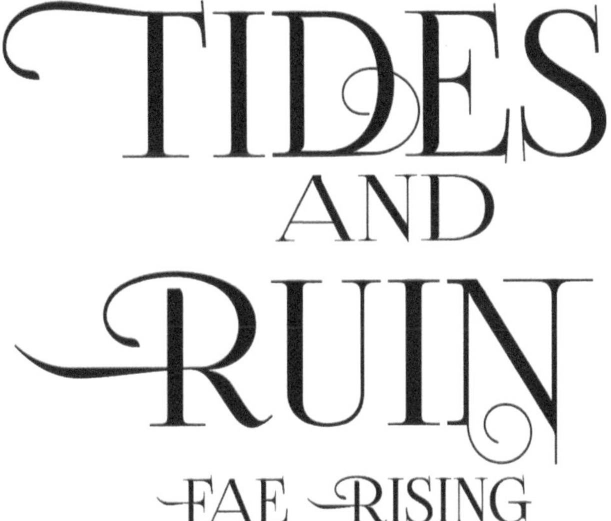

TIDES AND RUIN

FAE RISING

MIRANDA LYN

COPYRIGHT

Fae Rising

Cover Designer – Tairelei – www.facebook.com/Tairelei/
Copy Editor – Second Pass Editing
Art - Alrun art

CONTENT WARNING
Violence, Language, Sexual Situations

ALSO BY MIRANDA LYN

FAE RISING

DEDICATION

To women everywhere. You are enough.

ALEWYN
THE BOG
HE MISTS
WIND COURT
WESTERN GAP
DREGAN MOUNTAINS
EASTERN GAP
MAZE FOREST
TRESA
HYTHE
ROCSBREW
ERAST
MARSH COURT
HRUNDEL
NAGA RUINS
DUNES
FLAME COURT
SEA COURT

FLAME COURT
EFI'S AISLE
PRISONER'S AISLE
SEA CASTLE
THE SEA COURT

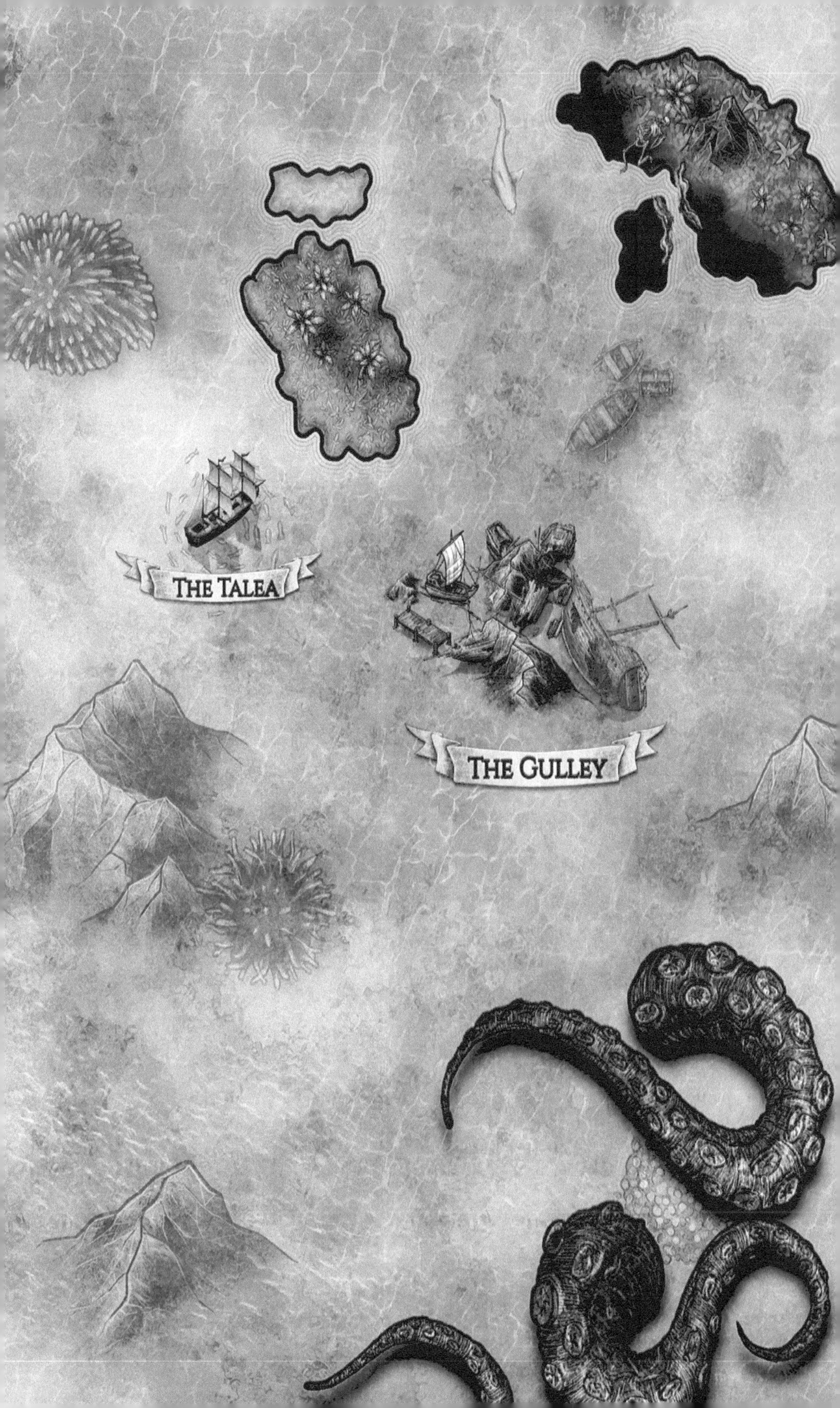
THE TALEA
THE GULLEY

PROLOGUE

KAITALEN

A *very long time ago…*

There was blood in the water. Far, far below me. The angry ocean moved as a draconian dancer, gracefully vicious and without apologies or permissions. Another victim claimed by the greatest villain of all. I sat atop a smooth rock cliff and watched below as a tiny prick of crimson melted into the cerulean blue of the sea, growing like a wave.

I was not a hero, only a boy. If Greeve were here, he'd dash into the water and save the poor soul. Or Fen. He would blast away the bad guys with his magic. Me? I could only sit here, biting my lip as I stared into the angry sea while it stole life from someone. Eyebrows drawn, I wondered if it was a damsel. Or a mom. Or a baby. I winced, closing my eyes to push that horrid thought from my mind.

I peeled them open and looked again, listening as the water crashed into the cove of cliff walls. An inky sensation crept over my skin as guilt sank into my empty belly like a giant boulder. Maybe I wasn't a hero and maybe I was afraid, but I still moved to my feet and inched toward the looming edge. The fresh saltwater air turned to static as the hair on my arms and the back of my neck stood straight up. Something strange, like a feeling of desperation, snaked around my body. But it was not my own. Then I heard it, traces of a whimper from within my mind. So faint, I might have missed it, had I not been holding my breath. Someone needed help.

Pushing the messy blond curls from my eyes, I sucked in three quick breaths and launched myself from the clifftop. Regret poured over me as that heavy boulder in my gut made me ten times heavier. The furious sea came racing toward me and I had to force my body to react. Narrowly making it into a diving position, I slammed into the bloodied water. I saw nothing at first but murky red, like a paintbrush dipped in a rinse cup. Kicking my feet, I surfaced only long enough to take a deep breath and plunge back in, pressing through as doom jolted me.

Help! Please, help me. The shrill sound of a young girl's voice was wrapped in frantic desperation in my mind.

I kicked harder and faster than I ever knew possible, becoming one with the saltwater. It flowed over my heated skin in a caress as I moved, giving me the sense my actions were not my own. As if someone had stolen my will. Still, I swam until I felt the ocean sand below my fingers.

This way, the voice pulled me. I darted to the left, concentrating on holding my breath, while swimming as rapidly as I could. After several long minutes below water, the instinct to gasp pushed into my mind. Nevertheless, I swam. Lungs burning. A hand, tiny and pure white, came into view, waving through the murky water. Invisible coils wrapped around me, jerking me forward. A small girl, sea fae, was wrapped in layers of knotted rope, cutting so deep into her long tentacles, the blood poured from her, staining the sea.

Shaking with uncontrollable fear, from the sea creature or the prospect of drowning, I wasn't sure; I pushed on, tangling fists into the coarse ropes as I tugged.

Something sharp! the girl screamed in my mind. Of course, she was right. I blindly ran my hands along the sandy bottom of the ocean, searching for anything to help the creature. I'd have to free her in order to free myself from the compelling power she used on me.

Moving my hands over a slimy creature as it slithered away, I cringed. Refusing to give myself the time to think about what I'd just touched, I continued until finding what I believed to be a serrated shell. My lungs burned. I'd die trying to save her.

Returning to the sea fae, I sawed the coarse ropes holding her down until, one by one, they let loose. The moment she was free, instead of shooting away from me, she sank to the seafloor. Turning to leave, that pull to save her faded from me. But I'd come this far. I reached my hands out to grab the stranger and drag her through the water to the surface. Gasping for air so rapidly, each breath was like swallowing a thousand shards of glass. My muscles ached. I coughed and choked and didn't think I'd ever take in enough air again.

I'd jumped from the cliffs without considering how to get out of the deep water with the girl. Searching for someone to help us, I contemplated screaming, but of course, no one came to the cliffs. We were tucked into a cove, the crashing waves far louder than my measly yell. I'd have to swim around, dragging her, though my muscles were protesting and heavy exhaustion weighed on my body.

Gritting my teeth, I settled the matter in my mind. I wouldn't leave her behind to save myself, and that was that. The tumbling waves shoved us dangerously close to the jagged rocks in the water.

I swam. Forever dragging that little sea fae behind me as I tried to be stronger than the swells of the furious sea. She squeezed my hand once as we moved, but other than that, she was lifeless. Going carefully around the cliffs and toward the sandy bank, I slowed, willing my feet to kick through the pain so I could reach land before I passed out. My heart pounded in my chest to the beat of a hollow drum. King Tolero must have told me a thousand times not to jump from the cliffs. He would skin me alive if he knew what I'd done. I wasn't about to die in the water and prove him right. My stubborn will alone would save me. *I am not just a boy*, I chanted into my mind. *I am a hero.*

That tiny hand slipped from mine twice and I had to turn back for her. I still wasn't at a point where my feet touched the bottom to walk. She was so light, so easy to pull, yet I couldn't hold on. She slipped away again. I turned back to get her, but she wasn't right behind me as she had been before. Pounding heart leaping into my throat, I dove in, searching for her. She was gone. As if she hadn't been there at all.

I searched for ages, trying to find that poor girl, but she disappeared. Vanished. Maybe I wasn't a hero after all and I'd imagined every detail. Or maybe she'd died anyway and slipped away to the Ether. I closed the final gap and crawled onto the red sands of the Flame Court beach. Placing my hands on my knees, I caught my breath. She was there; I knew she was. I jerked around to study the water, the waves, the ripples, anything.

Marching back to the castle, toes covered in gritty red sand and clothes dripping from head to toe, I winced when I noticed the cook.

Loti, with her silver hair and pressed apron, met my gaze, a hefty rolling pin in her hands as I approached. "And just where have you been, mister?"

"There was a—" I stopped myself. She wouldn't believe me.

"A what?" She whacked her hand with the rolling pin, meaning to be threatening, though she would never harm a hair on my head.

"I saw a treasure in the water so I swam out to investigate."

"Ah. And you didn't think to take your britches off?"

"No… I…"

She eyed me, scanning up and down my sopping wet mess. "And where's your treasure?"

"She—it disappeared." I dropped my eyes to my sandy toes as my ears burned with embarrassment.

"I see. Well, in you go. Best have a dry set of clothes on for dinner, Kaitalen."

I darted for the door. "Yes, Loti."

Late that night, with a full belly, warm in my oversized bed, I thought of the girl. I willed myself to remember what she looked like, though I couldn't quite get the picture right. Hadn't her hair been dark? I tossed and turned, struggling to hear her voice. Nothing. As if someone had plucked her from my memories. A soft breeze blew into my room at the castle, blowing the light fabric that framed the open balcony. The only sound for hours would be the endless waves of the ocean as they lulled me to sleep.

I woke before the sun as I felt drawn to the sea once more. Like a tether around my waist, she pulled me there, just like the day prior. Avoiding the kitchen, I ran straight for the water. Though I avoided the cliffs, I tossed my old boots to the side, shoving my socks into them and rolling up the cuffs of my pants. I stepped to the edge of the clear blue water, the foam from the waves tickling my toes as I stared. And waited.

The crescent moon hung low in the sky, surrounded by a million twinkling stars that stretched all the way to the horizon, their reflection showing across the water as if the world were a never-ending expanse of sea and sky. I could live here, I thought. The rich waters called to me, even now. Begging me to plunge headfirst and live a thousand lives below the surface. I could be a pirate, sailing the seas, plundering. Or a merfae, guarding Queen Morwena's grand castle of bones.

I swallowed hard. Not the last one. The sea queen was scary. Queen Efi had warned us to stay far, far away from her. Yet, here I was, on the edge of her kingdom, wondering why I shouldn't just dive in. I took a step closer, the water now lapping at my ankles.

Are you afraid of something? a girl's voice cut through the air.

"No." I spun in a circle, looking for the source. Nothing. "Where are you?"

A giggle erupted in my mind. *I'm in the water, of course.*

"Well, I'm not going in there." I jammed my hands into my pockets and stuck my chin out. "You can't make me this time."

I could if I wanted.

"You better not, 'cause I brought my sword and I'll chop you."

Another giggle. *No, you didn't.*

I started to walk away. "Just leave me alone."

"But I have a gift for you," she said in a sing-song voice, halting me.

"What kind of gift?" I asked slowly as I turned back toward her.

"You don't have to be afraid of the water, little boy. You can come in."

I shook my head. "No, thanks."

"I will make you a deal. You get in and I'll show myself."

I scrunched my nose, considering her offer. I wanted to remember what she looked like. "Maybe."

"You and I both know your heart, Kaitalen. You've always loved the water. Now, I have something from the sea to give you, but I'm not coming up there. Come down here to get it."

"Fine! But if I die, I'm going to haunt you from the Ether."

Another giggle. "Deal."

I peeled my night shirt off and stepped out of my pants, naked as the day I was born, then dove into the midnight water, shuddering as my small body acclimated to the chill. Catching a tiny, glowing light in the distance, I swam. I didn't know how, but I knew that's where I needed to go. Magic, I guess.

I followed the light until it grew bigger and bigger. Until it vanished, and a small girl, with jet black hair and tentacles for legs, smiled sweetly at me. "Hello, Kaitalen."

It's just Kai.

She stuck her bottom lip out. "Aw, but it's such a sweet name."

You can hear in my head?

She giggled, the balls of her cheeks turning pink. "It's a charm, see?" Holding out her hand, she showed me a bracelet I recognized from the day before.

I watched her black tentacles move like snakes through the water. *What are you?*

"Well, that's not a very nice question, now is it?" she asked, the calm smile melting from her face.

Where's my gift?

"If you're going to be a jerk about it, I'll keep it for myself. How about that?"

Okay, fine, I said, treading the water to keep myself from floating up. *But I will run out of breath soon.*

"No, you won't." She reached forward and touched my shoulder. Sinking to the bottom of the ocean, I'd lost the desire to gasp for air.

"What did you do?" I grabbed my throat, realizing I'd just talked underwater. My feet hit the ocean floor, a cloud of sand billowing where I'd landed.

"Relax. It's only temporary," she said, her hair moving around her as fluidly as the tentacles. "Two days. That's how long I was stuck in those dangerous ropes. I didn't think anyone would come to save me." The orneriness left her eyes as she remembered her own capture. "But you did and so you shall have a gift." She held her hand out, fist closed.

"What is it?" I took a step backward.

"It's my gift. Do you want it or not?"

I shrugged. "I guess, but if you turn me into a sea monster, I'll eat you."

"You are very annoying, I've decided. Just take the gift as my official thank you for saving me. I might have died. It's the least I could do." She dropped a translucent green rock into my hand.

I studied it, turning it over and back again. "A rock? I save your life, as you say, and you give me a rock?"

"It's sea glass." She laughed. "May it bring you more luck than it did me."

"Does it have power, like you do?"

She lifted a shoulder and rolled her eyes before vanishing. Losing the ability to speak and breathe underwater, I kicked off the seafloor and swam for the surface as frantically as I could while the echoes of that little girl's laughter trilled through my mind. I reached the beach, just as the blazing sun was lifting from the horizon.

You are a hero, I heard her whisper as I threw my discarded clothes on and bolted to the castle with the sea glass gripped in my hand.

Every day after that, no matter the weather, no matter the trouble I got myself into, if I could put my feet in the water for even a minute, I found peace. It was a great unknown, and I was an explorer of all things. That's what that little girl gave me. It wasn't the simple trinket I wore embedded into the ring on my hand, but it was the spark of my ever-growing obsession with the sea and everything hidden within its mysterious depths.

CHAPTER 1

LYRA

Many, many years later….

The salt of the sea was like a soothing balm to the crevices of my scales and the grooves between my bones. Deep-rooted in the ancient history of Alewyn, the ocean, no matter how vast, would always be home. Not a god, but a great entity, divining life and death along her tides and within the coldest, darkest parts of her. When I was a kip, just a baby siren, I only stole when necessary for survival or when my father told me to, but over time, the world honed me into a creature far more skilled and dangerous.

My target, an old ship, glided across the tumbling waters, the pirates aboard oblivious to my presence. I swam closer. High-pitched notes of a pocket flute lingered in the sea sprayed air as a limp flag tried and failed to blow in a breeze so faint, it could not lift a wisp of my waist-length hair. The ship's underbelly was covered in rigid crustaceans, and any sailor worth his salt knew this thing would sink within the year. The signs were obvious, the slow creak of the boards, the chipped paint on the bow. I might as well relieve them of the fortune they would lose to the sea.

My skin came alive as the huntress in me thirsted for her next treasure. Tightening the muscles in my core, I waited until the ship was in just the right position before I leaped from the water, my beautiful, dark purple tail transforming into fae legs, and landed on deck, sinking into the shadows. Grand entrances were fun, but this would be an in and out job. Stealthy and quick. Water dripping from my hair plinked onto the weathered floorboards. I ran my hands down the ends of the blonde locks, helping to alleviate the excess as it dripped down my simple shirt and riding leathers. At least I'd been wearing black the last time I was in my fae form.

Hidden, I memorized the scattered pattern of the rough crew, their motions as predictable as the tide. The patchy sails failed to push the ship at a respectable speed. Orders were shouted over strewn coils of rope while the lookout slept in the bird's nest, his limbs hanging over the edges of the wooden bucket high above me.

Today would not be a blood bath, though I might have preferred it to sneaking about. I pressed my back against the stacked barrels full of sloshing ale, contemplating the drip where a cork was haphazardly shoved in. Someone had been in the captain's lager, and I'd bet he had no idea. I stepped over the twisted ropes and kicked the cork with my foot until it shot out of the barrel, its contents spilling out onto the main deck.

As the crew came rushing in, I created enough of a distraction to sneak below deck. While most captain's quarters were above deck, Hollis was just the soft-of-heart male that would prefer to reside amongst his crew. The belly of the ship smelled of mold and vomit and I held my breath; the air settling on my tongue as I crept. The stores were in a final stage of rot and that meant only one thing: a desperate captain, dependent on selling his prized treasure. Something he'd saved and coveted for so long, he'd let his ship decay, worried only for that fortune. A rookie mistake, my father would say. I pressed into the spacious quarters, scanning the open room that resembled a small study.

"I knew you'd come."

A brown leather chair faced away from me. Hollis wasn't stupid. I hadn't been discreet while asking questions at the docks and word traveled fast through the Gulley.

"We can skip the small talk, Hollis. Either hand it over or I'll take this ship down."

The words hung between us as he inched around in his chair, leaning forward to rest his elbows on the desk covered in parchment and empty glass ink bottles. As always, his head-to-toe black leather and kohl-lined eyes complimented his dark locks. He was delectable.

"You'll pry it from my cold, dead hands first, Lyra."

I shrugged. "Who says they have to be cold? I don't have that kind of patience." Plopping into the seat across from him, I swung my boots onto the smothered desk, brown ale still dripping from the soles. My voice remained as neutral as my face. "Shall I sing you a song, Hollis?"

"Don't." He leaped from his chair, sending it crashing into the wall behind him. "There are forty fae on this ship, more than enough to take on a single siren." His gaze dipped to my chest for only a moment before he turned away from me again.

He couldn't resist me. None of them could. I was a siren of the sea. Crafted by the gods themselves to seduce a male with only a glance. They wanted me before they even knew me. Before they had time to learn how dangerous I could be. Perfect curves and sensual features, so irresistible, only the blind would not bow, and even then, I had my siren's song to lure them close. My long nails, as sharp as knives, clicked together as I waited for him to turn once more.

"You know you prefer to look at me, Hollis. If only for a moment." I brought my fingers to the buttons of my shirt with a half-smirk. "Shall I undress?"

He couldn't help the way he leaned toward me—how he licked his full lips, even though he didn't want to. I had morals. Boundaries. I would not take from someone that would not freely give. But I would pull that desire forward, enhance it, stroke it.

"Lyra, don't do this. You aren't this selfish. If you take the Eye,

Vexyr will send the others, as I've nothing to pay his tithe." He struggled to keep his strained voice steady.

"Turn," I purred.

His eyes glossed over as he faced me. Though my song was not as strong or long-lasting as Queen Morwena's enchantment, it was enough to seduce a simple fae. A wave of yearning poured over my body at the sheer thought of seducing Hollis. His perfect chocolate hair tucked behind his pointed ears, the shadow of a beard along his sharp jawline. I stood from my seat and moved closer to him. The smell of fear permeated the air as I moved a nail down the straps of leather crossing his chest and pressed myself against his body.

"We could play first, pet. If you'd like?"

"You would force me." He struggled against me. "You would let that control burrow. What right do you have to this power?"

Flaying my dangerous nails, I grinned. "By birth alone."

He made a guttural sound I couldn't make out. I stood on my toes and licked a soft trail from his neck to his earlobe. His knees buckled, and he landed hard on the cracked wood floor.

"What a good boy you are. Shall I reward you?"

He looked up. A plea embedded in his golden eyes. As he reached up to unfasten my pants, I stepped away.

"Tsk, tsk, Hollis. You must wine and dine a lady first. Go find me a glass of red, pet."

He released a raspy breath and jumped to his feet, rushing for the door. As soon as his eyes weren't on me, he halted, my power dissipating. His shoulders sank like an anchor to sea. "I thought we were friends, Lyra."

I sighed, shaking my head. "Friends are weakness in a cruel world. You'll do well to remember that."

He nodded and left the fetid room, defeated, without putting up a fight. That should have been so much harder. Another pirate and I might have thought him suspicious for conceding so easily, but perhaps he was just smarter than he looked. Hollis' days as a pirate were coming to an end and he must have already known that. He'd either move into the Gulley, though there was no dignity there and he was far too soft for that, or back to one of the three mainland courts to start a new life. His best option was probably settling down in the rolling hills of the Marsh Court.

I rubbed my hands together and circled the small room. Few things were out of place for a captain's quarters. Maps were pinned to the wall with worn edges, empty bottles, tomes of leather-bound books haphazardly stacked on a broken bookshelf. A small box with a blue jewel sat on a shelf. I opened it carefully, only to find a heavy metal compass. I chucked the compass behind me, but kept the box. It was pretty, and I was a collector. A painting on the wall across from me caught my eye and I couldn't bite back my smile as I pulled and it swung on its hinges, revealing an iron safe behind.

Coiling anticipation settled in my gut. Closing my eyes, I shut out the world as I turned the dial back and forth and all the way around until the vibrations in my hands assured me I'd entered the right combination. I opened the door with a click, and though it appeared empty, far in the back, on the bottom shelf sat Isla's Eye. A deep red ruby the size of my palm. I wasn't sure if I'd have sacrificed a ship for her, but Hollis and I were not the same.

I slipped the smooth jewel into my pocket and didn't bother shutting the safe behind me as I made my way to the exit. A calm sense of readiness poured through my veins as I placed my hand on the door and pulled it open, expecting exactly what I saw: the entire crew of forty, armed with weapons, and ready to take me out.

"And to think, I was going to let you keep your pockets full."

"Cover your ears," someone shouted.

"Too late." A melodic note burst from my lips as toned and clear as the first time I'd used my siren's call.

Jaws dropped; angry fists relaxed. Many of the seafarers inched toward me, infatuated, if only for a moment. I continued to sing as I shimmied through them, walking the deck as if I'd owned it. Plucking several coins from threadbare pockets on my way to the plank, I could nearly hear their hearts skip beats as I passed. Collecting more tiny treasure than I'd planned, I ended my song and waited for them to come back to reality just to see the startled looks on their faces before I leaped overboard and disappeared into the rolling wake of the dilapidated pirate ship.

CHAPTER 2

Leaving Hollis and his furious crew behind, I went straight to the Gulley. Though it would never be found on a map, it was a home of sorts for wayward pirates, fallen fae, and a plethora of other sea creatures who sought pleasure in shared misery.

Sitting on a wobbly stool, I stared out of the dust-caked window of my favorite tavern, watching the cloaked crowds move through the graveyard of sunken ships resurrected on iron stilts or propped on jagged rocks protruding from the ocean. The old ships were linked with questionable rope bridges, and I could always tell the newcomers versus the regular crowd by examining which bridges they trusted to walk down and how scared they were to fall into the midnight waters below. Lit only by swaying lanterns hung from the bows of the dilapidated vessels, above the doors, and from hanging ropes, the Gulley at night was never a place one should venture alone.

"Been a while, Lyra. What'll ya have?" Adair asked, thrumming her fingers on my table as she waited for my order. The wiry, green hair growing from her long, pointed ears twitched as another patron slid a chair across the floor.

"Same as always. I want the red, dry. And tell Merk if he waters it down, I'll empty his favorite hiding spot before he has time to move it. Again."

She shook her head to hide her crooked smile and walked away. She knew I wasn't joking though, and Merk, the stingy tavern owner, would be moving his diminutive stash of coins, anyway.

"This seat taken?" A gravelly voice broke through my thoughts as I studied the movement out the window once more.

"Yes," I mumbled, not bothering to look. Until the table shifted, and the foolish stranger sat down anyway. I turned in my seat, the death glare on my face unmistakable. "Trouble with your ears?"

The pirate soaked me in from the moment he could see me fully, his blue-gray eyes making a sweep up and down. Tight black curls framed his face, his broad shoulders and muscled arms giving him far too much confidence.

"None at all. Thought you should get a look before you cast off a good time." He twisted the evada pearl in his ear as he shared a handsome smile with me.

Rage, pure and searing hot, raced through my pulsing veins, so loud the world faded away as it flourished. I wound the rest of my body to face him, our knees touching. A gasp across the room brought the hushed tones of the others to an eerie silence as I rested my hands on the stranger's thighs, digging my long nails in until they pierced the leather he wore and his skin broke. His smile melted, face turning ashen as I held my chin high and hissed.

"Tell me, love. What was it that encouraged you to sit down? Was it the inviting look on my fucking face?" He shook frantically, looking down at my bloodied nails and back up to my eyes. "Then enlighten me, what was it, so I may be more direct next time."

I reached forward, grabbing his balls in my hands, the seam of his pants ripping. He howled, but no clear answer came from his trembling lips.

"In the future, when a female tells you no, do society a favor and listen. Because I can guarantee you, these," I squeezed tighter, "certainly aren't big enough to keep me company." I twisted and leaned forward until my face was inches from his. "No means no, understand?"

With a mug as red as the burning sun, he squeaked, "Yes."

Releasing him, he stumbled backward and out of the ship, running into Ori at the door. She took one look at him, and her head snapped to me. Her long, blue hair whipped across her face accompanying the glare.

"Dammit, Lyra. He was beautiful. What do you think this is? The Feral Boar?"

The room sprang back into motion as I shrugged, and she plopped down across from me. "He had a small dick. You're fine. And look, he bought you dinner." I slammed the coins I'd swiped from the creeper onto the table.

"Oh, goodie." She clapped and waved down Adair. "I'll have what she's having."

I drew my eyebrows together. "You hate red wine."

"I'm trying to broaden my horizons," the mermaid said, studying the coins she'd picked up. "We can't all steal our fortunes, Lyra. I have to settle down, eventually."

"Oh, right, and having a glass of red wine in the Gulley is going to bring all the good males forward." I looked out of the window again as Adair set our glasses down. "Just bring the whole bottle, would you? It's going to be a long night."

"Of course." She smiled, swiping the coins from Ori's hand. "Cook's got potatoes and scurry on the menu."

Ori scrunched her round face. "Scurry again?"

I kicked her under the table. "That'll be fine."

"Ow," she whined, leaning down to rub it. "What was that for?"

"I'm gathering info on a job, and I have it on good authority my next mark will be here tonight. I don't give a pixie's ass what's on the menu, that's what we're eating."

"Oh." She scooted toward me, whispering, "Who's the mark?"

"I don't know."

"Well." She pushed her hair over her shoulder, but it immediately fell forward again. "What are you stealing?"

"You know, Ori? You'd be the worst thief on the planet. Discretion is a virtue."

"Name one person in here that doesn't know you'd steal their last breath if only to make yours longer."

"That sounds like you're calling me selfish." I tapped my finger on my chin and scanned the room. "That guy."

Her head turned to the fae I pointed at in the back corner of the room. She laughed. "That guy hasn't moved in over a month. I'm pretty sure he's dead under that cloak and the single reason this place smells so dreadful."

"The single reason?" I snorted, wiping my finger along the rough tabletop, and showing her the grime. "I highly doubt that."

"Okay, but seriously, who's our mark?"

"*Our* mark is non-existent." I rolled my eyes and went back to watching the movement out of the window, half tempted to clean the dust with my hand.

Ori scooted closer, circling the top of her glass with her finger. "One time, that's all I ask. One single time I want to come with you."

Our food arrived steaming hot, but the sour smell of the scurry took over our table. Ori scooped it up, held it above her plate, and turned her spoon upside down, letting it slosh back into the muck. She audibly swallowed and forced a smile as Adair set the wine bottle between us. The waitress always kept her distance from me, as most people did. It'd been ages since I'd pickpocketed for no reason, but some reputations were hard to shake.

We ate in silence until the silver bell above the door peeled and Ori grumbled as her sister walked in.

"What is she doing here?" she asked under her breath.

Narina, not quite used to land legs, stumbled bow-legged to our table and sat down, ignoring Ori as she leaned into me, a conspiratorial look on her face. "I hoped I'd find you here."

"Why? Did you get lost on your way home?" Ori asked, scowling.

"The Gulley is not on anyone's way home, Ori. Mind your business."

"Okay," I said, laying my hand flat on the table. "I'm not doing this again with you two." I turned to Narina. "I think what she means to say"—I cut Ori a glance—"is what are you doing all the way out here? You're leagues away from the castle." I glanced down at her trembling legs and back to her innocent mermaid face.

She ran her fingers through her short, pink hair and smiled sheepishly. "Queen Morwena has a message for your father. You know how much I hate searching for his ship."

"Lie. You hate *him*. You'd rather walk the Gulley than deliver a message to Turrik," Ori scoffed. "Sounds like you."

A cloaked figure crossed through the glow of an orange lamp in the misty distance.

"I'd love to stay and chat, but I've got to go. Play nice." I turned to Narina, snatching the note from her fingers. "I'll make sure he gets the message."

I slipped out of the lifted ship and onto a trusted rope bridge before either of them could argue. Narina lived in the castle and attended court with the queen. Even though they were siblings, Ori hated her. They were both holding on to past transgressions and Narina had dug her tail into the sand, refusing to forgive. Or maybe she was just a bitch. I didn't care. I didn't have time for their squabbles.

I'd received another anonymous letter. The same sender as always, scripted in gold lettering, offering me a job; the payment always the item stolen. It was a challenge at first. Taking jobs that had nothing to do with my father. Fun even, as thieving usually was. But this was the first time the item was something other than a rare jewel or a treasure map. This time, it was personal, and I would not be keeping the recovered treasure.

The cloaked figure stepped onto a swaying walkway across from me. Most of the nefarious patrons of the Gulley were cloaked so, while he blended in, I had spent an exuberant amount of time memorizing the usuals. I was always looking for newcomers—the ones that never saw me coming until it was too late. And this one, in particular, had a sweeping tail. A trait he didn't think to hide as he carried a most coveted treasure. One I'd be happy to lift.

He turned sharply and moved in the opposite direction, likely checking to see if he'd gained a tail. Another one. I kept moving, knowing the bridge he'd have to go down next was weak and he'd end up turning around or plunging into the waters below. Passersby maintained a wide berth, but that was never personal here. I pushed my hood forward, hiding my face. More than once, I'd been stopped mid-hunt by a siren's admirer. There was a reason my kind had long since vanished.

As predicted, the target turned and came back my way. Just as he was passing by, I conveniently slipped on a loose plank and slammed right into him. *Damn.* His front pocket was empty. I allowed my hood to fall, showing my face.

"I'm so sorry. These bridges can be tricky."

"Indeed, they can be," he said, grabbing my arms to steady us as the rickety bridge swung from the momentum of my embellished clumsiness.

The instant his eyes met mine, I saw it. Not the fear of a siren, but the lust for one. Not everyone was smart, which worked in my favor.

"You're beautiful." His voice was low and raspy, sensual, actually.

He stood at least a head taller than I did, and though the bridge had steadied, his strong arms remained on mine.

"You can let go now, sir," I said, my voice sheepish as I batted my long lashes, sharing a genuine smile as he fell into my web.

"Oh, forgive me." He dropped his hands but stepped closer.

Gods, he was gorgeous. A strong jawline, pouty mouth, and dark lashes matched the brown hair and skin. My body responded to the way he parted his lips, a whisper of a smile upon them. Any other might have stood before him in fear, knowing what he'd done, but I'd dealt with bigger monsters than him my whole life. I lived with one.

"I forgive you," I answered, a lusty smile on my face as I held his gaze.

"Please, let me make it up to you."

I giggled, rubbing the abrasive fabric of his cloak between my fingers as I kept that sweet smile. "What did you have in mind?"

He glanced around us and bent down to mutter in my ear. "Something very shameful."

"I have no shame." I reached up and licked his beautiful lips. "None at all, in fact."

He cleared his throat. "I have a room."

"I thought you might." I winked, letting him take my hand and guide me through the Gulley, though I could have gotten us there faster.

Rigg's was the only place worth staying, and even that was questionable on most days. Still, as I pinned him to the door, my body pressed firmly against his, I didn't mind at all. A private room would only allow me precious time. I unpinned his cloak and dropped it to the rug-covered floor. It fell with ease, dust billowing from where it landed silently, indicating empty pockets. His eager hands were all over me within seconds, releasing buttons and pulling the shirt up. He held my breasts, kneading as he kissed my collar bone. I tilted my head, basking in the pleasure of his tongue on my neck. There was no need for this to be a quick job. Thank the gods.

He lifted and carried me across the room and to the freshly made bed. A small leather case shoved below a throw on the chair caught my eye. I knew he'd been here already, as he didn't stop and ask for his key, but I'd wager that was what I'd come for. Especially as he ripped his pants off and threw them against a wall, though I'd checked the pockets. I could use my siren's call to end this now, but as he continued undressing me, my adrenaline building, I didn't see a reason for it. I would get what I needed. As soon as I was done getting what I wanted.

Now naked, his perfectly muscled body hoisted above me, I continued to smile sweetly at him as I took his length in my hands. He groaned at the simple touch. The sound darting straight through me and into my siren's heart. Lust was a very specific language I spoke fluently and without pause or abandon. I lifted my hips from the bed, pushing his tip down my slit so he could feel just how wet I truly was. How easily this fae body could satisfy him. Again, he moaned, reaching to stroke between my legs. His kisses were calm and gentle. Far sweeter than anything I wanted. I bit his lip in return, licking the tinge of his metallic blood from my lips as he slammed into me.

"Faster," I sang, using my siren's call on him for the first time. Blissfully obeying, pleasure wracked my body as he moved in and out of me quicker than he'd likely moved in his life. "Harder," I panted, hardly able to breathe as he pushed for my gratification solely. Tip to hilt, over and over, until I was screaming with unbridled euphoria.

He pulled from me just as I exploded, planting his tongue between my legs while I trembled. I did not move away as he tasted me, building that tension once more. He was ravishing, slipping his fingers into me as he relentlessly stroked me as if it were a lock and he, the only fae alive, with the key.

I rode another wave of ecstasy, siren satisfied, the mark still drunk with lust and eager for his own release. I rolled him to the side and sang once more.

"Do not move, pet." I pulled my naked, satiated body from his and dressed as he watched me with hooded eyes.

Gorgeous, but not nearly the proper male I'd met on the bridge. I'd never pegged him for anything more than what he was though. A sick bastard.

I lifted the carefully placed throw from the only chair, revealing a cherry wood box, polished to a gleaming finish. His eyes doubled in size, though he was still under my spell.

"You might have fooled the world, sir. But a siren always knows."

I opened the box and my stomach lurched as I reached inside for the stolen siren's song. Captured in a glass jar, no less. I closed my eyes for only a moment, imagining what this poor soul must feel like, her power missing. Knowing that her entire existence sat in the hands of a sleazy male.

"Be grateful I didn't cut the dick from your body, just so you could begin to imagine what she felt when you took this from her. Instead, I will take something else from you. Stand."

He did as he was ordered, trembling as I took my hidden knife and cut the tail from his body. He might have been still, but the piercing scream of pain, followed by the deep red trail of blood running down his ass, gave me just the sense of justification I needed. It wasn't enough. It would never be.

I swept out of the rented room, lifting my hood, and falling back into the hall's shadows as the mark ran naked from the chamber, trying to catch me, a trail of blood following him as he screamed.

CHAPTER 3

Sharpened claws gripped my throat as I thought of Vexyr putting his hands on the recovered siren's song I now protected. With my father's tithe due, I had no choice but to see him, though I'd rather arm wrestle the Kraken. There were no safe places in the Gulley, no one I trusted more than myself, except perhaps my father, though undeserved, and he was halfway to the castle. As the night passed, I had no desire to remain here longer than necessary.

Keeping my cloak wrapped tightly around me, I slipped the small jar from my pocket, the orange glow from the stolen song hidden beneath the fabric. I could feel it. Hear the pulse of music within the tiny grains of magic. I shoved it between my breasts and kept walking because I was not the only skilled pickpocket around and I refused to be a victim of distraction as my bewildered mind reeled.

A mist from the sea slickened the ropes, spraying the wooden planks. The wind pushed and pulled, causing the maze of bridges to sway and the ships in the dock to test their anchors. Those ships, like the fae, were never meant to be dormant. The sea liked to remind the sailors of that from time to time.

Nighttime had settled over the Gulley, bringing the rows of elevated ships seemingly closer together, as the vilest of fae came out to play. The shifting crowds on the swinging bridges made them more dangerous by the minute, and the glowing lanterns and silver moon in the open sky never quite gave enough light.

I gripped the prickly ropes harder, maneuvering through the hoisted village, cautious but confident as the song pressing into my chest gave me a sharp sense of purpose. Stealing a siren's song must have taken an exorbitant amount of magic and a subdued siren. I'd only heard of such a thing happening one other time, as a kip. A bedtime story from my mother, laced with heavy words and vile warnings. Some I took to heart and others were fleeting. She was the only siren I'd known. The others remained in hiding. She was vicious by nature, a battle-ax of a female, though I'd never heard her use her song. Perhaps I was too free with my own, but a weapon was a weapon, and she was no longer here to judge me.

Thrumming music poured from every direction, causing me to sway. To feel it so deeply within my body rocked my core. Seducing me in all of its orchestrated chaos. I pushed my hood away, showing my face, so those near would keep a distance. My reputation preceded me, and it was always a blessing on a crowded night.

Vexyr's place was the easiest to find, sitting at the farthest end of the pirate's village. Polished with gleaming black paint and meticulous golden filigree embellishments, his ship sat intact with red sails down, meant to look as if it balanced between rigid stone peaks protruding from the ocean. He had two identical ships. His castle among the lowly peasants in this shit hole town, and the one he lorded over on the waters.

Gods help anyone that ever found Vex chasing their wake, though. It was impossible to get in or out of the Gulley without passing his place—unless you jumped into the patrolled water below. Which I'd done more times than I could count, preferring that over Vexyr's odious gawking.

As a siren, I lived for the inevitable lust of others, relished in it, but from him? This vile scoundrel that forced the sea to take a knee from a pirate with no title? Disgusting.

I climbed the steps to the deck of his hoisted ship and snarled at the stalwart guard until he shifted to the side, letting me pass.

"He's in a mood," the other guard with feathers down his arms warned under his breath.

"He's always in a mood," I hissed before shuffling through the half-dressed females, lazing about the ship like statues, meant to be worshiped.

They glared. There was no question who Vexyr coveted above all else or why. A skilled thief, able to influence the mind and walk on land or swim in water without charms or pearls because of my mixed heritage. I was a treasure he longed to collect, which made my coming here even more dangerous.

I crossed through the languid crowd lounging on the quarterdeck and cringed as I let myself into the captain's quarters, not at all surprised to see him alert and waiting for me, a disciplined guard standing just behind him. He was no fool. His henchmen had let him know I'd arrived the moment I was spotted in the Gulley.

"Lyra, my lovely. I wasn't expecting you." The broad-chested beast of a high fae sat casually in his oversized chair behind a barren desk. The jagged scar on his face gave explanation for his eye patch as it traveled down, distorting as a wicked smile spread.

"Lie," I answered, holding his gaze as I sat in the tall chair opposite him. "My father's tithe is due. I've come to pay as I always do."

He lifted a chained pocket watch from his leather vest and studied it as he ran a hand through his thick brown locks. Not to check the time, but to bring my attention to the iron key hanging from his neck, or perhaps the charm set into the ring he wore. The skeleton key gave him the unrivaled power to rule the seafarers like a god below the queen. Some said he was in her favor, others claimed he was so elusive she didn't know the Gulley even existed. Nor did she care to, most likely. I leaned forward, my siren longing to steal the key he taunted me with from his neck. The key that could open any treasure, they said. The key that every pirate wanted.

He smoothed a hand down his chest and placed the gold watch back into his pocket, patting his heart as he shifted and cupped his fists on the archaic desk between us. "I've forgotten the day, it seems. What have you brought me this time, lovely?"

I pulled Isla's Eye out of my pocket, the sizable ruby catching in the light from a flickering sconce mounted on the adjacent wall. Without a single command from his puppet master, the guard circled the desk, holding a silk pillow in his palm. Dropping the gem with no care, I bit back a smile as both fae flinched at my carelessness. As if that priceless stone would have shattered on the dusty rug covering the softwood planks of this ship.

The grandeur ritual for turning over stolen goods to a pirate lord was oddly appropriate for Vex and his lack of genuine propriety. He snapped his fingers and held his palm out for the guard, who promptly handed over the jewel along with a long-handled jeweler's loupe. Several moments passed as he examined the deep red gem, then nodded with a grunt and sent the guard from the room, taking my treasure with him.

Vex cleared his throat. I hadn't realized I was scowling at the door, my siren protesting the ease at which I handed over our stolen goods. I whipped back around; all traces of emotion removed from my face as I waited for permission to leave.

"As you know," he began, standing to gaze down at me. "It's my duty to look over the"—he paused, stroking his chin— "seafaring folk. It brings me no pleasure, I assure you, to take the items you find so dear." My mind flashed to the tiny jar pressed into my bosom, but I kept my face neutral as he continued. "If I'm not mistaken, that was Isla's Eye. A most valuable treasure, was it not?"

The smile he failed to hide turned my stomach. Vexyr was not an ugly fae. In fact, if not for his sour face and revolting nature, he was attractive. I'd fought my baser needs a time or two, knowing the moment I gave into him, he'd think he had some kind of claim over me. I would never be claimed. Never anchored down like my mother.

I held my tone flat, blinking slowly. "It was."

"It seems to me, I had a deal with Hollis to deliver that exact treasure in exchange for six months' tithe. I'm sure you can understand my confusion, as you have delivered the item with no such guarantee."

I shrugged, sinking back into the hard wooden chair. Whatever game he wanted to play; I wasn't interested. I flared the daggered nails on my hands, examining them as I swallowed my glare. "Hollis had trouble holding on to it."

"Undeniably, he did." He stepped around the desk, adjusting his vest as he moved behind me, gripping my shoulders with his massive hands.

Every ounce of me wanted to pull my song forward and take him to his knees, if not for that fucking charm on his finger. A tithe from a siren long ago, giving him immunity to the power of our songs. I imagine she gained a lifetime of freedom from him for such a gift. I clenched my teeth instead.

"The problem is, my lovely, Hollis was under my protection at the time of this trouble, which means you broke my law. Again."

He squeezed harder, and I sucked in a quick breath. His giant fingers dug into my burning skin. Anger, boiling low in my belly, rushed to the surface as he touched me without my permission. He was a male. They were disgusting creatures meant to be taken to their knees at the whim of a female. I swallowed the rage teetering on the brink of control. A siren was at the mercy of no male.

He'd never tried to punish me before, seduce me, yes, but never punish. I weighed my options. The small knife hidden below my waistband was inaccessible, and he knew it. I could take his heart. That was the single thing I'd held over him, but I couldn't fight a crowd of his men to escape and they'd be ready. They'd kill me before I could even get my mouth open to sing.

Vex had taken many private audiences with me, giving everyone else all kinds of erroneous ideas. They did not see me as a threat. His hands lowered onto my collarbone, brushing his coarse knuckles along my neck. I could only think of my safety as he got closer to the song tucked only inches from his disgusting fingers.

I'd have to play the game I was best at, the only tool left in my arsenal. I stood and faced him, planting a knee in the chair so I could be nearer, but hoping the high back would create enough of a barrier between us.

Pressing both of my palms against his chest, I pouted. "I thought of only you, Vex. His ship is going down. It's a wonder it still floats. He's been telling everyone of the deal you made him, and it was only a matter of time before someone else stole the Eye and didn't turn it over to you. If he didn't want to be a target, he shouldn't have made himself one with no regard for your desires." I paused, sliding my hands up mere inches, forcing back the recoil. "I thought I was doing you a favor."

His dark eyes raked my curvaceous body. I felt every bit of their movement. Studying the pattern of the stitching on his collar, I gritted my teeth as he let that moment hang between us.

"Well," he said, reaching to my face. "I suppose that changes things, doesn't it?"

Swallowing, I lifted my eyes to meet his. "I knew you'd understand. There are certain desires even I can't fight. The thought of someone else getting hold of that jewel wasn't an option."

"And what am I to tell Hollis, Lyra? That I do not keep my promise of protection? That I allowed a simple female to break my own law?" He licked his lips, moving in toward me.

Simple fucking female, my ass.

"Are you not Lord of the Sea? Are you not the maker and breaker of the rules? Do you answer to him?"

"Why do you play this game with me, siren? Give me one night. One night to worship your body as it should be." He moved the chair away with his boot, pulling my body flush to his own. "The things I could do to you."

I slipped away; desire still heavy on his face as I made my way toward the door. "You know what I am, Vex. My needs and wants are not my own most of the time. Besides, do you not enjoy your female audience on the deck? You've acquired such a gathering."

His hands turned into fists at his side. "Meer dalliances while I wait for you to come to your senses. I'm going to lose my patience with you,

Lyra. You are a treasure to be won and I am the king of treasure." He tapped his chest, indicating the key that swung from side to side as he stared at me.

"You are so free with your compliments it's a wonder the line outside your door is not longer." I pushed open the door and looked back at him. "Six months, then?"

"One," he barked.

"I've given you a treasure you'd traded six months' tithe for."

"One month and I won't send the brigade after your father's ship for breaking my laws."

Arguing would get me nowhere, and I was so close to my escape. I gripped the knob so hard I thought it would break. "One month, then."

"I'll be here, waiting."

As I stormed through the mass of nosey pirates on his ship, my mother's words rang through my mind. *Never sleep with a powerful fae unless you wish to be lorded over.* Vex fell right into that category. Though I wondered how thin I could wear his patience before he took our freedoms.

Vex was the only way to ensure safety on the ocean waves. If you paid him tithe, you were safe from looters and rival pirates. If you angered him or failed to pay, he would put a bounty on your ship and a bigger one on your fallen body. My father hated him; his ship, his only pride and joy.

He was the only male I worked for. It was the life I knew, and his boat was the last piece I had of my mother. At one time, I think he loved me. Until she died and he forgot how to love. I took over her role: treasure hunting while he spent his life mourning her loss, gathering secrets as plentiful as wealth for him to lock away in his secret room. Guarded with powerful wards, I'd never stepped foot inside.

I pulled out a short cord I'd swiped from Vexyr's deck and tied it around the bottle and then my neck. When I plunged into the sea, my body taking its true siren's form, I set off to the rendezvous point the last gilded letter had directed me toward.

The chilly depths of the ocean were dark, a near-impossible feat to navigate by sight alone. The hypersensitive scales along my body were a tool, if not a weapon, allowing any slight movement in the water to warn me of nearby danger. Fortunately, most fish stank. I also used that in my favor. I'd followed many currents of cool water pushing into the south, keeping my sharp eyes peeled for outlines and the shadows of landmarks I'd mapped over years of traveling with my father as he anchored through the ocean, sticking close to the southern coastline.

Though my father was a high fae from the Wind Court, he preferred the warmer climate of Flame Court—just not the people. Instead, he worked for Queen Morwena, delivering items she requested. I was his tool—the thief—and he, the faithful servant of an unforgiving queen.

The turquoise glow of a familiar reef appeared before me, its rigid texture and vibrant color a deep contrast to the smooth, sandy bottom of the sea. I darted to it, desperate to rid myself of the song. Unsure of how long it would be until I could expect a messenger to retrieve it, I circled the reef. Sitting idly in still waters always made me skittish. Anyone that respected the ocean and ventured her dark depths knew better than to let their guard down.

I kept close to the jagged walls of coral, their color matching the beautiful tones of the shallowest part of the ocean. My deep purple tail blended into it like a shadow. Though it was night, some creatures had no problems seeing prey in the dark. I didn't have to wait long until a sea fae approached, a golden band circling his bicep, his bottom half mere tentacles.

He searched the waters around us first before he stopped in front of me, crossing his arms over his chest. "My name is Arman. Our mutual acquaintance has sent me to retrieve an item." He held his hand out expectantly.

Narrowing my eyes, I studied him. He didn't flinch, though he waited before a siren. *Why?* I moved my fingers over the fibers of the cord at my neck as I pulled away from him. "Tell me who you work for."

"Even if I wanted to, I'm unable." He pointed toward the golden band on his arm.

Charmed. Damnit.

"Sirens are a rare breed. Why should I trust you with such a thing?"

Arman dipped his chin, as if he'd expected my response and held another letter out for me, scrawled on fabric, untainted below the water. The gold around the edges of the note was a match of the others I'd received.

Lyra,

Arman will deliver the song back to the siren who has lost her way. Your payment has been delivered to your room, unseen by your father. Until next time.

~A.T.

The letter was signed as they all had been. I lifted the necklace from my body and though it still felt wrong to hand a siren's song to a stranger, I did as I was instructed, if for no other reason than to rid myself of the heavy weight it carried. Though I couldn't escape the knowledge that someone knew how to steal a song from a siren. I should have asked Mr. Tailless more questions. He would be long gone by now but the question remained: who was he planning to deliver that specific item to in the Gulley? If it were Vexyr, he would have gone there first.

CHAPTER 4

Home. Though not exactly. There was a difference between living *on* the ocean and *in* it. Within the belly of a swaying ship, with water just out of your grasp, or submerged in the water, comforted by it, soothed by the motion of the great lulling sea. I'd taken my first steps on this ship. My mother said it had happened beneath the full moon. I'd swam far sooner than I'd walked, she'd added. Naturally. I was different. Unique.

"Sirens don't accept mating bonds nor do we take husbands," she'd said to me. "I am rare, as are you."

The thought of that siren's song brought back so many haunting memories of my mother as I walked the familiar planks of our ship, named by her. *Talea*. There were days when I'd close my eyes and the loss of her would strike anew. The only salve to that wound was showing the world how vicious I truly was. Taking whatever I wanted and apologizing to no one.

Cut from the same cloth as my mother, I didn't feel bad for the fae I injured, nor would I any. Males were used for pleasure and breeding. My mother, however, left everything about being a siren behind to grow old with my father. Though I don't recall them ever being overly affectionate, my father mourned every second of her loss, becoming a shell of the fae he once was. Nearly obsessed with her memory, he locked her journals and mysteries away into his warded room on his prized ship.

My father's ship was the largest I'd ever seen. A source of immense pride, but also the familiar tiered decks I'd grown up on. The sails were creamy white, but as they caught the light from the sun, if you were looking just right, you could see the threads of gold laced within. Great wooden masts erupted from the ship's decks, so wide at the base, I couldn't wrap my arms around them. We'd measured my growth as a kip by notches in the wood. I'd lived so many hours of my life on the quarterdeck, leaning over the carved railings and staring longingly into the tumultuous sea, dreaming of the cool saltwater.

I strolled through the halls below the ship until I reached my door. I thought about seeking out my father, but I just didn't have the desire. Not tonight. I couldn't bear to look at him, drowning in his own sorrow. The loss of my mother was tragic, even after all these years. She'd crafted me into the perfect thief, showing me when to be ruthless and when to be vulnerable, but I sometimes wondered if I was the only one that saw that side of her. She was the only other siren I'd ever known. There were memories of hers that she would let slip sometimes of others she had met, but it was up to her alone to teach me the way of our people. How to lure fae into a trap; how to obtain what I wanted by whatever means necessary.

My father had spent these last years—not searching for her unknown murderer—but desperately seeking a way to be closer to her. Clinging to her memories within her journals, wishing she could be by his side once more. He sickened me. Loving her more in death than life. Forgetting the world around him, especially me.

He was the planner, the procurer and curator of secrets. She had been the quiet executioner. We followed his direction, going where he told us, stealing what he desired. My mother and I were the tools to his craftsmanship. Amassing a great treasure, hidden away, so that one day we might leave the sea and live like royalty. Only one fortune had eluded him. The Kraken's. And one day, I thought we'd find that too. Until my mother died, and the world changed.

Turning the knob to my room, I looked over my shoulder to make sure none of the lessers on the ship had followed me. My father had acquired all males over the years, and I had to believe that wasn't a coincidence. As my mother spent her time teaching me how repulsive they were, it was easy enough to steer clear and see them for nothing more than what they were. Indebted workers. Given free food and board to keep the ship in pristine condition.

Reaching my hand below my pillow and finding something solid, I pulled out a palm sized blue stone and basked in my victory. It smelled of the messenger, which meant he'd been sneaky enough to get onto my father's ship. That was no small task. An ember of respect for the creature grew within me. Pushing my bed to the side, I rolled the rug over and raised a floorboard. After I sat and listened to the silent hall for several minutes, I lifted the trapdoor below and dropped the jewel into my secret stash. I'd been amassing quite a treasure thanks to A.T., and I reveled at the fact that my father, the king of gossip, had no idea.

Shoving everything into place, I stared out of the circular window in my dark room, into the ocean beyond. The great expanse was more than I could ever dream into existence. The memories hit me hard today. Without removing a single item of clothing, I leaned back onto my bed and fell asleep, dreaming of angry pirate lords and hands grabbing me from every direction. Of drowning and my body turning slowly to salt. I woke, shivering and drenched in sticky sweat.

After a bath, the sea minerals refreshing my mood, I changed and met my father at the table he requested set up every morning for breakfast on the main deck, while he called orders to the lesser fae we allowed to live with us as they saw to our needs.

"Finally," he drawled, hardly deeming to look up from the worn map in his hands. "How long has it been, Lyra? Two days? Three? I have need of you."

I swore he'd aged centuries since last I looked into his forlorn face, his loose hair blowing in the morning breeze, the slight curl matching my own; though his was black as stone and mine so blonde it could be silver in the right light.

"What am I to acquire this time, father? Will it be the moon? The stars?"

"Do not speak to me like your mother. I will not tolerate it."

I could argue. Had argued. A thousand times to pull him from his stupor. Nothing worked. He obsessed over one thing and one thing only. Something he'd never have. I had never considered my parents mated, but maybe his obsession was his way of avoiding The Mists. Perhaps they had been, and I'd never known. Never cared.

"Yes, father," I managed, taking a piece of dry bread from a lesser's waiting tray. "What are we after today?" And by 'we', I meant me, of course. "Narina came to the Gulley to let me know the queen was asking for you."

"Keys." He dropped his map, leaning forward to watch for my reaction. It was always his favorite part of this game we played. That and the victory. "Lichen sent a second messenger shortly after who was *not* afraid to approach me. He requires a ring of keys for our queen, and you'll need to venture to Halemi to get them."

"You're joking," I scoffed. "I'd rather fight the Kraken. Halemi is so droll."

A hint of a smile touched his eyes. I wasn't sure if it was because he agreed with me, or he loved to force me to do things I didn't want to do. It always seemed to be the latter.

"Bring the keys back to me and we shall deliver them together."

"No. I'll get the keys. I have no desire to visit the sea castle."

He pulled the map back up to cover his face. "You will accompany me."

Conversation over.

I grabbed the letter from the table and stormed off, not bothering to say goodbye as I leaped into the ocean, my purple tail scarcely making a splash as I swam toward the Flame Court. In this form, I kept a simple matching band of fabric tied around my chest, as was the fashion, though I would have preferred topless.

I think I hated my father. He never asked, only commanded, and as taught by my mother, I hardly said no. Even in death, I didn't want to disappoint her. But he showed no care for me at all. Only himself. Always himself. Perhaps that's where I gained my charming personality. Still, I did his bidding, if only to have a sense of identity and purpose in a world that cowered before me. As they should.

Flying through the comfort of the ocean, swimming so fast that the world passed me in a blur, was a thrill. It taxed the muscles in my body, always pushing harder, becoming swifter. The ocean was my healing balm, but it was also my playground. I darted through schools of leisurely fish, exploring the sea floor, moving through familiar shipwrecks and rainbow-colored reefs. I skimmed the top of the water heated by the sun, letting it tan my skin as I listened to the calls of the whales and the chittering of mating dolphins. Horny bastards.

Dodging and weaving, I avoided abandoned nets and camouflaged hooks attached to fishing lines. I explored discarded barrels from ships and lazed through the faster moving currents, letting them carry me along as I left all my troubles in the world behind and focused on my next mission.

A mark. I'd memorized the letter, building him in my mind as I went. A set of keys. What a long swim for something anyone could have stolen. There was more to the story for sure, but it wasn't my place to question. Especially the queen. Rumor had it she'd been spending a lot of time on land and away from her castle. Maybe it had finally caught up to her.

I neared the bay, swimming past the little isle the Elder King frequented. Mourning the loss of his fallen wife, just as my father did. If they weren't entirely different, I'd think they were the same fae. Both so consumed with loss, they'd forgotten to live. As if another soul was more important than their own.

Blinded by the scorching desert sun, I stepped out of the water, taking my fae form. I wrung the droplets of water from my hair and kicked the red sand from my boots as I took the long way, avoiding the castle and heading toward the city. The sun would dry it soon enough.

Halemi was busy, buzzing with news of the prince's return and his red-haired mate. After ten minutes of meandering, I knew enough of the local gossip to hold a conversation with a stranger. With city buildings as close together as could be, it was easy to hide among the small alleyways when needed. I swiped a cloak from a passing cart with a wobbly wheel and noted how unaware the southern kingdom was. No one seemed to care how close they came to a stranger; how free they were with their opinions. High fae and lesser fae carried conversations as if they were friends. Stepping into the Flame Court was akin to opening a book of someone's fantasy world. This was not the world I knew it to be. However, it was a pickpocket's dream. Which would come in handy once I found my mark.

I'd casually studied faces, knowing from the information provided, he'd be well built, carry himself well, dressed fashionably or in uniform, and I'd imagined he had a stern face, maybe a scar or two, though the description hadn't mentioned it.Avoiding the same gossip over and over, I soon picked up on other pieces of important information. Something my father would be very interested to know.

The Elder King had locked my queen in his dungeons. That explained why Lichen had sent the messenger. But it begged the question… Was I now aiding her escape?

A coup, they said. Though I could hardly believe it. Morwena was cunning, had been since birth—murdering her own parents to take control of the sea. Stealing her birthright and wearing her bloodied crown crooked and all. She was a legend. Conniving and calculated, brilliant and viscous. She was everything I strived to be, with a title attached. I never wished to lord over people, preferring my own life away from others. I thrived in seclusion, but she would always be an inspiration.

Spying a decent-looking tavern, with no broken windows or cracked walls, I dropped three coins onto the bar I'd swiped from the barmaid's loose apron as she'd passed.

"Wine. However I can get it."

I kept the hood around my face, but the tail of my braid still fell over my shoulder. I didn't belong here and most of them knew it. But several northerners walked the roads, so as long as I matched my father's harsh lilt of the Wind Court, no one would ask too many questions.

Served in a mug, rather than glass, the yellow-tinged wine sloshed as it was set before me. I peeked over the edge and eyed the barmaid. I'd never start a fight in the southern court. Aloof as they may be, any fae in the bar could likely kill me. Instead, I moved to the back and sipped my drink as I waited for information. And it didn't take long.

"Big as an ogre, I tell you."

"Nah, Rhan, don't go telling lies. She's only a flit of a girl but she dropped the giant yesterday. Fucker fell right on his back, and she leaped up on his belly. He laughed like nothing else as she took a bow and ran off. Quite the mate the prince has. Pretty little thing."

So, the faerie prince of the kingdom had found a worthy mate. Another valuable piece of information. I finished my drink and left the tavern, following the crowd toward the lists. As the cheering grew louder, I tried to rein in my excitement. Not for the show, but because I knew he'd be there. Maybe fighting, leaving his belongings in a discarded pile. Easy. So fucking easy.

The crowd seemed to part for a group of high fae walking in my direction, and I sank back into the masses as I laid eyes on the faerie prince. Not my target, but a tall draconian warrior kept to his right, oozing danger, dark and fierce. I looked to his other side and my jaw dropped as I recognized my mark. The commander. Though not scarred, his strong build was as I'd pictured, with messy blond curls falling over his face, covering one of his blue eyes, as his noticeable smile took my breath away. This was not the demeanor of an army commander, but I knew it was him. Without a doubt. Reaching into my pocket, I pulled out the crushed paper. His name scrolled across the top in rushed handwriting. The commander of the Flame Court army. *Kaitalen.*

CHAPTER 5

Not sexy. Just a mark. A pretty little mark that I could take to his knees with want for me. The siren in me stirred. More than that, she swam in circles, purring as she laid eyes on that gorgeous male, running his fingers through his hair as he laughed with his friends. He had no idea what was coming for him. My body moved before I could plan. I barely had time to lift my hood before I crashed into him, my hands swifter than his awareness. Pure toned muscles more solid than I'd been ready for. It was only a second, but a full lifetime, as we collided. He looked down at my face with no reaction, then turned back to his friends as he continued on his way, steadying me with his hands without giving a second look. Not one.

The undulating crowd moved around me as I stood there, astonished. He'd seen me and not stuttered. Hadn't gazed back. And worst of all, he'd blocked me from taking the keys from his belt without even realizing he'd outsmarted me. I couldn't… *What the fuck just happened*?

Pulsing dread melted over me and I struggled to swallow as invisible fingers gripped my throat. Something was wrong. I turned, grabbed a pudgy little lesser fae by the collar, and brought him close to my face.

His surprise transformed to desire, shoulders loosening and green eyes glazing over as he looked at me. Took me in. I shoved him away and stomped off, hiding within the confinements of a nearby alleyway, kicking the compacted red sand below my feet as I fumed.

He'd seen me. I knew he did. I peeked around the corner of the building just in case he was just slow in the head, and it was taking him time to process. A war injury maybe. But no, he'd been swallowed by the crowd as he and his comrades moved through the fae and into the famed Flame Court lists.

Pinching the bridge of my nose, I replayed the encounter and drafted a different plan in my mind. I swept back into the crowd, more confident this time. It was a fluke. He had been so distracted by the adoration around him, he hadn't really seen me. Taking down the hood of my stolen cloak, which was beginning to suffocate me in the heat, I unclasped it and swung the heavy fabric over my arm.

I was exposed. Far more than I cared to be, but as the eyes of the surrounding males, and some females, began to fall upon me, the familiarity brought me back down from disbelief. A stroke of luck on his part. That's all it was.

Approaching the lists, the fae along the stands made way for me as I passed through, hoping to get to the fence line where the three towering males stood. The lists, which was essentially a sand-packed arena, was a playground to the Flame Court. A place to train, to fight, to prove something to the rest of the world.

The lines of fae rumbled as someone with wine-colored hair and a lean body walked out into the training grounds below. A hush fell over the crowd, and I found myself as enthralled as the captivated audience. She studied a wall of weapons, opposing another female with long chestnut hair. The prince's mate and a sparring partner, it seemed. I squeezed up to the fence, several fae down from the group of males. The prince kept his eyes locked on his mate, a salacious look on his face as he watched them prepare.

The opposer turned for only a moment to look at the draconian at the prince's side. As she brushed her hair behind her ears, I noticed something was different about her. My eyesight was not as keen above water, but her *eyes*, I thought. They were feline. She stood with no weapons, waiting for the other to begin. I watched the one with red hair pull several wooden knives from the long wall of weapons. I needed to focus on the mark, but gods help me, I couldn't look away. She moved like a mermaid below water, each step a dance of enchantment as she fluttered through the arena, flicking weapons at her opponent, who seemed to disappear and reappear, dodging some and taking them at full force other times.

The crowd was still. Like a painting, like the last note of a song when the instruments stop, not daring to take a breath should it halt the show. I could steal from every person here and they would have no idea until the spell was broken and by then, I'd be long gone. Now would be the perfect time for me, if I hadn't been at the very front of the fence, all eyes fixed over my shoulder on the new future queen.

Still, I moved. Small steps to the side, acting as if I could not see over the fae in front. Closer and closer I lurked until the handsome commander was just out of reach. I turned again to the show, allowing myself to disappear to anyone that had watched me move. The prince's mate tumbled to the side, whacking the other with a knife in the chest so hard, the draconian beside my mark turned away. His eyes locked with mine. A breeze seemed to pick up and relax. His face gave away nothing as he looked back to the arena, then to me once more, then back, enthralled with the opponent, it seemed.

The commander leaned against the gate, his upper arms crossed along the top, creating a barrier so he couldn't see his belt line, which was perfect for me. I stood beside him now, and it only slightly pained me that he didn't notice.

Using the cloak as a cover, I slipped a hand beneath the commander's eye-line and grasped the dangling keys locked to his belt. The clip required barely a flick, and they were mine. But just as I locked my hand onto the ring of keys, the commander turned to shove the draconian and, once again, I lost my chance. Not only that, but as he turned, my arm twisted, and I went with him, putting me between the two males.

Turning first to the draconian, I pulled my song forward, whispering as I sang, "Look away." I was worried his kind would not fall prey to my magic. Draconians were a mysterious dark breed of fae that lived by their own laws. But his eyes glazed over as he did as I instructed. I turned back to the commander and lowered my dark lashes. "Forgive me," I said in a smoky tone. "I was just sliding by and seem to have been caught in your tussle."

Kaitalen looked down at me, his eyes meeting mine through his mess of blond curls. I reached up to place my hands on his chest when he said, "My bad," and stepped to the side so I could pass.

I stumbled backward and dropped my awkward hands. He moved away from me. Not toward. Away. What the actual fuck? I was a siren. I had one fucking job. I stepped closer, singing, "Look at my face," hoping only he could hear me.

But he didn't. He just swung his arm over the stupid draconian's shoulder, writing me off as he said something into his ear about a gale.

I stomped away from the sand-packed arena, absolutely stumped. I must've blinked a thousand times, wondering if that really happened. I'd failed. For the first time in my life, I hadn't acquired the treasure. I hadn't allured the mark, and he had no desire for me. None. I stormed through the city, a scream locked into my throat, as frustration took over for the confusion.

A male pulling a cart behind him stepped right into my path. I did the only thing I could think of.

"Stop," I commanded him, holding his eyes as my power so often needed. Stepping closer, I let his eyes rove over my body as I dropped the cloak. "Tell me, sir, do you have a female at home?" He shook his head fervently. "I'd never take from another female," I whispered as I circled him, stepping just out of his eyesight to be sure he was still interested. "Would you like to touch me?" I murmured into his ear from behind.

Again, he nodded, reaching for me. No ring.

"The gods must have blessed me." He grabbed my waist and pulled me flush against his towering body.

We stood in the middle of a road, fae passing us by without much of a second glance.

"What do you carry in your cart?" I asked, rubbing between his legs to confirm his desire.

He swallowed, trying to hide his precious nerves. "N-nothing. I've just delivered."

"Have you." Smiling, I pulled him around the wagon.

He was a bit less fit than my usual rendezvous, but he was attractive enough, with tanned skin, short brown hair, and dark eyes. The exact opposite of a certain commander. He would do.

I stepped into the back of the wagon, pulling the canvas material over the top. I didn't need the privacy. In fact, I'd have a glorious time letting him bend me over the cart, but I was hiding from a certain blond.

With absolutely no couth, giant fumbling fingers undressed me. Aggressive. I liked it.

"Will you make me purr, pet?" I asked, unbuttoning his pants, not bothering with his shirt. I didn't need a bare chest. Only something long and hard slamming into me, reminding me that I was still very much a desirable creature.

"Yes," he grunted, rubbing the slit between my legs as I lay back on the rough wooden slats of the cart.

"Taste me," I sang, tilting my head back as his mouth closed over me, his unpracticed tongue only hitting the mark occasionally. "Here," I pointed. "Lick me here until I scream to the gods."

He came at me with renewed purpose, but when I closed my eyes, there was blond hair and blue eyes staring back. I gasped, pulling away. He linked my legs with his arms and pulled me back to his mouth, doing only what I'd demanded. But it was wrong. It felt wrong. To have his hands on me.

"Stop," I commanded.

He submitted without pause. I dressed and though his eyes watched me, he said nothing as I jumped from the cart and strode back down the road.

I didn't let myself consider why something was changing. Why I hadn't enjoyed being worshiped and obeyed. Why I'd pictured the commander only moments after meeting him.

This day was entirely fucked. I wasn't, unfortunately, but the day was. All because a male seemed to have been wholly immune to me and I'd never encountered that in my life. If it was possible, I had a serious case of blue balls as I stomped my way back toward the sea. And that's exactly where I should have gone. Except I couldn't let it go. I couldn't. So, I spun on a heel and headed straight for the castle. The letter said he resided within. I needed to know more. I needed to know everything.

I walked through the gate and across the bailey as if I were meant to be there. In my fae form, with no evada pearl, there was no reason to suspect me of anything more than calling on someone within the castle. I'd learned if there were enough people and you acted like you belonged, more often than not, fae tended to take that at face value and not ask questions. That would get me into the castle, but likely not very far through it.

Stepping into the palace was odd. Full of so much color and life, though, I'd pictured something different. Dark and sad and full of mourning for the fae queen that died so long ago. Instead, it was opulent. Emerald greens and ruby reds splattered through the paintings and the furnishings in the entry. I looked around in amazement for only a moment, allowing myself a bit of curiosity before I tucked it all away and become a fae on a mission.

I walked with my head up through the halls, having no idea where I was going. When someone passed me, I simply mirrored their chin dip and kept strolling. Until I hit a dead end and had to turn, smacking into a servant with a long nose and calculating eyes. I called my song forward, wasting no time.

"Take me to Kaitalen's room."

Her eyes became heavy as she reached to touch my face. I let her.

Her desire only made the song more powerful. She'd have to look away and the song would lose its luster soon enough. Fortunately, his room was not too far from where I'd hit the dead end.

"Go away," I sang into the servant's ear as I let myself inside the commander's room.

CHAPTER 6

Males were repulsive creatures with no care in the world for personal hygiene. Heaping piles of clothes that smelled worse than a boneyard littered the commander's room. One wall was open to the elements, leading to a balcony with nothing but sheer curtains blowing in a slight breeze. Even that didn't deter the stench. I moved to the balcony, the desert sun warming my skin as I oriented myself. His room sat in the northeast corner of the castle on the third floor. I could scale the wall to let myself in for the job. Manageable, though not ideal.

I studied the array of weapons strewn about the room with fascination. I was nowhere near skilled enough to recognize the purpose of them all. Nothing like the prince's mate. Curved blades hung on the wall like art, and for some reason, it worked. I could see him here. He smiled. A lot. Which told me he didn't take life too seriously, though with his position I would gather he was more observant than he let on; that was far more dangerous for me.

There were no books in sight, but he did have a few flasks of heavy amber liquor. Though the rest of the room was absolutely disgusting, his bed was made, his closet was tidy, and there was a picture of a young female on the otherwise empty bedside table. I only glanced, but assumed it to be a lover.

Three soft knocks on the door gave me enough time to dart under the bed before it swung open. This was a castle. I'd never be able to use my song on the prince or the king and therefore, needed to keep my exposure to a minimum.

"Kai?" a feminine voice called out. "Oh, for goodness' sake. What have I told you about this mess, Kaitalen?"

I peeked from under the bed to watch a tall, slender fae gathering his clothing from the floor. She gagged and I smirked as she lifted the black and furry peel of a fruit from the floor.

"They do not pay me enough for this," she said as she dumped the pile into a basket, turned back to examine the rest of the strewn clothes, shook her head, and left.

I didn't blame her. Because, fucking gross. I rolled away, avoiding the black stain left behind from his discarded food. Opening the door a fraction, I waited until she disappeared around a corner. As if I was meant to be there, I swung it open before striding out of the castle without a second glance.

My queen was somewhere within, but I wouldn't be her rescue party. There was a difference between stealing the keys meant to free her and orchestrating a dungeon escape from the Elder King's castle. I crossed the bailey, unbraiding my hair as if I hadn't a care in Alewyn.

I'd discovered several things: the commander was a drinker, he didn't spend any time with the learned arts, and if needed, I could get to his rooms from the outside with the right rope and grappling hook. I had one on the ship, but I had no plans to return to my father empty-handed. Instead, I sought the tavern closest to the castle, marked it for tonight, then found an inn.

The Flame Court left my skin crawling with discomfort. High fae and lesser fae canoodling like equals. I much preferred the division in the sea. Merfolk, the high fae of the sea, with titles given to certain favorites, and everyone else, lesser. Servants. A proper caste of a proper society. Each with their place. My father, favored highly by our queen, preferred it the same as I did. My mother had no opinion, though she showed no problems having servants on our ship.

I saw myself to my room, turning down the aggressive passes from the inn keeper. His wife was unamused and, given any other circumstances, I might have taught him a lesson, but I had bigger issues than an unfaithful pig.

Peeling my clothing off, I sank into a cool bath, preferring chilly water to sweep the sweat and sand from my heated body. I could hold my fae form in the water if I wanted to, but I didn't see a need, so I let my tail drape over the edge of the deep bath, the purple scales catching the sun pouring in from the small window. Water, in any capacity, calmed me. Each drop that fell from the sky, poured into the ocean, all connected somehow, just as I was connected to it. I pulled my hand from the bath and let the dripping water from my fingertips fall into the basin, rippling in tiny circles. Like fate, one minuscule disturbance to the surface and everything around it changed.

I thought of the commander and leaned my head back against the cooled edge of the bath. I thought of the way his curls fell across his vision, the way he looked at me, though he hadn't seen me at all. I remembered his smile and the laugh that paused the world.

Gritting my teeth, I pushed it all away and focused solely on the keys at his belt. Two loops in, three iron keys. I groaned, remembering how I'd missed them in the first place. How careful I'd been, and then angry and careless. Not again. He was just a mark. Just another beautiful fae in a crowd of them.

Tearing myself from the bath, feet below me once more, my heart twinged a little as the water drained away. I'd need something different to wear for the evening, which meant visiting a neighboring room or two. Within minutes, I was behind the locked door to the adjacent room, trying on a questionable number. It was slightly big, and I'd be pulling the top up all night. I needed something more… secure. There were toiletries on the counter so I borrowed them, dropping them into a pocket before breaking into the next room, only to find a male bathing himself. He hadn't questioned his own locked door when I giggled and pretended I'd let myself into the wrong room. Tiny brains.

There was one final door, though I could hear the throes of passion from the hall. I pressed my back against the wall, steadying myself. It was one thing to be used to feet; it was quite another to remember my fin was gone. I hated that feeling. I stepped away, resolved to let myself into the room, taking what I needed and leaving without being caught. My song was just the backup plan.

The locked door was no issue. A hard turn to the right, pulling out on the spindle with enough pressure and a simple slip of a hairpin, I opened the door with ease. I could have used one of my long nails, but I preferred to keep them strong. I lifted slightly, hoping the sharp squeal of the hinges would be eased by the minor adjustment, though I wasn't sure they would have heard anything over the woman's wails. Whatever that male was doing to her was very, very good. Even my siren stirred as I entered the steamy room.

Heavily patterned carpet and over-worn furniture greeted me. As expected, boots and leather, and even some silky numbers were strewn about. A small hall led to the larger sitting room and then to the left the bedroom. Sauntering through the room, I plucked pieces of soft material from the floor until I'd acquired most of the female's clothing. Though less curvy than I, her light garment, typical for the Flame Court, would do nicely.

The moaning female paused as the male grunted. A sure sign the end was nigh. I dashed past the open doorway to the lover's bedroom and toward the exit, but froze as she called out. "Are those mine?"

Unsure if she was addressing the male or me, I rushed to the door, but the male came stumbling out. Floppy ears hanging and stark ass naked. No wonder she was so happy. His eyes burned for me the moment he let them wander. A swell of desire rose within, only because I'd just listened to what he could do to a female. Curiosity was such a salacious bitch. Especially as I stared down the lesser fae, his massive member standing at attention, but I had to put myself in check. Now was not the time.

I curled a finger, gesturing him forward. Sliding my hand over his chest, I leaned in and whispered, "Go back. You've not seen me. Only in your dreams, pet. But whatever you're doing to that female, do it longer and harder. Until she is so spent, she falls asleep on you. Then let her rest, feed her, and do it again. Worship her."

With his long dark hair and that infamous southern tanned skin, he stepped in, his eyes glossed over. "I could worship you as well. Join us."

I smiled and walked out the door. Of course, he could have. Maybe later. I sauntered down the hall and back to my room, feeling quite satisfied with myself. I stepped into the soft blue skirt. The material was nearly see-through, and the slit in the side came all the way to the waistband. The top covered only my breasts, though it had gossamer sleeves. I lined my eyes and tied half of my hair up, letting the rest of the silvery locks cascade down my back. I stared into the mirror, shifting from one foot to the other as I admired the curves of my figure. We would see how the commander responded now. And if he didn't stop in his tracks, falling over himself for me, then he was just not interested in the female variety. Love or not, that had never stopped them before.

Looking out of the circular window of my borrowed room, I watched the bustling travelers on the main road until the sun set. Pushing carts, guiding horses, laughing in groups, whispering in others; not a care in the world in the Flame Court. What lives they must all lead, so unaware of the rest of us, unafraid.

By nightfall, I thought enough time had passed that I could set my plan into motion. I followed the compacted red sand roads through the evening crowd, across the street to the tavern closest to King Tolero's palace.

A hundred eyes turned toward me as I slid my hood down and smiled sweetly, walking through the packed room to the back, pressing against the wall as I slipped into one of the few open tables left in the place. They stared, and I let them. Lust-filled eyes and rosy, heated cheeks as they all pictured what they wanted to do to me. What I could do to them. It was sad, really, their inability to hide that strong desire.

Longing that smothered the room like fog over still waters in the early morning. This was my power and also my curse, as I was learning.

He wasn't there. I put in my order with a stumbling barmaid and picked at the seam of my cloak as I waited. A ruckus began by the entrance of the bar, pulling the attention away from me long enough for a male to stumble into the seat across from mine, his hairy body blocking my view of the door.

"Yer new," he slurred, setting his mug of ale on the table, a languid smile slathered across his high fae face. Deep brown eyes stared back at me, waiting for mirrored adoration.

"You're inept." I scooted to the side of my chair, trying to see around him.

"Oh, I like them fancy words... Inept." He sat up straighter, smoothing his long beard as he smiled. An imaginary crown of pride atop his unwashed hair. "Indeed, I am." He turned to his buddies, watching from another table, and wiggled his eyebrows. "She says I'm inept."

They all roared with laughter as he beamed, leaning across the table to take my hand.

I smiled pleasantly, keeping my voice down. "It's not a compliment, you ogre. Go find someone else to bother."

His face dropped like I'd struck him, and he jerked my arm, pulling me to him. Anger rang through him as he pulled a knife from his belt and slipped it beneath my chin. I panicked for only a moment, knowing I'd have to use my song in this crowd, until his head slammed forward, crashing into the table between us. The commander stepped into view, though again his eyes were not on me.

"That's twice this week, Erb," he hissed into the fae's ear. "This time, don't bother coming back."

The male slumped to the floor, a small trail of blood dripping down a gash in his head. The commander scowled at his buddies, and they dragged the drunken fool through the tavern and out the door, apologizing as they went. I studied Kaitalen, his shoulders carefully rising and falling as he clearly tried to contain his anger.

"I'm sorry," he said as he kept his eyes on the door.

I could smell the bite of alcohol on him, hear its sway on his swollen tongue.

"It's not your fault." I kept my voice soft and alluring, though I didn't seem to matter.

He took a step, and I leaped from my seat, conveniently letting the cloak pool to the dirty floor, revealing the curves of my body. His sharp eyes swept over me once. Finally. But he hesitated.

I used that chance, tugging on his arm. "Let me buy you a drink. Please. For the trouble."

He turned to look at the draconian he'd arrived with, who nodded subtly, but the commander shook his head. "Not tonight, doll."

My heart skipped. The rejection from this male was infuriating, but there was desire in his eyes; a flicker of a slackened jaw. He was fighting it harder than I'd ever seen with remarkable self-control. Like he'd spent his life hiding his true feelings, it didn't faze him at all. I watched him walk away, affirming this would not be the end of this night as he slightly faltered walking to his seat.

I'd wait. All gods damned night if I had to. Even though he certainly did not have a ring of keys attached to his belt, they couldn't be far, and I had nothing but time. I sipped my wine and watched as one drunk after another stumbled out of the door. A few fights broke out and all of them ended with the commander taking charge. The male behind the bar kept his mug full, and I'd never once seen them exchange coin. A nod, a silent conversation maybe, but never payment.

In an effort to eavesdrop, I left my seat, sidling up to the bar and laying down two coins. While I waited for him to take my order, I stood as close to the commander as I could, knowing I'd placed myself, again, in his sights.

The draconian's back was to me as he kept his voice low. "It's not all bad. Having a mate is like finding yourself."

How poetic.

"I can't even look at a female right now," the commander grumbled.

Clearly.

"I don't want to be alone forever," his words slurred. "But I don't want to go through the shit you and Fen do, either. Are you happy?"

A dark chuckle filled the space as the draconian lifted his mug to his lips. "Never been happier."

Sliding that piece of information into my brain, I placed my order and moved back to my seat on the opposite side of the room. Fear of commitment was second nature.

I kept my eyes on another figure sitting a few tables from Kaitalen with his back to me. He'd picked three pockets since I'd been here, and though never completed well, the drunks hadn't noticed and he was slowly amassing quite a stash of coins, snatching a full satchel from the last patron. I had half a mind to steal them from him myself, just to show him how it was done, but I was more curious to see how observant the commander and his buddy were.

The draconian surveyed the remnants of the tavern, his eyes briefing over me before our stares met. He clenched his fists on the table and leaned in to whisper to the commander as he continued his study of the room. Kaitalen looked at me and grinned as he stood from his table. He passed the pick-pocketer, and to my astonishment, leaned into him, wishing him well, then stepped away, stumbling toward me once more. He'd actually done it. He'd lifted the stolen goods from the cloak draped over the back of the male's chair without him noticing. Sharing a thumbs up with his dark friend, who rolled his eyes, he plopped down next to me.

"I know a secret," he said by way of greeting, his words far less comprehensible than before.

"Do tell," I purred, casually sipping my wine.

"You have a cloak."

I nearly spat my drink at him. I swallowed, refraining from laughing as I said, "I'm sorry, what?"

"It's ungodly hot in the desert most of the time, yet you have a cloak. That is," he paused, squinting his eyes for the right word.

"Questionable?"

"Yes," he yelled, throwing a fist in the air in celebration. His eyes doubled in size. "You're pretty."

"Tha—"

"I'm pretty too," he beamed. "We could be pretty," he hunched over while whispering, though hardly anyone was left in the bar, "together."

I smiled. An actual smile, no guise required. The commander was clearly off duty for the night. I wouldn't say he was pretty, though. Perhaps children were pretty. Girls maybe. But not him. He was sex incarnate. A beast of a man whose voice reverberated directly to the clenched muscles between my thighs. I didn't just want his hidden key. I wanted all of him. Every hardened inch. *This* was the epitome of my siren's prowess. Not only a mark for the kingdom, but my own mark. I yearned to drag him below the sea and keep him for my own pleasure.

Leaning my chin on my hand, I patted the seat next to me. "Sit with me, pet."

He took a step back, face becoming serious as he looked at the chair. "I don't pay for sex."

"Good gods." I leaped up. "Does this look like a brothel to you?"

He grimaced, blinking rapidly as he examined the room, before turning back to me, confused. "This is Gillie's."

Circling the table, I leaned all the way down, gathering my cloak from the floor, the high slit in my skirt doing exactly what it was meant to do as my leg slipped free of the fabric on full display. I stepped inches from the commander's face so my words could not be mistaken.

"If this body was ever for sale, not even the Kraken's treasure could pay for it. My consent is my own, my body is my own, and believe me, Commander." I moved closer, his breath on my lips as I whispered, "I could fuck you four ways from yesterday and you'd never touch another female again in your life."

He pressed his forehead to mine. "You're pretty."

What a simple-minded fool. Still, I couldn't help my smile.

"I'm headed back, Kai. I trust you can find your way home?" The draconian stood at the door, no expression on his dark face, nor hidden behind those shadowy eyes.

Kai swung his heavy arm around me and looked back at the drac. "I don't pay for sex," he answered.

The draconian burst into laughter, the deep guffaw nearly causing me to join. I'd wager they had a bet about my occupation and, though the commander had won, he'd also lost. The last patron left, following the draconian.

We crossed the sticky floor and got as far as the door before the male behind the bar stopped us.

"Okay, Kai?" he asked, staring at me carefully, though in no way vulgar.

"Need help with the clean-up?" the commander asked.

"Not tonight, my boy," he answered. "Enjoy your evening."

"We're pretty," he replied, flicking a finger between us as he pulled me out the door.

I'd checked three of his four pockets as we walked. No keys. He stopped me in the middle of the street, pulling me to his chest as he tugged the clip from my hair, letting the half that was up fall down my back in waves. He pushed his hands into my hair, massaging my scalp with tender fingers as he leaned his head on mine.

In that moment, that one second, this wasn't a job. He was just looking at me. For me. A wisp of vulnerability ripped through me as he swept his hand behind my neck. I found myself moving to my tiptoes to let him kiss me. To let him ravage me. Except he didn't. He brushed a single soft kiss onto my lips and then looked only at my eyes as if he were trying to find the real version of me within their depths. As if he were searching for something he knew was in there.

"This is going to sound weird, but I think I can see where the sea and sky meet," he whispered. "In your eyes."

I lifted a brow, running a nail down his chest as I enraptured him. Similar to a coiled serpent, I waited for the perfect moment to strike. "What does that look like?"

He closed his eyes, drawing in a long breath. "It's like watching the water dance within the reflection of the sky." He jerked, stumbling away from me as if a spell had been cast and cleared. He shook his head, aware of the alcohol now coursing through his veins. "Don't get too excited. I am not the one for you or anyone else."

"I'm not the one for you either, pet. There are no commitments here. You can still take me home." A job. A mark. A key. That was all.

"Nah." He turned down the road and pulled me behind him, marching like a fool. "Let's find someplace else to go." His walls were back.

Thank the gods. "I've got a room," I offered, pointing to the inn we'd just passed.

He pivoted and continued his marching straight into the inn. It was the most childish, ridiculous thing, but I laughed anyway as I let him pull me along, giving him directions until we were standing alone in my room. He paused for only a moment, waiting for me to change my mind as his eyes burned into mine, my skin searing beneath his gaze. Reaching for him, I'd never come alive so fast in my life. His hands planted on both sides of the door, effectively caging me in. Hot kisses trailed my neck as he pressed his large body against mine.

"Wait," I panted. "I need a minute."

"Thirty seconds," he growled, struggling to step away.

I headed for the bathing room to remove the knife hidden under my waistband. I'd checked his last pocket to no avail and now I'd have to use my song on him. I needed to try again.

Stepping back into the room, my heart dropped as I found the commander face down on the bed, snoring, the liquor finally making its claim. I shoved him. He cracked an eye open, mumbled something illegible, bopped me on the nose, and fell back to sleep.

I shoved him again, rolling him to the side, but he'd passed out. Slapping his cheeks a few times, I let myself fume. Why did I even care?

It was time. I had to let my fascination with Kaitalen go and focus on the job. He wasn't moving for the night, and he didn't have the keys. Which meant they were probably in his empty room in the castle. Changing back into my regular pants and shirt, I swiped the coins he'd taken from the pickpocket, and I left that room for the final time. Maybe he didn't pay for sex, but he was paying for the room.

The city slumbered as I moved like a shadow through the night, the full moon my only companion until I reached the castle. I got within feet of the gate before a massive giant stepped into my path. Calling my song forward, I gained quick access, and an escort as I was let into the castle. He'd forgotten me by the time he turned away and I wondered if that was because of my song, or his soft mind. I knew the way to Kaitalen's room and wasted no time letting myself in.

It had been tidied, but I still searched everywhere. An expert thief, I'd leave no trace of having been here. Sliding my hand between the mattress, I found nothing. I checked every pocket and stacked box in his closet, and pulled out all his chest drawers, searching one by one. Then tried the bottoms and sides of every drawer for a hidden compartment. Gritting my teeth, I moved to the bathing room, but when I heard the door slam open, I froze.

My mouth went dry as my heart rattled. I was sneaky, quick, and quiet, but I was not a fighter. My father was confident I wouldn't need training because of my song, but if that were the prince or even the king, I was in trouble. So, I sank back into the shadows and willed my breath to move slowly in and out of my lungs. I'd lived hidden on a boat for three days once, completely undetected. I could do this.

I'd spent careful minutes combing the commander's room without a hint of detection. Whoever was in there now was hunting far more carelessly. The drawers crashed to the floor, a mirror broke, and sharp voices scolded each other quietly. One voice I recognized, though I would not reveal myself to him.

"If there isn't a key, then what?" Lichen asked.

A muffled voice answered, "She gets out tonight. The guards are handled. If not the commander's key, then someone else's."

"And how many keys do you think there are for the dungeons?" Lichen was annoyed, and the tone was well delivered.

"You live here, I don't. You play this game for her. You tell me."

The female was not amused with his attitude, though I couldn't say I blamed her. Probably one of the queen's selkies.

"I will only suffer this life until our queen is freed, and that smartass female is captured. Do not condemn me for a life I do not want. I've played my part for a long time."

"Nothing in the closet. Check under the bed and then we go," the female answered, ignoring him.

"You're not even going to check the bathroom?"

"If you think we need to, then be my guest, but when was the last time you hid something where the cleaning staff would be most thorough?"

Lichen huffed and within minutes, they were out of the room. He either didn't trust my father to secure the key, or I'd taken too long. That grated on my nerves more than anything. The mess they'd left behind was a disaster. I wondered if he would trace this chaos back to me, waking up alone in a hotel room. Oh well.

There was nothing else I could do if I didn't want to start searching the guards. As Lichen had said, the queen was getting out tonight one way or another. Finding the key was pointless now. So, I snuck out of the castle, having to use my power three times before I found my way back to my comfort zone. To the hypnotic ocean that called me into its swells with fluid fingers and its own siren's song.

My father was going to be furious.

CHAPTER 7

The smooth waves pushed over my deep purple tail, illuminating the silver flecks within the scales like the night sky. I glided through moonlit water, needing no landmarks to find my way. For a moment, I considered avoiding going home, unsure of how my father would react to my failure. I'd never let him down. Never failed a job. I could find treasure buried in the bottom of the ocean for years and haul it back. But this was more than that. The commander must have had a charm that resisted my song. But the only jewelry I'd noted was the ring with sea glass on his smallest finger. Sea glass would never hold magic powerful enough to resist it. *But it must have.*

Our ship was anchored where I'd left it, which didn't always happen. Sometimes, my father would move and leave it to me to find him. He'd used that trick to teach me how to navigate the ocean when I was a kip. The massive game of hide and seek my mother abhorred. It was the only time my father had shown pride in me. Perhaps that's why I'd become so good at it.

I climbed on board our giant ship. One of the largest in the south, for sure. His usual perch on the deck was empty, and I guessed he'd gone to bed hours ago. So, I went below, pausing for only a moment outside of his door before deciding the news of my failure could wait until the morning. Falling face-first onto my bed, I closed my eyes only long enough to yearn for the touch of the commander once more before I drifted off to sleep.

"Wake." My father stood above me, deep circles around his eyes as if he hadn't slept at all. I knew that look, though. He was fuming. "Where is it?"

I looked at his outstretched hand, then sat up, swallowing the lump in my throat. "I failed."

"Speak up," he yelled. "Surely, I've misheard you."

"I didn't get the key, Father. The commander was resistant to my song and the Flame Court was humming with the news of the queen's capture. I couldn't reveal myself to many or I would have created a lynch mob. She made them all leery of sea fae."

"You should have done what was needed, no matter the price. She will have my head now, and I have you to thank for that."

"At least then you can join my mother and stop all this wallowing," I snapped.

Hard fists tightened at his side as he glared. "Get out."

"You can't be serious."

"Get. Out. And don't come back here until you've changed your attitude. I don't need a failure on this ship. Failure breeds failure, and I'm not in a catching mood."

He stormed off; his disappointment not surprising me at all. I'd lived with it my whole life. A constant companion. I'd ached for my father's approval. I couldn't steal it. Couldn't draw it forward. More than rubies and gilded boxes. More than all the salt in the sea. It wasn't his love or adoration I craved, only his approval. I couldn't use my song on him; our shared blood prohibited that. Still, something buried deep within me wanted to plunge my fist into his chest and take his aching heart into my hands.

Although, perhaps then he'd see me.

I changed, considering where I'd go. There weren't many options. I could go to the mainland, but it made more sense to stay in the Gulley. It was just a few days. Only until this blew over.

I leaped silently into the water, plummeting straight to the seafloor, and settled below the ship long enough to steady my heart and to remind myself I still respected my father, though sometimes I didn't know why. Maybe I loved my mother and in that, I trusted my father by default. But I also hated him.

The Gulley was busy with patrons milling about the bridges. I swam to the long, floating docks, jumped out of the water, and landed in my fae form, dry as a bone. I ran my fingers through the tangled mess of my long blonde hair and tied it into a braid, pushing it behind me as I avoided the larger crowds and found my way to the inn. There was only one here and the last time I'd come, I'd left a tail in the waste bin like a discarded dinner.

I sent a message to Ori, letting her know I'd be staying a couple of days, and expected her to show up within the next few hours. She loved the idea of doing something dangerous, but she'd worked the docks, making questionable friends and even more dubious lovers since leaving castle life behind.

I crawled into the creaky bed; the springs screaming their age as I moved, kicking my boots off and pulling the stiff blanket up to my shoulders. The stench was dreadful, and I had to toss the dusty thing away. For a brief second, I considered leaving and heading to the Flame Court inn, if for no other reason than a comfortable room. Certainly not for a dreamy-eyed, mysterious commander.

As expected, Ori banged on my door within a few hours. "Wake up. We're going out."

I dropped my chin, eyes heavy as stared at her through the crack of the door. "Do I look like I want to go out?"

"You're a siren. You always look like you're ready to go out." She pushed herself in. "I'm not sitting in this smelly ass room. Let's go."

"Aren't you a ray of fucking sunshine?"

She twirled her hair with her finger, smiling. "If I spent my life moody and broody as you do, I'd be miserable. Like you. Now, get up."

I pulled the pillow over my face, instantly gagged, then tossed it across the room, dust flying as it landed in the dark and moldy corner. Ori laughed, pulling me by my hands until I was on my feet.

"Don't leave anything behind, Lyra. This place is disgusting. You can stay with me tonight."

"Tempting, but no. I like my space."

"Don't say I didn't offer," she said, curling her lip as she ran a finger down the wall.

"Where to?" I asked, pulling my cloak from the hook on the back of the door.

She laughed, putting her hood up. "Well, the Feral Boar doesn't sound very appealing, now does it? Merk's of course."

The small bell above the door rang as we entered, crossed the familiar tavern, and took our usual seats, surrounded by recognizable faces. Faces I'd never had a conversation with, but were always there. Adair didn't bother taking our order. She set two glasses of red down and waited. I placed three coins on the table and slid them toward her. She wordlessly gathered them and hustled away.

"What's her problem?" I asked, swallowing half my glass in one gulp.

"No idea." Ori shrugged, mirroring my commitment to inebriation.

"Next round's on me," she said as the bell above the door chimed and two larger males walked in, paying the rest of the room no mind. She shifted in her seat uncomfortably, covering her face. "Sweet baby boggarts, Lyra. Have you ever seen them before?"

"No," I answered, turning to look out the window.

"What is wrong with you?" She fluttered her hand in the air between us. "Do your… thing."

"I'm not seducing strangers tonight, Ori. I'm not in the mood."

She rested her hand on her chin and scowled. "I hate when you're in a mood."

"I failed a lift," I mumbled into my glass.

Her head fell off her hand as her eyes doubled in size. "You what?"

"I failed." I looked back out the foggy window.

"I didn't even know you could do that." She was trying to hide a smile. "Relax. People fail all the time. It's a shock to you, but the rest of us are used to it. It's not that big of a deal. What happened?"

"I don't know. Truly. There was a male and—"

"A male? I am shocked." She pressed her hand to her chest in mock dramatics. Then lowered her gaze. "There's always a male with you. It's how you function."

The two strangers from the table deigned to look our way and while Ori swiped her hair over her shoulder, smiling widely, I could only roll my eyes and glance away again.

"I'm going to get more drinks. You stay here and sulk. Be right back."

I raised my hand to call Adair, but she snatched it from the air. "No, I insist. My ass looks great today and I intend to show it off."

That pulled a smile from me as she stood and sauntered across the bar, commanding all eyes on her with the swing of her hips. She returned with four glasses of amber liquor on a tray.

"You're a terrible friend," I said, before lifting my glass and throwing it back as the two males joined us.

"Eager, I see," the male that slid in next to me said, jutting his broad chest forward.

"Hardly." I snorted, trying not to compare his blond locks to Kai's.

"Lyra," Ori snapped behind a forced smile as she lifted her glass to the others. "Cheers, boys."

She didn't waste a second, letting the alcohol burn as she threw her hand in the air and gestured to Adair, who promptly turned her back and ignored her.

"We know what my issue is tonight, but what's yours?" I asked as I eyed my friend. She never played the desperate card.

"Nothing. It's nothing." She scooted closer to the other male, running her finger along his forearm as she lowered her lashes. "What's your name, handsome?"

"I'm Kit. That there's Blan."

I scooted my chair back as I stood. "Okay. I'm definitely going to need more alcohol if we are hanging out with Blanket tonight."

Standing from the table, I lost my footing and swayed, tracers filling my vision. I snapped my head to Ori; but she was so busy entertaining her guests, she hadn't noticed. None of them had. Strange.

"You okay?" Adair asked, handing me two glasses of wine. Her eyes flashed to the table and back to me.

"What?" I asked, following her glance.

"You stumbled. You look flushed. Are you okay?" She pressed her hands on her hips, though didn't come closer.

"Of course," I snipped, walking back to the table, feeling light-headed. When was the last time I'd eaten?

I plopped down into my seat, the wine sloshing on the table. Kit hadn't looked at me. Neither of them had. I dropped my hand off the table and turned in my chair, the motion just enough to check his coat pocket. Empty. But something was strange.

"I think I'm going to head out."

"What's your trouble had?" Ori asked, tilting her head in slow motion.

"What?" I asked, though my tongue swelled in my mouth. I stood, my vision blurring. "I need..."

A hand wrapped around my wrist, and I jerked my arm away. My heart rate increased, panic taking over my senses before I could call my song forward.

"Don't touch her," I heard Ori say as the world went numb and then completely black.

There was nothing for so long. Only darkness as I slept. Until cold water caressed my face. Instinctively, I changed forms, though the voices were muffled, and still, I could not see. The sea pulled me, begging me to come alive, to break through the fog in my mind. Surrounded by the desperate ocean, an instinct deep within me brought my song to the numbness of my lips. I opened my mouth to force the power out. But a deep-searing pain caused the world to still and fall fast and far away.

Nothing would ever be the same again.

CHAPTER 8

Every porous groove in each of my bones ached as my quaking heartbeat rattled me awake. *Gods. Oh, gods.* I held back the scream in my fiery throat as I jolted, immediately aware of the greatest devastation of my life. I couldn't think. Couldn't process the absolute ruin as the world fell around me. Discarded in the back of some darkened cave, I urged my aching body from the seafloor, only to sink once more, my heartbreak overwhelming as my tail weighed me down.

Biting back a wail, I lunged, hauling myself up as I screamed, urging my body to cooperate. I swam desperately for the surface. The prickle of sunlight lacerated my eyes as I came out of the water and sobbed until my throat was raw and aching. Until my face burned from the tears that fell. The benefit of crying in the ocean was that it would never betray your tears. Salt for salt, we were the same.

My song. They'd taken my *song*.

My body was a foreign shell, my soul the only thing familiar as my throat threatened to close entirely, refusing to let me swallow the aching lump. Staring down at my trembling hands, I wondered what I was, if not a thief and not a siren. Though I still had my tail, the loss of my song felt like a missing body part. Like a severed limb on the inside. My father's hateful words rang truthfully in my ears. *Failure breeds failure*, and so it had.

A sadness unlike anything I'd ever known inched its way down me like a permanent weight, pulling me back to the bed of the ocean as my body refused to do anything but mourn. I felt the crack in my heart. Tiny at first, and then achingly growing as time slowed, and I lost all sense of self.

I dug through my memories, desperately trying to remember what had happened. Then I recalled Ori, and icy fear gripped me as I came alive once more and started moving, lost but desperate to find her.

South. I'd go south, following trails of warm currents, the smell of the desert sand baking in the heat, the ocean guiding me instinctively, as it did all creatures of the sea. Hours later, the sun faded beyond the western horizon and the Gulley came into view. Still defeated, a small part of me contemplated surrender. To turn my life over to Vexyr and let him protect me, as I was no longer able to protect myself. What did I have? Long nails and a pretty smile? What would that do in the grand scheme of things? Nothing. I was broken. Damaged beyond repair and, quite honestly, he probably wouldn't want me if he knew the truth.

I hauled myself onto the dock and let my fae form come forward, uninterested in the great show of transitioning just before I landed on the long, empty pier. No longer concerned with having a single set of eyes on me, judging me, as if they knew I was no longer the confident, powerful siren I'd once been. Still, they seemed to know. The eyes that watched me, the shoulder that slammed into mine as I walked along the rope bridges. The glares from the deck hands and shady pirates I'd seen a million times. I could have been walking this deck a naked fae, unattractive to even the lowest of lows. And what a terrible feeling that was. Perhaps my lack of confidence shed a new light on the world around me.

I stood outside of Vex's ship for only a moment before I turned away, unable to bring myself to do it. To say the words the world would eventually know. Unable to allow my heart to break any further as I begged him… I swallowed the churning bile in the back of my throat. I would not beg, no matter the circumstances.

Searching the docks for Ori, I checked her regular perch first where she ordered the ships in, and when she didn't turn up there, I went straight to the rented room she kept in a stationed ship. It was a home of sorts for shop workers and owners that didn't have rooms available among their wares.

I knocked three times on her door before it finally swung open. A half-dressed and half-asleep Ori answered, her evada pearl nearly the only thing intact. She froze, realizing who was knocking, then looked over her shoulder before stepping out of her room and whispering to me in the hall.

"What happened to you?"

I folded my arms over my chest. "You're asking me? The last thing I remember, we were at Merk's and the world was spinning. The next thing I know, I've woken up in the back of a cave in the middle of nowhere. I've got bruises all over. What the fuck happened, Ori?"

"Good gods, Lyra. I have no idea. I haven't seen you in four days. You were slurring your words and said you were going home and then you left, insisting we let you be alone."

I swallowed my gasp, noting the ringing in my ears as the world slowed. *Four days…*

A muffled grumble came from behind her door, and I eyed her as adrenaline rushed through me. "Who's in the room, Ori?"

She stumbled, an attempt to block me. "It's no one, just some guy I've been seeing on the docks."

I stormed past her, hoping to find one of the fuckers from that night so I could demand answers. I threw the door open so hard the handle punctured the inside wall. Hollis stood in the room wearing nothing but a look of sly contentment as my eyes swept over his naked body.

"What's the matter, love? Jealous that your friend doesn't have to use magical powers to take someone to bed?"

I turned back to Ori, but she only shrugged. "I thought you'd be mad."

"Why would I care if you're sleeping with the riffraff?" I slammed the door shut and stomped away.

She didn't bother following. Because why would she? We weren't really friends when it came to our personal lives. We went out. I fed her need for males' attention, and she fed mine for feminine companionship. I expected no less from her. Hollis was pissed I'd taken Isla's Eye. If he thought bedding Ori would become some form of revenge, he was sadly mistaken.

The creaking of the docks below my feet created a comfortable ambiance as I wandered the Gulley aimlessly, lifelong regrets biting at my heels. My mother had warned me about flaunting my power. I hadn't listened, and my entire life had changed in one single night, but I couldn't tell a soul. I'd been robbed, defaced, and the truth was my own burden as I tried and failed to formulate a plan. The inevitable would have to happen. I would have to go home and tell my father. If for no other reason than for him to help me get my song back. He was the collector of secrets and curator of knowledge. He probably already knew something, and if not, he'd know where to ask.

Wallowing as I wandered, when Vex stepped into my path, I almost ran right into him.

"Hello, my lovely. Where are you off to?" he asked, his tone light, playful even.

"I'm not in the mood to play your games today, Vex," I growled, stepping to the side to move around him.

He lunged sideways, blocking me again as he reached forward and rested a hand on my shoulder. "The sun is shining, the gulls are chirping, and it's such a still day on the water."

"Well, I'm not a pirate, so I don't really care how pissy the ocean is. I've got shit to do." I twisted my body so his hand fell from my shoulder. There was no point trying to walk away. He would only follow.

"Tell me what's happened, and I'll see it fixed." He pushed his finger under my chin and forced my eyes to meet his. I noted the twinkle and couldn't help but step backward. His happiness was jarring.

"My business is my own. I've got a mark to find. Now, if you wouldn't mind." I threw my hands on my hips and tapped a toe on the walk as I waited.

"I know what you're doing. Trying to keep me chasing you. You're worried I'll get bored once you finally cave, but worry not, my lovely. You'll always be the only one for me. I have a feeling you'll know that soon enough. One can only resist for so long."

"Oh, yes." I rolled my eyes. "I can feel my disdain wavering, even now."

He leaned in, a smile growing as he whispered, "Can you?"

"Nearly." Though I thought the deep-toned sarcasm evident, he dipped his chin and moved away, finally allowing me to pass.

For a moment, I pictured myself slashing into his chest. Ripping him to shreds for touching me. Destroying him as thoroughly as I felt ruined, consequences be damned. I pictured the life leaving the eyes that pinned me. That idea alone carried me away.

I hustled down the walk, jumped in the air, and transformed, diving straight to the bottom as I put as much distance between Vexyr and I as possible. The trip was shorter this time, each thrust of my tail toward our ship more dreadful than the last as I pushed on. Sorrow settled over me like a second skin, as if the word failure was painted across my face for the world to see—for my father to see before I even spoke a word.

I landed silently, taking in the vastness of the ship, the lack of wind through the air, the smell of salt and sea life. Following the shine of the planks down to the ship's lower deck, my eyes landed on my father. He stood with his back to me, studying my mother's journal, again. As if the first thousand times he'd flipped those pages hadn't been enough for him to feel close to her. Though not at all the same, that absence he felt was parallel to my own. The gold of his belt buckle scraped against his desk as he whipped around, my presence startling him. He clenched his teeth, his words careful as he spoke.

"My daughter. I trust you've replayed these last days in your mind enough times to understand why failure is unacceptable."

I stepped closer to him, pushing away the urge to kill him. "I've never once thought failure was acceptable. My mother taught me better than that."

"Indeed." He pulled the journal to his heart, a forlorn look passing over his features as something stroked his memory.

My next words were so hard to get out, they were like barbs on my tongue. My voice was barely audible. "I've lost my song."

A pause. An unbearably long pause that sucked the air from the world as I held my breath and waited for his response. He hung his head for a moment, and I clenched my teeth, balling my fists as I readied myself for the hateful words that were sure to follow.

"When was the last time you saw a siren?" His jaw ticked.

"I've never seen another, aside from mother."

"Sirens are rare and hard to find. A fool would have you believe Zariya exists. But you are not a fool, are you? To believe in a fabled city of sirens. Your mother knew it was a myth and so do you. Others are not so bright." He paused, tapping a finger to his chin. His voice was so quiet I stepped closer to hear him. "There's word on the wind that someone is collecting siren's songs. I should have warned you to be more careful; it must have slipped my mind." Something strange caressed his features. A flicker of hatred before his face became blank, his eyes as hard as steel. A look I'd seen a million times as a kip when he did business. When he scolded my mother. As if a light had been turned on below his skin. "I know more. A way to help, should I choose to do so."

Hope filled me as I willed myself to relax. "Do you mean it?"

He pulled away, turning his back again. "You will obey me as you've always done and when I decide it's time, I will tell you where the answer lies. Do you understand?"

I took a step toward my father, seeing only red. What a dreadful bastard he truly was. Using the loss of my song as an excuse to own me. Once again, the desire to kill settled beneath my skin. I'd been lenient for far too long, letting him dictate my world. With a crucial part of me missing, the only thing I wanted to do was destroy everything. Even this unbalanced relationship with the only other person I had.

He tapped his fingertips together and watched me carefully. "How many cities are there below the sea, girl?"

"None. The sea is vast with small colonies, but no cities."

"Why is that important information? Use your brain for once."

I'm positive my disdain matched his as we squared off. He so enjoyed pushing my buttons. "Hunting a species is more difficult when they are spread thin."

"Then learn your lesson, girl, and stay away from other fae. I am the only one you can trust now. You've put yourself in a compromising position often enough that someone finally wised up and took advantage. This is your fault, Lyra. I'll help you retrieve your song, but it won't be soon." Fueling my anger further, he pulled a letter from his pocket. "The queen has summoned us both. Now we must answer for your failure to do her bidding. She gave us several days, but since you've been… gone… we'll have to go in the morning. Leaving me no time to find a way around her wrath. You will make that up to me."

I clenched my jaw so hard I thought my teeth might crack. I'd lost my song. The single most useful power I had to do his bidding for years, and instead of getting it back—though he held information—we had to go see the queen. And after that? I opened my mouth to protest, but what could I say? I had failed him. And if this would be my punishment, then so be it.

Without a word, I walked down to the hull of the ship. I stuck my arms out and dragged my honed nails down the walls, leaving deep gashes as I rounded the corner and strode into my room. As a kip walking these halls, they'd seemed so large. A castle on the water, I'd thought. But now, they were closing in fast, and like the world itself, threatened to swallow me whole. I'd be his servant from now until he gave me the information he knew. I didn't consider my father to be a liar, but certainly manipulative. Didn't we have enough lesser fae slaving on this ship?

Shoved beneath my pillow was another gold-lined letter. I froze, checking the hall before shutting my door. How did my father not know? He collected information as thoroughly as his treasure. Still, I could no longer fulfill these orders. Without my song, I had no security blanket. Nothing to protect me should I be caught. I'd lost my entire identity in one night. I crumbled the letter without opening it and tossed it into the bottom of my closet. That life was behind me now and would be until my father agreed to help. I'd never learn a thing on my own. He'd see to that.

The next morning, we stood next to each other on the starboard bow. I could have said a million things, but only hatred would escape my lips and that would get us nowhere, so instead, I jumped into the water. He joined me a moment later, his evada pearl in his ear as he swam next to me.

He couldn't navigate under the sea, so it was up to me to guide him along, and I loved that single upper hand. His pearl made it possible for him to breathe underwater, to stand at the bottom of the ocean and speak, but it did not give him a tail or tentacles or fin. Over the years, I'd learned that was an incredibly rare trait.

The long night had turned my will to iron. I'd laid in my bed and remembered every lesson my mother had taught me about the wishes of males, and the only thing my father had done was prove her right. As I let the salt of the sea restore me, soothe my heart, and secure my doubts, I knew. I'd walked a fine line, letting my heart decide what was right and wrong. No longer. I was a siren, gifted to Alewyn by the gods to bring a male to his knees and revel in the power of a female. As I gripped my father's hand tighter, I pictured the world crumbling beneath me. I would drown this fucking world. If only to be the last one swimming.

CHAPTER 9

Nothing about Morwena's castle was warm or inviting, and that reminder of how ruthless the sea could be was just what I needed as we got close to the ivory bone-covered palace. I raced along the mineral-coated tentacles sculpted from ancient carcasses and waited for my father, who always swam the last league himself. He smiled as he approached, and I held my scowl.

Swimming the winding halls of the castle used to unsettle me. My mother and I were the only sirens to ever come to court and, though we were always greeted with fear, we held our chins high, our eyes sharp, and our nails sharper. I pictured her now as we moved toward Morwena's throne room, always a force to be reckoned with. I didn't understand then, but now I was learning. Now I was seeing the ways of the wicked world. The fire in my soul was akin to that of the queen before me.

I swept into the throne room as if I owned it, just as I had been taught. The sea fae filled the room in a rainbow of colors. They wore shells in their hair and pearls stuck to their faces. The only clothing to be seen were narrow strips of fabric covering the females' breasts. It seemed the bare-chested males, with hair, fins, and tails of all colors, all rose a little higher when I entered. The females cowered, pulling their lovers closer. As if I would take a paired fae from under their nose. As if these males were something to be desired.

My father stayed beside me; his face twisted into reverence as he beheld our queen. Bending low at the waist, his arm before him, he greeted the freed leviathan wrapped around her throne of bones and crustaceans. With her only in half sea fae form, the upper part still fae-like, she seemed even more menacing than usual. I swept a bow as well, though I didn't think she would see the gesture, anyway.

A selkie leaned over to whisper to her. Only then did she realize we'd walked in. The other idiots in this room were dumb enough to be fooled by her. She was so blind in this form she wouldn't see a Kraken, even if he struck her in the face. That's why she kept dry rooms. Because our sea queen preferred her land dweller form.

"Turrik," Morwena crooned. "Where have you been?"

"Caught between the reaper and the deep, my queen."

She held her composure as if she'd been expecting such an aloof answer. "You were to acquire the key to free me, and yet you failed. Explain."

"Easily done, Your Grace." He smiled as he swept the tails of his jacket behind him in the water, building the anticipation for a story he'd damn well rehearsed for a week. Hiding behind the clothing only *he* chose to wear in the sea, he began. "I'd heard your betrothed was having trouble in the Wind Court. As you know, I spent many years there. I sent a crew north to see if he needed a hand with his… uprising."

Morwena laughed. The room followed shortly after and I waited, a scowl on my hardened face, to be dismissed.

"The rebellion in the Wind Court." She laughed again. "That fool can never keep his fae in line." She shook her head, tightening her coils. "As you can see, I had no need for your key, anyway. Lichen was able to assist, so all is well. Please do come join my side, my poor selkies have missed you. I've got quite a treat for our guests today."

My heart dropped as I felt the lie in her words; the hunger in the selkies' gray eyes as they floated beside the queen's council on her dais. She was livid. I watched my father join her side, and I noticed the clench and release of his fists. His fear struck the water, the vibrations apparent to even the lesser fae as he moved closer. She would toy with her food, though. There was time, perhaps. If only I could think of how to save him. Not for the value of his life, but for the rescue of mine. I needed my song back. I needed to know whatever he did. And then he could rot.

The hunter in me wanted to coil around him, refuse to let her close, protect what was mine. But as I swam to a dark corner, hoping the others would somehow forget about my presence, I realized I might have to pull off the greatest heist ever. Stealing a fae from under the queen's nose.

I'd need a commotion, something to distract them all. I crept down the side of the room full of lingering sea fae, willing them to face forward as a mermaid dragged in an auburn-haired female. Her eyes swept the room until she was addressed by our queen.

"Something catch your attention?"

Only then did I realize she'd captured the prince's mate. Ara, they'd called her.

"Just wondering how you eat fish when you literally are one."

I tried desperately to hide the smile threatening to come forward. I didn't hate the sea queen. In fact, I respected her ruthless nature. She embodied what I strived to be. Commanding and merciless. I simply hated the idea of being below anyone.

"No matter," the queen answered, her blonde locks slithering in the water around her like serpents. "I've brought you here today because I've come to a rather disappointing conclusion."

Ara kept her tone bored. "It wasn't just a rash?"

Not an ounce of fear radiated off the prince's mate as she went head-to-head with Morwena. Even I couldn't help but smile at the suicidal comments she made, clearly unattached to her own life as she continued to anger the queen.

"You are insufferable, girl."

"We all need goals, Morweenie."

The queen grew upon her bony throne, rising to look further down at her nuisance. The crowd silenced. "King Autus will never stop hunting you. He's after the Wild Hunt and some damn door. I hoped that would keep him distracted, but alas, it has not."

Moving slowly, more concerned by the selkies carefully eyeing the space than the queen, , I sidled down a smooth stone wall until I was almost to the door in the back of the room. I'd have to move all the way to the front on the other side to get to my father, but so far, the mouthy high fae was proving to be a perfect distraction for me.

"Guess you should have kept your mouth shut about me. Then he wouldn't have known."

The entire room moved uncomfortably as we waited for our queen to rain down fury upon her. To shred her to pieces before she spoke another word. My own excitement at the impending murder grew. She'd deserve it for speaking to our queen that way. I'd seen her do far worse for a much smaller slight.

Instead, Morwena cackled and slumped back into her throne, which was potentially even more worrisome than an initial attack. She was playing with her prey, just as she would with my father.

"Oh yes, but you know how royalty can be. Always trying to show off the upper hand."

"Or fin," Ara retorted.

Her guile was admirable, if not incredibly stupid. As was now shown on Morwena's face. Say what you wanted about our queen; she would not tolerate someone making a fool of our kingdom. Her kingdom.

I made it past the door before a great boom reverberated through the castle and an unsettling feeling moved over the room.

Morwena's head snapped up. "What was that?"

Just the distraction I needed as I continued my path, the sea fae near me inching away as I advanced. Their fear fueled my determination. Morwena must have known what the sound was before the rest of us because she shouted for her guards. Obedient selkies moved with the merfae soldiers. I'd made it as far as a group of servants, listening to the persistent distress in the room before the queen flew from her chair and attacked the prince's mate, who had somehow freed herself from her chains.

Unable to move as the crowd backed toward the wall, I watched Morwena tighten her coils. I caught the movement of the prince out of the corner of my eye and smiled as I realized this was a much bigger coup than the queen had bargained for.

The hall doors slammed open and following closely behind the commander's draconian friend was perhaps the most shocking thing of all. A three-headed beast. The notorious hydra. Her eyes were as dark as the black sands of the Cliffs of Mar. Her three serpentine heads, all terrifyingly identical, were reminiscent of dragons. A myriad of colors, ranging from blue to silver scales, covered her body, giving a beautiful sheen, as if her skin hid diamonds beneath. Barely fitting into the room and trumping the queen leviathan's size, she held only one fae in her sight.

The surrounding servants whispered their surprise, convinced Morwena had staged the entire thing. They huddled in close, their chains rattling as they moved backward. I looked at the group of advisors floating, dumbstruck, as they watched the chaos ensue. The general crowd of merfolk observed with quiet confidence, unfazed. They'd spent too much time within the walls of this castle. Too much time forgetting the great dangers of the sea. And karma.

I thought we'd see the most epic battle the sea had ever known, but after only a pause of realization, my body smashed into the wall behind me as great magic rippled through the room and the castle walls started to crumble.

The sudden awareness of our queen's death flashed through the entire court, not just the room, as was the way when a sovereign died. The shrill sound of a chorus of mermaid screams echoed throughout as they swam toward each other, the room erupting into madness. I couldn't see my father at the dais anymore and as I moved to search for him, the doors slammed shut. The hydra dashed across the space. Rumored to have been the thing of Morwena's childhood nightmares, she'd told the world she'd slayed the beast, when clearly, she'd only royally pissed her off.

The room went utterly still, not even a blink as the hydra covered the body of the prince's brave mate. The draconian moved toward the prince and together they seemed to prepare for their own battle against the behemoth.

"She's mine," the prince growled as he stepped closer to the hydra, his muscles straining as he fought for control of himself as his mate was captured.

"She is of the world. She belongs to no one." The three heads answered in unison. "Take a step closer and I will have you for lunch. Only she will decide her companion. Not you or anyone else in this room." The hydra's heads snapped toward the dais, my father hidden in the mix as they moved toward a door. "No one leaves," she hissed as her great tentacles stretched around the perimeter of the room, pushing everyone closer to the center.

The group of selkies, Morwena's personal lackeys, hid behind the throne. Wary eyes met each other as we floated and waited while the hydra stared us all down. A flourishing knock on the doors caused the room to shift in uniform curiosity as the hydra moved enough for them to open and the most glorious sea god I'd ever laid eyes on swam into the ramshackle room like a golden savior. His blue pearlescent tail glimmered with laced tendrils of gold and only lent to the godliness as he whipped his blond locks from his face and cleared his throat. Only then did I realize. Only then did the world below me shift. *Kaitalen.* The closest thing I'd ever seen to the fallen god of the sea.

One of the hydra's heads turned in the direction of her captive, having a conversation too quiet to overhear. She motioned toward the draconian and let him within her coils as another one shut towering doors behind the commander. After a pause, the prince's mate was freed, and their group stormed to Lichen, screaming for an antidote.

So, the queen had not only captured the prince's mate, with Lichen's help, she'd poisoned someone important. Gauging by the face of the prince, I'd say it was likely his father. I guess if you messed with the

Flame Court, you'd eventually get burned, or eaten by a great sea creature, it seemed.

I swam only a bit farther, still stuck amongst the lesser fae bound in chains as Lichen, hidden at the front of the room, was killed and then promptly eaten. They'd finally realized he was a traitor living alongside them. Years and years of his life he'd give to our queen for the chance to live among us, to advise her as he'd hoped the Elder King would have once done. All for him to die before Morwena had allowed him the freedom of the sea.

The prince's mate addressed the crowd long enough to give the hydra permission to eat us all. Then, with little hesitation, the draconian swam forward, his muscles rippling as he looked ready to kill while grabbing Ara and vanishing into a trail of a million bubbles. The prince followed up her statement, appointing his commander in charge before he also vanished.

The scandalous sea fae in the room would have scattered, had it not been for the hydra's newfound control. She held her tentacles locked in place, blocking the exits as she seemed to grow larger than life.

After a quiet conversation with the hydra, Kai circled the room, analyzing what would be done now that the Flame Court's presumed princess essentially ruled the sea. The selkies from behind the throne began to move as one, latching onto their infamous spears.

The commander didn't so much as bat an eyelash in their direction. A subtle tilt of his head and the hydra was on them, devouring them all before they could pray to the gods for their twisted souls. They joined the queen in death as closely as they had followed her in life. A poetic and fitting ending to their lives. I'd never liked them. As a kip, they would stalk me in the castle halls when I'd come to court. They'd report anything I did to the queen and if I'd done something she didn't like, she'd call my mother forward, making sure everyone knew how much she disapproved of both of us. Which had never bothered my mother as much as it had me.

The sea vibrated with fear as the commander took his role and, within seconds, controlled the room. He continued his thorough observations and as he moved closer to me, panic gripped me by the shoulders. With my face flushed, I swallowed that voice inside that begged me to flee. There was nowhere to go, and I knew he would recognize me. He'd know instantly I was the one from that night and would assume I'd freed the queen. I was no longer worried about the trouble my father would find himself in. Instead, I focused on inching backward, attempting to blend into the chained lesser fae. Though as a siren, I hardly did at all.

"Why are these fae in chains?" he asked, pointing at the surrounding crowd.

The room was silent. Utterly still, as every sea fae remained loyal to our fallen queen and said nothing. A vein formed in the commander's neck as he turned, running his hand through his hair as the muscles in his back twitched with fury. Still, he did not raise his voice.

"My name is Kai. I am the commander of the Flame Court army, and it seems we are all going to spend a lot of time with each other. That works better if we aren't plotting each other's deaths. So, I will ask again, why are these fae in chains?"

"Forgive me, sir." One of the lessers at the front of my group swam forward, pulling the hat from his head, showing an oddly placed set of gills. "We wear these chains because we are slaves. To the crown for being born, what we are."

The commander swam closer to the male with dark hair and even darker eyes. He looked to the next and another as he shook his head, squinting. "What the fuck is this? Who can remove these chains? Who has the key?"

The room looked toward the group of advisors; my father included. One by one, they turned toward him. They would condemn him for not being one of them. Not officially, that is. He had wined and dined with the highest of this court on many occasions, but he still had two legs. Even so, as my father stepped forward and stared down the commander, my heart soared as he lifted his chin and growled. He would not bow to a land dweller, and neither would the rest of us.

Kaitalen moved so fast, it was like he had been born with that beautiful, powerful tail. He had my father by the throat in less than a second. "These fae are guilty of simply living. What is a lesser fae in the sea? Anyone other than a merfae? Unless the queen showed you favor? Disgusting. You will tell me where the key is, or I will use you as my next example. My king condemns none of you, but only as long as you cooperate." He held his voice calm, though his eyes were on fire. "Where the fuck is the key?"

Gasping, my father patted his chest. He'd held the key for the queen. Why didn't I know that? But like so many things, he was the procurer and curator of secrets. He also was not at court, so naturally, not an easy target. It made sense. In that moment, I was reminded that I hardly knew the fae that had raised me at all.

The commander threw my father to the floor, snapping the long chain he'd pulled from under his shirt. Shame flooded my father's face as his cold eyes met mine. I could all but hear him say the words. *Failure breeds failure.* He blamed me, even now, as if my failure had somehow created his. Defiance roared to life within me as he gritted his teeth and moved to stand.

I pulled away from the mass of lesser fae waiting to have their chains removed. I only managed far enough to bump into a familiar face with cropped pink hair.

"Come with me," Narina whispered, taking my hand and pulling me slowly down the wall and into another group.

Mermaids. I could blend in with them. Though curvier and far more vicious by nature, if I tucked my sharpened nails behind my back and held a dumb, forlorn look on my face, maybe I wouldn't be lumped in with my father. At least, that was the plan as Kaitalen began to section the room, the hydra at his side; the ultimate enforcer as he sorted through us.

He approached our group, and I avoided looking in his direction as he scanned us all. I was fucked. There was no way he was going to forget me. My hair blonder than his. My cheekbones more defined than those around me. Eyes that could melt a soul. Our history. That moment we'd shared in the street. One look and I'd be tossed out with the others. He'd know why I was there. He shifted to the mermaid next to me and I bit my tongue, waiting for the anchor to drop. But it never did. He looked me up and down one time without interest and then carried on to the next.

I clenched my jaw so tight my teeth ached. He hadn't noticed me. Not a gods damn hint of recognition in his eyes. And fuck me if I hadn't been staring deeply into them as he scanned my body like it was the same as all these fawning mermaids. He winked at the dark-haired female next to Narina and I had to swallow my utter annoyance.

The commander continued his careful evaluation of the room and started giving orders. Several moved forward to help him and I wondered what my father must have been thinking as he and Morwena's closest advisors were ushered out, the hydra uncomfortably close as they swam away.

Within the hour, Flame Court soldiers were swarming the room, reporting to the commander, and scouring the castle as everyone that actually belonged waited, huddled together for instruction. There would be a revolt, without question. Some of the merfae were already whispering. But as the hydra returned and loomed close, we could do nothing.

"You're all to find rooms for the night. Most of the west wing of this castle is intact. The east wing was not so fortunate. If your rooms were among those destroyed, you're to see …" The commander turned to the red haired merfae beside him. "Sorry, what was your name?"

"Jof, sir." The fae threw his hand up to salute the commander.

"Right. See Jof and he will help you find another room. You're not to leave the castle without my permission and there will be no exception to this rule."

Several angry sea fae looked scorned enough to murder him, and several more eager enough to fuck him. I was, unfortunately, a member of both parties. Because gods help me, that male was always meant to be an entity in this pulsing ocean. Though likely, she'd already laid claim over him as well.

"What's your plan?" Narina asked as we were dismissed.

"No plan. Going to find a room to commandeer and figure it out from there."

"You *could* sneak off if you wanted to," she said, her eyes glued to Kai.

Moving my hands through my hair and down my waist, I sighed. "Maybe."

I swam away, headed straight to the west wing of the castle to find something suitable. My mind became a single track with two goals. Free my father and get far away from this place.

The power Ara had within her was astronomical. The ceiling of the throne room was severely damaged with an intricate webbing of cracks threatening to bring it down due to the explosion of magic. But upon wandering the fallen castle, I found she'd left nothing unscathed. Jagged stretches of broken walls lined the hallways, those that still stood. Dust clouded the water so thoroughly it was like swimming through a thin sheet of mud.

Sweeping what seemed like a hundred rooms of the ramshackle castle under the guise of finding a new room, I searched and searched for my father. Kaitalen's presence, even when he was nowhere near me, was so uncomfortable it was like I could feel him behind every corner, see those eyes within every shadow. When I blinked, I could feel his hands on me, his fervent lips pressed to mine; and that was perhaps the biggest problem of all, especially without my song to protect me from his wrath.

CHAPTER 10

Scheduled patrols moved up and down the dilapidated hallways as others found their rooms. I slipped inside a locked room easily and rifled through a stranger's belongings. Finding nothing more than a handful of coins and an empty chest, I sat on the stiff bed, waiting for time to pass. For a plan to come to me because I would *not* be staying in this castle.

My father didn't deserve the effort it would take to help him escape. If I could find a way to recover my song without helping him, I would. But the easier answer was to help set him free, demanding the payment of my song for the act. I wondered if I could somehow con the commander into giving up Turrik's location. Though I'd rather kill him for leaving me wanting in my own rented room.

There wasn't an easy solution here. Not without the power I'd once had. I'd never known the freedom it provided me. How did normal people even live like this? I studied the pattern of bones lining the wall until there were more than a handful of silent minutes beyond my borrowed bedroom door. I pulled it open and, finding the curved hall dark and barren, slipped out and continued my hunt. Careful not to make a sound, I listened for hushed tones, feeling the simple vibrations of the water.

It became a job as the huntress emerged, seeking her treasure. Shadows called to me, comforted me, as I sank into them, avoiding the mixture of sea fae and Flame Court fae that patrolled the underwater castle. Tall ceilings and winding hallways were my only companion as I searched. Rounding a corner, I saw a glimpse of the hydra's tentacle turning in the distance. I darted forward, hoping to catch her scent, if not her direction. But she was fast, and three dead ends later, I gave up. Huffing, I turned and slammed into a wall of muscle.

"Looking for someone?" the commander asked, staring like he'd caught me naked.

I shot around him and placed my back against the closest door. "No. Just wasn't paying attention and passed my room."

"That's your room?" he asked, lifting an eyebrow.

"Yes." I scowled, sticking my nail in the locked door behind my rigid back.

He swam closer, a smirk on his face as he tilted his head to the side and studied me. He talked to me as if he'd known me forever, yet looked at me like he'd never seen me before. "You're sure?"

I heard the click and turned the knob, nearly falling into the stranger's space as the door swung open. "Home sweet home," I lied.

"A tour, then," he said, still smiling as he let himself in.

"Don't get your hopes up, land dweller. This isn't a dry room."

In fact, it wasn't much for a room at all, nearly the size of a closet with nothing more than a small bed and tall dresser shoved in a corner, though it didn't quite fit.

"Ah yes, the dry rooms. I wasn't expecting those in the sea castle."

"I'm surprised your brain is big enough for expectations." I spun around, hiding my face at the slip of the tongue.

He chuckled. "And yet here we are."

"Morwena preferred her fae form. The leviathan just didn't wear the crowns the same way. The dry rooms were for her pleasure, but also land-dwellers stayed here. It's not like the Sea Court is only made up of sea fae."

"Noted. But why do things not just float around here?"

I pinched my brow, unsure if I'd heard him correctly. "Uh. Magic? Have you never been to the Sea Court?"

Ignoring my question, he swiped a frame from the bedside table and turned it so I couldn't see, pretending to study it. "Who's this?"

I searched the room for clues, but there was nothing. I yanked the frame away, unable to glance at it before I had to answer. "That's my late great-grandmother and it's fragile."

"She was a looker." He beamed.

I set the frame down and cringed as I saw a fully bearded male standing in fae form on the starboard bow of a small ship raising a flask.

"And these? Also yours?" I whipped around to find him holding a massive pair of stained underpants he'd lifted from a chest of drawers. Must have been a land dweller.

"Nosy." I snatched them and stuffed them back inside, embarrassment pouring over me as I had to look away, my brain refusing to function at a normal level.

"These your teeth under the bed here?" he asked, hands where his thighs would have been as he searched below.

My soul left my body as I lunged to hide whatever he'd seen. He burst into laughter, and I realized he was joking. The dick. I jerked upright and jammed my hands across my chest. "Are you quite finished scouring my room for all the bad guys in this castle, land dweller?"

The smile faded from his face as his wall went back up. Walls were good. I could deal with walls. I arched an eyebrow.

He scowled. "Where have I seen you before?"

Fire erupted from my ears at his shocking admittance that he didn't recognize me. I'd suspected, of course. But to hear him say it, when I hadn't forgotten him for a second, infuriated me.

"How would I know? I certainly don't go gallivanting through the courts. I can hardly stand to be here."

He moved closer. "Then why are you here?"

"Am I being investigated for something, Commander?"

He swam closer still, his ocean blue eyes threatening to swallow me whole. "Should you be?"

Whatever had sparked between us in the Flame Court resurfaced as we faced each other, inches apart. The words my brain tried to form in retort turned to seaweed as I stared. I hated him for it. The only defense I had was to hide behind my power of seduction. But that was dangerous territory with this male.

I moved away, plucking a small skull from a shelf as I kept my back to him. "I've done nothing wrong. Will that be all?"

He followed me, pulling the skull from my hands and placing it back on the shelf. "Will you tell me if you're in trouble here? If someone's forcing you to be here against your will."

I flinched, unwilling to admit anything. "Don't jump to conclusions, Commander. The only one giving me trouble right now is you. *You* are forcing us all to be here. Or are you so simple minded you've forgotten?"

A second strike upon his face as he moved to the door.

"If I let these angry fae leave, they will go directly to our enemy and join his forces. We can't have that," he said pulling it open, his tail catching it from hitting the wall. He turned back as if he meant to say something else, but instead, he glared at me and swam away.

Whatever was between us, or wasn't, I think he felt it, too. He had to have recognized me, but he remained detached. Playing a role, I supposed. Still, I had zero interest in colluding with the commander. We did not stand on the same side of the line drawn in the sand. We were both here because we had to be. That was all it could ever be. Seducing him would only be a dangerous game.

After giving him several long minutes to disappear, I hunted the hallways once more, taking extra caution to avoid all interactions with the other fae. I'd keep that room for now. It would provide solitude more than anything, although the voices carrying through the walls from the room beside me were not ideal. Even on our ship, at least I had peace and quiet.

I tried to remap the maze of halls in my mind, remembering

where'd I'd been and what I'd known of Morwena's castle when it was still intact. I'd never quite realized how tall the ceilings were or how chaotic the halls were, some leading to absolutely nowhere. Just random paths with no purpose. Unless there was more to this castle than met the eye.

Two days passed as slow as sea grass growing on the ocean floor. No sooner had the Flame Court taken over than the commander had been called away. Word of the Elder King's death spread through the castle like blood in the water. Only those connected to the Flame Court cared, but I wondered in the commander's absence how this news affected him. That poison had come from Lichen's hands, working directly for the Sea Court, but I couldn't find it in myself to feel guilty for it. To blame anyone but Morwena and her betrothed, Autus, for their manipulative minds. Fae died all the time, and it had nothing to do with me. The only problem would be if the commander came back here with a score to settle. But after two days of searching for my father to no avail, it seemed he may not return at all.

By the third morning, the repairs had advanced to secure the structure of the castle, though who knew what would become of the Sea Court. I discovered Narina and her band of friends in the dining hall. Scattered tables of all sizes filled the room, each decorated with obnoxious amounts of flowers and pearls, swaying in the slight current of water. Morwena had an eye for all things beautiful and, though I found them a waste of perfectly good prizes, even I would admit they were pleasant. Green tendrils of floating seaweed hung from the vaulted ceilings; some plants so low they blocked the magical light in parts of the spacious room.

I hadn't bothered fraternizing with the others, convinced I'd be leaving soon, but as the time dragged on, curiosity got the best of me. My current company droned on about who would rule the sea and the sad state of things now that the Flame Court had stepped in. Within minutes, however, the conversation turned to the commander.

"Isn't he gorgeous?" the mermaid closest to Narina asked, fanning herself.

"I heard he's a beast in the bedroom," someone else said.

"How could anyone here possibly know that?" I mumbled, remembering him ass up on an inn bed, snoring contently.

She shrugged, taking a bite of her food. "Fae talk."

"Fae gossip," I countered, rolling my eyes.

"Draea said she saw him sneaking out of her friend's room this morning," she answered, watching me for a reaction she wouldn't get. "Can you blame him? He's been living above the surface for ages. I'm sure someone like you is just bummed he hadn't been able to find your room."

My head snapped to the side. "Someone like me?"

Narina bolted from her chair. "Chel don't."

"What?" the red-haired mermaid asked. "Surely a siren needs a male every night, or she shrivels up. I heard you rip their hearts out with those claws when you're done fucking them." She leaned in. "Is it true?"

"Sometimes," I answered lightly, grazing her neck with my nails. "Sometimes we do it before."

I left the table, letting them all eye my full body before I swam away, pride smothering the anger in my soul at the hateful taste of her words. I could have the commander if I wanted him. I didn't. And as far as I knew, he still hadn't returned, so he certainly hadn't been in a mermaid's bed last night.

Before I could leave the room, the guards filed in, the hydra on their tails and the demon himself behind, bare-chested and as gorgeous as ever. *So aggravating.*

"Morning." Kai cleared his throat, seeking attention he didn't get as the murmurs of the rest of sea fae drowned his voice out.

They did not respect him. The mermaids sat in awe, except for Narina. She leaned back in her chair, arms crossed over her chest as she looked over the newcomers with obvious skepticism. She tipped her head, a condescending smile upon her lips.

"Morning," he shouted, barely gaining a response again.

I had to stifle my laughter as the hydra tilted her heads back and screamed at the room to shut up. We would not go quietly into submission. At least that had remained the same.

"Today I will have a small interview with each of you and then you'll be sectioned off into teams to help around the castle. There are no more slaves. No more servants. If you don't help, I will find something else to occupy your time. This castle will remain in shambles and eventually decay, or you can build it into something you're proud of. Your choice.

"We don't have answers. The sea is vast, there are a lot of sea fae within it, and I'd like to go forth peacefully. That being said, my friend here," he pointed to the hydra, "will now hunt Autus supporters. Show of hands for all the windy lovers." He rose his hand and scanned the room. "No? Not one? Okay, then. I'll see you each one by one at my table."

He flashed that smile, and I could have sworn a mermaid fainted as he swam by and sat alone at the only round table with no decorations. He thrummed his hands along the tabletop until a line formed, the sea fae submitting. Perhaps we would go quietly.

I begrudgingly took my place in the line, waiting forever as it crept forward, full of fae with no desire to work, and no option not to. I couldn't wait to see what the mermaids would get stuck doing. With the hydra on patrol, it wasn't like anyone here was going anywhere. Though I had full intentions of finding a way to do just that.

My turn came. Several had stormed off after their heated conversations, but Kaitalen looked as calm as ever, a smile still plastered on his good-looking face. Wondering if that smile was his armor and his laughter his walls, I sighed heavily, unamused, as he gestured to the chair opposite him.

"I'm fine here."

His lips formed a thick line as he dragged his eyes over me. The room faded away, and that look felt like fingers roaming my body as they once had, pinning me against a door. My breath caught. He shrugged and looked down at his notes, clearing his throat.

"Whatever floats your boat. What are your skills?"

"Seduction." I tilted my head and lowered my lashes as I moved closer.

"Still working on that one, I see. Anything else?"

I'm confident my jaw hit the seafloor. It would always be a game of wits with this one. I flared my hand open, letting my nails show. "I can pick any lock, steal anything I want, and rip your heart out, Commander, so don't tempt me. Just put me wherever and leave me alone."

"Perfect." He didn't bother looking up. "Kitchens. Next!"

"Wait. What? I'm not a cook."

He folded his hands, looking at me as if I were a kip and not a full-grown siren. "Well, shoot. All the spots for common thief are taken. Surprising, I know. Find Leora, she will help you."

I jerked my arms to my hips. "I don't even know who that is."

"And yet you live in this castle." He finally met my eyes. "What does that say about you?"

I bit the inside of my cheek so hard I could taste blood. "That I'm not social. What happened to the queen's advisors? Surely they've earned kitchen duty."

"Not that it's any of your concern, but I have moved them to another location, so as not to… inspire revolt."

"Oh yes, we wouldn't want anyone *inspiring revolt*."

I swam away about as gracefully as the rest of the scorned court. This would not end well for the commander, and I couldn't wait to watch him fail. I knew where the kitchens were, but I had other shit to do. While the castle was busy with their newly appointed jobs, I searched for an exit in the maze of halls. Three lefts and a right from my stolen room, and I'd found another dead end. That was four I'd discovered. Frustrated, I whipped the dead-end wall with my tail. But rather than something solid, a hollowness echoed from within. A blessed, glorious hollowness.

I jerked my head over my shoulder, confirming I was alone, before rubbing my hands up and down the wall, looking for a lever of some kind. Finding nothing, I moved to the floor, searching for a pattern in the mounted shells. Still nothing. Desperate, I swam to the top, hunting for a hinge at the ceiling or a hint of light, but instead, I found a small impression in the corner. I pressed the indentation and waited as the wall rotated, giving me only seconds to slide in before it closed.

Blind due to the lack of light, I placed one hand along the wall, one in front of me, and swam. There were no sounds in my secret hallway, but that didn't matter as long as there were also no sea monsters. And while I wouldn't put it past Morwena to hoard them in hidden passageways, there was nothing to indicate I was anything but alone. The water was still, apart from my movements, and there was no scent beyond that of the usual sort.

Inch by inch, I made my way down as if swimming through an inky shadow. I let myself become distracted, trying to build a world around me in my mind. It was only a hallway. Ground below me, ceiling above. I focused on the steady beat of my heart as I glided; until one heart beats became two. I jerked to a stop. The thumping growing louder as someone drew near. I had seconds to find a way around a person I couldn't see, hoping they couldn't see me, either.

A sharp inhale from the stranger was all I needed to know where they were. I shot toward the ceiling, praying to the gods I didn't find spikes or even knock myself out moving too fast. The rapid heartbeat faded away, and I used that as a sign to get the hell out of there. Whoever was roaming the secret halls was just as afraid as I was. Only a fool would swim blindly in a castle crafted by a beautifully demented sea queen.

As I glided through the water, a welcoming light grew in the distance. Within minutes, I'd cleared the space and found myself at the opening of a cave. It seemed odd Morwena would not have this entrance guarded, but then she was dead, so maybe she had, and when the commander took over her army, they hadn't been forthcoming with that information. Which worked all the better for me as I bolted from the cave and navigated my way back to our ship.

Nothing had changed. Even the gold trim of the paint remained sparkling. The quartermaster paced the deck as the lesser fae cleaned what likely didn't need cleaning. How boring their lives must have been. I had no doubt my father had charged them with reporting any odd behavior from me, and if I freed him, they would do exactly that. So, rather than alerting them to my presence, I went to his study and shut the door quietly behind me. If he had information from an outside source about my song, it had to have come from somewhere. Unable to access his warded room, and unable to read whatever it was he locked away in my mother's journals, the only answer was a deep scouring of the rest of the ship.

Pulling the bottom drawer from his polished desk, I only found stacks of ledgers and years of debts he'd placed upon others for trading information. Not a single journal, no book of secrets here. He'd kept nothing but those scripted books, scrawled with her elegant handwriting. Everything else of hers was tossed to the sea in a fit of rage a month after she died. He'd never given me an explanation, and we'd never spoken of it since.

The desk was always the first place to look. I knew it and he did too, which was why there was nothing inside but those meaningless debts. What did he care if others learned who owed him? He was far too cunning to keep important names in there.

I moved to the bookshelves, pulling them each out one by one and flipping through, then replacing and repeating. A folded paper fell from one, but it was blank. I put it back where I found it. Skilled as he was, he'd likely planted certain things to see if someone had rummaged through his office. And though he could never be sure it was me, he would be free, and we were already on poor terms. Playing thief in my father's study felt familiar and foreign as I knew I couldn't use my song to turn away the lesser fae on the ship. They hardly had names to me, so there would be no doubt where their loyalties lay. To the man that offered them food and shelter.

I rolled the pristine rug from the floor and pried up loose floorboards. A box containing a few small trinkets I'd lifted was there, but nothing else. Putting everything back exactly as I'd found it, I left the study. I passed his room on the way to my own, but as the servants hustled around the ship, cleaning like my father would catch them napping, I ignored it for now, lifting my chin as I walked, my presence known to everyone on board.

I hated my room. It reminded me of everything I'd lost. My whole identity. I could stay. But I'd never free my father and get my song back if I did. He'd be at the mercy of the commander and his land-dwelling soldiers. That loss of control just didn't work for me. I showered, spending extra time to sort through the knots in my long hair. As I studied my naked body in the mirror, I wondered if the losing my song was more than that. If I'd somehow lost my siren's ability to enthrall males by looks alone. But I'd seen how the others gazed at me. Lust filled their eyes as they were pulled to me. It was only him. Just the commander who resisted. And it was infuriating.

I grabbed something simple from my closet and when the letter I hadn't bothered to open rolled forward, I knelt to pick it up. The gold on the envelope assured me it was another job I couldn't do right now, but curiosity got the better of me as I opened it and pulled out two pieces of crumbled paper.

Lyra,

Trust no one. Even those close to you. I've included something valuable.

~A.T.

The clear warning on the paper caused my mind to race as I tried to remember whether I'd gotten the letter before or after someone stole my song. I flipped to the second page and nearly dropped the message. Scrolled in the most beautiful handwriting was a journal entry. My mother's. Dated long before I was born.

Talea and I played by the boundary. A ship came in and I really wanted to use my song to pull it to us, but she snatched my hand and dragged me away. I think there was a male on board. Maybe I'll go back one day while the rest of the sirens slumber. If I'm brave.

What the actual fuck? So many questions swarmed my mind as I stumbled backward, falling into my bed. Talea… she'd named this ship after someone important to her. Someone she'd never mentioned to me. *A.T.* had my mother's journal. Potentially from her youth but my eyes were locked onto that 's'. She'd told me stories of other sirens, but never indicated she'd known them. I assumed it was passed down knowledge. We were so few, sirens had been reduced to a bedtime story. Rare as Zariya, the fabled city of gold they'd once hailed from.

My mother had even wanted to use her song. It couldn't have been her, but it had to be. I knew that writing. She'd left her life in journals. Journals my father hoarded. Except for this one. I flipped the page back and forth, searching for anything else. A small doodle of a ship with great sails was drawn in the corner, and that was it.

So, my father was a ruthless asshole, but my mother had her own secrets. Ears ringing, I stashed the letter in the hidden compartment below my bed and promptly left my room.

The hallway between the rows of rooms on the *Talea*, clearly named after someone my mother had known, was narrow. The smell of wood polish and rotten fish filled my nose as I ran, trailing my hands along the walls to the deck, gasping for the fresh sea air. Unsatisfied, I leaped and crashed into the ocean, letting the sea comfort my skin and scales as I sank, needing to bury my hands into the sand. To feel the truth of the only constant I'd ever known. The ocean was a ruthless, fearful bitch, but she'd never lied about her role in this world.

I'd found myself swimming back to the hidden tunnel before I realized where I was going. Maybe I was playing a role as well, pretending to be a guest of the queen, but she was dead, and no one cared what I was doing. My father still had answers. More than I'd ever known. He could be hidden anywhere in the world. If I was going to get answers from him, I was going to have to sweet talk a certain mouthy commander.

CHAPTER 11

Even though there was a chance the cave that transitioned into a hall to the palace could be occupied, I couldn't swim up to the guarded front doors, so I'd have to take my chances. The pitch-black path was still and silent. Like the other side, the wall above the sealed door had a place to push a mechanism, engaging the door to swing open. The castle was bustling with the day's activities, mostly repair work, if the banging and shouting were any indication.

I considered hiding in my room, but I needed to find out where the commander had moved my father, and the only way to do that was to play his game. So, I reported for duty, swimming to the kitchens, surprised to discover them empty, save one lone little sea fae, glowing with light and humming a song as she prepared some kind of meal.

Letting myself in, I cleared my throat to introduce myself when, from a pantry, Kaitalen emerged, chewing on a thias, the long white vegetable crunching as he smiled that annoying smile.

"Oh look, you've decided to join us."

"I don't recall you giving me a timeframe, Commander."

"It's Kai, if you don't mind, and immediately was the time frame, pretty little thief."

"Aw, you think I'm pretty?" I placed my hand to my chest, sarcasm my second language. "How sweet."

"No, but you do. Wasn't that one of your two life skills?"

"I'm trying really hard not to hate you right now. That handsome face is helping, but only just." I did want to hate him, but an idea formed in my mind, and far be it from me to deny such a genius plan.

"Look a little closer. Maybe it will help." He patted the top of my head before swimming past to join the glowing sea fae lighting the kitchen. "This is Leora. She's running this cookery now. But she's done for the day." He turned to face her. "Thank you again for taking this on by yourself. It won't happen again."

"It was a happy day." She was the size of my arm with a small tail and perfectly round cheeks. She glowed bright orange, her bottom shaking as her high-pitched voice carried through the room like a song.

Kai crossed his arms over his chest, pinning me with a stare. "We've had two additional guests join us and they have not had dinner. You will make it as your contribution to today's work."

I swam closer to the commander, sticking out my lower lip. "But I'm not a cook. Perhaps there's something else I could do."

"And I am not a ruler, yet here we are. Better get started."

"I can help you." Leora flitted around the kitchen while the commander and I held each other's glares.

He tilted his head toward the pantry he'd come from. "Ingredients are in there. I'm sure whatever you can manage will be fine."

Refusing to let him have the win, I helped myself to the pantry, snatching a basket from the pile at the door. Annoyed, I grabbed one of everything and shoved it in. After I had several things I somewhat recognized, I pulled two sea slugs from a jar and went back to the kitchen, hoping he'd left. Instead, he sat his happy, tail-covered ass on the counter and traced his midnight blue scales, humming as I got to work. Yanking a knife from a hook on the wall, I chopped whatever I'd grabbed into small pieces.

"That doesn't—" Leora started, but I shot her a lethal glare and she promptly shut her mouth, swimming closer to Kai.

I used several seasonings. Some I knew I hated and one smelled so bad, I added extra. After multiple sounds from Leora, as she tried and failed to direct me, I submerged half the food into a hot container so it could warm, then readied the dishes, threw on the slugs, and slammed the plates down on the table.

I made it to the doorway before the commander stopped me. "Going so soon?"

"I keep forgetting this is a prison now." I spun so quickly the current of water pushed Leora into Kai. She jerked her body away and swam out of the room.

"It is not a prison. But as you've just made our dinner, I thought we'd sit together and enjoy it."

"*Our* dinner?"

"Yes. I was too busy dealing with a group of angry merfae to have dinner. And you were too busy avoiding the kitchen. So now, we eat."

I scrunched my nose. "I'm not eating that."

"Why? You wouldn't have purposefully ruined it to get out of kitchen duty now, would you?"

"No," I said sweetly, sitting down at the table.

This was bad. So bad. There was no way in hell that food was going to be anything less than poisonous. Still, this was also a battle of wits. Round two with the commander and this time, I'd win.

"Fork?" he asked, holding out a utensil.

I shared a fake smile and lifted it from his hand, ignoring the spark when our fingers touched. He sat across from me, watching as I dipped the fork into the mush I'd created and held it inches from my mouth.

"Cheers," he said, scooping his bite.

As one, we placed the vomit-inducing food into our mouths and gods help me, it took every ounce of strong will I had not to move my face a muscle as I chewed, then swallowed the vilest food I'd ever tasted in my life. It was awful, and he damn well knew it. But rather than letting me win, he simply scooped another bite and stared me down, daring me to eat more. I felt the brick tumble in my stomach from bite number one, but I would not concede.

The screeching of the fork against the plate potentially gave away my hesitation, so I scooped fast and shoved in the bite, not bothering to taste it. I swallowed and stared down the commander as he chewed. And chewed. And chewed. Then a gulp as he swallowed.

"Tasty," he lied, taking another scoop.

And so the battle continued. We both suffered in agonizing silence, refusing to let the other know they'd won the most ridiculous fight on the planet. Maybe he was stubborn, but so was I, and I would not back down. Though my stomach didn't agree with me, I heard his rumble and barely held my unamused expression as I took another bite, eyeing that fucking sea slug as the color drained from my face. I'd eaten a slug once when I was a kip and was sick for days.

I glanced at the captain's face as he seemed to mirror my thoughts, staring down at that little beast as it moved along the plate, leaving a thick trail of clear slime behind it. Perhaps some considered it a delicacy, but as I longed to get the taste of whatever concoction I'd just eaten from my mouth, the very last thing I wanted to do was follow it with that.

"What's the matter, Commander? Never had a sea slug before?"

He looked over his shoulder as if Leora would appear and save him and then back at me. "Just feeling full. That's all." He swallowed audibly. "I sure wish there was cake."

"Mmm. Too bad. Something sweet sounds delicious." I poked the grayish slug with my fork, trying and failing to sound sexy in any capacity.

"Perhaps you could show me how it's eaten first. This being my first time and all."

"I've just witnessed you shoveling that food into your mouth like you haven't eaten in days. It works the same. Open mouth, throw food in, try not to vomit."

"Anchors away," he mumbled, picking up the slug. It slipped from his fingers, leaving a trail of slime, and he tried to hide his retch as he snagged the disgusting thing back up and shoved it in. I watched as he turned from a sun-kissed god to a murky green color, holding his mouth closed.

"I can't believe you ate that thing," I said, shoving my plate away.

His stomach gurgled, and he held a fist to his chest, cheeks puffing out. I thought for sure he was going to throw up, but he let out the longest belch I'd ever heard, then smiled and stole the sea slug from my plate, popping it into his mouth and holding my stare as he gulped and grinned like a child.

"Commander?" An unfamiliar voice in the room jolted both of us. "I need to speak to you."

Kaitalen waived his hand through the air, looking a bit queasy, but in control. "What is it, Jof?"

I recognized the lesser fae as the one who'd helped him in the throne room after Morwena died. Up close, the texture of his leathery gray skin shimmered under the magic that lit the inside of the castle. He swam toward the commander, tucking his hands behind his back, just below his fin, as he lifted his chin and stared at the wall. "Sir, I believe we need to speak in private."

"Jof. It's fine. You can sit at this table and speak to me like a normal fae. I am your equal." He pushed the chair out. The guard eyed me as he took the seat next to Kai. I wasn't leaving unless asked, so I sat back in my chair and waited, hoping this was going to be informative.

"I think the one thing that was a problem is still a problem and we probably need to do something about it."

Kai flicked his eyes to Jof, then back to me. "You're dismissed, siren."

Letting false hurt show in my eyes, I pushed off the table and darted out the door, then halted, falling into the shadows as I rested my back against the wall, listening.

Kai let out a long sigh. "What is it, Jof?"

"It's Cohv, sir. I think he's still going to be a problem. The... talk you had with him didn't seem to do any good. I found him parading through the halls, his entourage chattering on about the same things.

They don't believe a land dweller should command the sea. They don't trust you."

"I know. And I can't blame them for that. If my king died and the usurper took over, I wouldn't go silently, either. We need them to see this is the right way on their own while maintaining peace. I have no idea what will become of the Sea Court. But if we let them go, campaigning for Autus' army, we will see them again on the opposite side of the battlefield and that's the one thing we don't want. The only thing we can do right now is continue to watch them and keep them busy."

"I'll continue to monitor him, sir."

The commander's voice seemed tired already. "Thank you, Jof. You're a good soldier."

Convinced they were only going to stroke each other's egos, I darted away. I swam through the broken halls, making my way back to my room, then turned the lock and made it halfway to the bed when a firm knock halted me. Expecting it to be the commander, wallowing in apologies, I swung the door open with ease.

Only it wasn't the commander. Instead, a muscle-bound merfae leaned into the entry, his long blue hair wafting around him. Cohv. He flashed a perfect smile, dimples showing in both cheeks as he lifted an eyebrow. "Care for some company?"

"I didn't realize the queen kept whores in her castle." I flicked my eyes down and back up. "That actually explains a lot about the male ego around here."

The smile melted from his face as his color changed to red. "I'm not the whore around here. That title belongs to you, siren."

I studied my long, dangerous nails as I smirked. "It seems like you're the once soliciting, or did I misunderstand your meaning?"

He pushed into the room, leaving the door wide open as he swam for me. Though outwardly, I kept calm, my heart beat like a thousand sails in a storm. My song would have stopped him, but it was gone, and I only had one other line of defense. A deadly one. I stayed where I was, ready to aim for the heart. But before he was close enough to reach, firm hands grabbed him by the shoulders and yanked him backward, tossing him through the room and back out of the door.

Kai didn't speak a word to me as he left, slamming my door shut behind him. He'd come. And though I hated to admit it, he'd saved me. Because now I was a damsel that needed saving. There was a reason the sea gifted her precious siren with a song. Beautiful melodies that would save them from a male that thought he could take what did not belong to him. Gritting my teeth, I was once again reminded of why I so desperately needed to get to my father.

I waited only a few seconds before opening the door a little, not at all surprised to see the commander there. His back to me as he heaved, clearly coming away the winner of a fight.

"Commander?"

"Do they come often? The males?"

I shrugged, but he kept his back to me. "No more often than I can handle."

He turned then; his eyes sad. "You shouldn't have to *handle* it."

"No. I shouldn't."

"You could stay somewhere else. Somewhere safer than this room."

"I'm fine here. For now."

He released the tension in his shoulders, letting whatever plagued him fade away. As if he'd locked his feelings into a box and simply moved on. I knew that feeling all too well.

The face of a hardened commander returned. "You understand why I sent you away earlier?"

I smirked, playing my role as well. "You don't trust me, and you shouldn't."

"I'd like to put you in the kitchens as a cover story for my real use of you. Thief, wasn't it?"

The surprise on my face was not an act. "You want me to steal something for you?"

He looked both ways down the hall before jutting his chin toward my room. I slipped to the side and let him in, shutting the door behind him.

"As long as I'm in charge of this castle, I decide when you come and go. When you sleep, when you eat, when you work. I have a job for you tomorrow. You will prove yourself worthy of my trust and acquire something for me. Understood?"

"You sure take your job seriously, don't you?"

He leaned close to me, whispering, "You have two options. Fall in line or I'll put you there."

Maybe I didn't have my song, but I was still a siren. I was born and bred for this. He had come back. He'd protected me. And I could see it in his eyes. His desire was growing. He fought it, but so did I. Because we both had a role to play.

"I'd love to see you try."

I didn't realize we were moving until my back was to the wall, his nose inches from my own. We'd been in this position before. My eyes flicked to his lips and back to his eyes.

"You're not going to try to kiss me now, are you, Commander? Because that wouldn't make you any better than the last fool that pushed into my room."

I pressed my palm onto his chest, squeezing just hard enough for him to understand he wasn't the only powerful one in this room.

"I wouldn't dream of it," he sneered, backing away. "Lock your door, vixen." The tension vanished as quickly as it had risen the moment he turned to leave. "I'll see you in the morning. I hope you're as brave as you claim."

I fell asleep listening to the distant sound of my siren's song haunting me. My heart breaking at the phantom notes that ebbed and flowed with the steady current of the sea. Holding my eyes shut tight, I buried my face in the pillow until the pounding in my head became pounding on the door.

"I'm coming." I snarled, trying to push my body into motion after a hard night's sleep. I yanked the door open to find the commander leaning on the door frame.

"Ready?"

"Don't tell me you're a morning person too."

He beamed. "Morning, midday, night. I'm good *all* hours of the day."

"I haven't even blinked thirty times today, Commander. I'm not in the mood for flirting or fighting with you. Where are we going?"

"Aw. Our little siren is a grumpy guppy this morning."

"Har har."

"Oh, and a pirate. Fun times."

I snorted. "You aim to annoy people, don't you?"

He snagged a piece of debris floating in the water and fumbled with it in his hands. "I come by it naturally."

He drifted backward, waiting for me to shut and lock the door. We meandered down the hallway, his chin high no matter the looks he took from others we passed. They didn't dare give me those looks. Most kept a safe distance.

"I thought I'd introduce you to a new friend of mine. See if she needed any help today since the kitchens are clearly not a great place for you."

We passed several patrols, whom he greeted by name, making small talk as he continued.

"How the hell do you know every single sea fae, yet you've been down here for what? A couple of days?"

"I know them because I've taken the time to get to know them. These are all people of equal importance. But I could see how you wouldn't understand that." He peeked at me from the corner of his eye, waiting for me to take the bait.

I refused. "Naturally. So, what's your plan, Commander? You're going to come down here and keep us all locked up? Do we have an end date to this madness?"

He shrugged. "I have no idea. I'm not in charge of the plan, I'm just here to execute it."

"What happens when all these sea fae tire of your little game and turn against you?"

He stopped, turning on me with his commanding gaze. "This is not a game. These are lives. This is a war. Maybe I'm patronizing you because I find you interesting, but don't get me wrong, siren. I will do what I have to do, because saving those that you consider lesser is the right path." He moved closer to me. "What makes you think you're better than Leora?"

I looked up at him, letting false fear show, though my eyes drifted down to his chest, my fingers tingling. Murder was my last line of defense. But he wasn't angry. Firm, but so passionate, I had to collect my thoughts.

"I didn't—" I shook my head, trying to find a satisfactory answer.

His voice softened as he held my gaze. "I'm not blaming you. You're a product of your raising, just like everyone else. But I hope to open your eyes to a better world."

"You won't move the ocean with a dream. These fae are not so easily swayed."

He pulled back. "Maybe not the ocean, but I'll do what I must to keep the sea fae from joining Autus at any cost. Because that's what's been asked of me, but also because that's the right thing to do."

I trailed behind him, wondering what that kind of enthusiasm for a cause felt like. "It must be incredibly exhausting, trying to change the world."

"Some days. But other days, it's rewarding." He pointed in front of us. "We are headed to that door at the end of this hall. I'm going to check in with the guards on rotation in this wing, but let yourself in and I'll be right behind you."

"Why does this feel like a trap?"

A bark of laughter followed a sly wink as he swam away. "I have no idea."

CHAPTER 12

The room he'd led me to was empty except for a few chairs and one long table anchored to the floor. With nothing else to do, I rested in a seat and waited for the commander to join me. Sitting in a chair underwater felt so formal. But then, we were in the queen's half destroyed castle and she had preferred her high fae form. I found myself studying the walls for charms that would turn this into a dry room. The floor rumbled below my chair and I watched, dumbfounded as the entire opposite wall rotated and the hydra swam in, all six of her eyes staring me down as each of her serpent-like tentacles slithered into the room behind her. The once empty space was now incredibly crowded as she crept closer.

My heart raced as I swayed my tail back and forth to soothe my jittery nerves. Every instinct I had, everything I'd learned about staying alive in a sea full of dangerous creatures, told me to escape. Her faces twisted into what might have been smiles, had it not been for the rows of teeth. A flutter filled my stomach as I felt every bit of judgment from the beast before me.

"Siren," she said by way of greeting as she continued to come closer.

I reached into the pit where my song had once been and felt instantly hollow. A sharp reminder that I was nothing but a fraud as I sat here, playing Kaitalen's game because I was a glutton for punishment and needed him to play mine as well.

"Hydra," I answered smoothly.

She moved in until her center head was within inches of mine. "Where is Kai?"

"It might surprise you to learn that I am not his keeper."

A low growl came from behind clenched teeth as her middle head, the size of my whole body, collided with me and pressed me back into my chair.

"Oh, look at this, you've met," Kai said, entering the room as if he enjoyed the show. "Playing nice?"

Slowly, so fucking slowly, she backed away, that center head glued to me as the others greeted the commander.

"Friend of yours?" I asked, the disdain as clear as I could make it.

"Hydra, this is Lyra, Lyra, this is… oh." He pushed his hands flat onto the table. "Do you have an actual name?"

The room seemed to darken as she commanded the space, growing, if that were even possible, stretching her tentacles longer, leaning into him to answer. "I am as ancient as the sea itself, created from the first grains of sand as they wept, forming the ocean in which we live. I've halted gods and defied the wind, lived a thousand lives, and yet only this one. I am Doriahs, serpent of the sea."

"Doris. Got it."

He winked at me, and I bit the inside of my cheek as the hydra corrected him. "Dor-ai-us."

"Oh, sorry. Door eye us."

"I want to like you," she said in retort as she backed into a corner.

"Is there a purpose for this fun little meeting?" I asked, tapping my long nails on the lengthy, marbled table.

"We're going hunting. The three of us. Together. I thought we should get to know each other first."

I pulled my head back, giving Kai a pointed look. "I'm not going hunting."

"You are." He gestured to the door and when I didn't move, he pinned me with a hard look, offering no choices as he left me in the room with the beast.

I leaped from my chair, following him promptly down the hall, arguing the entire way out of the castle and into the deep waters beyond. The hydra, stretching to full size, terrifying me as we went.

"This is ridiculous. Did the mermaids not put on enough of a show for you? Did none of them strike you as warriors?"

"These mermaids are not warriors. Yet. But today, I don't need a warrior," he answered, swimming on.

"At least tell me where we are going." The sun lit the sea as we swam in familiar waters. My instinct was to turn and swim away, but with Doriahs close by, no one was going anywhere without permission.

"They are ahead, Kai," the hydra warned.

Blocking the sunshine from above sat a cluster of pirate ships, all anchored close to each other. A meeting of pirates on the sea was rare. Most handled their dealings in the Gulley. The hydra had been hunting, indeed. I halted, letting my shoulders drop as I backed away.

"They are trading slaves on those ships," Kai said from beside me.

"Maybe the memo hasn't gotten around about that being frowned upon now?"

"It's time to see whose side you're on, Vixen. I plan to save these fae, but there's a book on one of those ships that I need. I'm told it has information regarding more slave trading. You're going to acquire that book for me."

He could have punched me in the gut, and it would have shocked me less. The world started closing in as I tried to refuse and couldn't bring my song forward. I turned to escape. The hydra stared me down. I was a skilled thief with my song, but what was I without it?

The commander swam in closer. "That bravery wavering?"

"You'd have to be a madman to try to steal from a band of pirates during a parlay. I'm good at what I do; I might even be the best, but I'm not an idiot. If you want me dead, Commander, just order your pet to do your bidding and be done with it."

He put his hands on my arms, his eyes flicking between mine as I tried to settle my heart. He'd trapped me into this plan just like he'd trapped my father. He was the enemy.

"Draw the line, Lyra. I won't force you to do this. But I will ask. Because those are innocent lives up there and raining an army down upon them on their territory is allowing for more death than I'd like to see."

"Is it a command or not?" I needed him to trust me, but gods, if I had to weave through a group of pirates without my song to protect myself… The water became heavy as it pressed in on my body. Sheer panic and doubt threatened to sink me.

"Not. But honestly, I thought this would be fun for you."

Once upon a time, it would have been. That was the worst part. Weeks ago, this would have been the quickest way to win me over. But now, everything had changed, only I couldn't admit that to him or anyone. I would not be weak, not to him, but also not to myself.

"Tell me what you know."

He pulled away, his face strictly business as he drifted back and forth in front of me, rubbing his jaw as he spoke. "There was hardly any information found in Morwena's rooms and the advisors aren't willing to see reason or provide us with anything useful. But there was a message intercepted about this hand-off. This is a two-part mission. You're going to find the book that's supposed to contain names, and then Dory over there will take them all down."

"And you?"

"Supervisor. And if you get into trouble, savior."

"So, you want me to just randomly get onto one of those ships, sneak around until I find a book, and if all hell breaks loose, then what? Caw like a fucking bird until you show up and hope we both don't die before the hydra smashes the ships to pieces and kills us all, anyway?"

"Well, when you put it like that, it sounds awful. You're a siren. I'm sure you've used that magic of yours to get yourself out of a tight spot before."

"You assume. You have no idea. But I'm going to do this and then you're going to owe me, Commander."

"I don't like open-ended deals."

I narrowed my eyes, pursing my lips. "I don't like near-death experiences."

"Fair."

"Take some kind of cover; these are probably sea fae. If they suspect anything, they are all bailing into this water."

"I'm not entirely helpless, Vixen. Plus, I've got Dorthiasy back there."

I smiled, his humor lightening my fear. "She's going to kill you one day."

"She could try." He wiggled his eyebrows, and I swatted him before swimming away to peek at the ships from above the surface, deciding which one to infiltrate.

Since they were all of equal size, I had to look for familiar faces. They'd probably all frequented the Gulley enough for me to sort them out, but the problem was staying out of view of the lookouts in the crow's nest. All five ships had crew members watching the waters from above for approaching ships. It didn't surprise me that they had no one below. You'd have to be out of your mind to approach a gathering of brigands.

I couldn't get a close view so I had to come into the west, hoping the glare of the sun off the water would block me enough to sneak passage onto a ship, and then I'd just have to wing it. This wasn't a first for me, but without my song, I had nothing to get myself out of a pinch—other than a hydra and an overconfident commander lurking somewhere below.

I jumped onto the deck, landing silently between the curved wall and the cockboat. The riding pants and a tight black shirt I preferred to use in fae form helped me slink into the harsh shadows on the deck. Pirates were always drunk on the ships. I peeked around the small boat tied to the deck to study the crew, noting several familiar faces. Simmonne's ship would be where all the pirates came to eat and drink after business was handled. He kept quite the reputation in the Gulley for his after-hours antics.

From here, I could see the other ships better and within minutes, I'd narrowed it down to two that likely had the book. All the ship decks were full of cages, and while that might be easy to navigate, I'd have to rely on the lesser fae not giving me away as I crept along the decks.

To my astonishment, most of the fae in the cages were not sea fae. If the hydra attacked these ships, they'd sink and drown, and then it would have all been for nothing. But was that my problem? Kai had asked me to get the book, he'd said nothing of my part in freeing these slaves. Cursing silently, I leaped back into the salty sea and dove for the commander, who was not remotely hiding.

"Are you okay?"

I looked over my shoulder to make sure he was talking to me. "No. I've been killed, and this is my ghost visiting you now to deliver a warning."

"Did you get the book?" he asked, ignoring my sarcasm.

"No. There's a problem. Most of those locked up fae are lesser fae, but they are land dwellers. She takes down those ships and they are all going to drown."

"I see." He moved his hands through his hair as he looked up to the surface.

"That is the party ship," I said, pointing. "Once the sun goes down, most of the pirates will move to that one. I'd bet on it. And those two over there are the likely sources of the book, but they also carry the most cages. There are some on those other two ships, but they seem the least likely targets, based on the crews."

"You can tell just by looking at the crews."

"I've seen them around," I answered, not meeting his gaze.

"We have to free the caged fae and worry about the book another time."

I bit my bottom lip, considering what I was about to propose. Each move I made from this point forward would be to gain back my power. My options were limited. "I have an idea, but it's going to require commandeering one of those ships and it's risky as hell."

He looked at me funny and then just chuckled. "You sound like Ara right now, which should be a giant red flag."

"Your call, Commander."

"I guess I have to trust you, siren."

I took his hand and pulled him toward Doriahs. "Stay here and make sure those ships don't leave until we get back."

"Easily done." Her terrifying smiles shook me to my core as she swam away.

"I hope you're used to that tail, Commander. Because it's time to test your swimming skills."

I'd never worked with a team before, aside from my mother, but as we sped through the ocean side by side, there was a foreign joy laced in the wake we left behind us. We raced, sharing quick glances as we made it back in record time, stopping only long enough for him to demand entrance.

"The pearls should be in this room," he said. "Wait here."

Intrigued, I peeked around the propped door, only to find him standing there waiting for me to do so with his sculpted arms crossed over his bare chest. His eyes held mine until I caved and whipped around, drowning in his gaze. The sound of the quiet laugh he shared only with me twisted something inside as I remembered that I was merely getting close to him to free my father. I closed my eyes but saw only his as I waited.

He carried the chest full of evada pearls all the way back to the waiting ships, refusing to let me take a turn. We left the trunk with the hydra as the final bit of light fell from the sky. Total darkness took over, leaving only the orange glow of the lanterns along the ships and the stars above reflecting in the water.

As anticipated, most of the sea fae had gathered on Simmonne's for a night full of drinking, the air filled with low laughter and folk music. Kai and I helped ourselves to the first empty ship. He stumbled backward, taking in the sight of the lesser fae crammed into cages like wild beasts for slaughter.

I pressed my hand to his back, steadying him as I whispered. "No more than two hours and their lives will be their own. Let's go."

We had a plan. I'd distract the sea fae on the ships, Kai would break the locks and free the lessers. That all went to shit in a ship as soon as he came within arm's reach of the nearest pirate. He beat him senseless, and I said nothing, keeping my eyes turned away as the commander took his rage out on the poor bastard.

I made it to the first cage and used my nails and a hair pin to pick the lock while speaking to the lesser fae inside the cage. Eyes wide, they stared at me, nodding as one while I spoke. "There's a scary ass sea monster overboard. She's harmless as long as you don't piss her off. Get your friends and get in the water. She has evada pearls. Stick them in your ears and swim as far and fast as you can. Follow the moon. Keep it directly in front of you until you hit the shore with deep red sands."

The lock clicked, and I swung the cage open, cowering at the shrill of the hinges. Only one of the three males on deck turned, and the commander had him down before he could gasp. And so we went, cage to cage, freeing the fae. The sound of their plunges into the ocean was masked by the tumbling sea water lapping against the sides of the ships and the sea spray spritzing the deck.

We finished two boats, Kai hiding the knocked-out pirates into the captain's chambers to be discovered later. The third boat was empty. We searched the hull, the captain's quarters, and each of the storerooms below for hidden fae, but there were none. I found something, though. A certain book I'd have to decide what to do with. My father would gut me if he knew I'd turned it over, and I was certain I'd open the pages and find his name. The faces of the lesser fae on our ship came to mind, but I shook my head, pushing them away. Now was not the time to question my morals. The fourth ship was much like the first two and after we'd cleared that one, both exhausted, it left our final and biggest hurdle.

"Are you sure you want to do this?" he asked for the third time.

I straightened my shoulders and lifted my chin, hardening my face until there was no question of my resolve. "I'm not afraid."

CHAPTER 13

I had to rely on my charming personality to cause the distraction we'd planned. Kai hated the idea, insisting we use the hydra, but that didn't work with her protecting the freed slaves.

I hopped onboard Simmonne's vessel, right into the middle of the drunken pirates, snatched a full mug from the closest bearded fool and drank the whole thing as I threw the cloak I'd snatched from the second ship from my shoulders and waited for lust-filled eyes to fall upon me.

Sauntering across the pirate-packed deck, I slipped onto the lap of the fae playing a flute and curled his hair around my fingers as I leaned in close. "Play me something catchy, pet."

As the song began, I moved through the males, stealing hats and rubbing chests, my body pulsing to the music as fluid as the ocean. I lost myself for a moment, entertaining the crowd as they reached for me on instinct. For a moment, I remembered I was a powerful seductress, enrapturing an entire group of males as my hands trailed down my electrified body. They all wanted to fuck me, and as my eyes landed on the commander, sliding between the cages on the other side of the deck, he stood there frozen, watching just as the others did. I turned away from him, hoping it would be enough to push him to keep going, but I could still feel his eyes burning for me. It was so hard to look away from him, to keep my gaze on the ones I was meant to entertain when, in my soul, I knew I danced for him—the only one that thought he could resist me.

Fire surged through my body as our eyes met over and over. I bit my bottom lip, rubbing my breasts, and he stumbled forward. Straddling a high fae sitting on a barrel as the others whooped and hollered at their friend's luck, I closed my eyes and pictured Kai's body below me as I moved my hips in and out and back and forth. I pulled away from that male and continued to work the crowd, their hands reaching and touching me. And I let them whilst planning their deaths for being such cruel and vile creatures.

This was the work of a siren. Maybe I didn't have my song, but I had this power: to stop a male with a single look and bring him to his knees in awe of me. Perhaps the commander had done me a favor, and didn't even know it. He'd shown me that my song was only a small part of what I really was.

I caught sight of a mess of blond curls leaping over the side of the ship, which was my sign to back away. But as a throat cleared behind me and large hands circled my waist, I froze, recognizing Simmonne's voice.

"I did not know the siren thief would be joining us," he whispered into my ear. "You wouldn't happen to know where all my slaves have gone, now would you?"

My spine went rigid as his hands clasped tighter around me. I spun, facing him, and wrapped my arms around his neck, nuzzling his ear. "I'm only here to play, pet. What use have I for a shipload of fae?"

I pressed my lips to his as he collided with the railing of the ship. Before he could register my movement, I jammed my hand into his chest, my honed nails the perfect tool, as I gripped his beating heart and yanked it free. Still pulsing in my fingers, I dropped it onto the deck and turned to face the others.

"I forgot to introduce you all to my friend. We call her Doris."

A great harmony of hydra screams came from the ocean. I waved goodbye and jumped overboard just as she wrapped her tentacles around the massive ship and snapped it into pieces.

Kai was at my side in an instant, taking my elbow and pulling me through the sea, toward the mass of land-dwellers we'd freed.

"Never again," he fumed.

I held out the notebook he'd requested. As he pulled it from my hands, we said nothing more as we met up with the swimming land dwellers and guided them through the dark waters and straight to the Flame Court.

I wanted nothing to do with whatever information that book held. I just wanted to get the hell out of there, still able to feel that warm heart pulsating in my hand, the rip of skin, and look on his face as I murdered that fae. I'd killed before, would likely kill again. But sending a soul to the God of Death, was always haunting.

We made our way back to the sea castle, his tail brushing mine several times as we swam, though I could still feel anger rippling from him. I'd pissed him off and the only thing I could think about was whether he'd still trust me with the location of the advisors, if he was angry.

I'd done everything he'd asked, had risked my own tail to do his bidding, and this was the thanks he had for me? I'd take his heart too. Should have just started with that and let the sea show the land who was more vicious. Who really held the power here. I let the space between us grow as I swam behind him down the hallway toward our rooms. Several mermaids lingered just outside his door, and they shot daggered looks at me as we passed by together.

"Find somewhere else to mingle," the commander barked, causing them to scatter like a school of fish.

Something about the tone of his voice, that powerful authority, stopped me. He had such a way of pulling that side of him forward when it suited him and tucking it away when it didn't.

The entire hallway emptied and before I could even utter a word, he cut through the tension-filled space and wrapped me in his arms, his fists buried deep within my long hair. Without a second of hesitation, his sinful lips were on mine, burning the memory of Simmonne away forever as he smothered me in his lust, moaning as his hands trailed down my arms, leaving embers of need in their wake. He pulled his lips from me, only to graze his teeth along my neck, sending a wave of desire through my body as I wrapped my arms around him, groaning as I tossed my head back.

My heart stopped pounding, falling faint within my chest as he overwhelmed my senses. As the only thing that mattered transformed into this male, worshipping my body. Time stood still. My body tingled. I pulled him closer. He pushed me against the wall. There was not an inch of me that wasn't desperate for him. That wasn't possessive and searing with need.

"Wait," he managed, halting, though his chest rose and fell harder than it should have, his beautiful swollen lips parting. "Stop." He pulled away, resting his forehead on mine. "Sorry. I'm sorry."

"We're either going to fuck or fight, Commander. It's one night, not a lifetime," I answered, moving the blond curls from his eyes as I ran my fingers down his cheek. "I need nothing more than one night."

He closed the gap, his lips soft as our bodies pressed together. "One night," he agreed, nodding as he bit my bottom lip, brushing his thumb over my breast. "Come with me."

He grabbed the back of my neck and pulled me in for another kiss, his hands frantic as he explored my body. As his tongue stroked mine, his muscles threatening to overpower me in that embrace. I couldn't help but let my eyes fall shut and just release all the barriers for a single moment, lost in Kai's lust. In his perfect kiss. His tongue massaged mine, grazing my teeth as he pushed for more, sucking on my bottom lip and moaning against my mouth.

He pulled away only long enough to unlock his door. "Do you have an evada pearl with you?"

Unwilling to give him any information about myself, I nodded as he pushed the door open. A shimmering barrier told me all I need to know. He moved through first, removing his pearl as the magical wall held the water back to his dry room. I pretended to adjust a pearl as I followed, swimming through the magic and changing into my fae form on the other side.

No sooner had I entered the room than he came for me again; his deliberate hands pushing my tight black shirt over my head. He kicked the door shut and pulled me by the hand through the sitting room and into his bedroom. My eyes swept the place as quickly as I could, but it was hard to take my attention from the beautiful male stroking my body. Later. I'd worry about it later.

He slid to his knees and held my waist as he planted soft kisses on my navel, carefully tugging at the top of my pants. Though not graceful, he was certainly skilled, never taking his plump lips from me as my bottoms dropped to the floor. He licked slowly up my naked body as he stepped out of his clothing. Experienced hands massaged my breasts, flicking a nipple before he closed his mouth over it to soothe the sting.

I let him lay me on the bed, looking at me through the curly blond hair that always covered his brow. He licked his lips and crawled slowly over me, his muscles not at all taxed as he held his body above, closing the space and kissing me again. He was so gentle, the siren within me was ready to rip him to shreds for want of him. I moved my nails down his back, lightly at first, until he snarled, biting my bottom lip before pulling away.

"All the things I want to do to you. Tell me what you want, Lyra."

"Not Vixen?"

Lifting an eyebrow, he smirked. "You certainly are."

I narrowed my eyes, the tremor of his salacious voice moving straight down my spine. A male that didn't just grunt and groan, then roll over and pass out, was rare indeed. I moved my fingers into those wild curls.

"Don't hold back. Not for a second. I want all of you. I want to feel you inch by fucking inch."

A wave of shock poured over me as he obliged. I hadn't had to use my song, and yet he intended to give me exactly what I wanted.

"I'm going to make you regret that request."

He hooked his arms around my fae legs and dragged me to the edge of the bed, bringing his fingers to my inner thigh. My skin was on fire by that single touch alone. Every touch, each phantom kiss, burned into my skin as he worshiped my body. I released a long breath, trying to hold still, to keep from attacking him until he was buried deep within me. I had to remind myself this was a game. One I was well-trained in. Kai was still my mark, and though he was sure to be a good time, I couldn't let myself forget why I was here.

But his kisses became feral, his tender lips replaced by teeth grazing my skin. An ache of desire grew so heavily, all thoughts of anything but passion and pleasure left me. He massaged my entire body, but avoided the only spot I wanted him. He sucked and teased the inside of my thighs until I grew so sensitive, I thought I might explode the moment he reached my core. But he didn't. He refused, moving back down.

"Touch me," I begged.

His ragged voice crawled down my spine. "Tell me where."

I reached my hand down, stroking between my legs. The sensation of contact made my toes curl. "Right here, pet. Taste me."

He lifted my fingers and put them in his mouth, groaning at the taste of my desire. Finally burying his face between my legs, he licked my lips before taking my clit into his mouth and devouring me whole. The orgasm was there, waiting. It did not need to build or climb. The moment his mouth, fiery and hot, closed over me, I was done. Falling as he slipped two fingers inside and expertly navigated the explosive orgasm. He did not relent, did not pull away as I tried to move. As my legs trembled. Instead, he bit the inside of my thigh and something about that pain mixed with pleasure took me right back to the peak of another orgasm.

"Enough of this." I purred once my exhausted body settled. "I've seen what you can do with that tongue; let me see what you can do with the rest of that body."

He pulled away, a smirk on his face. "I'll take you fast and hard, or not at all."

I smiled as I crawled backward on the bed. "I've always preferred my pleasure laced with pain."

"Perfect." He pressed the tip of his shaft into my opening.

Clenching my jaw, I held his gaze as he pushed forward. I arched my back, feeling the burn of stretching around him. He held his thumb against my clit, massaging in languid circles. Fire lit his eyes as he slammed forward with no more warning, pushing himself to the hilt and giving no pause as he withdrew and drove inside me again. He never stopped massaging me, never once forgot of my pleasure as he moved his muscle-carved body. He was a warrior in every sense of the word. His body a tool he knew exactly how to work.

As he changed his pace, I raised my hips to meet him and Kai took that as a sign that I needed him deeper. He lifted my leg, resting my calf on his shoulder, testing just how limber I could be as he leaned down to kiss me, stretching those muscles as he continued to fuck me. Pain laced with pleasure, just as I had asked.

I couldn't have held back if I'd wanted to. I no longer had control over my body. I was his entirely as he stroked me, stretched me, and filled me to the brink, overwhelming my senses until I couldn't hold back my scream. I'd ensnared a sex god. Addled thoughts coursed through my mind as I tried to remember anything beyond the unbridled pleasure of Kaitalen swaying those beautiful hips as he worked my body.

"Come for me again, little vixen," His voice was more strained, but nevertheless, commanding.

Still in control as my body willingly obeyed. As I rode the waves of the greatest orgasm of my life, his skilled fingers still flicking the bud at my entrance.

"Gods, you're beautiful."

I pulled away, rolling over. Pushing my ass into the air, I looked over my shoulder, smiling wickedly. "Harder, Commander."

Needing no more provocation, he slammed into me once more, kneading my curves as he pulled out slowly and shoved back in. He groaned. A hard smack came across my ass. The burn from the impact spread and, as I tossed my head back, he gripped the ends of my hair, crashing into me over and over again. Until neither of us were breathing, both strained until we erupted, finally satiated, as if he'd commanded my body in time with his own.

If this was a battle of wits, as he so loved, he likely thought he had won. But I had a plan to get close to him, as close as he'd let me. Unable to help the smile on my face, I let a single fact settle on this day. One taste of me would never be enough for him.

CHAPTER 14

I slipped out of Kai's oversized bed and traipsed around his rooms. The dry rooms in the castle had been planted for diplomats from other courts who visited, and rumor had it the queen's room herself was dry. Kai's sitting room was a breathtaking creation of vaulted domed ceilings with images of sea fae and creatures painted in various shades of gold. Heavy crimson drapes covered a wall that was actually a thick window, giving the most spectacular view of the sea. Even in the darkest part of the night, I could still see the schools of fish that drifted by, and tendrils of seagrass swaying in the deep, dark water. The glass below my fingers was cool and inviting. I could have stared all night. Instead, a firm hand wrapped around my waist as Kai nuzzled my neck.

"You have the most beautiful view, Commander."

He spun me around, lifting my chin with a knuckle. "Indeed, I do."

Before I could protest, he was kissing me. Those lips of perfection could easily sweep me away as quickly as his pretty words. I did, however, need him to fall into my trap, and that meant I could enjoy him just a little longer. I slid my hands up his bare chest and locked them behind his neck, letting his tongue captivate me.

He pulled away, his eyes shifting between my own with a flare of concern. "Are you okay?"

"Of course." I forced a laugh. "Why do you ask?"

"Tonight, the ships, that was a lot. It was dangerous. Necessary, but risky."

Staring out the window once more, I forced myself to reply. "It was an order, wasn't it? But I think the fact that you stopped and asked makes all the difference."

"That is my job. Before all else, I'm here to do my king's bidding. I offered you an out because I wanted to see if you would take it. If you would back down." His words were slow and calculated as he'd built a picture of presumptions in his mind.

"You'll find I never back down."

Taking his hand, I pulled him back to bed. He fell in first, pulling me behind him as he wrapped me tightly in his arms once more. Something about that sense of security, along with his soft slow breaths upon my ear, carried me off to sleep.

I woke to the shrill sound of heavy curtains sliding along a steel rod. Rather than sunlight filling the room, I stared into the depths of the ocean once more, entranced as I studied the sun kissing the tops of the water like a spider web in motion.

"Breakfast?" Half-naked Kai stood in the doorway, holding a tray for me. "I'm not sure how they do it, but there's a grocer that brings me dry goods. I'm not the best cook, but I have a small kitchen here. Do you like coffee? I toasted some—"

I held a hand up, halting his rambling. "It's morning. Be less perky."

"But I like perky."

He stared at me with a half-smile until I rolled out of bed and wrapped a sheet around myself. I strolled to the door of his bedroom, lifting the cup from his tray as I traipsed into the sitting room and slumped onto the couch.

Setting the tray on the coffee table, he took a seat beside me, looking through the papers I'd already gone over secretly last night. I waited for him to realize there was nothing important before I reached for the buttered toast.

"I have an idea," I said, taking a bite of the warm bread.

"That sounds dangerous."

"No more dangerous than wrecking a parlay on open waters."

He smiled, every tooth showing as he wiggled his eyebrows. "That was just a little fun."

"You play your parts thoroughly, Commander. Domineering and in charge or the wise guy with a dashing smile."

"It is pretty dashing."

I took a sip of the bitter coffee, closing my eyes as I inhaled the dark roast.

"Your idea?"

"Oh, right, sorry." I set the cup down, turning to face him. "What if I spy for you in secret?"

He scratched the back of his head. "Why would I need that?"

"The sea fae already fear me. I proved myself to you when I didn't back down last night. What if I keep an eye on what's happening with the castle residents? You said yourself, we all have to stay here so your king knows we aren't joining Autus' army. I can promise you they will not fall in line as easily as you hope."

"What if they get the wrong idea? I mean… You're pretty, and I'm pretty, right?"

He watched me carefully as realization struck. "Oh, my gods." I lifted a paper from his lap just to roll it up and strike him with it. "You've said that to me before. You *did* recognize me from the Flame Court."

"I have a trained eye. Of course, I recognized you. But it sure was fun watching you squirm."

"I think I hate you all over again.," I couldn't help but smile. "It could work, you know. We can keep our interactions sparse and secret."

"You're asking me to trust you. That's a big ask in a foreign kingdom."

I lifted the tips of my hair, studying them instead of Kai's face as I considered what it would take for him to let me close. "I heard a rumor that Cohv isn't your biggest fan. I'm sure I could keep an eye on that, if you needed."

His jaw clenched. Faintly, but enough that I'd seen it. "What's in it for you?"

"War is coming, and I'd rather be on the winning side." I crawled across the couch, planting myself in his lap. "You need an ally. You need someone you can trust. I have no loyalties here."

"I saw the way they looked at you on that ship last night. And Cohv when he tried to bust into your room the other night. I know the sick things that go through these males' minds." He looked away. "I don't have a lot. I'm the bastard son of a mother that didn't want me. But I can offer you protection. I can make sure you're safe too."

Maybe it made me an awful person because I knew one day I'd betray him, but I kissed him anyway, nodding as we sealed the deal.

He pulled away, his face turning serious. "No thieving, Lyra. Follow the rules or you'll force my hand at a punishment."

"Would that include more spanking? Because I could get behind that idea."

He lifted an eyebrow, considering, and then shook his head with a grin. A knock interrupted us. He looked back and forth between the door and me.

"You don't expect me to answer it for you, do you?"

"No. But you're wearing a bedsheet."

I looked down and nodded, letting it fall to the floor and pool at my feet as I stood. "Good idea. I should be caught naked in your rooms."

"What?" He leaped from the couch and yanked the sheet from the floor. "We're trying to be discreet about," he waved a hand between us, "this." Another knock sounded as he wrapped the sheet around me and tugged me to him. "Let me get one thing clear, Vixen. I don't share. You can traipse around this castle however you wish, but don't get any ideas about letting another male touch you."

"Oh, I'm property now. Got it."

He leaned down and nipped my bare collarbone. I bit my lip to keep from reaching for him, instead vanishing into the bedroom to dress.

When I returned, I realized they must have had a long conversation at the door, because Jof, the orange-haired fae with gray skin, was only now entering the dry room.

He fell to the floor, not quite getting the timing right on his evada pearl, and I hid my smile behind my toast as the commander helped him up. His eyes locked with mine for a second and then pivoted back toward his new commander.

"I'm so sorry to interrupt. I can come back later."

"Not necessary. Lyra works for me. We were just discussing her new duties."

"I have news, sir." His eyes flicked to me again and I wondered if anyone had ever given him a lesson in subtlety.

"You can speak freely in front of Lyra." Kai pinned me with a look as if to tell me he was trusting me with whatever Jof was about to say.

I nodded once, and we all moved to the sitting room.

"It's Cohv," he confessed, though reluctant, as if the words were hard to say.

"How many conspirators do we think Cohv has at this point?" Kai asked Jof, who sat nervously on the couch. With his evada pearl, the gray skin was gone, replaced by something as pale as the moon. His orange hair remained.

"There are six that I know of."

"Do you have names?" I asked, genuinely curious.

He worked his hands in his lap.

"Don't be nervous, pet. I won't bite." The high-pitched and shaky tone of his laughter forced me to almost feel bad for him. Which gave me a superb idea. "Jof, have you met my friend Narina?"

"Oh yes," his voice became steadier. "I've known her for years. She's from here."

That explained the nerves. He hadn't told the commander that he knew I wasn't, and he probably knew more than that.

"Right, well. I had just come to visit her the day the queen died. I'm not from here, as you know. She's been a friend of mine for a long time, though. And of course, you know my father."

He nodded his head, dabbing a bit of sweat.

"I've been avoiding him for years. Since my mother died. Terrible old fae."

"I didn't realize your father was here," Kai cut in.

I shrugged. "Oh, he's not anymore, not that I'm keeping track of him these days."

I wondered if Jof would connect the dots and say the words I was avoiding, but apparently my act of openness was enough to ease the tension as his shoulders melted.

"You know… Narina would be a great source of gossip. She might know something. We should plan a dinner, just the four of us. I don't want everyone finding out about my new position, but we can trust her. We don't have to tell her anything, just let her talk."

Kai turned to Jof. "Thoughts, soldier?"

I snorted. Naturally, he didn't fully trust me.

"It couldn't hurt. They are getting more aggressive with the other sea fae. Eventually, they will start joining just to avoid the consequences if they don't. We can't fit everyone onto the island with the other advisors."

"Right, then. Should we say tonight?"

Standing, I held my face as neutral while shuffling through my knowledge of local islands. "Works for me."

Kai laughed. "I hope you're not planning to cook."

"Of course not." I said behind clenched teeth. "I thought you might do the honors with a land dweller meal."

"I'm sure I can figure something out, pet." He exaggerated that last word so much, even Jof had to know we were testing each other. As we always did.

"Let me get this straight. You and the commander slapped the salmon and now you want me to have dinner with him and that merfae? In his dry room, no less." Narina lounged in one of four high-back chairs in her suite, her pink tail swaying lazily back and forth as she studied her trimmed nails.

"I know it's a—"

She thrust her tail through the water, whipping around. "Of course, I'll do it."

The excitement in her eyes shocked me, but I kept my face neutral. She'd made that far too easy. We had a history, but I was closer to her sister, Ori. Mostly just because she'd left this place. Narina and I had been friends once. Maybe a loose definition of the word, but I could play the part now. Try to be the friend she wished I was. I needed her to trust me, and that started with dinner.

Narina was my only connection to the rest of the sea fae in the castle. She always knew gossip and who was where and when. She was the perfect mark for my new position as spy. Even though that was also just a role. Keeping all the lies and strands straight in my own mind would be the most difficult part of this task. I reached inside, feeling the void where my power once was, and knew I'd step on anyone to get that power back. To take back control of my life.

Narina leaned forward, crossing her hands in her lap as she looked around her room, searching as if someone might pop out at her. Twisting her face into a half smile, she whispered, "I can't believe you're … you know… with the commander. Chel will be so jealous."

I leaned back with a look of indignation. "Have you met me? Why are you so surprised?"

"I've spent over twenty years trying to talk you into moving to the castle with me. Court is fun, and the males more so. But what have you always told me?" She lifted an eyebrow, waiting for an explanation.

I huffed, keeping my voice neutral as my glare. "You've known me forever. Don't be daft. It's not like that. I'm not planning on leaving the freedom of the ocean. Not even for that sex god."

She wiggled her eyebrows. "That good, huh?"

I groaned. "It should really be a sin, Narina. He's … attentive."

She giggled and clasped her hands. "Do you think he'll give up his life on land for you?"

"It was one time. Calm down. I have no intentions of repeating it. You sound like your sister right now." She balked, and I instantly regretted my words. "I'm sorry, I didn't mean—"

"It's fine." She shook her head, instantly a million miles away. "I'm over it. She was right in the long run anyway, wasn't she?"

I hated getting involved, preferring to withdraw from these sensitive conversations on purpose. Narina and Ori were the closest thing I'd had to friends since I was a kip. My mother had insisted I interacted with others my age, and they were the only ones available. Twins, but nothing alike.

"Have you seen him?" I asked carefully.

"No, and I hope I never do. Someday I may forgive Ori for proving what a whore he truly was, but never him."

"Do you think that's why she won't come home? She feels guilty for seducing your betrothed?"

She moved to her closet and started sorting through the rows of fabric. Dressing in the sea court was so much easier than on land. A simple cover and off you went.

"No. She was happy to leave, or so it seemed. And she definitely won't come back with the queen dead. She loved her more than our mother, you know. Ori's happy to seduce the pirates. She wants to be you, Lyra. Can't you see it?"

"There's nothing glamorous about the life of a thief using her good looks to steal from males."

She pinned me with a look. "Your good looks and your siren's song."

Even the mention made my stomach roll. "That's a good color." I left the chair to pull the yellow fabric from her hands. "It would be beautiful with your pink hair."

"Who are you?" she asked, putting back the green she'd held in the other hand. "I love you because your openly shitty attitude is a nice change of pace from the bitter and conniving bitches I usually deal with, but if this some new version of you, it's weird."

Crossing my arms over my chest, I leveled my glare. She was right. I'd done too much trying to seem normal. I wasn't normal, and she knew it. "Your hair looks ridiculous when it's that short and you have a senseless amount of lip stain on."

"There she is." She laughed, swimming behind a folded screen along the wall.

I admired Narina's room for being over the top with extravagance. Sure, her parents had once stayed here in the castle as well, but she and her sister had always been given certain allowances. A large, gilded trunk sat nestled at the foot of her four-poster bed, overflowing with jewelry and long strands of giant pearls. I'd eyed that chest as a kip and had stolen from it many times.

"How's this?" Narina twirled through the room, the yellow tied behind her trailing down her back.

"Looks good to me. It's a dry room, though. What will you have on when you put your pearl in?"

"Just a plain white shirt and I'm wearing those doeskin leg coverings."

"Riding pants," I corrected.

"If one should be so lucky."

I turned my back to her, moving to the door as I wondered who she was planning on riding.

"I'll see you in an hour?"

"I'll be fashionably late," she promised.

Dinner was simple, but Kai had tried. Narina and Jof pushed food around their plates more than they ate it, sharing embarrassed glances, although the salty fish and crisp potatoes were quite good. I'd eaten land dweller food my whole life, living on a ship, but dry food was an acquired taste, which was evident by the faces of our guests.

Kai remained happily oblivious to their disgust as he enjoyed his dinner. Through the awkward silence, I cringed, scraping my fork across my plate as we sat there. Remembering this was a job, I shifted in my chair, pushing my hair over my shoulder.

"So, Narina. I heard Chel has a new merfae she's fawning over."

She swallowed, perking up as I'd obviously guessed at something she wanted to talk about.

"Oh no. Chel still has eyes for…" She paused, glancing at Kai before turning back to me. "Someone else. But Drea may be off the market soon."

She looked toward Jof. "You know Drea, right? Yellow hair, orange tail."

Jof jumped in his seat, shocked to be addressed at all. Wiping his mouth with his napkin he nodded.

"Right, well anyway, she's been hoping to get to know Incar better, following him around and basically stalking him, so imagine all of our surprise when she showed up to dinner the other night with Venzo." Her eyes were as wide as her smile as she looked at each of us, waiting for a response she clearly wasn't getting.

"Incar's brother?"

"Ohhh," I said, nodding and dragging out the word. I had no idea who she was talking about, but the point was, she was talking.

"Exactly," she said, throwing her head back and laughing. "Can you imagine? And poor Incar."

"Poor Incar?" Kai asked, folding his hands on the table. "Sounds like he wasn't interested."

"Of course, he was." She giggled. "He was playing with her. Hoping to keep her interested by ignoring her."

Jof shifted uncomfortably in his seat as I hid my sly smile behind my wine glass. At least I wasn't the only one uncomfortable with boring gossip. I filled Narina's glass with more wine and forced a smile as she continued explaining that Venzo and his cousin had gotten into a fight and how one of the mermaids wasn't talking to her because she'd wanted to be with the younger cousin. By the time she was done, I think we were all struggling to keep up with the latest news from the socialites of the castle.

Kai nudged me from under the table as she prattled on and I jerked up, not realizing I'd started to fall asleep. He pinned me with a glare and tilted his head toward Narina. She was talking Jof's ear off. He'd been staring wide-eyed, clearly still uncomfortable but too polite to mention it.

I cleared my throat, halting Narina as I turned to Jof. "So, what did you do before Morwena's death?"

He dropped his fork. "I'm sorry?"

"Oh." I looked at Narina, her wide eyes an indication that I'd asked something wrong. "As in for work? In the castle."

"I was a slave."

"Oh… Sorry." A forced apology was not helping as I glanced at the others, shaking their heads at me. "What? I didn't know. He's a merfae. I assumed he was better than the lessers."

Narina kicked me under the table. My head snapped to her so fast she slid back in her chair. She'd forgotten who she was dealing with. We were friends, but only just.

"No one is better than anyone else," Kai said flatly.

"It's fine." Jof placed his napkin over his plate. "I'm not ashamed of where I've come from, only for the fact that this kingdom was so cruel in the first place. I never fit into Morwena's mold. Never complied with her hatred of others. So, into the chains I went."

"It's still quite sad." Narina placed her hand on Jof's forearm resting on the table and smiled at him as she tucked her pink locks behind an ear. "I bet you're happy to be working with the commander now."

I could spot an act from a mile away. I had been born to lure and lie my way through life. She'd made coming to dinner too easy and now she was openly flirting with a fae she probably looked down on. Something she would not have done weeks ago.

"It is a good job."

Every ounce of my soul wanted to call Narina out, just to see what she would say, but that's not what I was doing here. Instead, I reached for my glass of wine and finished it in one sip, letting myself sway a little too far as I leaned against her.

“Is the castle gossip exhausting for you, Lyra?”

“Not at all,” I answered.

“I hear the commander has quite the entourage of mermaid fans.” She giggled, leaning back onto me.

“Oh, that’s not gossip.” Jof chuckled. “I’m sure there’s still a gathering outside his door.

Kai beamed. “I’ve asked the guards to keep the halls clear.”

His meaning was clear. He didn’t want anyone knowing I was in his rooms. I bit the inside of my cheek, studying the party around the table. Jof was simple. He wanted to impress the commander. Kai, not as simple, his dual personality more confusing than anything. But then, so was the mermaid, giggling like she had when we were kips as she played her role. This dinner could not have been more of a farce, and the sad thing was perhaps Narina had them all more fooled than I did.

CHAPTER 15

Never in my life had I laid in a bed with the same person twice. Sex, in all of its glory, was just a means of pleasure. Males were the bitter skin of fruit before plunging into the sweet juices of the center, be it the look of betrayal on their faces when they realized the truth of a siren, or the hidden treasures I'd acquired along the way. I'd never used my song to force a male into sex, but I'd never needed to, either. They were always willing and ready. But as I lay alone in my bedroom that night, I found myself wondering whether Kai had taken one of those mermaids into his.

Forcing those thoughts from my mind, because it didn't matter what he chose to do on his own time, I became more and more aware that I either needed to get my father out as soon as possible, or go hunting on my own. The problem was, without my song, I couldn't force anyone to tell me a thing. I felt trapped and only hoped that feeling wouldn't call me to do desperate things. The only other person I knew with secret connections was whoever A.T. was. And I didn't know them at all. Had no way of reaching them.

I stretched across the bed, feeling less like myself than I had in days. Jof had said the advisors were on an island. Maybe I could talk Kaitalen into exploring the ocean. I could get him to lead me to the island, since it was probably the only place other than the castle he'd been. We'd agreed I'd still keep my other duties as a cover.

Leora, the little glowing sea fae, was working in the kitchens with several other mermaids when I entered. Her eyes went wide as she backed away from me, colliding with the counter.

"Good morning, Leora."

The orange glow she emanated dimmed as she dipped her chin to me. "I wasn't sure you'd come back."

My mouth formed a line as I realized I deserved that reaction. "Well, I'm here now. What am I supposed to do?"

She looked at the other mermaids, who had gone still, watching. "I have most of the jobs covered."

"Well, most isn't all, now is it. I'll just do whatever she's doing." I crossed the large kitchen and picked up a knife, slicing the vegetables strewn along the table, just as the mermaid with black hair was doing.

"Oh no." Leora swam forward, pulling them away.

I set the knife down. "Am I not good enough to chop your vegetables? Gods. I hate this castle. I'm just trying to do my job like everyone else."

Leora shrank a little as she answered. "No. These have already been chopped. You'll make them too small."

"Oh."

Perking up, she swam around the counter and patted my hand. "I'll think of something for you to do tomorrow. Why don't you take the day to get to know the castle better?"

Eyeing her suspiciously, I backed toward the door. "Well, if you insist. Do you know where I might find the commander?"

"Oh, he's gone to the Flame Court for the day."

Perfect.

I was sneaking out of the castle within the hour. Since there was no tithe due and no father giving me orders, I could swim. As far and as fast as I wanted. Wherever I wanted. The relief of the open waters was instantly soothing until somewhere far away I heard a voice as smooth and soft as honey ringing through the water like a whisper on the morning wind.

I jolted to a halt, spinning as the song created a physical response in my body. A twitch of my tail and heat crept up my spine, around my neck, and into my mind, clouding my thoughts and capturing control as it lulled me into an intoxicated forward motion. There was a promise on the water, deep within that voice, luring me into something so beautiful, my heart ached with need.

I jerked, a warning passing through me. Gritting my teeth, I felt ripped in half between desire and fear. This was wrong. So wrong. Yet fighting it was like battling a final breath in fae form. The last drop of water leaving me as a siren, writhing on a beach just before death. Still, I pushed away.

The song disappeared in a tail flick, and with my heart racing, I did the only thing I could think of as I sped to the Gulley. For the first time in my life, I was desperate to get out of the water. Afraid of that suffocation consuming me. Someone had just tried to use a siren's song on me. Not only should that not have been possible, I'd also been incredibly weak in resisting. Perhaps it wasn't a siren at all, because where would she have come from? The stolen song, returned? Another bit of proof that they were out there somewhere. Maybe it was only one. But I was not alone. I was rattled, but not alone.

I never thought the view of the Gulley would comfort me, but it did. Merfae were scattered through the water on the east side. I watched them heave down a ship to a dangerous degree as they cleaned the vessel using long poles. Likely the ship needed repair, or they wouldn't have bothered. I swam around in a distance for a better look, wincing at the gaping hole. She bilged on her own anchor. I can't imagine the captain was happy about that one.

I preferred to enter the Gulley through the docks, but hated passing Vexyr's overbearing ship looming as I passed. His men were trained to look for me. I nabbed a discarded cloak from a merfae working in the water and slipped into the crowds passing on the rope bridges. For a moment, I'd forgotten the demeanor one needed to traipse through this place. Some parts were so familiar, and others were beginning to feel foreign as I realized I no longer had the protection of my song or the threats of my father.

He held a rapport with many of the captains, which meant someone here had to know something. He was a collector of information, but it always came from someone else. The Gulley was the hub. I needed only to look in the right place. Unfortunately, my gut was telling me the right place was stalking Vexyr's ship. Not the one perched on the cliffs, but the one in the water, where the real business happened.

His guards patrolled the water like starving sharks seeking blood. They were hunters, which was why falling into the waters below the Gulley was so dangerous. While most of the patrons could remove an evada pearl and swim away, that wasn't always an option.

Thinking of the guards and how many times I'd used my song on them gave me an idea. There were no alleys here though, nothing was hidden in the pirate's village until night, so I'd have to be creative as I hunted. Anyone that knew my song had been stolen wouldn't be afraid of me using it on them. I'd only have to hunt down the unfortunate souls that learned the hard way not to fuck with me.

The last time I'd walked the Gulley I'd sworn everyone knew. I had felt the judgment and disdain, the close proximity of fae that once feared me. Cloaked, with my braid tucked below the hood, they had no idea who I was. I could pull the hood, but then I'd risk Vexyr, so instead, I went to the second best place for gossip and fearful fae. Merk's.

The obnoxious brass bell above the door chimed as I walked in. I kept the hood high, my claws hidden, and sat in a seat that wasn't my usual. When Adair walked my way, I simply shook my head, and off she went. I waited, just as the figure in the back of the room always did. Ori had teased that a dead person laid beneath that cloak, but I knew better. I'd seen the rise and fall of shoulders every time I'd stopped.

The heavy door opened and closed three times as I counted the dark wood panels lining the floor. I listened to voices and the cadence of footfalls, waiting for something familiar. One fae I could have used was so drunk he probably wouldn't have cared about my threats no matter what I'd said to him. Two others were quiet, and I didn't dare risk looking up and exposing myself.

The hue of the sunlight coming in through the filthy windows changed as the hours passed, and I knew I still had to swim all the way back to the castle and come up with some excuse for my absence if the commander returned before me. Lying was a sport, though, and I'd spent my entire life practicing. I could handle him.

Desperation settled in, and at the risk of exposing myself, I decided to use the one target I didn't want to. I waved a hand in the air, and Adair walked over. She'd seen my nails, if nothing else.

"Where have you been, stranger?" she asked, thrumming her fingers on the table.

I lifted my chin enough to look into her eyes. If she was going to lie, I would see it right there. "I've been keeping company elsewhere. I've lost something that belongs to me, Adair. Tell me what you know of it."

She shook her head, her stare as steady as ever. "I don't know what you're talking about."

At least she was smart enough not to use my name. "Don't make me use my song. I'd hate to do that to you."

Fear. A single flinch across her face and the ghost of a backward step told me all I needed to know. If there was talk of my song going missing, it wasn't happening here.

"I don't know anything. I swear it."

"Thanks, Adair." Dipping my chin, I stood to go. "I mean that."

I was out the door and down to the docks faster than I'd ever traveled the Gulley. I needed to get out of there before he caught me, and it was only a matter of time before that wasn't possible. I couldn't deal with Vexyr yet. The lack of protection was also a lack of identity. I'd never felt so exposed as I jumped into the water, staying in my fae form until the very last second before swimming as fast as I could away. I considered checking on the *Talea*, but my father's ship would have to wait.

The mental exhaustion from being in the Gulley was taxing. I'd always had to watch my back there. But I'd never realized the security my song gave me until it was gone. Feeling destroyed, such a fraction of the person I once was, I pushed myself hard to get back to the castle. Only as I approached did I realize something about it felt safe. And that in itself felt wrong.

Coming to my hidden cave, the lack of guards surrounding the castle in the distance giving me pause. Kai would never leave it unguarded, but few remained, from what I could see. I dashed into the secret entrance and then into the abandoned hallway.

As I rounded a corner, droves of sea fae filled the space. Crumbling halls we hadn't been able to use before had been cleaned and restored. Whoever was doing all those new jobs was making progress, and quickly. As we were pressed together and ushered down the corridor, I searched for a familiar face but found none.

Slipping away from the crowd, exhausted and only wanting a bed to lay my head on, I jerked when a familiar arm slipped through mine.

"Everyone's been called to the ballroom. Your lover will notice if you're not there."

I rolled my eyes as I let Narina spin me back the other way. "He's not my lover. It was a one-time thing, and for pixie's sake, keep your voice down."

She winked and dragged me down the hall with the rest of the imprisoned sea fae. We made it into the old ballroom, but rather than elaborate décor and peppy music, there were tables lined up around the walls and a fierce-looking commander floating in the middle of the room, glaring at me. I lifted my chin and smirked as he swam closer.

"Where have you been?" he hissed, keeping his voice quiet as he moved in. He preferred close. He preferred to wreck my comfort zone. And I didn't hate the way he looked at me while he did it. "I've been back for hours. I had something to discuss with you, but you weren't here."

"She was with me," Narina answered. "I didn't feel like working today either, so we took the day off and did … girl stuff."

His eyes shifted between us, but eventually those broad shoulders relaxed, and he turned away.

"He's moody," Narina said as we watched him go.

"I hadn't noticed," I answered, my nails pressing firmly into the palms of my hands.

I'd skipped the day, but so had she. Based on the sly look on her face, I'd say she had been doing something far more sinister than 'girl time.' Whatever the hell that was.

"I've ordered you all here this evening to be completely transparent with you. The things happening on land are not good. Everyday, information is coming in that leads us to believe war is on the horizon. War changes people. It changes the land, the sea, the hearts of us all. You think you'll never have to do something until a time comes when you don't have a choice. You may say you'll give your life in service to another, but when it comes down to it, will you really?"

He swam closer to the crowd. Curious faces drew serious as the murmuring of voices fell silent. "We will have more Flame Court guards move down to the castle and we will be sending more sea fae to Halemi so you can train on land. I won't force you to fight. The new king will not force you to fight. But I will ask you to, on his behalf.

"This evening, we will start with the basics, seeking those of you with natural skill to take the first round of training on land." He crossed the room to a table full of multi-length spears, lifting one extra-long one with a curved blade on the end rather than pointed. "My guards and I are here to train you. As you can see, we have filled these tables with weapons. Several nights ago, I watched a female as she was attacked under the sea. She got away, but only just. It's time to learn to fight, as you should have learned long ago. Move about the room, find a weapon that intrigues you and let's begin."

Reluctant at first, the fae stared at the commander as if he'd grown two more heads. But as his team of guards spread throughout, examining the weapons laid upon the tables, the sea fae moved. I felt eyes on me as I found a table with different length whips. I lifted one and ran my hands over the black leather that wrapped around the thick base of the handle.

"Interesting choice." Kai's words were like a feather moving down my spine.

"It's not a choice at all," I answered, setting the whip back down.

"Afraid?"

"Show me," I purred, moving closer as I swept my arm over the table. "How does one use a whip correctly?"

He moved away, circling the table several times as he examined the whips while stroking his bottom lip with his thumb. "You want to choose one that isn't too long when you're new to this. It takes an incredible amount of upper body strength to use a whip with precision. It's not just in your arm strength, but here," he said, brushing his fingers over my core as he glanced to the side. He'd have to play this game carefully or the others would notice. Pulling a weapon from the table, he pressed it into my hands. "Take this and let's see what happens."

"There are other uses for whips, you know." He moved closer but I backed away. "Careful, Commander. You wouldn't want anyone to see you giving me special attention."

Fire lit his eyes, but he swam away, pointing to another table. "I'm happy to take you up on that whipping lesson later, but for now, your goal is to knock this glass over. Extra points if you can break it."

"Must you watch?"

He nodded. "You don't want to start with bad habits and continue to practice with them. I'll get someone else to help you if you want, but you need to be trained."

I dropped my hands. "I was fine."

"What?"

"I know you were talking about Simmonne grabbing me on the ship. That wasn't below water, it was above, but I was fine."

He crossed that personal boundary again, leaning so close I could nearly feel his beating heart. "You didn't use your song. You failed to use a weapon at your disposal. You weren't fine. And it will never happen again."

The tension in his eyes as he accused me was crystal clear. He'd noticed. My cheeks flushed. I needed to hide the dangerous truth.

"I don't use my song." I pulled my arm back and cracked the whip, shattering the glass at the table. He eyed me carefully but said nothing. I shrugged and pushed the whip into his chest. "Not my first time."

I left him floating, dumbfounded, as a mermaid swam up and asked to go next. He handed her the whip, but as he moved to follow me, I shook my head and sought out the table full of spears. Three guards were explaining the logistics of throwing one, how to hold it and why it was better to learn to use it without throwing it, but simply perfecting the thrust.

I glanced out of the corner of my eye at the commander, now encircled by mermaids and other females interested in learning whatever he'd teach them. His smile was wide as he worked with the sea fae, and I could see why he was chosen as Commander. Not because he was ruthless, though maybe he was, but more so because he seemed to actually enjoy weaponry and the teaching tactics. His muscles rippled as he flicked that whip through the air in demonstration, but for some reason, their collective reaction to him grated my nerves.

Why should I be jealous of a gaggling bunch of mermaids? How did the commander know exactly how to get a reaction out of me every single time he wanted?

Chel, the mouthiest mermaid of them all, reached forward and let her hand brush his for a moment too long as she took a whip from his hands. He smiled at her and that was all the fire I needed to storm out of the ballroom. I was too tired. My mood was erratic, probably because of all the stress of the day.

Shutting my bedroom door, I sighed, finally able to just be in peace for a moment's time. I hated all of them. Hated how being here made me feel. I didn't want to be a part of something bigger. I just wanted to be left alone. He could have his mermaids.

A single knock on my door turned my stomach. I couldn't handle any more. Not today.

"Lyra, open the door," Kai barked.

I hauled myself off the bed and turned the knob, slowly. He was in my room, slamming the door shut in an instant. Urgent hands pushed me against the wall as his lips crashed into mine, forceful and passionate. All the tension and jealously vanished like the last ray of sun on a long day.

I moved my hands up his chest, burying them into his hair as our tongues brushed each other. He bit my lip and I let out a moan, fiery desire shooting straight through my body.

"Gods, I want you," he panted, untying the dark purple band across my chest. I twisted my tail around his, lost in the sensation of my scales rubbing gently against his.

"I want—"

Another knock came. I pressed my hand over Kai's mouth as I pulled my body away. I smirked as he waited. Frozen.

"Unless you want to meet your maker, go away," I answered.

A throat cleared. "Uhm. It's me, Jof."

"I said what I said."

Kai pulled my hand away from his mouth, kissing the tips before he pushed away and cracked the door open. "What is it?"

"Sorry, sir. I know you said not to interrupt, but one of the mermaids is caught in the harpoon net again and she won't let the guards get near her. She's asking for you."

Kai squeezed his eyes shut and tilted his head back, growling. "I'll be there in a minute."

Shutting the door, he turned back to me, an apology on his lips.

I held my hand up. "It's fine. I should probably get some sleep, anyway."

He said nothing, but nodded and slipped out of the door, leaving me wanting him more than I ever had. Damnit.

CHAPTER 16

Training again. Crammed back into the old ballroom, I tried to stay at the back of the crowd, watching and listening as the guards provided information that could be valuable to me later. They wanted us to fight for them. To die for them. They seemed to miss the most important point. We just wanted to live for ourselves.

"Each table will now be assigned trainers. You have half an hour to decide on your preferred weapon before working with the trainers on proper use. If you learn nothing else today, learn to defend yourself."

I looked around the room, realizing for the first time, apart from Jof, only females filled it. Kai had a penchant for them, apparently. As he swam directly to me, I considered cutting around him and doing my own thing until I could sneak out, but he moved into my path and crossed his arms over his chest, leaving me with no choice. Egotistical males.

"What's your issue with females?" I asked as he led me to a table.

He pointed. "Let's start with this one."

"Fine, but answer."

He took my hand, rubbing the underside of the wrist before he secured a stiff piece of material that fit like a glove all the way to my shoulder. "It isn't that I don't think women are strong or smart or anything like that. You all deserve to be cherished and loved. My mom abandoned me when I was young. Too young to be able to protect her or myself. I lived behind a bar in a tavern until I made friends with Fen. I have no idea if she's even alive now. She left and she's never tried to find me." He picked up a tiny knife and shoved it into the contraption. "I wish I knew she was safe. I'd protect her now if I could. Maybe I'm compensating."

"Even though she left you?"

He smiled sadly. "It's easier to love her if I don't think about that part."

"Well, I've always been able to protect myself. My mother trained me when I was young, before she died. I'm not a soldier. I can protect myself and that's always been enough."

His eyebrows creased as he looked at me with sympathy. Why had I said that? I didn't need his pity.

"What is this thing?" I picked at the apparatus, hoping to change the subject. Boundaries. Walls and all that.

He let the moment pass and pointed. "This piece is the bandolier, and these," he lifted the little knives, "are water picks."

"Oh, I've been eyeing these. Do you mind if I join you?"

Chel nudged in beside us and I rolled my eyes as Kai dipped his chin and pulled a second bandolier from the table.

"Slide your hand in like a glove. You'll secure the straps here and here."

"Could you help me?" she asked, smiling far too sweetly.

He wiggled his eyebrows and smirked at the redhead. "Of course."

She giggled as he carefully slid the long glove up her arm. My soul left my body as I pictured ripping her to shreds while she flirted with him right in front of me. But then, of course, no one knew we'd been sneaking around. And I'm sure if she did know, she wouldn't care at all.

"Do you think this one's a bit too big for me?" she said. "I'm smaller than the siren. Maybe we should trade."

"Oh. Good point." Kai turned to me and removed the contraption without a word or a glance.

I bit my tongue so hard I could taste blood as she glared at me behind his back.

Oblivious, Kaitalen removed her first glove and slid mine onto her arm. He tossed me the other as he fastened hers into place. She had to know I couldn't touch her here in the castle. That's the only reason she'd be brave enough to look at me like that. The commander's protection wouldn't last forever.

Shifting us until we were side by side, he moved in front to demonstrate. Though she probably didn't realize it, I could feel the fear emanating off her body. Her confidence was wavering, which boosted my own as I lowered my chin and stared down the commander, daring him to look away from me.

Chel stretched her arm, moving slightly away at the action. "I think mine is a little too tight; could you check it for me?"

He swam over to investigate, moving his hands down her arm. Unable to control myself I coiled to lunge, but just at the last second, Narina slipped between us, pinning me with a look as she declared she'd also like to learn about the contraption.

Kai helped her put on the last remaining glove and continued his lesson.

"These are called water picks." He held the tiny, pointed knife up to show us. "You load them into your wrist bandoliers like this." He pressed the small blade into a concealed pocket on the strap he'd tightened on my wrist. "You'll load the entire strap." He clicked each one into place, then tightened a second strap over them. "And once they are all secured, you pull down on this lever at the bottom of the brace, and that will cause a spring-loaded reaction when you release. These are far more powerful weapons under the water, but they will work on land, should you ever need it."

"Like baby spears," Narina said, twisting her arm to look at the band.

"Yes," Kai answered, jolting forward to point her arm away from people. "But these are weapons and dangerous. You should be careful."

She cowered. "Right, sorry."

"So, what are we shooting?" I thrust my arm out, pointing at a glass similar to the one I'd hit with the whip.

"Calm down, siren." Kai pushed my arm until I was pointing at a row of cushions stacked up, resembling a sea fae with an oversized tail. "Aim and flick your wrist, but—"

I didn't give him time to warn me; I just jerked my wrist up and the tiny knife grazed my finger as it shot across the room, a tiny prick of blood dissipating into the water.

"Mother fucker." I pulled my hand to my chest, then away, afraid to stab myself by accident. "Get this thing off me."

Chel laughed and I turned my arm toward her, ready to shoot again. Kai grabbed my wrist and yanked it away.

"If you'd listen, you have to keep your hand in a fist, or you'll block the knives.

"Who would have guessed?" Narina mocked, not bothering to hide her smile, as she knew Chel was close to death.

I closed my hand and flicked my wrist again. The tiny dagger flew from the weapon and landed so hard in the single cushion, they all toppled to the seafloor.

"Oh, my turn." Narina was so excited, she yanked back on the lever and released it, then jerked her arm out and twisted her fist. When nothing happened, she turned to Kai. "I think mine is broken, Commander."

He moved in close to investigate. "Ah." He pulled back on the lever again. "When you pulled this, you didn't wait for the click. I forgot to mention that."

He pushed the small piece back and without warning, Narina shot him, a tiny dagger slamming straight into that cerulean blue tail of his.

She gasped and backed away, disappearing into the crowd of sea fae that moved toward us as the commander barked and blood began fogging the water around us. I pushed the fae back, looping his arm around my shoulder. Jof swooped in on the other side, and we swam toward the door.

Someone shouted, and I looked over my shoulder just in time to catch Cohv swimming over to Narina's side, though he hadn't been in the room only moments ago. He'd tried to attack me in my room, was causing trouble for Kai, and now just happened to appear as soon as the commander was injured. I could have taken his heart right then, had it not been for the blood in the water.

"I'm telling you, it's just a scratch. Let me go." Kai pushed against Jof, who in turn shoved him down farther.

We'd made it to the healer's hall and into a small room, which felt more like a dark cave lined with shelves of vials and sea plants. He fought laying on the table, but Jof wasn't having any of it.

"I'll fight you, Commander. Right in front of the siren if you force me to. You've got a rip in your tail. You don't know what that could mean. You need a healer."

"Here." I plucked a flask from a shelf and handed it to him. "Drink this and shut up already."

Kai twisted the lid off, and as the liquid moved down his throat, he relaxed. He handed the flask to Jof, and the lesser fae didn't hesitate in draining the remaining liquid.

He wiped his mouth with the back of his arm and returned the flask. "Will you listen to me now?"

"Don't start with this again. It was an accident. That mermaid didn't have a clue what she was doing."

Jof's eyes flicked to me and back to Kai. I could tell he still didn't trust me, but I found it more interesting he didn't trust Kai. If anything, it was a reflection of how badly the lesser fae had been treated.

"You have to be more careful."

Kai lost all expression on his face. "I assure you, Jof. I am more than capable of handling myself."

"We can talk about this later," Jof said, just as the door opened and the healer entered.

An older sea fae, with likely hundreds of years of knowledge, came in, his face stern as he moved directly to Kai on the raised platform in the middle of the spacious room. Jof and I swam away, giving the healer distance, but as he eyed Kaitalen, disdain clear on his face, we scooted back in.

There was more going on in the castle than I could commit my time to. I needed to find my song, which meant gaining access to the island my father was on somehow, and I couldn't care about the rest.

But then there was Cohv. And Narina being more suspicious than anyone. I hadn't mistaken his proximity to her. There was plotting happening behind the commander's back and, though Jof was trying to warn him, he wasn't listening. Which was very dangerous. If Cohv somehow managed to take over the Sea Court, he may very well have the advisors on the island killed and start a war with the Flame Court in the meantime. Or we would end up joining Autus.

"Lyra?"

I jerked my head up, realizing Jof and the healer had left, leaving me and Kai alone.

"You okay?"

"Yes, I'm sorry. It's been a weird day. I didn't even hear what the healer said."

"That's because he didn't say a word. Just slapped some salve over it and swam away. Jof is chasing him down."

"Either way, that fin isn't getting any better today. Best to get you back to the room."

"No. I need you to help get me to the Flame Court. There's a healer there that can fix this right up."

"Woah. I'm just the spy. I shouldn't even have helped you come here."

"You were the closest person. It wasn't odd that you would help."

"Have you met me?"

He didn't answer, only stared me down.

"Fine, but I'm not going to the castle. I'll get you to land, and then you're on your own."

"Deal." He grunted, pulling himself up.

We left the castle just as seamlessly as we had the night of the pirate ships, only I was much more aware of the looks from others. Either complete adoration or utter hatred filtered our way as we swam away, moving first to the surface, then along the top of the water. As soon as we were close enough to stand, he removed his earring, and I changed into my fae form.

"How do we suddenly have clothes on?" he asked, genuine curiosity in his question. "I haven't really asked anyone how the evada pearls work."

I shrugged. "Magic, I guess. Whatever we're wearing in each form last is what appears when we swap between them. I don't question the logic. I'm just glad I'm not naked each time."

"Well, that makes one of us." He ran his fingers through his soaking wet hair. "I'd really prefer if you came with me. With Cohv down there, who knows what state I'll find you in when I get back."

I looked down at his pierced leg and then at his face. "You're one to talk."

"It was an accident."

"Don't think you're fooling any of us with that answer."

He raised his eyebrows, pulling back. "You really think your friend would do that?"

"If there's one thing I've learned over the years, Commander, keep your friends close and your enemies closer. I'm not saying she's an enemy. But I trust no one."

"No one?"

I left that question hanging in the air for longer than I should have. "I am learning to trust you," I lied. "Trust takes time to build." Not a lie.

"Indeed. I accept that challenge."

I crossed my arms over my chest, hoping it strengthened the wall.

"I'll meet you back down there. I'm not afraid of Cohv. If anything, he should be afraid of me."

"Oh, right." He tapped his chest. "Because of the heart removal thing. Got it."

"Insulting me does not build trust, Kaitalen."

He straightened, something foreign flashing across his face. But then he blinked, and it vanished, the walls back in place. "I'll check in with you tonight."

I leaned down, plucking the seashell from the sand. "Here. Take this. Something to remember me by in case Cohv decides to kill me before you come back." I tossed the seashell, hoping it would ease the tension.

He caught it effortlessly, forcing a smile as he turned and limped away.

I leaped back into the sea, making my way to the castle and directly to Narina's room. I knocked but she didn't answer. Just as I was about to let myself in, she swam around the corner, the smile plastered across her face faltering when her eyes landed on me.

I gave her a knowing look and she dipped her chin once, looking over her shoulder before she opened her door to let us in.

Without giving her a moment to conjure a story, I got in her face. "Tell me everything and don't leave a single detail out or I will use my song on you, and you won't like what I force you to do."

"Lyra, I—"

I held a hand up. "From the beginning, Narina."

She moved away, but fear shuddered through the water. "I guess I just assumed you were playing with the commander like you usually do."

"There's more going on with you that you aren't saying. Continue."

"I … I can't tell you. You'll just go to him."

I gripped her by the arm and shoved her against the wall so hard a picture came loose from its hook and slid to the floor, breaking into pieces. "Whatever you imagine will happen at the commander's hands will be nothing compared to what will happen at mine. I need information. Now."

She trembled in my grip, squeaking, as she opened her mouth to speak. "Cohv is Morwena's only descendant. He doesn't like the Flame Court coming in here and commanding the sea like it is theirs."

"So what's the plan, Narina? What do *you* have to do with it?

"I'm... we're... I'm to be his queen."

I released my grip, stunned.

Misreading my shock, she pushed away. "And what do you think will happen to you when I tell him you've put your hands on me?"

I whipped around, the anger on my face unmistakable. "You shot the commander on purpose."

She grunted, a whisper of a smile caressing her lips. "Of course, I did. I missed, but there will be another time."

The world rocked below me. Not at her words, but my reaction. This was not my battle. This was not my concern. Would Cohv make it more difficult for me to free my father? Perhaps. But I'd shown my hand way too early and now I needed to backtrack.

I moved away from her, slumping onto the bed, my eyes glued to the floor. "You're sure he can do it?"

She didn't move, didn't take the iron from her voice as she snapped, "He can and will. And now you don't have me to show you favor."

I gripped the sheets, willing my heart to slow. To play the role. Though all the roles were beginning to mingle in my mind. The daughter, the interested lover, the friend, the thief, the siren. So many roles. So many holes I was digging.

I looked up, locking her gaze. "He has my father, Narina. I'm only trying to set him free. I don't know who to trust anymore, but I won't stand in your way."

"And the commander?"

"He's just a mark. I don't care about Kai. Just the job." The words tasted foul on my tongue.

Her features softened as she reached for my hand. "You can't turn your back on your friends, Lyra. You attacked me."

"It's not like it's the first time that's happened."

"Well, we aren't kips anymore. And this is serious."

I shook my head. "I had to have to the truth. I didn't think you'd tell me."

"Why wouldn't I? Especially since you're on our side."

I nodded, covering my face in mock humiliation. "You know why. I don't trust people. Your sister called me selfish, and she was right."

She'd never agree with her sister. A fact I knew well and used to my advantage as she plopped beside me on the bed, leaning her head onto my shoulder. "She's wrong, Lyra. You're only trying to help your father. No one can fault you for that."

Resting my head against hers, I sighed. "Thanks, Narina." I let the moment linger, if only to convince her of my sincerity, before I continued. "So, what are we going to do about this commander and his soldiers?"

"Well," she said, perking up. "I will make sure Cohv knows you're on our side and you just keep doing what you're doing for now. You can be our eyes. A spy!"

"How strong is his power?" I rubbed my hand down the deep purple scales in my lap, a pattern I'd memorized a long time ago.

"Power?" she asked, turning toward me.

"Well yes. If he's a descendant, he must be able to enchant people. That's what marks royalty by birth."

"Oh that. Yes, well… he's working on it. Apparently, it takes time to develop when you're not a direct descendant. He's got a friend researching it for him."

I moved from the bed, turning to look down at her. "I'm so glad to have you. Living in the castle, having a constant friend nearby is something I'm still trying to get used to."

She got up, wrapping her arms around me in a hug. "You can be scary when you want to be." She laughed nervously. "I'll let you know what Cohv needs you to do as soon as I talk to him. Remember to try to get any information you can, in the meantime."

"I promise."

CHAPTER 17

"Are you always a giant baby, or is this just a fun experiment?" I asked Kai as he moaned from his couch.

"I aim for giant baby every single day."

"Mission accomplished." I held a drink of rum out to him, and he swallowed, winced, and handed the glass back, indicating he wanted another. I obliged. "So, I talked to Narina."

He choked on his second drink. "Already? You didn't want to wait for me?"

I set the decanter on the low table and moved to the chair. "I'm supposed to be your eyes around here, right? Plus, she wasn't going to talk in front of you."

He wiggled his eyebrows, a trace of ease from the drink lifting his muscles. "I can be pretty persuasive when I want to be."

"So can I." I winked and sipped my wine.

"What did you learn? Anything valuable?"

I'd thought about this for a while. Whether I wanted to play both sides or stick to only one. In the end, I decided telling Kai would solidify his trust in me, so I told him everything. His demeanor changed gradually as I recalled the conversation.

"This is the kind of thing I should be reporting to Fen, but he's got a lot on his plate right now." Kai ran his fingers through his hair, his elbows sitting heavily on his knees as he hung his head. "We do everything together. We're a team."

"Honestly, this shouldn't be a surprise. Cohv hasn't exactly been candid with his hatred for you. If the king is too busy, it looks like you've got a new team now."

"You're sure he doesn't have power?"

I nodded. "I told you everything she said. He's got a few followers but so far, no enchantment."

"For now, eyes open. We watch and wait. If they corner you and make you report on me, make something up. I don't care what you say. Don't make yourself any more of a target, Lyra. We'll figure out who his team is and keep them separate as much as we can." His sad eyes flicked to me. "Thank you."

I gestured between us. "New team."

He smiled, then stood and walked perfectly around the table, filling my wine glass, never taking his eyes from mine. My breath caught. That single look from him called my desire forward as if he'd commanded it at will.

"Some injury." I snorted, gulping the wine to break his stare.

"It's healed, actually. But I'd prefer the sea court to think I'm injured. They'll underestimate me. Which is why when we go to dinner, I'll be far too drunk to notice anyone's scheming."

"I think I like your style, Commander." I lifted my glass and clinked it to his. He was falling into my carefully laid trap and right now I hovered from above, watching him fall.

"I think I like you, little vixen." He smiled.

I stood, setting my glass down as I wrapped my arms around his neck and kissed him. The desire was there, but mostly I needed to stop him from his confession. My guilt was already budding, and we had so much further down this road to go.

For such a powerful male, he was far more layered than I'd expected. Caring and secure. Whether I liked it or not, something was blooming between us. And I had to stop it. I just didn't have the strength to pull away.

His kiss deepened, spreading fire through me until yearning pooled low in my belly. He knew instantly the salacious thoughts that entered my mind as he pulled my shirt over my head and squeezed my breasts. I pressed my body into his and, feeling his need equaling mine, I moved my hands over his growing erection.

"How much time do we have?" I asked, my breath hitching as I pulled away from his heated kiss.

"Eternity," he answered, lifting me from the floor and walking us over to the couch. He laid me down, pulling off my loosely fitted pants as his eyes locked onto the apex between my writhing legs.

He didn't pause a wink as he moved to his knees, taking the sensitive bud into his mouth as I ran my fingers through his unruly hair. He licked between my folds, and I arched my back, moaning at the sensation of him worshiping my body.

"Do you like that?" his voice rumbled.

"Yes." I could barely put the word together, the need for him growing, my thighs aching for release.

He pulled away, his eyes burning into mine as he licked two of his fingers and pushed them into me, using his thumb to rub in a rhythm that would soon destroy me.

"Tell me how it feels, Lyra."

That smoky tone of his commanding voice was nearly my undoing. But I couldn't. I was climbing a hill of pleasure and as I reached the top, a moan escaped as everything wrong in the world faded away and for just that moment, it was him and I. Nothing else mattered. My legs shook as all my muscles reacted to the orgasm he'd so brilliantly orchestrated.

Kai moved above me on the couch, his slick tip pressing into my opening. He waited, watching me, until the final waves of my orgasm vanished. Then he slammed into me. Hard. I gripped his back, my nails digging into him. I watched as his face twisted between pleasure and pain. He thrust in an uneven pattern, keeping my body guessing as it responded to him, as he wrapped my hair around his fist and pulled.

A thousand pricks of agony collided with a million waves of pleasure within my body, and without a warning, another orgasm built. There was nothing tender and sweet about this. Purely feral, we thrashed like beasts until we came together, grunting and panting until the moment passed and he slipped away, claiming he needed a shower before we left.

I was grateful for the space. The time to reflect on my decisions and make sure I wasn't burying myself as I walked this steep edge. But no matter which way I turned, I'd fall if I didn't stay the course. So, I did.

All eyes were on us as we entered the great dining hall that night for dinner. We arrived amidst a group of guards, blending with other sea fae, so it didn't look obvious that we had arrived together. Kai was dramatic, swimming sluggishly as he made his way to the head of the table. He swayed in his chair, eyelids heavy as he smiled easily. Clearly, he'd spent many of his days drunk. He played the part so well, at one point, when he dropped his spoon, even I was convinced.

Jof must have been in on the act as well because he watched the room carefully, but was poignant in his decision to not correct the commander in front of the sea fae lining both sides of the long table. Narina sat close to me, and two seats down from her on the opposite side sat Cohv. He observed Kai closely, whispering to the merfae with a bright green tail beside him as he sneered.

By the third course, Cohv stood from the table, moving toward Kai. I watched the commander's subtle movement as he slipped a knife into his palm. The merfae leaned down, whispering something into his ear. Kai laughed a little too loud and Cohv's face turned red as he swam out of the room, far angrier than I'd seen him.

"What did he say?" I asked.

A nearly imperceptible shake of the head was his only answer. The rest of the night was uneventful, apart from Narina practically shaking in the chair beside me until she just couldn't sit still any longer and bolted for the door. There were traces of fear in the water. Not concern. That's when I realized Narina may not have chosen to follow Cohv. She may not have had a choice at all.

I thought to follow her. To make sure she was okay. I replayed the conversation in her room in my head, looking for anything that would indicate she didn't want to be involved with Cohv. I was so focused on her perception of me, I hadn't considered reading between the lines.

Not wanting to make it seem like I was on either side, I stayed in my seat, watching the crowded table as intently as Jof.

Kai, still pretending to be drunk and injured, reached for my hand and tugged me closer to him. My heart dropped as I realized everyone was watching us. The sham would be up. But then I caught a glance of Chel, practically lighting me on fire with her angry glare, and smiled, tilting my head as I leaned into Kai and stroked my nails possessively up and down his arms.

"What did he say?" I asked again, noting our proximity allowed for a private conversation.

"He threatened Leora."

Holding back my gasp, I asked. "Why? She's literally the most harmless fae in Alewyn."

"Because he knew he would get a reaction out of me."

"What did—"

"Commander?" The sweet voice of the red-haired mermaid grated on my nerves.

"Yes?" he asked, slurring as he looked up at Chel.

"Would you mind helping me back to my room? I hate to go alone when Cohv stormed off so angrily. He scares me."

"Actually, I was just leaving. I can take her, Commander," I said, raising an eyebrow at him as if daring him to argue.

"You're a gem," he answered, turning away from us both.

Chel whipped around, nearly smashing her tail into me as she pushed out of the room. I followed, my smile wide as I abandoned her in the hallway, moving silently as I listened for voices. I lingered outside of Narina's silent room for long enough to decide she'd either gone to bed or wouldn't be returning tonight.

I wasn't sure where Cohv's room was, but I was finally alone and while I had every intention of catching Kai in his rooms later, I took the opportunity to head to the library. I'd started there when Kai had left for the Elder King's funeral, but hadn't found time to come back. I refused to give up, though.

Books were protected by magic, as most things were below water, and if I could find anything about siren's songs—any history on sirens at all—I needed to.

As I entered the circular room, I remembered why I hadn't returned. This wasn't going to be a quick job. Beautiful cases held thousands of books lining the rounded walls from floor to ceiling. A small table and two chairs were the only provisions for seating. So, I began.

Night after night, I slipped away, quietly searching the stacks of books for anything that could help me get my song back.

On the nights that Kai didn't stay in the Flame Court, we slept together. One of us always seeking out the other. But as I began to wake up in cold sweats, panting and terrified, I knew I wasn't going to be able to keep up the charade forever. The loss of my song was starting to affect me physically. Knowing it was out there somewhere and not being able to find it haunted me. And I could only lie to Kai about my nightmares for so long.

"Tick tock, Vixen."

I rotated sideways in the floral printed chair in Kai's sitting room and hooked my legs over the arm, picking at my long, lovely nails. "I told you, I don't want to go."

"I promised Leora she could sit with us. Us is plural." Kai pointed to me and back to himself. "You. Me. Us."

I groaned, staring at the ceiling. "Fine, but just dinner and that's it. I'm not going back to training."

"You will go back, but I won't force the issue tonight."

"It's so cute when you think you can tell me what to do." I stood, walking toward the door.

"I woke up this morning hoping you'd recognize how cute I am." He smirked and let me lead the way as we left his rooms.

Our nights together were long and passionate. I cherished my time alone only because I needed space to remind myself repeatedly what I was doing. Why I was pretending. It was much easier to hate, and ultimately betray, a person when they were vile. But Kai wasn't. Being forced to spend so much time with him was becoming more and more difficult. I couldn't fool my heart, and that was the problem.

I didn't hold his hand or let him pin me against the walls in the hallways when there was an audience, but when there wasn't, we could hardly keep our hands off each other.

I laughed at all his nonsense and taught him things about the sea. I could do everything he needed; be everything he needed. But I'd always be the villain at the end of this story. And that truth had begun to haunt me.

Just as he'd said, Leora sat at the place beside me where Narina typically sat. She fussed over the presentation of the meals on the plates, shaking her head. But as we began eating, she listened to everyone compliment the dishes, though they didn't know the cook sat among them. Her warm glow became brighter.

"Would you like to go back to the kitchens for work?" Kai asked as I smiled down at the little sea faerie. I hadn't been back since I'd been excused for chopping the vegetables too small.

Leora's face turned up slowly, a smile spreading as she nodded at me.

"Actually, yes, I think I'd like to try again. With a bit of training this time."

She squeezed my hand, hers so tiny it reminded me of a kip's. "I would be so happy to have you. I can teach you all the things and you can nibble on snacks and taste the sauces. It will be so good." Her bottom shook in her seat, and only then did I realize she'd been sitting on a box to appear taller.

"It's a date."

Kai smiled that infectious smile, and I tucked my hair behind my ear as I stared. His soul was so good. Someone tapped my shoulder and I looked up to see Narina floating behind me, her frantic eyes darting all around us. Leaning down, she whispered so quietly into my ear I could barely hear her.

"Cohv wants to speak to you. He's waiting in my room. He says it's time for you to turn over the information you've gathered."

"Narina, you look terrified. What's wrong?"

She shook her head and leaned in again. "Don't tell the commander. Just come as quickly as you can." She swam away, leaving me to decide my next move.

"What is it?" he whispered, jaw ticking. He knew.

Barely moving my lips, I smiled as I answered, "I am to report to Narina's room right now to tell them what I've learned about you."

The hesitation on his face was clear. He didn't want me to go. "Be careful."

"I'll be fine. They think I'm on their side, working undercover."

"Still. It's best to be prepared." He grabbed my hand under the table and placed a knife into it.

"I've got one hidden on my fae form. If I need it, I'll just slip my pearl off and snag it."

He covered his mouth with his hand, pretending to yawn. "I'll see you in five minutes."

There was no question in his words. He'd follow me, just to be sure I was safe. And I couldn't argue. He would have never agreed otherwise.

Swimming through the sea castle, I arrived at Narina's familiar door within minutes. I raised my hand to knock, but the door behind me opened and I spun to find Cohv, with several other merfae floating beside him. He twisted his mouth into what might have been a smile, had it not been for the fist flying for my face. I tried to dodge him, but wasn't fast enough. He connected squarely with my jaw, and as the pain spread through me, another grabbed my arms while Cohv shoved a massive piece of cloth into my mouth.

They were afraid I'd use my song, and had I held the power, I would have spat that fabric out and done just that. But unwilling to reveal my secret, I mumbled instead, throwing my body like a fish on a line as they wrestled me down the hall and into another random room.

Panic rose in my throat as they tied me securely to a chair. Cohv turned his back to me, spear in hand, and stared at the door. Narina drifted in a corner of the room but wouldn't look at me.

"He'll come. Don't worry. If our little siren is good at her job, he's already fucked her enough to be desperate for more."

I hated that running joke. It seemed the easy insult for my kind. Even Hollis had gone there after I'd found him in Ori's room. Bastards.

"But why tie her up?" Narina asked from the corner. She rubbed a fresh bruise on her arm. Had that been there at dinner?

"You can never trust a siren. Don't be an idiot. She's just as much on our side as the commander is."

Narina's sad eyes flashed to me, and I could see the apology in them as she sunk back in defeat and waited just as the others did, though she was the only one without a weapon. Shifting to my fae form wouldn't help us. Without the ability to move my hands, I was useless.

Boiling rage like nothing I'd ever experienced filled my senses, but it was not my own. I wondered if the feeling was radiating through the water. It was Kai, and he was as mad as the Kraken.

If he came storming into this room, he'd be met with three spears in the gut before he could get a word out. It wasn't a tiny space, but it also wasn't ideal for a fight. Especially one against three. And Narina, for whatever her role was in all of this.

I studied her out of the corner of my eye as I watched the door. I knew she didn't want this. She'd gotten in way too deep and couldn't see a way out as she shook with fear, taking in the reality of the web she'd spun. She had been overconfident in her room, caught in the lies of a wishful fae. I was torn between feeling sorry for her poor taste in males and wanting to rip her throat out for not warning me. But with that bruise on her arm, and the fear in her eyes, she had always been just a pawn.

Another wave of fury. He was close. I didn't know how I knew, but I could feel it. Feel him as if he was on the other end of an invisible line, linking us. I squeezed my eyes shut and prayed to the gods he would not come barreling through that door just to meet his death.

I knew I shouldn't have cared. If Kai died, it might make finding my father easier. Freeing him easier. Times like these reminded me that a beautiful female could not survive in a world full of males who never saw her for more than her body. Narina being the prime example.

The door flew open so hard it fell to the floor. Chaos ensued. Kai, Jof, and several others came surging into the room. He glided over the top of them in one graceful arc, in no way concerned with their weapons, as he attacked Cohv from behind. The others fought as well, but I couldn't take my eyes off the seething male that landed punch after punch, not bothering with weapons.

He paused long enough to look at me, noting the bindings and the growing bruise on my face before continuing his assault, one after another. Bones crunched, the tumultuous water clouding with someone's blood. Cohv rolled away with a grunt, reaching for his weapon that had sunk to the ground beside him. My Flame Court warrior yanked it out of his hands, whipped it around, and buried it in his throat before he had a chance to fight back.

A small yelp came from the corner as Narina watched the male she'd meant to marry die. I could see the relief in her eyes, though, before Jof took her hand and escorted her from the room. After that, there was too much red to see anything else. The others were already dead. Whatever their plan here was, they'd failed to a miserable degree.

"It's not enough," Kai heaved. "I don't care what his death means. It's not enough. I need to kill him again."

I could see an outline of him throwing the spear to the side as he fell before me. "I shouldn't have let you come. I should have gone in your place. I'm sorry. I'm so fucking sorry."

He carefully untied the bindings at my hands, and as soon as they were free, I yanked the cloth from my mouth. "I'm fine. I was never the target. It was always you."

"I'm responsible for this because I made you the target. They would have never touched you if Narina hadn't known we'd been together. We've been careful, but not enough." He wrapped his arms around my waist and lay his head against my abdomen. "Forgive me."

"There's nothing to forgive." I frowned as I stroked his hair. "You're wrong. He threatened me the first night in the castle. You saved me then and you saved me now. Cohv is no longer a problem. He attacked me, beat me and tied me up even though I was never his enemy. He's been abusing Narina. If she lets us, we can tell people that as well. The small fire he was trying to build is gone and it's his fault. He will never be a martyr."

"All good, sir?" a soldier asked from behind us.

Kai rose and took my hand. "Fae died today, soldier. That's never good. But today it was justified."

With that, he pulled me from the room and led me back to his.

He slept with me wrapped in his arms and I couldn't help but succumb to the panic. I was lying to him about everything. About being half-fae, not having a siren's song, my intent to free my father and the only reason I was even in the castle. When these walls came tumbling down, I was going to be buried alive.

CHAPTER 18

I spent the next two weeks learning how to truly work in the kitchen. The early hours prepping and the late nights washing had Kai ready to go insane with my absence. So tired by the end of each day, I crawled into bed, more spent than I'd been in my life. Doriahs was gone more than ever as the days passed. She spent her time rounding up sea fae, forcing them to report to the castle. Most stayed. She was back for now, though.

I was to start training with Kai on land soon. The ordeal with Cohv worked out in our favor, just as I'd told him, but there was an edge of fear in our secret rendezvous. He didn't trust I was safe. And that was non-negotiable for him. He needed that confidence.

"We have a special job today," Leora said as I did the morning prep work. "Since it's just you and I, we're to deliver food to the advisors that have been locked away."

The knife in my hand slipped and I nearly cut myself as I realized what she was saying. I looked up, trying desperately to hide my excitement. "What do we need to take?"

"We will do the normal lunch menu and double it, along with some extras I've been storing away for the trip."

I flew through the morning routine, doing everything as precisely as she asked. I'd finally learn where my father was. I would be able to sneak away, free him, find my song and get the fuck out of here before I couldn't find a way to separate myself from Kai.

He was a dangerous vulnerability. My father would never approve. And he could never know. He would use Kai against me. Somehow, he'd find out something about him to twist and turn until I ultimately gave up everything, just like he'd already done with my song. This castle held nothing of use to me, of that I was certain.

Kaitalen swept into the room and before I could back away, keeping a friendly distance, he grabbed both sides of my face and kissed me soundly. Leora gasped and I jumped out of his arms, my eyes twice their normal size.

Realizing what he'd done, he turned to Leora, grabbed her face and planted a big, wet kiss right on her tiny glowing lips.

"Good morning, ladies. I'm heading to the Flame Court for a day or two. Something is going on up there and Fen's called a meeting."

"So, you're kissing everyone goodbye?" I managed, trying desperately to hide my laugh.

Leora hadn't moved from her spot, but she was beaming, lighting every crevasse of the kitchen.

"Oh no. That was just hello. I have something bigger planned for the goodbye."

He darted for Leora. She yelped and scurried away, giggling as she dove into an empty basket.

"Okay, okay. Truce," he said, holding his palms up so she would come out. "No more kissing the sea fae."

She slowly emerged from her hiding spot, still giggling. "I'm not sure why anyone would want to, sir."

"Here." He pulled a long chain with a small blue charm on the end that I'd never seen before from around his neck and handed it to her. "This will open the gate. In and out, though. Don't linger. They are still dangerous. Also, don't call me 'sir'." He shuddered. "Makes my skin crawl."

"You are so dramatic," I teased, unable to stop myself.

He winked at me. "I mean it. Be careful. Autus must be up to something dangerous. My tracking skills are strong. If something happens, I'll find you."

"I'll be where the sea meets the sky," I joked, referencing that place he'd said he'd seen in my eyes.

"The horizon? Meet you there." With that, he was gone.

Leora sighed heavily, smiling as she glowed so brightly, I had to shield my eyes. "You two are so romantic."

"He's an idiot," I answered as I took the large container we'd been packing from her hands. "And there's no "us." Don't get excited. Let's go so we can get back soon."

I eyed the charm she dropped around her neck and moved toward the door.

"Oh. Hiding it are we? Fine. Fine," she said, following. "We have to find Doriahs. She's to accompany us."

"Of course, she is." I laughed. "Kai would have it no other way."

Leaving the castle with full permission was nowhere near as fun as sneaking away. Though I'd nearly always traveled west, we went east, Doriahs carrying the heavy load as if it was nothing. She spun and twirled through the water, causing Leora to laugh with delight as we swam. She struck up a conversation with herself, each head answering the most ridiculous jokes until even I was laughing at her unusually light-natured humor.

It took several hours to get to the island. I'd begun building a mental map as soon as we left the castle, but after traveling so far underwater, I wasn't convinced even I would find it again on my own.

"Aren't you coming?" Leora asked when I stopped before we reached the island.

"I'm going to check the perimeter while Doriahs watches your back."

I couldn't tell them I knew my father would call me out. So instead, I stayed back as Leora dragged the food across the beach. She waved the charm in front of the latch of the gate and the hydra's great arms stretched out of the water to slide the gate open, as if they had done this together many times. Though one of Doriahs' heads hissed in my direction when I didn't follow her in.

"She's perfectly fine," I said, more to myself than her.

I couldn't see what happened from behind Doriahs, so I swam around, searching for another way onto the island. The far side was made of sleek black rock cliffs and a thick maze of giant kelp filled the shallow waters surrounding the island. This made it near impossible to swim through without getting my tail tangled. Unless using the gate, getting onto the island wasn't happening.

I rushed back to Doriahs' side, knowing she'd seen me casing the place. "What?" I asked, shrugging. "Don't tell me you didn't circle it to make sure there was no way those assholes were getting out either."

"Of course, I did," she hissed.

All was still and quiet for a moment, and then the hydra was surging toward the beach, reaching in to pull Leora away. Using one of her long tentacles, she shoved the charmed gate shut.

"Are you okay?" I asked Leora when the hydra finally released her.

"They attacked me." She shook as she forced the words out. "I brought them food and still they attacked me for being lesser."

I pulled the little faerie into my arms. Not a shred of light came from her body. "You are not the lesser fae, Leora. You're not. It's them, with their hateful hearts and closed minds. You're kind and good. I'm sorry I didn't go with you. I will next time. I promise."

She shook her head. "I'm never going back there. Never ever."

"You don't have to," I assured her as I hugged her again. "I'll make sure of it."

Doriahs didn't speak a word the entire way back. The journey there had been much more pleasant than the one home. When I entered my room, I almost expected the suspicious hydra to follow and force me to give her answers. But she didn't. So, I crawled into bed and wished my life wasn't so fucking complicated.

My dreams started as a haze of blue eyes and firm muscles holding me, but they soon changed into something far more sinister. It was no longer Kai above me, but Vex. He stroked his hand down my cheeks and licked his lips.

I called my song forward and the siren responded callously. "Move your hands, pet." He did as I enthralled, no longer immune to my song, as he released me. "Now step away."

I stood and dressed myself, his eyes burning into my body with every inch I moved. Standing before the door, I looked over my shoulder and sang once more. "Take yourself into your hands and stroke. The moment before you come, stop and wait for the sensation to fade away before you start again. Never stop and never climax." I walked out of that room and into the water.

I woke drenched in a cool sweat, the gaping void of my power more obvious than it had been in days, possibly weeks. The bed moved and I screeched, leaping away, pulling the sheet with me. Kai rolled over, wiping his sleepy eyes.

Heart racing, I relaxed my shoulders, bringing my hand to my chest. "I thought you were going to be gone for a couple of days. You scared me to death."

"I figured I could just go back in the morning. Sleeping in a bed with you, waking up to you… It's so much better than sleeping alone in the castle."

Though he was being genuine and saying exactly the right words, I still balked, storming out of the room. "You're so clingy, Kai. This is my room. My space."

Even I hated myself for saying it. Loathed the way it made me feel dirty to be horrible to him.

"I'm clingy in a really cute way," he answered.

"Go back to sleep." I stared at the door to my room as I hung my head. The walls of this gilded prison were moving in on me faster than I'd cared to admit.

I waited. And waited some more. Until I heard his breathing slow and soft snores fill the space. I had to go. Had to get out of this place.

Unaware of the time, I decided I didn't care about the risk. Slipping out of the room, I dashed through the quiet halls, finding my escape route and leaving the castle behind as quickly as possible. It felt as though someone was chasing me, though I knew it was just my guilt—carefully laid plans coming back to haunt me.

My father's ship remained where I'd left it. I climbed on board and nodded once to the black-haired quartermaster. He dipped his head and stared back out to sea, the moon lighting the golden tones of his skin. It might have been the first time I'd looked into his face and seen him as an actual person. I clenched my jaw, unwilling to deal with the war within myself, as I moved to my room. I was losing who I was, and it was making life far too complicated.

Crashing into my bed, I heard the crinkle of paper below me. I didn't have to look to know what it was. Beneath the blankets and the sheets was a fresh letter from *A.T.* I held it to the light, wondering if I could glance at the words through the envelope. I'd decided that would be only a mild commitment to whatever the task from within was.

Failing, I opened it and read the letter. They'd asked me to retrieve the ring from Vex's hand. As if that were a thing I could just do. As if I wouldn't have done that already if I knew how. He'd been immune from my song my whole life. If only I could have just taken it.

I didn't bother forming a plan. Slipping the letter back into the envelope, I hid it with the others. This was one job I would not be taking. Regardless of the reward, I had too many other things to worry about than a mysterious person with pretty handwriting.

Thinking of that ring created a tingle in the back of my mind. A feeling like I'd forgotten something lingered there. *Vex's tithe!* I shot out of the bed, cursing the stars as ran to my father's warded room. I'd thought maybe he would have somehow released the ward. Would have known I needed to get in there. But alas, it was still sealed shut with no handle, only magic. He'd been hoarding piles of treasures and maps and anything else he found of value behind that door. Maybe even information on who was stealing the siren's power. Or even how they were finding them when I'd never seen another.

Frustrated, I clawed at the door with my nails, wooden splinters curling below my fingers as I dragged them down, leaving deep gashes.

They vanished in seconds. I hated how good he was. I'd searched the castle, the Gulley, the sea. Everywhere. And the answers were likely just beyond my fingertips. But my father hadn't deemed me worthy. That truth lit my blood on fire, sending wave after wave of anger through me as I grabbed the biggest, random jewel I could find in my father's bedroom and left.

The sun had lifted in the distance as I swam toward the Gulley. Even as I counted how many days late our tithe was, I still took the time to appreciate the deep purples and pinks drawn across the sky. The horizon. Where the sea met the sky. That ping of hurt for snapping at Kai resurfaced and I started to hate myself as much as I hated my father. I could have walked away. I knew where the island was. All I had to do now was swipe that necklace while he slept and be on my way. He'd be crushed, but I'd be free.

Then I'd force my father to give me whatever information he knew before I freed him. Even then, I still might not. But if I knew my father, he'd pay anything, do anything, to be off that island.

The creaky dock was empty. Pirates weren't known for being morning people. Aside from the occasional drunk sleeping in his own vomit, the walkways were also clear of patrons. Confident I'd catch him asleep, and thus possibly a bit groggy, I didn't hesitate to let myself onto Vex's hoisted ship, banging on the captain's quarter doors.

After a few muffled sounds, the door flew open, revealing a naked and red hot Vexyr looking ready to kill someone. He held my eyes as if daring me to look down. Unbothered, I held the stone I'd taken from my father's room out to him. "Our tithe."

"I conduct business during business hours. Come back then."

He moved to close the door, coughing in an attempt to muffle the sound of female giggles coming from within. I slammed my hand against it, wedging my boot forward so he couldn't shut it. "I have places to be today. I can't sit around waiting for you to finish getting your dick wet. Just take the payment and I'll be on my way."

He lowered his chin, glaring at me. "That mouth is going to get you in more trouble than you're worth someday and I won't be there to save you."

I dropped the stone into his hand. "I've never needed you before. I'm not sure why I'd start now."

Vex was dangerous. I needed to be careful with how far I pushed him. But I didn't know what else to do. If I waited here all day, Kai would know I'd been sneaking out of the castle. I couldn't count on Narina to cover for me again. She'd practically hidden away in her rooms and refused to come out for more than the evening meal, and even then she kept to herself.

So, ruffling Vex's sails and hurrying on my way before it caused too many questions was my best bet. My only bet. I left the Gulley as fast as I had come, guilt swirling within my mind like a breeze. It was there, but not something I noticed unless I focused on it. And I didn't want to think about how guilty I'd felt for leaving Kai the way I did. He'd done nothing wrong. But then he hardly ever did.

None of that mattered. My identity was still a mess. Half land dweller, half siren. Was I still half siren? With my song missing, was I anything more than a pretty face? A phantom of what I should be? A full siren was still half, wasn't she? Half merfae, half siren. It wasn't the same. I'd never be the same.

My mother hadn't used her song, but at least she'd had one if she needed it. I'd used and abused mine until I didn't know how to live without it. Feeling guilty for treating Kai the way I had wouldn't make a difference at the end of this. I needed my song back. And I could trust no one but myself to make sure that happened.

Awareness shivered down my spine as I swam through the sea. A whisper of a foreign feeling, yet as familiar as my own conscious. A tug, maybe. Focusing on the feeling, I hid beneath a large mass of vibrant coral. Something was coming. The ocean was warning me. I waited, scanning the water for movement. A flash of golden hair and blue tail swam past me and though my heart dropped into my stomach, I pushed off the coral and crossed my arms.

"Are you *following me*?"

Kai whipped around, looking at the bottom of the Gulley in the distance and then back toward me. "Fancy seeing you here."

I threw my arms up. "You're totally following me."

He opened his mouth, shut it, then opened it again. "You're not supposed to be out here."

"Yeah, well, I'm not a fan of being locked away in a prison all the time. I belong in the sea. I should be able to swim for hours in one direction, turn and go the other way. I should be able to leap from the water, kiss the sun, and land back among the waves without being told what to do.

He ran his hands through his hair, swimming closer to me. "That's fair. I didn't know you cared to leave the castle. You could have just told me. I would have come along."

I shook my head, rolling my eyes. "How did you find me?"

"I assumed you'd be where the sea met the sky. I was just headed there now."

I snorted. "You'd have better lucking finding Zariya."

"Zariya?"

"Yeah, it's not… it's not real. It's just a made-up place... A figure of speech… Never mind. What are you doing here, Kai?"

"I told you I was an excellent tracker. You were pissed this morning. And when you didn't show up for kitchen duty, Leora got worried."

"Well, I'm fine. I'll be back soon."

He lifted a shoulder. "Okay."

"Okay? You aren't going to argue with me?"

"Nah. I'll see you later." He lifted his tail and turned, headed toward the Gulley.

Naturally, I followed. "Where do you think you're going?"

"I mean, not that it's any of your business, but I'm going to check that place out. I've never been this far into the ocean before."

"You're not going to the Gulley."

He stopped short, a lift appearing at the corner of his mouth. "Why not?"

I felt stupid for challenging him. He'd go for sure now. "Uhm, because the ocean is full of pirates that would kill you for sport. The Gulley is where the vilest like to hang out. You're too pretty to leave there unscathed."

"Yet somehow you managed." He smirked.

I couldn't help but mirror his smile. "I don't trust something in that compliment."

"Because I'm not going to listen and I'm going there, anyway. Hey, just like you. Maybe that's why we get along so well."

He turned to leave, but I grabbed his arm and yanked him back. "Seriously, Kai. It's dangerous."

"Then come with me."

He wiggled his eyebrows and swam off, leaving me no choice. Once again. With Vexyr up and already mad, it was more dangerous than ever. I couldn't let Kai die in the Gulley, no matter how much I wanted to kill him.

CHAPTER 19

"Woah, these are weird," Kai said, making the rope bridge we were standing on sway dangerously far back and forth as he looked at me, laughing like a boy.

"Okay, child. Calm down or we'll both fall in, and I promise I won't save you."

He steadied the bridge, but not before he jumped a couple of times just to be an ass. "I wonder if I can figure out how to make one of these go from my balcony to Greeve's. I think he'd love that."

"Oh, so he's also an immature stalker?"

"Uhm. Yes."

Turning, I waved my hand through the space in front of us as we looked over the Gulley. "This is it. The whole place. Only one ship is open right now. Most of the ruffians sleep until the evening. They come out to fight and fuck and then hide back in their holes. The sun is not their friend unless they're sailing. But they come here for… other things."

"What's open?"

"What? No. I meant we should leave. There's nothing more to see."

"The Feral Boar? What's that?"

I shook my head, studying the sloppily painted sign he pointed to. "That is not happening. It's the worst of the worst. Even I won't go in there."

"You say that like you do a lot of dangerous things," he answered, moving down the rope bridge as if he didn't care for my warning.

"You know what? Fine," I called out. "Have fun. I'll be at Merk's when you're done exploring. If you're not there in an hour, I'll assume someone threw you to the sharks. That's what's in the water below, by the way. Have so much fun."

I wiggled a few fingers at him and headed to the only place I thought I might hide from Vex. Which was ridiculous because he probably already knew I was back.

It was early. Merk's was empty, save for the hooded figure that hung out in the back, two pirates passed out at their table and a bright-haired mermaid leaning over the bar as she gossiped with Adair. The barmaid looked up, jutted her chin toward me, and then went back to her conversation.

Not thirty seconds later, the bell chimed over the door and the mermaid dropped the drink in her hand, the glass shattering into a million pieces as she took in my broad-shouldered, charming stalker, sliding his fingers into his pockets as he examined the room.

He didn't acknowledge me, only marched forward, and began picking up pieces of glass as the mermaid blushed and giggled at something he'd said. Probably something stupid. Adair, green hair standing on end, came around the counter with a broom and Kai took it, cleaning the mess as they sat back and appreciated the show.

I dug my long nails into the table, refusing to interfere, though it felt like he wanted me to. Like the way he handed the broom back was a test. Or the way he leaned forward, whispering to Adair, who snorted as she laughed and gestured to the bar, permitting him to help himself. Which was ridiculous. I turned in my seat, resting my hand on my chin as I looked out of the window, ignoring the commander's shenanigans.

Something was wrong. Off. It wasn't just the feeling of my lost voice, but something else. I didn't want to care that he flirted with others, but I just couldn't help that feeling of betrayal.

A tray of drinks landed in front of me as Kai plopped onto the seat across the small table. "I want a pirate hat."

I didn't bother looking at him. "Have you ever even been on a ship before?"

"I don't think that's a requirement. I mean, I'm not sure, but I don't think so."

"It is."

"Why are you ignoring me?"

I finally shifted in my seat to challenge him. His eyes were genuine, his face serious, as if he hadn't been talking about a costume three seconds ago. "I'm not ignoring you. I'm patronizing you. You wanted to come here, and we're here. Get your fill. Entertain all the mermaids, Kaitalen. Just let me know when you're done."

Reaching across the table, he took my hand. "Are we hiding this even here? This far away from the castle? Lyra, being kind to someone you don't know doesn't mean you're entertaining them. Nor does it mean I was flirting with them."

"Gods damnit, Kai. Can't you just be a dick for five seconds? Say the wrong thing, do the wrong thing. You make the rest of the world look bad without even trying."

"The majority of this world is shit." He leaned back in his chair, hooking his arm over the corner. "Although, I am basically perfect."

I bit my lip to hold back the smile. He was teasing, but gods if it wasn't sexy. "How do you do that?"

He spun the tray he'd sat down. "Do what?"

"You never take the world seriously. Nothing bothers you unless it's violence. It's like you're two people."

He lifted a drink on the circle tray and sat it in front of me, then took another and sat that one in front of him. "Let's play a game. I've made this tray full of drinks. All different. Some are not so pleasant." He pulled out a deck of cards from his pocket. "I'll deal a hand. All you have to do is say whether you think my hand is better or yours. If you get it right, you pick my drink, if you get it wrong, I pick yours."

"You answer my question and then I'll play."

He shuffled the cards. "My brothers aren't truly my brothers. They are my family by choice, but not by blood. Fen has the most amazing magic and Greeve does, too. I'm ordinary. I've spent my life shoulder to shoulder with two of the most incredible people. They have always been the heroes. I've carved my own identity by being the funny one, I guess. Sometimes laughter is the greatest way to deal with something."

"Sometimes laughter is a façade and people use it as a shield against the rest of the world."

"That too." He dealt each of us five cards. "Do you know how to rank hands?"

"Yes. But I see you've already picked my drink."

"First drink goes to fate," he answered, studying the cards in his hand as he spread them around.

I lifted my small pile and, finding only a pair, set the cards down and watched his face. The corner of his mouth lifted only a little bit. He'd gotten something good.

"Your hand is better than mine," I said, flipping it to show him.

Tucking the cards to his chest, he leaned over the table to see what I'd gotten. "Oh. Winner."

He laid his three-of-a-kind down on the table, picked up his drink, and swallowed the whole thing.

I waited for a reaction to see if it was good or bad, but he didn't show a sign of anything. Just picked up the cards and re-dealt them. This time I had two pairs, but he lifted the corner of his mouth again and I had to think about how many things beat that. It had been a while since I played.

"My hand is better," I said.

He laid his cards down first and I followed, beating his one pair. Though I could tell by his face, he'd thought he had the upper hand again. His little smirk was giving him away.

"You win. Pick my drink, Vixen."

I spun the tray just as he had, surveying the glasses for options. "This one." I plucked the one with sloshing green liquid and scrunched my face as he took the drink, showing no reaction at all.

"What the hell? I thought there were some bad ones in there?"

His eyes glowed with humor. "There are."

"You pick the higher hand this time," I said, tucking my hair behind my ears as the game suddenly got serious.

"Oh no. It'll be my turn as soon as you get it wrong."

He dealt the cards, and I tried to keep my face as blank as possible as I lifted them straight from the table. This time he didn't smile. He had a terrible hand.

I bit my lip, laying my cards down. "My hand is better than yours."

"Drink up." He set his cards on top of mine.

"You tricked me!" I jumped from my seat, staring down at his flush. "You knew I was reading your face."

"I knew you were staring at me with immense adoration. That's all."

Shaking my head, I lifted my glass from the table and slammed it back as quickly as he had. The drink was fruity, with a hint of dark liquor and crème. "Mmm. Delicious."

I wiped the inside of the glass with my finger and licked the crème away as he watched me carefully, desire vibrating between us. I sat back down. *Let the games begin.*

He dealt the cards, and this time it was his turn. He looked only at his hand, never once considering my expression. Instead, he said, "Mine is better." And laid his cards down.

"You just happen to get a four of a kind?" I tossed my cards. "You stacked the deck."

He tapped his lips with his thumb, then spun the tray. "You watched me shuffle."

When the tray stopped spinning, he grabbed the glass closest to him and handed it over.

"This is kind of unfair since you know what's in the drinks."

"Try it," he said, his eyes alight with excitement. "I'll choose blindly next time."

I tilted my glass to him in mock cheers and brought it to my lips mumbling, "As if you'll win again." The drink was strong and bitter, but the taste afterward was nutty and smooth. "Not bad. Not my favorite."

"You deal this time," he said, shoving the cards in my direction as he studied my eyes. "Getting a little tipsy?"

"No." My heated cheeks were from his stare, not from the drinks. "Pick up your cards."

He shook his head, eyes locked with mine. "Yours is better."

I smirked as I shifted in my chair. "You don't even want to look?"

"No."

The tension continued to build as he watched me lift my cards. I looked over the top of them, trying to hide my face. Why was it so hot in here? Warmth swarmed my chest, moved down my stomach, and stopped achingly low. I showed my hand, and he flipped his.

"Ha. I win."

"Indeed, you do." He rubbed his hands together. "Pick my poison, love."

That last husky word sent a shiver down my spine. Losing my ability to think straight, I lifted the red liquid and handed it over. His face, though he tried to keep it neutral, looked about as enthused as it had when he ate that first sea slug. I bit my lip to keep from laughing as he lifted it to his mouth. Winking at me, he downed the drink in one gulp, gasped, then took a white glass left on the tray and drank that too.

"Dragon's pepper," he panted, sticking his tongue out as he sucked air into his mouth and pointed to the white glass, "Gana milk. More."

I jumped from the table, noting the light head, and carried the glass to Adair. "Do you have any more Gana milk? My... friend is an idiot."

She laughed, and the mermaid beside her giggled. "Yeah, we watched."

I thought I caught a shift from the silent hooded fae out of the corner of my eye, but when I turned to see, they seemed to have frozen once more. Adair cleared her throat, grabbing my attention. She gave a subtle shake of her head and sent me back to the table with a tray of wine, cheese, and more milk.

Kai drank the second glass in one gulp and I sat down, sipping my wine as he shoveled cheese into his mouth.

"There's one more glass," he said, looking at the nearly empty tray.

"I'm not touching that. It's green and it looks thick."

The deep red from the pureed dragon's pepper still colored his lips, and a few beads of sweat gathered on his forehead. He looked down at the drink for several long seconds before gulping and lifting the glass. "Well, we can't let it go to waste."

As he raised the glass to his lips, I reached forward, resting my hand on his forearm. Taking the green drink from his fingers, I dumped half into an empty glass and handed it back to him.

"Together?"

"Such a romantic," he sang. "Cheers."

I smiled, taking the drink at the same time he did. The smile melted from my face as his grew, watching me. I gagged. Lurching as I gripped the edge of the table with my hands and closed my eyes, forcing myself to swallow the sour drink.

"Helps if you don't hold it in your mouth."

I lifted an eyebrow, smirking. "I rarely hold things in my mouth, but I'll keep that in mind for future reference."

He jerked, his knee hitting the table. "How far into the future are we talking? I've got something you could practice with."

I moved in closer. "Do you, now?" I stood from the table and held my hand out to him. "Let's go find it."

Needing no further provocation, he dropped a bag full of coins on the table and led me out of Merk's.

We moved swiftly through the Gulley, but just as we were jumping into the sea, I caught Vex staring us down from a ship anchored on the dock. Red faced and gripping the railing so tight it looked as if he'd snap it in two; my stomach froze even as Kai and I swam away. He'd seen Kai's face. Without a doubt. And that was going to make things far more complicated.

I thought about going back. Making an excuse to Kai and explaining the situation to Vex, in hopes of smoothing this over before he did something stupid. But I'd only be digging the hole I was in deeper by lying to Vexyr again. Because as much as I might try to convince him that Kai meant nothing, it was a lie. He was beginning to mean more to me than most things in this world. And that was the terrifying truth.

So, we swam on, spinning around each other, letting our tails intertwine as we stopped for prolonged kisses and unsatiated touches. I let him lead me through the ocean, and he never faltered. His sense of direction was impeccable. Pulling me onto the shore, I switched forms smoothly.

He stepped back, clothing dripping as mine was dry. "Okay, explain it. You didn't touch a pearl."

I was caught. I'd been so distracted by his closeness, his needy hands, and my treacherous heart, I'd forgotten to be careful. The truth was the only way forward.

"I wasn't completely honest before because I wasn't sure if I could trust you, and then I just didn't know how to say I had lied. I'm sorry."

"Do you trust me enough now to tell me?"

I nodded. "I'm half siren, half-fae. But not merfae like other sirens. My father is a land dweller. I have the power to change at will."

"Like a shifter?"

Shrugging, I took his hand. "I guess?"

"Okay, well, that's not a bad lie. I thought you were going to reveal something terrible."

That statement was far too close to home for comfort, but I tried to keep my emotions neutral.

"Do you remember when you said sometimes laughter is a façade and people use it as a shield against the rest of the world?"

"Yes," I answered, growing more and more uncomfortable as I let him lead me toward the Flame Court castle.

He stopped short, brushing the hair behind my ears and rubbing my cheeks with his thumbs as he looked down at me. "You were right. It usually isn't even genuine. But with you, it always is. I never feel like I have to pretend with you. I've never felt more like myself. When we fight, it's real. When we make up, it's real. You're real."

I hooked my hands over his wrists, swallowing the heavy guilt. He was right. The depth of what was between us was more than the lie I'd let it be in my own heart. I couldn't tell him everything. Couldn't tell him it had started because I was setting him up to get onto that island. But that didn't matter right now. The only thing that mattered was him.

"I have another confession to make. And before I say it, just know I'm more confused right now than I've ever been." I glanced between his eyes to see he if showed any part of understanding, but he only blinked, staring so far into mine I thought I might fall if his hands weren't already on me. "This. Whatever is going on between us, it's not surface deep. I miss you when you're gone. I want to touch you even when I'm near you. Even when you're right in front of me, it's not enough."

His hands dropped to his side. He walked three steps away, then spun back as if he would say something. Then turned again before closing the space between us as he wrapped his arms around me, lifting me from the ground as we spun, laughing more purely than I'd ever heard him laugh before.

"I feel it too." He grinned, burying his face into my neck as he put me down, all traces of the alcohol from earlier gone. "Let's be together, Lyra." He leaned down, his mouth so close I could feel his breath on my lips. "You and me against the world."

I shook my head. "It has to stay between us for now. You know how they will react at the castle if they think we are together. I'm still the bad guy down there."

"There's no cost too high. I don't care what they think."

Wrapping my arms around his neck, I moved to my tip toes, pressing his lips to mine. "I just need a little time to figure it out in my mind. I've never done this before."

He nodded, staring at me through those ocean eyes. "Whatever it takes, love."

He kissed me slowly. As if it was the first time, and he needed to memorize every inch, every tiny sound I made. As if the world had paused just for him to show me without words how much my confession had meant to him.

Too soon, he pulled away. “I’ll be right back.”

Turning on a heel, he jogged into the castle. I stood there for ages, staring up at the massive golden domes at the top, gleaming in the sunset.

Eventually, he came back with a satchel thrown over his shoulder. “I have something to show you.”

Following him, I watched the colors in the sky, listened to the symphony of noises from the wind and the waves, and kept walking as he pulled us up a hill. We stopped, peeking over the edge of the cliffs below. The ocean waves were so strong, the spray caught the breeze and dampened my clothing.

Kai spread a blanket out behind me. “I thought glasses might break, so I brought mugs. I hope that’s okay.” He handed me a cup and poured a deep red wine inside.

“It’s perfect.”

He lowered to the ground, patting the blanket between his legs. I sat, leaning my back against his chest as we watched the gradual fade of the purple sunset in the distance, as if someone was slowly blowing out a room of candles. His arm wrapped firmly around my stomach, and I decided, for this one night, I’d let myself forget the lies I’d woven to get to this point. I’d forget the part of me that was missing. I wouldn’t think about anything else. I’d focus only on the person behind me. The fae that was changing my world into a brighter, happier place.

“Do I make this more difficult for you? Balancing your worlds?”

He chuckled, shaking his head. “Difficult does not mean impossible. One day, there will be a line drawn in the sand and you’ll be faced with the impossible. Impossible is where heroes are made. Where dreams are answered. Impossible is where my passion for you comes from because nothing is perfect, except for this.”

I sighed, letting the weight of the world fall from my shoulders as I lived in the moment. His heart beat in the same rhythm as mine. His breath whispered across the tips of my ears.

"I fell in love with the ocean right here," he said.

I traced my finger across the arm at my waist. "Why right here?"

"Well, I was practically raised by a tavern owner until Fen's mom died. And then, even as a boy, I think I felt like I lived in his shadow. But out here, I got to be alone. It wasn't so bad, moving into the castle, becoming something like a son to the king. But sometimes, I needed a moment to remember where I came from. To remind myself that not everyone had riches and freedom. So, this is where I came to remind myself what home really was. Until it became home."

The rumble of his deep voice carried me away as I pictured a sandy-haired little boy, running wild across the red beaches until he made it to this spot, lifting his hands to conduct the waves as he fought for control and a place in the world.

"So that's why you love the sea so much. Because in a way, it's been a home to you, just like it's been for me."

"I want to give you something," he said.

I turned in his arms, placing one leg on each side of him so I could see his face. "What is it?"

He pulled the ring from his finger. "It's nothing powerful. There's no magic or myths associated with it. It's not even valuable. But it's mine and I want you to have it."

He handed me his sea glass ring. Though simple, with rough edges and a smooth top, it was beautiful.

I held it up to let the budding moonlight seep through the stone. "Where did you get it?"

"The first time I ever saved someone, she gave that to me as a reward and told me I was a hero." He smiled sadly. "I never saw the girl again, but it inspired me to join the ranks of soldiers. I worked every day to be strong enough to be a savior, just in case. I moved up the ranks while Fen completed his schooling and Greeve trained with special wielders. They had their strengths, and I learned to have my own, because of her."

I held the ring back out to him. "You should keep it. It means so much to you."

He shook his head. "Not as much as you do. Not anymore."

I slipped the ring onto my finger and kissed him gently before pulling away. "I'm not so sure you don't have a magic ability."

"That good in bed? I know. It's a gift."

I smacked his arm. "No. I mean, you tracked me down in the ocean, then you brought us all the way back with no problem."

"Oh, that's not magic. I'm just really good with direction."

I leaned in, resting my forehead on his as I wrapped my arms around him. "So, when I say you'll find me where the sea meets the sky, you really can?

"I'll always find you." His lips grazed mine. A kiss, but only just as he teased, running his fingertips up my back so lightly, I almost didn't feel the touch. He shifted to my thighs then, sending an ache through me as his fingers moved like a prayer against my body. I'd never wanted my clothes off so fast in my life.

I slipped my hands below his shirt and lifted it over his head. The absence of his soft touches lit my skin on fire as my siren stirred, demanding the feel of his hands. After our clothing was gone, and we lay naked under the blooming stars, facing each other on our sides, he continued his stroking against my skin as he held my stare. He knew what he was doing as he skipped his fingers down my spine, crossing over to my thigh as a wry smile touched his lips.

"What's that look for?"

"I'm just not in a rush. I want this night to last." He rolled over, tucking his hands behind his head as he looked up at the expanse of stars that peeked through the world smothered in a thick blanket of darkness. "I thought when Fen and Greeve met Ara and Gaea, I'd be left out again. And I'm not. It's hard not to run through the streets screaming how I feel to the world."

I snuggled up to him, wrapping a bare leg over his. "And how do you feel?"

His breath hitched. "All my life I've lived in a bubble of unearned luck. Things have always worked out, but this? You? You are luck personified. You are everything I never hoped to dream for. When I first saw you on the street in Halemi, I had to fight every single nerve in my body to keep from falling to my knees. But even then, I couldn't fight it. I drank and drank in that tavern, trying to numb the pull to you."

I giggled. "You were very drunk."

"I still don't pay for sex, though. Just in case you were wondering."

I crawled on top of him. "I wasn't." Moving down his body, I took him into my hands and stroked, relishing in the guttural sound that followed. "What was it you said? Not to leave it in my mouth?"

"Oh no, you can. In fact, please do."

Obliging, I moved, tasting the salty tip before taking as much of him in as I could, running my tongue over the veins and ridges of him. I held his stare as his face strained. Those bedroom eyes squeezed shut as he tossed his head back, grabbing my hair as I fulfilled my earlier promise. A need like I'd never known built between my naked legs.

He grabbed my arm, halting me. Rolling us over in one smooth motion, he slid down until he sat at my opening. My skin was on fire. A single stroke from him, and that would be it for me.

"Touch me, Kai. I need you to."

He thrust forward, rubbing himself against my clit. My back arched in response.

"Like that?"

I shook my head. "No, pet. I need you inside me."

He teased again, only brushing as he leaned down, taking my nipple into his mouth. Rather than biting, as he liked to do, he moved his tongue in circles. Keeping me guessing as he took his time. I lay there, letting him torture me for as long as he wished, hoping as he did, that the night would last forever.

When the teasing and the building were over, he looked down into my eyes as he moved so slowly inside me, I felt every bit of him in perfect detail. Our breathing matched as effortlessly as our heartbeats as he made love to me. Because that's exactly what this was. Eyes locked, slow and steady, exploring the way we felt about each other.

It was as if we could conquer the world together. Or burn it down. We could sail a thousand seas together and never find a storm. As if each star in the vast sky wished upon us. I felt the ring on my finger as I gripped his back. We were perfect. And nothing else would ever matter beyond that simple truth.

Except maybe the lie that chased us both.

CHAPTER 20

Monsters chased me. Roaring and screaming so loud my ears throbbed in pain. I ran, looking over my shoulder as I opened my mouth to sing. To demand them to stop. Instead, my stomach rolled and I vomited; another creature growing from the bile to join the chase.

I had no song. I had no way to protect myself from the beasts that would catch and kill me. Talons as sharp as knives swiped through the air, latching on to my skin and shredding it. Teeth gnashed at my heels as I tried and failed to escape them. Every fear I'd ever had paled compared to this. I couldn't catch my breath. My feet grew numb from running. Stumbling forward, I tripped and landed face-first into a million shards of broken shells. The sunlight faded as the monsters closed in. My body convulsed in fear, shaking so hard I thought I'd vomit again.

But then it was warm hands on cool skin. The monsters faded away as sleepy Kai came into view, studying me from his dry bedroom in the castle. He lifted the back of his hand to my forehead.

"You're sweating. And you were screaming. Are you okay?"

Having locked my muscles as I dreamed, every part of me ached. Cold sweat caught the chill in the air.

"I'm okay." I swallowed, but my throat felt like I'd been eating sand. "Just a bad dream."

He pulled me close, letting me lay in his warmth as I waited for my heart to stop racing and the hideous faces of the gruesome beasts to fade away. I needed my song. I needed to find a way to tell Kai I'd been using him all this time. That he had to let my father go free so he would agree to help me get it back. But I knew it would break him. After the night we'd had on the cliffs a week ago, I couldn't bring myself to do anything but love him thoroughly and let him love me back. Even if we hadn't spoken the words aloud. I couldn't fight the pull to him. It had become almost impossible.

Content and safe in Kai's arms, I fell asleep again.

Far too soon, he shifted, waking me. I rolled to face him, kissing his neck, his chin, his pointed ears until his chest rumbled and he flipped me over, overindulging his siren, as he so loved to do.

"Training today," he teased as he stood from the bed, stretching all his glorious muscles. "No getting out of it today. We're going up to the lists."

"I'm going to go because I know it will make you happy, but I'm also going to bitch about it the whole time. You've been warned."

The Flame Court was aptly named. I was standing in a sizzling pot, waiting for the fiery sun to relent. The lists, typically lined with crowds of fae looking for a show, were empty, except for a group of sea fae and four soldiers that worked patrols in the castle. The sea fae were becoming softer as Kai won their favor with his effortless charm. He hadn't reached that level of sympathy beyond the castle walls, but as he said, now wasn't the time for conquering. Besides, Doriahs had been adding to the castle population daily.

"Bend the knees," he reminded me.

"It's too hot to ask my brain to remember what my legs should do, and this sword is heavy."

"That sword is crafted to slice through the air in perfect form. It's not heavy. You're looking for excuses. The minute you stop making excuses for yourself, it will become easier."

I mumbled but bent my knees as I watched his moves and blocked his sword as metal sliced against metal.

"Why aren't we using the wooden swords like everyone else? Those look safer."

"Because you don't want to come up here every day and practice. It's a gradual transition from wasters to real swords, but you're learning basics with a real sword to skip ahead. Chin up."

He circled me as he called a mermaid with an evada pearl over, handing her a real sword. "If you're not careful, you'll hurt each other. Do exactly what we've been working on. One swing left, one right, then two steps back for a break. Don't deviate or I'll have to chase down Tem and I'm not sure he's here right now."

"Got it," the yellow-haired mermaid said as she adjusted her top. She gripped the sword with two hands, and Kai had to correct her.

Holding my core tight, I tried to focus on the fight. It meant a lot to him, and I didn't want to waste anyone's time. Besides, if I never got my song back, I'd need a way to defend myself, even it if was just the basics.

He had let the other soldiers train me first, keeping a distance as he watched without making it obvious. These days, it didn't matter how much we tried to stay away. We could hardly keep our hands off each other.

"Elbows," he called from the side. "Keep everything firm, ladies. Muscles wound and ready to move. Watch your opponent. Their eyes and feet will tell you a lot."

The clash of our swords sent a vibration through my aching arms, almost as painful as the shriek of the sharp note that rattled through my ears. My arms would hate me by the end of the day, without a doubt. Sweat dripped from my forehead, running straight down into my eyes. I stepped back, the sting blinding me. The mermaid hadn't noticed I'd moved, and the tip of her sword rattled against the heavy chainmail Kai had insisted I wear.

"I'm sorry. Oh, gods, I'm so sorry. I wasn't watching your feet." The mermaid's voice shook with fear. "Are you okay?"

"Let's take a break," Kai barked.

"I'm fine. Truly. I just need a drink."

He crossed the dirt-covered ground to a wooden table in the distance, bringing back a drink and damp towels for all three of us. I swiped the cool fabric across my forehead and the back of my neck, the relief nearly orgasmic. I moaned in pleasure and noted the way his ears perked.

I didn't catch the mermaid's name as she sank back into the crowd with the others, taking direction from Jof. Studying them and the obvious distance between me and everyone else, I wondered if I'd said or done something to scare the mermaid away, but then I considered who I was. The fact that I'd always pushed everyone away. I guess that's what made Kai so different from me.

"Serious question," he said, stepping in front of me to block the view of the others. As if he could read my mind. He kept his voice low, but I could see the excitement in whatever he was concocting in that mind of his.

"Go for it," I said, taking a final swig of the water.

"How do mermaids have sex? The mechanics I mean. Where's my dick in water? Where does it go?"

Spitting the entire drink all over him, I doubled over laughing until I was choking. He rushed forward, patting me on the back as he held his infamous smile.

"You cannot be serious. You need the talk?"

He nodded. "I think so."

"I'll make you a deal. You let us call it for the day and get out of this ungodly heat, and I'll tell you."

"Answer, then one more round with just me, and then we can go."

"A compromise from mister bossy?" I placed my hand against my chest in mock surprise. "I'm shocked."

"I'll take that as a deal," he said, waiting as if I held the secret to his entire existence.

"If I told you I laid eggs and you just had to fertilize them, would you believe me?"

He grinned wide, shaking his head. "Not a chance. I've seen too many handsy sea fae to believe that one."

I drew back. "Have you, now?"

"Don't change the subject."

"Fine." I let out an exasperated sigh. "But for the record, I've never had sex in siren form, and I have no intention of trying it out, so don't get too excited."

"You hate fun."

I laughed, wiping the sweat that had reformed on my brow. "No, I don't. And besides, I'm not sure if the magic that turns you into a merfae works this way. Basically, when I have a tail, I have a section of scales that slide apart like a pocket. So do you, potentially. Out comes the big guy and that's pretty much how it works."

"Oh, we are so doing that." He rubbed his hands together in excitement. "It's negotiable, right?"

"No." I bit back a laugh, trying to keep the façade of moody siren in place. "But personally, I think sharks have it much easier."

He froze. "Wait. How do sharks do it?"

My eyes doubled in size. "You don't know? Sharks have two penises, the female has a hole, he basically just bites her, rolling her to the side. Double the action."

"What?" He stepped away from me. "What? This cannot be true. Jof!" He waved his friend over. "Tell me right now. Do sharks have two penises?"

The small bit of color drained from the poor general's face as his eyes flashed to me and then over his shoulder, as if he was afraid someone would hear us. "Yes, sir. But doesn't everyone know that?"

"Oh yeah, totally. We were just making sure you knew. You know, just in case."

I bit my lip as he sent him back to work. "You really are a child, you know that?"

"Did you expect any more of me? Honestly?" His eyes twinkled with delight as he handed me the sword once more.

"Not even a little bit." I took my position, only then realizing he'd effectively lifted my spirits. All the silly came from the best, most wholesome place. And I think I was starting to love him for it.

We progressed as he'd taught me. Graceful, like a dance to a song sung from our synchronized weapons. Somewhere in the trance, as we spun and stared at each other, I got swept away in the motions. My body moved on its own as I concentrated more on my foreign waves of feelings than the way my feet shifted or the stiffness in my arms. Stepping in and out in a pattern I'd never learned, we continued as one, as if our souls led us in a careful dance.

The crowd cheered, breaking the daze, and we stepped away from each other. We'd somehow moved into the center of the training area and everyone else had gathered around us to watch.

Kai stepped in, taking the sword from my hand as he whispered, "You are a dream."

I wanted to kiss him so badly I could feel my lips tingling. Could see the same desire in his pointed look as he caught his breath.

"Everyone is dismissed," he yelled, commander once more. "Jof, get these soldiers back to the sea."

The scattered sighs of relief filled the air as we gathered together and started our march back to the ocean. I'd lingered at the back of the line, not quite welcome amongst the others. As we walked through the city, an arm reached out and grabbed my wrist, yanking me into a shadowed alley.

"Kai," I whispered. "We'll get caught."

He didn't care, locking my arms above my head with one hand as he pressed his body into mine against the bricks.

"Do you see that spot right over there?" He tilted his head toward the street. "That's where I first saw you. The first time in my life I thought I wouldn't be able to hold my composure."

I bit down on his earlobe, grazing my teeth down his neck, trailing kisses along his jawline. "Do you see that spot in front of the tavern?"

He released my hands, lifting me so I could wrap my legs around him, using the building for leverage. "Mhm."

"That's where we stood together the first night. I swear time stopped that night. The world vanished and it was just you and I."

He paused his greedy hands and leaned his forehead on mine. "You felt that too?"

I bit my bottom lip, nodding.

He lowered me to the ground, burying his hands into my long hair. "I wish we could be together all the time. No secrets, no more hiding."

I looked down at the ground. I didn't deserve that with him. Not until I'd told him the truth. The charm had to be hidden in his rooms. If I could find it and get the information I needed, maybe he'd never need to know that I'd lied. Maybe there was still a chance to save this thing between us.

"Soon," I promised. "How long until your meeting with the king?"

"It started ten minutes ago." He wiggled his eyebrows at me, and I shoved him away.

"You're late. Get out of here."

"Yeah, yeah. I'm going." He swooped back in for another kiss. "I'll meet you back in your room. Merfae sex is on the table."

"Who is Vexyr?"

Kai's blunt question came from nowhere as he readied for dinner that night. Which basically meant drinks in his room back at the sea castle with Jof and sometimes Narina, although tonight she was absent.

"Why do you ask?" I kept my voice light and slightly uninterested, though my heartbeat probably gave me away.

"Remember the journal you stole from the slavers? His name was written several times."

"Doesn't surprise me." I sipped my wine as he refilled his glass. Jof, as always, had water. "He likes to lord over some of the pirates and cause issues from time to time."

Kai pinned Jof with a look. "Once this stuff with Autus is handled, we need to take care of that."

He'd need to be warned of Vexyr's true nature before he chased him down. Judging by the death glare Vex had given Kai when he saw us, once they did meet, it wasn't going to end well. But thankfully, Kai hadn't noticed him, and this was not a problem for today.

We entered the dining hall unceremoniously. Kai had asked every sea fae that could be rounded up to join us. The meal was simple, but at the end, as he swam high above us all, demanding everyone's attention, I realized I'd forgotten to ask about the meeting with the king.

"Thank you all for coming tonight. I never thought we'd cram thousands of sea fae into this room and you'd all be willing to listen to what I had to say, but I can't tell you how proud I am to see you here. That I can look around and see those of you that once wore chains finding your own path."

He looked down at Leora, who shone so brightly the room twinkled.

"I think he means me," she whispered.

His shoulders remained stiff, but his eyes became sad as he continued. I could feel his nervousness through the water.

"We are going to war with King Autus. We may have more time, but there's no way to know for sure right now. I implore you to look into each of your hearts and decide if you will stand with us. If you'll leave the sea for the time it takes to help the world find balance. I know things are delicate. I know they aren't perfect. But my time here has taught me how willing you are to help this world become a better place.

"I'm proud of you all. Even if none of you take a stand to join this war, you've accepted me and my soldiers into this place nearly seamlessly. You've shown me what it's like to want and make change for yourself. The sea fae I've met are some of the most inspiring fae in Alewyn. But I'm not here to dish a thousand compliments. I'm here to formally ask the Sea to join the Flame. To fulfill King Fenlas' call to arms. I can't promise you'll all live. Death is a part of war. But we need you. This world needs you."

Chairs and eyes shifted through the room as Kai paused to look nearly every one of them in the eyes. To let the weight of his heavy words spread through the room. This was the first time I'd let myself realize what was coming. War. Before, it had been a thing somewhere in the future that wasn't connected to me. But as I sat amongst thousands of sea fae staring at Kai as he begged for help, only then did I understand that he would be on the frontlines of that battle.

CHAPTER 21

Everything was changing at such a rapid pace. Somberness hung heavy in the water as we realized there would be no choice if we wanted to keep the peace that had begun to settle into the sea. Still fragile and certainly nothing to celebrate just yet, real change had been made through all this time. But death and murder were seductive traits for fae. I didn't think we'd ever be able to break away from our true nature.

"It's really good," Kai said with a mouth full of the food I'd just made. "You did this on your own?"

I pulled a checkered cloth from Leora's hand just to smack him with it. "I'm learning."

A commotion came from down the hall as the king and future queen of the Flame Court came barreling into the kitchens. Their faces were tight, especially Ara's. Her jaw twitched as King Fenlas looked only at Kaitalen.

I wondered whether I should bow or something, but they were in such a rush, no one seemed to focus on the niceties.

"We need a meeting. Now."

"Ara?" Leora's voice was kind, softer than normal, as she studied the king's mate. "Are you okay?"

Ara forced a smile, her auburn hair nearly brown beneath the water billowing in waves around her. Her eyes glowed silver. As if that unbridled power we'd seen nearly destroy the castle fought against the brink of her control. Something was definitely wrong.

"There's a room at the west end of the hallway. Let me grab Jof and we'll meet you there." They left swiftly and Kai turned to me. "Come with me?"

The problem was, the more people he introduced me to, the more people I'd have to expose my lie to. Lying to multiple people was an inevitable way to be caught if one wasn't careful, and now was not the time to bare my soul to Kai. Not when the king and his future queen were here for something serious. There would be time for the truth. For asking for all his forgiveness later.

Still, I agreed, following him as he found his general and we entered the meeting room.

"Can I get you something?" Leora asked Ara, who paced the meeting room floor, stirring the sand below her feet as the world seemed to weigh her down.

King Fenlas spoke first. "We need a full report of the sea. Who is with us, who is going to fight against us?" He didn't take his eyes from Kai.

"The sea is vast, Fen. The court doesn't sit in one spot. They roam. We've got a few thousand, maybe a little more willing to fight with us. The others either haven't seen us or won't talk. Morwena kept prisoner camps. She was forcing anyone that wouldn't fight with her into chains."

Leora beamed, fitting right into the conversation. "We've set them free."

"And the others?" King Fenlas asked.

My heart plummeted. I knew what he meant. *Who* he meant. A muscle in Kai's jaw twitched. I wasn't sure if it was because of my response to the question or his own feelings as pure hatred rattled around me. I had to remind myself that Kai hadn't introduced me. I was there just as casually as Jof, two of his soldiers, and Leora.

"The hydra's been hunting. She's brought back anyone that didn't piss her off enough to get eaten. We haven't kept them chained up, but they are all under guard at Morwena's largest camp, which is on an island."

He meant the advisors' island of course, but I wondered at his words. Had he been adding resistors to the island? He'd never mentioned it, but then I hadn't asked. I avoided questions about the island, leery of becoming suspicious.

"Why would she use an island?" Ara asked.

Her body vibrated with that foreign power and my fear rose to the surface. If this lady exploded right here, we'd all be done for. And she certainly looked like she was about to burst.

"She had the water gated off with charms," Kai answered. "She was forcing them to share evada pearls. Only the strong survived."

It was then that I looked at Leora. Really looked at her. The scars on her tiny wrists. The sadness in her eyes, hidden with a smile. What else had she endured under Morwena's rule? What else had my little friend been forced to suffer through?

Ara stepped forward, gripping a chair. "Have we done the same?"

Gods, did she even know Kai at all? Of course, he would never do such a thing.

"No. We've tried to treat them kindly, though they haven't reciprocated. Leora was attacked twice, so she had to stop going when food is delivered."

I swallowed, darting glances toward Kai. Twice. I never knew about the other time. I'd been so wrapped up in my own life. I'd left her. Worked in the kitchens only when it was convenient until recently. Her bright light vanished, throwing the room into near darkness.

"Take me to them." Ara commanded the entire room like it was a weapon in her hands. There would be no argument.

"They… They are dangerous," Leora whispered.

"So am I."

The hydra was already waiting as we approached the island. I stayed far back, waiting with several of the soldiers Kai had asked to join us, as the king's mate swam forward to talk to Doriahs. Kai linked his hand with mine and I didn't pull away. Nor did I fault him for the worry on his features and within his soul. Everything was changing and, unfortunately for all of us, humor was not the answer.

The island looked the same as we had left it. Somewhere beyond the fence stood my father. Only leagues away from me, under the same glowing sunlight. Small waves crashed onto the island's shore as gulls cawed, tucking in their large wings before diving to eat the small mackerels that filled the water's edge. On the outside of that gate, one could have believed the world to be a beautiful place, with the clearest water and bluest sky. But that's how this world fooled everyone. Only danger lay behind the beauty.

Doriahs swam away from Ara, crawling out of the water. She writhed and shrieked, and I yanked my hand away from Kai, determined to save her from whatever had caused her madness. I got only a few feet, however, before the future queen demanded her to leave the beach.

The hydra put on a great show, leaping into the water, creating a giant wave that pushed us all back a little farther.

"What's going to happen?" I asked, staring at the back of the king's mate.

"I guess fate will decide from here," Kai said, swimming forward as he and soldiers walked onto the beach, following his friends.

I couldn't move, could hardly breathe as I watched. Doriahs came to wait beside me. Without her to open the gate, Kai pulled the charmed stone from his pocket and the soldiers slid the door open for the foreigners to enter.

He'd had the charm with him the whole time. In the pocket of his high fae form. A thousand waves of resolutions, guilt, denial and temptation, waved through me as I thought to search his discarded pants when we were alone.

An uproar came from the sea fae trapped on the island as they recognized the queen's murderer. They'd been shut off from the rest of us. Unable to embed their hatred any further.

"Why does this island intrigue you so much?" Doriahs asked with the giant head closest to me.

My ears began to burn. "What makes you think it intrigues me at all?"

"Answering a question with a question evokes doubt, siren."

Carefully navigating a conversation I wasn't prepared to have, I answered. "I just keep wondering what the sea would look like, had the advisors been left in the castle. What would have become of Kai if they hadn't had the intuition to separate these fae."

With two heads facing forward, keen eyes locked on the island, the third slowly blinked at me. "We're friends, right?"

I hadn't considered what the hydra and I were, but friends was an easy answer. I was terrified of her, however, I also trusted her. Because Kai trusted her. But he trusted me, so that wasn't saying much. "Yes, I think so."

"Then I'll tell you what I think. The fae on that island all deserve to die. They smell of rot and hate. Of murder and a thirst for power. They are of no use to this world but to poison it, should they be left to make their own decisions."

I nodded numbly as the seafloor rumbled. A great wall of water grew so high between us and the island, my ears rang. Panic set in. Kai was on that island and Ara was about to kill them all. Including my father. He couldn't die. Not yet. I needed him now more than ever. And she was about to take him. I swam.

I couldn't get around the wall. The water was fluid but somehow a solid barrier. I darted to the left, but there was no path through. To the right, I found the same thing. Defeated, I paused. All I could do was wade in the water and watch the giant wave, like it was being held by invisible hands. Then the water slowly collapsed back into the sea, killing no one, but wreaking total havoc on my emotions.

I couldn't keep doing this. Couldn't wait any longer to get my father off this island. Come hell or high water, I'd have to swipe the charm from Kai, free the person who didn't deserve it, and take him to his knees to get my song back. I refused to keep waking up in cold sweats, living like a part of me was missing. Like something inside of me wanted to scream to the heavens until I had nothing left to give because I was so broken and lost. Even with the wholeness I felt with Kai, my soul would not settle. He loved me. I had all the faith in the world that he would forgive me when he knew, when he understood why I'd never been complete around him. Why I still felt that lost sense of self, even in his protective arms.

"Are you okay?" Kai drifted beside me, though I hadn't seen him approach; hadn't seen anyone leave the island as I coiled my problems around my mind, resolving to stick to the plan.

"Are you? I was so worried about you when she… when that happened."

"Ara would never hurt me. She would never hurt anyone that didn't have it coming. I promise."

I dove beneath the water without responding, racing back to the castle. Not because I had to get away from him. Not because I was about to ruin everything if I wasn't careful. Not because I was breaking my own heart just thinking about what he'd say if everything went wrong. With every flick of my tail, I replaced all the walls I'd built around my cold heart. This was me. I was a siren, forged by the sea, a gift from the gods, and I would not deviate from restoring myself. This wasn't about him. It wasn't about my father. It wasn't about a shattering world, it was about retrieving what was mine, at whatever cost.

At the risk of being followed, I cut away from the group as they traveled together. Kai didn't chase me when I left and I was so far ahead of them, they never saw me break away. They didn't notice when I detoured and headed straight for my father's ship. At least that's what I thought, until my tracker called out from behind me.

"Tell me what's wrong." His voice was faint, but still there. Still racing towards me.

"Everything is wrong." I threw my hands up. "Don't you see? We've created a bubble at the castle, but it's not real. The real world is still set on destroying us. You saw her. That power she can barely hold back. The war is coming and you're leaving. And you don't even want me to come with you."

He pulled me into his arms. "I'm leaving, but not yet. There's still no way of knowing what King Autus has planned. The best thing we can do on any day is to keep living our lives. Keep pushing forward through whatever is happening."

"You sound like a soldier." Though he couldn't see them beneath the water, tears fell from my eyes.

He pulled away. "I am a soldier. But I'm yours. Forever. And no matter what happens with this war, the bubble we created will still be there after."

"And if it's not?" I hated that he couldn't figure out what my question really meant. Hated that he didn't just ask me for the truth. Because at that moment, I felt so vulnerable, I might have told him.

"We build a new one. Where the sea meets the sky."

CHAPTER 22

"Without getting into a lot of detail, Autus opened an ancient door and I have to go help the others shut it."

"Okay, but why does this feel so urgent?" I asked, sitting on the edge of the bed as Kai paced before me, running his fingers through his wild hair. I'd kept that wall up and I knew it was bothering him.

"There were creatures locked behind the door and he's set them free. I've met one before. It wasn't pretty and I'm still not sure how we lived through it." He fell to his knees before me, taking my hands. "I know you've been putting distance between us because you're afraid of what's going to happen. But have faith. I've spent my life preparing for these things. It's going to be okay."

I leaned forward, pressing my forehead to his. "Where the sea meets the sky?"

He sighed, the pent-up tension fading away. "I'll always find you."

"I hope so. I hope nothing will keep you away from me."

He reached into his pocket. "I need you to take this. Keep it safe. I'm not saying anything is going to happen. But if for any reason I don't come back, someone needs to have this." He put the charmed stone to open the gate on the island into my hand and I'd never been so shocked in my life.

Swallowing, I looked into his eyes. "Are you sure? Jof could take it."

"Jof has to handle everything else for me until I get back. I've got to go. Please don't go wandering the sea. Stay here, where I know you're safe."

"I've lived in this ocean for a long time, land dweller. I'm perfectly safe." My mouth twisted into a smirk as I clenched the small blue stone into my fist.

"I mean it." He kissed me soundly, the taste of his lips lingering long after he'd left.

Days passed. I paced the plush sitting room rug so many times, I thought the trail of my feet was forming. He'd given me exactly what I needed. I hadn't brought myself to take it, yet he'd put it into my hands. This was perfect. I could go to the island, find a way to free only my father, and be back before he even knew what had happened.

But I would still be doing something he'd directly asked me not to. I'd be using the charm he'd kept hidden and secure for months for my personal use. It was a betrayal of his trust. A lie taken shape as he followed all traces of truth back to the beginning of our relationship where I'd lied my way into his heart. He still had no idea I didn't have a song or that my father was on that island. He didn't know that when the nightmares of my missing song didn't haunt me, I'd lie awake at night, staring at the clothes discarded on the floor. Knowing where the charm he'd so freely given was, wishing I was strong enough to steal it away and never come back.

Leora. I needed Leora. Not to explain myself, but for the companionship. To remind myself of what I'd grown to love in this castle. Narina was a reminder of my past. Of my selfish ways, but Leora reminded me that I could be good. Could change. After I freed my father.

I found her at the table in the kitchen, snacking on sea slugs.

"I've never been more disgusted by you in my life," I joked as I joined her.

"I'll share?" she said, sliding the plate across the table with no resistance.

Scrunching my face, I turned away. "I'll pass."

Her glowing light beamed as she giggled. My heart had softened so much for that little sea fae. Even if I was a general wreck in the kitchens, and half the food I cooked tasted like decomposed garbage, she was always right there to encourage me to keep going. To keep trying. No one in my life, not even my own mother, had shown me such patience and kindness.

She plopped another sea slug into her mouth and wiggled in her chair as she closed her eyes and savored the food more thoroughly than anyone I'd ever seen. Taking her empty dish to the counter, she brought back a bowl of twisted sea knots. She knew they were my favorite. "The commander told me he might be gone for a while. Are you worried?"

"Why should I be?" I picked a sea knot and unraveled it, digging the tiny, sweet seed from the center and popping it into my mouth.

Lowering her chin, she pursed her lips. "Still playing that game, are we?"

I casually grabbed another knot. "We should have faith in him and trust that he'll come back. That's what he wants."

She nodded, swiping a handful of the snack and setting them in front of her in a pile. "I thought when I first met you I wasn't going to like you. But I like you just fine now. I'm glad we're friends. You've changed a lot, you know."

Ignoring the staticky guilt that rattled my ears, I simply shared a forced smile, knowing what I was going to do next. "I am going to have to miss kitchen duty tonight, Leora. Narina asked for a sleepover, and I couldn't say no. You know how she's been lately."

Her eyes squinted a little too long at me. As if she could feel the lie in the water around us. But she waved her hand in reassurance. "I can handle it. The new mermaids Kai sent to help are quite useful when they aren't gossiping."

"I know. I had to work with them yesterday." I rolled my eyes. "That Cora is bound to get herself in trouble with the soldiers."

Her light grew brighter. "I think that's what she's hoping for."

I rose from the table, knowing if she found out I was lying to her face it would hurt her. "I'll see you soon. Thanks for the snack."

I snuck through the heavily guarded halls, taking the path with the least resistance. Kai had never asked about my escape route. But then he never really forced me to stick around. He trusted I would always come back.

With each push of my tail, each drop of water that flowed over my body, I sank back into the siren my mother had molded me to be. There were no emotions, nothing in my path. My song was my mark, and I couldn't let anything get in my way. I'd deal with the aftermath later. Iron-clad determination soared through my veins as I swam through the ocean, stirring the part of me that was unapologetic, fierce, and devious.

I replayed memories of things I'd stolen. Of hearts I'd broken; hearts I'd crushed in my hands. Of friends I'd betrayed. I saw Hollis' face as I took Isla's Eye from his decaying ship. I replayed his spiteful words in Ori's room. I remembered my mother's face as I completed my first mission alone. My father's pride as I placed a giant emerald into his waiting fingers. This was me. This was who I was always meant to be. I'd lost myself in the bubble I'd created with Kai, but now I couldn't think of that. Only this. Only my target.

The underbelly of a ship in the distance caused me to pause. Something was happening on the island. If I swam to the surface, I had a greater chance of being caught by whomever was brave enough to step foot on the prisoners' shore. I was so focused on the new development; I nearly missed the giant hydra from the corner of my eye.

She hadn't missed me, though. She swam at me in record speed, all six of her eyes judging me harder than ever. She knew. On some level, she'd already figured me out. But I would not apologize. I would do what I had to do or die trying.

"Whatever you're planning, stop. There's trouble ahead."

"I've already made up my mind, Doriahs. I've got to get to the island. I'll swim forward and see what's going on."

She slithered through the water, circling me until I felt the pull of the whirlpool she'd created tugging at my scales, lifting my hair. "This is not a good idea. I cannot let you meddle. Kaitalen has asked that we only interfere if someone tries to open the gate. So far, the ship is only sitting there. That's all."

I held out the little blue charm, showing her. "Kai gave this to me. He trusted me with it. There's something I have to do. Just stay back and let me complete my mission."

Her serpentine body moved like a mass of snakes in the ocean. She pushed away, swam in, then pushed away again as she decided which of us to believe. "The nature of a siren is questionable."

"As is the nature of a hydra."

"True." She pulled to the side, letting me pass.

"I've got this under control, Doriahs," I said as I noticed the small glimmer of a red sail through the churning water. "Please don't interfere. It's important."

"I bid you well, Lyra. But use caution. There's a heaviness in the air. A bad omen."

"Good thing I'm not superstitious."

CHAPTER 23

Deep red sails waved in the distance, lured me in. Such danger indeed. Vexyr's ship sat outside the prisoners' island. The hydra was confident it was idle there, but I knew better. He wouldn't have conveniently docked beside an island holding valuable sea fae. He did nothing without an agenda, much like my father.

I swam close enough to reach out and touch the smooth, dark wood of the towering ship. Lifting my hand to block the sun, I studied the island, seeing no movement between the shoreline and the massive gate. I thought back to what Kai had said. These islands had been used to trap the sea fae that would not succumb to slavery or militia. This place was once full of rebellious souls and fae willing to die in denial of a maniacal queen. I hadn't truly believed she was wicked until now; as I considered the lives she'd stolen.

Muffled voices came from the starboard side of the ship. I swam closer, keeping as quiet as possible as I listened for any important information. The timbre of Vex's growl sent a small wave of fear through me as I remembered the last time our eyes had met. When he'd gotten his first glimpse of Kai and had likely painted a target in his mind.

"We had a deal. This was never part of the bargain."

Heavy boots thundered above as gentle waves lapped against the side of the ship. I closed my eyes to concentrate on the second voice, but I could only hear the pause as Vexyr showed his dominance, slamming things around. I swam underneath the ship, moving to the other side to try to hear.

"… because she is already mine. You sold your daughter before your capture, or have you forgotten? That was already a debt paid. I killed your wife for you. Lyra is my payment. I even gave her the time to choose me, as agreed upon. Time's up. There was no mention of a ride off this island. What will you pay for your freedom?"

My heart stilled at the words. There was no question who he spoke to. A thousand memories of my father mourning my mother came to my mind. It couldn't be.

"Yes, well, we had the timing wrong. I'm telling you she had a link to find the Kraken. If you could just give me back that first journal, I can find the treasure and pay you whatever your heart desires."

My father's voice was brittle and desperate. He didn't even try to bargain to keep me. He'd sold me. Just as those slaves had been sold in the meeting of ships all that time ago.

"I've studied the journal you sold your soul for when we first met. It wasn't worth the ship I gave you. Look into my eyes, Turrik. Do I look like a fool?"

Blood rushed to my ears as utter devastation crashed over me. The world spun and spun as the voices continued, but I couldn't concentrate on anything long enough to put together what they were saying. He'd killed my mother. He'd sold me. *He'd sold me.* All to search for a legendary treasure that was likely no more than a fable derived from drunken pirates. Less likely to be found than Zariya. Yet here we were. I was without a mother and, from this point forward, a father.

The shouting from the ship was not enough to pull me from the spiraling reality I'd found myself in. I'd come here to rescue my father. I'd sacrificed a relationship with someone that didn't deserve that level of betrayal. I'd found love and broken his trust to save a male that wouldn't even give the shirt from his back for me. My father probably didn't have a clue where my song was. Hell, he might've even been behind that, too.

I clutched the charm in my hand. I didn't need it. Didn't want it. The only thing I wanted was to go back to that bubble. Back to the place where the sea met the sky. Kai would've burned the world down for me, but clearly, I wasn't the same.

A shadow blocked the sun above and I looked up just in time to see a net fall over the side of the boat. Heart racing, I swam down as fast as I could. My tail caught in the weave of the netting and I slashed it away, pushing harder. Faster. Of all the nightmares in the world beyond what I'd just heard, being captured by Vex was the worst of them.

I wasn't fast enough. The weights of the net sank quickly to the shallow seafloor. I was trapped. My nails weren't serrated enough to slice through the thick cord, so I flashed into my fae form. Holding my breath, I yanked the small knife I kept in my belt and began sawing at the tangle of ropes at a painstakingly slow pace.

It wasn't going to be enough. I would have to do something incredibly stupid. Something I'd regret if Doriahs didn't figure it out. I pricked my hand, letting my blood cloud the water, hoping it would draw her to this spot. Then, reluctantly, I let go of the charm in my hand, dropping it to the seafloor. I had no idea how Vex had freed my father, but I refused to hand him the key to free the others.

The nets closed in, hoisting me overboard and dropping me like a dead weight. The faded black leather of worn boots plodded across the deck and stopped before me. I didn't dare look up. Instead, I hid my knife within my palm as I shifted to my fae form.

"Well, I didn't expect this to work out quite so nicely." The tip of a boot pressed into my side as Vex rolled me over, still tangled in the netting. "What are you fools waiting for? Free my catch."

Deckhands swarmed me, tugging this way and that until they were able to lift the netting above my head, untangling my feet as they yanked the cords away. A giant hand reached for my elbow, squeezing a little too tight as it yanked me to my feet. I couldn't look at him. I could only stare in utter shock at my father who would not meet my eyes.

"You sold me? What the fuck am I to you? Nothing?"

"You were always an accident." He spoke through his teeth, as he did when he scolded me.

His words cut so deep I thought I might be sick. "Maybe to you. But never to my mother. You were the constant villain in my memories. And now I know why."

He stalked toward me and lifted a hand, bringing it down hard across my face. "Failure breeds failure, girl. This started with you."

"No," I said, refusing to cup my cheek, to rub away the pain. "You were just the breeder. It started with you and your worthless plans. You're a failure, and I am, too. You destroyed me!" He said nothing more, turning his back to me as he always had. Hot tears streaked down my face. "You're a fucking coward. I hope the Kraken peels you apart, layer by layer."

"There's my fiery siren," Vexyr said, wrapping his heavy arm over my shoulder as he watched the show with pride.

I twisted away, still gripping the knife, hidden away. "I'll never go with you. If there had ever been even a small chance of that happening, you ripped it away when you murdered my mother. You're sick. And you know what's worse? The only reason you want me is because you think I'm some rare treasure you can collect. But you can never have me. And now I'm nothing. Not worth a single coin. Because that mother fucker won't tell me how to get back the song that was stolen from me."

Vexyr stepped forward, clutching my hair and twisting as he leaned over me. I flipped the blade out and tried to shove it between his ribs, but I was too slow, my brain too addled. He snagged my wrist, squeezing so hard the knife dropped from my fingers, clattering to the deck before he kicked it away.

"You will listen to me. You will sit in the hull of this ship until I join you. Each day, you will sit and wait for me. I will command you, and you will listen, or you will never get your song back."

I spat in his face. That was all it took for him to yank me to my knees, still gripping my hair. I reached up, digging my claws into his arms. Though bright red blood dripped from his arms, he kept his hands tight as he dragged me, kicking and screaming, across the deck.

"Sir," one of Vexyr's lackeys yelled from over the side of the ship. "She dropped this."

Vex threw me to two other crew members. "Hold her arms or she'll take your hearts before you can blink."

He stomped back across the deck, snatching the small blue stone from the sea fae that had come aboard.

The smile on that wicked fae's face burned into my memory as he held the necklace up to the sun, looking through his one good eye as he studied it. "Even your father was smart enough to keep his escape route hidden. You're proving quite useful already."

Tossing the charm back to the lackey he barked, "Take it back to the island and open that gate; only those that will trade their freedom to be in my eternal debt get freed. Everyone else dies. Meet me back in the Gulley when it's done."

He whistled over his shoulder, gesturing to the male standing rigid at the hull. A single nod and the crew were in motion, weighing anchor and adjusting sails.

"Take the siren below deck. I'll deal with her later."

Waves of pain shot down my arms as I tried and failed to twist myself free, kicking and screaming. "He'll come for me. He'll find me and he will kill you."

"Who? That land dweller? I hope he tries. I haven't been in a good fight for a long time, and he wrecked my slave-trading business in one shot." Vex paused, looking down at me, realization crossing his face. "I guess I should say you did, didn't you? You stole my book."

A terrible grin crossed my burning face. "I'd do it again too."

His guards blanched. No one spoke to Vex like that. It was just enough for me to rip away from them and launch myself toward my father. I'd tear him to shreds with my own damned hands. Vexyr caught me mid-leap, but still, I scrambled, still I yelled.

"Why did she stay with you? How could she?"

A smile far too similar to my own was all I could see before me.

"Because I stole her song. She never stopped fighting to get it back. Sound familiar?"

I went limp in Vex's arms. The fight within me dissolved in seconds. She'd never used her song and I hadn't been smart enough to figure out why. Why she'd let him treat her the way he did. Why she'd warned me against it, even though I never listened. I turned, ready to jam my nails through his chest cavity and tear out his heart.

"One more thing," Vexyr said as my arms were snatched again. He turned, stomping across his boat as he grabbed a large pair of bolt cutters.

Everything inside of me erupted, all the anger, all the sadness, the fear, the guilt, all of it.

"I was hoping I wasn't going to have to use these, but it seems you need a bit more breaking in."

I pushed and pulled, screamed and cried. Nothing stopped them as they clipped my nails, one by one. The pain so great, it nearly trumped my shattered heart. My nails were extensions of my fingers, made of bone. The final piece of being a siren had been stolen from me, and I truly didn't know whether they could be regrown.

Vex threw me into a room below deck. Though clean enough, it was nearly bare. He looked down at me, broken on the floor, and scoffed. "Where's that fire? Where's the siren that could seduce me with a look?"

"Go fuck yourself."

He tsked, moving toward the door. "I've no need for that. Plenty of willing participants, as you've so kindly reminded me."

The ship groaned, the creak of boards resisting the urge of the wind captured in the sails, ready to sweep it away. Shouting from above carried below, but I couldn't care. I hoped they all killed each other and left me here to rot.

Sometime later, Vex's quartermaster deigned a visit. I hadn't moved. He dragged a wooden chair with green velvet-covered arms and a tall rolling back across the room to sit in front of me, resting his ankle atop a knee as he lit a pipe. "He would like to know how long you will play this game, Lyra."

"My freedom is not a game. I am not an animal. I don't care what my father paid. I'm not an object he can sell, and I will leave this ship," I said behind clenched teeth.

"Well, see, that's the thing. Your father hasn't paid tithe in a long time. Everything you brought, apart from Isla's Eye, has been returned to him. You are his freedom. Which makes you the captain's wench now."

Steeling myself to get information, to get anything to help this all make sense, I asked, "How did you manage to get my father off that island? It's locked by magic." I chose not to mention the hydra I'd sent away.

He blew a puff of smoke into the air as he leaned back in his chair. "Your father had his own key to that island. He could have freed himself whenever he wanted. The sea queen trusted him with many things." He pinned me with a look that told me there was more I didn't know. "He simply chose to stay."

I sat up, pulling my knees to my chest as I pushed my hair behind my back. My sore fingers caught in the knots of hair created by the male that meant to keep me. A new wave of disgust settled into my bones. He'd put his hands on me. That fact alone would be his death sentence.

The door slammed open and Vexyr tossed my father into the room and followed him in. "Your father seems to think you will vouch for him now that he's called me all the way across this sea to rescue him from this island. Does he or does he not have a hidden room of treasure for me?"

It took me a moment to process the audacity of what he was asking. "You've got to be out of your gods damned mind if you think I'll do anything for either of you monsters. I don't care that you had to sail here, nor that he didn't die on that island. I don't owe either of you shit."

"Lyra," my father whispered, his face smeared with blood. "Please. I need your mother's first journal. I traded it years ago. Vexyr has it and I need it back."

"Don't you dare speak of her in front of me again!" I screamed.

"Well, that settles it," Vex said, crossing the room in three strides as he pulled a short, curved sword from his belt. "You wasted my whole day."

He ran the weapon through my father's stomach, and I watched, unfazed, as his worthless life left his eyes. When Vex turned to me, sliding the bloodied sword back into its scabbard, I knew justice hadn't been served. Not really.

"We are going home. You will become obedient, Lyra, or share his fate."

"You'll die first. I promise you that."

The punch to my face was the last thing I remembered on the journey back to the Gulley.

My father's body stayed in the room with me for two days. I considered going through his pockets, just to see what I would find, but I couldn't bring myself to do it. I closed his eyes and turned away from him. It didn't surprise me that he had gotten off the island himself. Didn't surprise me in the least that he hadn't thought to get a message to me but had instead turned to the pirate lord. It didn't even surprise me that he still thought I'd speak for him when it was over. He believed he'd had me under complete control, just like my mother. But something in me had broken. Even before his betrayal, I had never wanted him back. Only the information he'd claimed to have.

Eventually, the stench must have seeped upstairs because two pirates I hadn't seen before came and dragged him away. I stared at the blood-stain on the floor. A clock ticked in my mind as time passed. I thought they'd feed me. At the bare minimum. But I hadn't seen anyone since we'd arrived at the Gulley, Vexyr claiming he had nothing to fear as he meant to broadcast my capture and ultimate submission to the world.

I hadn't even tried to escape the ship. There had been no point. I knew how well guarded Vexyr kept it. How many eyes probably stared at the other side of my door, even now. Even if I managed it, where would I go? Back to our bubble? I was sure that had already burst.

My tongue stuck to the roof of my mouth. I'd hardly done anything more than lie on the tiny, two-cushioned couch for so long it was beginning to mold to my body. The only thing that brought me comfort was the small, sea glass ring on my finger. I'd held that hand to my chest, pretending it was his. As if I hadn't lied, hadn't betrayed him. Hadn't lost the one thing he asked me to keep for him. The deepest sadness I'd ever felt settled around me like a blanket.

But then absolute rage coursed through my veins. Changing to utter disbelief. Only then did I realize what that meant.

I wasn't feeling my own emotions. I was feeling Kai's. Time stood still. A thousand memories and sensations came crashing down on me as the truth finally rang free. *My mate.* For a moment, pure joy rattled through me. My own as I realized why I'd been so pulled to him. Why he seemed to be the only one that mattered. All that vanished as his fury took over. He must have found out. Must have realized that I'd left with that charm. That the island was likely empty. That I'd lied to him. Thoroughly. I wished I could disappear.

I should have been stronger. Smarter. I'd grown to be so much more with Kai by my side. Why couldn't I have been content? Why had that pull to find my song plagued me so thoroughly I felt the loss of it, even now? Frantic rage was the only answer down our newly discovered mating bond. A link between him and I.

I jerked up as the door flew open. Vexyr stalked in and dragged the green chair across the room, setting it on top of the bloodstained wood. He cocked a leg up onto the other and stared at me in silence until my skin crawled.

"You've brought this on yourself, you know."

He attempted to brush my matted hair from my face, but I slapped his hand away, the sting of my aching nails rattling down my arm. He stood. Veins bulged from his neck as he reached down, grabbing my shirt and twisting until he had enough of a grip to hoist me off the couch and yank me close to him.

"You've taunted me. Teased me every single time you've been in my presence, and now you shut down? Did you care for your father so much? I might have told you where we could start hunting your song if you weren't such a stubborn bitch. I guess I'll have to break you in first."

I stared him right in the eye. There was nothing he could do to me that was worse than what I'd had done to myself. He balled his fist and raised it in the air, gritting his teeth. He was so focused on me he didn't see the blur of a massive male barreling into the room before he was tackled to the ground.

I scrambled away just as Kai glanced up, locking sad eyes with mine. That single look said it all. The betrayal, the heartbreak, the confusion. But he'd come, anyway.

Fists flew, flesh pounded flesh. Kai rolled on top, squeezing Vexyr by the throat as his knuckles hammered into the pirate's bloodied face. Vex kneed Kai and used the momentary pause to roll, taking the top. I scrambled to stand, to try to pull him off, but an arm shoved me away and I wasn't sure whose. Kai got his legs under Vex and kicked him so hard he went tumbling backward, crashing into a side table.

I moved toward the door, set to run if I needed to. Two fallen bodies in the hall lay in a puddle of blood. I could hardly breathe as I watched my mate and the pirate lord battle it out, back to rolling around the floor. Kai took a hard hit to the face. Vex's eye patch was knocked away, showing only a rigid scar where his other eye should be.

"Kai!" I screamed as the pirate yanked a knife from his boot. "Right hand."

My mate turned just in time to grab the blade aiming for his heart. He twisted Vex's wrist and jammed the knife under his chin. Blood gushed as the metal pierced his skull. Kai ripped the knife out and jammed it in once more, roaring as his anger and sadness melded into one down the bond. He let Vexyr's limp body fall to the floor with a clunk as he held his back to me, heaving.

My world stopped as I watched those shoulders rise and fall. Every single moment with him flashed before my eyes as I wondered and dreaded what would happen when he turned around. What did he know? What would he let me say for myself? I pictured a thousand different scenarios in those few seconds and none of them ended well.

"Kai?" I whispered.

"I never told you my full name," he answered without turning. "That day on the beach, after your friend shot me, you called me Kaitalen. I'd never given you that name."

Heat burned my cheeks as I remembered the moment. I'd learned his name on the description card from Lichen, naming him as my mark. I opened my mouth to deny it, to coat my words in more lies, but I couldn't. Couldn't say a word as he turned around, breaking me with his tortured eyes.

"I loved you from the moment I saw you in the Flame Court. You were the first person that made me finally feel like I was enough. Not lacking." He straightened his heavy shoulders, removing the emotion from his face. "I must commend you for your incredible acting skills. I had no idea until I got back and found you'd left to free your father, that I was just another mark. Just another fool in your long list of males. Just a fuck you had to work for."

I crossed my arms over my stomach, the knot of sorrow throbbing.

"I… We're…"

"Mates? Yes, I've gathered that." His disgust turned my stomach. "Mates aren't supposed to do this to each other. I thought your song didn't work on me because we were mates. I guess I was wrong. You were just selfish, and I was blind."

"You weren't wrong."

He took a step closer, clenching his jaw. "Then prove it. Use your song on me."

"I can't," I answered. "I don't have it. It was stolen."

"Exactly," he seethed. "You could have told me. I would have helped you. We could have done it together. But you didn't because I didn't mean anything to you. I was never your hero, only the means to free your father."

He was silent for a long time, studying the floor. "Doriahs had to kill everyone that was on that island. I was responsible for those lives. I trusted you. And now they're all dead." Another pause. "I loved you, Lyra. It was never the sea that compelled me. It was you. Always you."

Twisting his ring on my finger, I searched for words, for anything I could say to soothe the aching soul we now shared, but there were no words worthy enough. His eyes flicked to my fidgeting hands.

Tears flooded his gaze, but didn't fall as he shook his head. "Keep it. It's run dry of any luck it ever gave me."

He moved past me, his shoulder grazing mine as he walked out.

Still at a loss for words, I hung my head and whispered, "If you ever change your mind, I'll be where the sea meets the sky."

Kai paused, but didn't turn back. Didn't give me one last look as he answered. "I'm going to war. I never want to be reminded of the sea again."

I thought I could hear the audible crack of my heart as he continued down the hall; his fading silhouette burned into my memory forever.

I stood there for several moments, processing. I deserved every word he'd said. Worse even, but I never truly believed he'd turn his back on me. I hadn't spoken, hadn't told him that it wasn't all a lie and that I loved him, too. Gods, I loved him.

I would have left then, but I couldn't walk away, leaving Vex's body with the skeleton key that had given him all his power. So I took it. Only then did I see the gleam of red on the floor. Isla's Eye. He must have had it in his pocket. Maybe he'd hoped to persuade me with jewels if breaking me in didn't work. That ruby was mine. It had been from the moment I'd swiped it from Hollis. I didn't leave it behind as I raced away from the Gulley and back to the sea castle.

I'd beg. I'd plead. I'd do whatever I had to do to get him back—to make him hear the words I needed to say. To tell him how sorry I was. If nothing else, then at least that.

CHAPTER 25

"I swear to the gods, Doriahs, if you do not get out of my way, I will spend my entire life learning how to kill you slowly. And if you kill me first, I will haunt the fuck out of you until you die and then I'll haul your carcass to the shore and let the creatures pick you clean."

She'd trapped me in a room, per Kai's orders, and I'd sat in there for days, screaming obscenities at her.

"You hurt him." Icy rage emanated so purely from her behemoth body.

Every instinct I had told me to swim away. To put miles and miles of distance between me and this predator.

"I hurt me, too. I get it. I know what I did. But how do I make that better if you won't let me go to him?"

"They are going to war. You will die. Then he will lose half his soul in the middle of the battle and probably die too. He told me not to let you follow him." She leaned in so close I could hear the shift in her bones and we were a single breath apart. "I will obey him."

"You know? That we're mates?"

"I could smell it on you both the first time we gathered in that room before we freed the slaves on that ship. I could see it in his eyes when he left. How he wanted you, even when he claimed he didn't. You don't get to hurt people like that."

I shook my head, refusing to let her win this. To cage me in like an animal. A thought struck me. "Did you like it? When Morwena locked you in that dark room for ages?"

She hissed. "I am not doing this to be malicious. I'm doing this for your own good. For him."

"What in the world could possibly be better for me than my mate? Better for him?"

She inched closer to the door. "You are many things, Lyra. But that is not one of them."

My body physically jerked at the words she used as a weapon. She might as well have slashed me with those teeth and ripped my heart out. The fight left my body as I collapsed to the floor. As each bone refused to do anything but crumble, I couldn't look at her. I couldn't even look at myself. "You're right. Just go. Leave me."

"I will not leave you."

"I don't need a fucking babysitter." I turned my back to her and brought my tail up, wrapping my arms securely around it.

"No." She moved until her great tentacles scraped against the sand and she was on my level, all three of her terrifying heads facing me. "But you need a friend and I would like to be one."

"I just threatened to feed your dead carcass to birds. And I wasn't even kind of joking."

She let out a breathy laugh. "I like my friends to be dangerous. It keeps me entertained."

I forced a smile and hung my head. "What am I going to do? He will never speak to me again."

"Perhaps you should start by figuring out why you lied in the first place."

"Someone stole my song. Right before we came to the castle, my father said he knew how to get it back. He said he wouldn't help me until he was ready. I thought I was supposed to save him. I was lost without my song. I wasn't safe."

"And then your father betrayed you, anyway. Just as you betrayed our Kai."

Hot tears pushed themselves to the surface and a new wave of guilt soared through me, threatening to shatter me once again. "I'm just as bad as my father was. Maybe worse."

"You're sitting on the floor, living through every wave of guilt and torment because of your actions. I would say that makes you a good deal better than your father."

"I need to speak to Kai, Doriahs. I need to say the words etched in my soul. If he turns me away after that, then fine. But I can't let those words be our last. He called me selfish, and he was right. So right. But I love him. And I need to tell him."

She shifted slightly, looking over her shoulder and then back at me.

"I can't leave the castle. With most of our trusted soldiers gone to help King Fenlas, I have to make sure it's secure."

I lifted my head and took in her words. Her contemplation. "I don't need an escort. I just need out."

"It's not safe. You'd have to cross the desert to reach the Marsh Court. You'd get lost before you ever made it. Or eaten."

"Nothing in this world is safe. I could be eaten by the Kraken just swimming these waters. It doesn't mean it's not worth trying; worth the risk." The moment lingered between us as she warred over the decision in her hands. "You wouldn't have to betray him. I don't need your aid to break free from this room. I only need your back and a fifteen-minute window, and I can be out of this castle and long gone before anyone even notices I'm missing. Leora barely leaves the kitchens and Narina would likely love to see me get lost. Apart from our dinners, she's been avoiding me since Cohv died."

"I do have to go check the fourth quadrant rotation soon."

"I would hug you if the thought didn't creep me out so badly."

"Keep your siren paws to yourself, friend."

I smiled for the first time in days. "You may be the only friend I have left."

All three heads spoke in unison, "Well, it's a good thing there are several of us."

"That's maybe… Let's not do that. With the 'all three heads at one time' thing."

She cackled and moved toward the door, her serpentine heads turning back to me. "You have fifteen minutes. Be safe."

"I promise. Oh, wait! Can you hold on to this for me?" I pulled Vexyr's key from around my neck. "It shouldn't land in the wrong hands."

She snatched it with a tentacle. "You had better come back for it."

"I will."

I deserved the flicker of doubt at those words, but she said no more as she left the room, leaving the door unlocked. She must have seen the damage done to my nails. I had the door open before she'd left the hallway. But she didn't turn around, only vanished around a corner in the opposite way I was heading.

I darted through the familiar winding halls, memories of Kai surrounding me as I arrived at his room. Spinning in a circle, I tried to remember what I needed from here. Why had I come to a room that never belonged to me? But it was him. His essence lived in that room. His laughter filled the empty space. I moved into the bedroom, lifting the blanket thrown on top of the sheets. It smelled like him. My gaze drifted to the bed, and I was struck with a memory of him worshiping my body, bucking into me over and over before pulling me into his arms and not letting go for the rest of the night. I thought of the words he'd said that I hadn't returned. *"I loved you, Lyra. It was never the sea that compelled me. It was you. Always you."*

I forced myself to leave the room and the memories behind. My heart ached more than I'd known possible as I swam in a fury of desperation with only the scraps of a plan. I moved through the castle and into the kitchens, catching Leora off guard. She scowled, holding a mixing spoon in her hand as she pursed her lips.

I held my palms up in surrender. "I know. I know. But I love him, and I have to tell him." Her shoulders dropped only slightly as I continued. "I'm sorry, Leora. I know he's your friend and I hurt him. But I'm trying to make it right."

"Why are you here?" Her natural glow was completely gone.

I'd only ever seen that two other times. I'd hated it then, and I hated it now. "I've never asked for help in my life." I swam across the room and took her hand in mine as I fell to the ocean floor and begged. "Please help me, Leora. I can't cross the desert on foot and make it in time. They have days ahead of me."

"And whose fault is that?" she snapped.

"It's my fault and I own that. But I can't fix it if I can't get there in time. I don't want him fighting in a battle with a broken heart. Just please help me, help him."

She softened, tugging me upward. "Anything I do will be for him. Not for you."

"That's all I ask. I know you spent time in the Flame Court. When I get there, I'll need to find a horse."

Pulling away, she went back to her mixing. "I was only in the kitchens for a couple of days to learn what they eat. It's terrible, by the way. If you go to the castle and ask for Loti, she might help you. Or whack you with her rolling pin. It's probably best if she doesn't know you hurt our Kai."

"Our Kai?" The words were out of my mouth before I could register them.

"Well, I'm not the one that let him fall in love with me so I could use him. He's my friend. So yes, *our.*" She shrunk away a little after speaking, the strain of having the backbone to speak those words taking its toll.

"I didn't know you had that in you."

"Was that Doriahs I just heard?" she asked, looking toward the door.

"Gotta go. Thanks for your help."

The little glowing sea fae shone brightly once more as she giggled.

I knew I'd never find a fae horse in the stables. Not with the entire southern army traveling north days ahead of me. But I wasn't foolish enough to think I'd catch them on foot either. So, I zipped out of the sea castle, swimming as fast as I could until I was in shallow water. After changing forms, I sprinted over the red sands toward the looming castle in the distance.

Having no plan, no idea who Loti was aside from someone Kai mentioned occasionally, I stopped at the first door I came to at the back of the castle and beat like hell on the wood until shouting came from within.

The door whipped open and a plump old female fae with a head full of tightly wound curls and an apron tied around her waist stared me down. "Half this castle's staff is off fighting to keep it safe. There better be an emergency to pull me out of my kitchens at this time of day."

"My name is—"

"Lyra." Her eyes narrowed as she crossed her arms over her chest and huffed.

"Have we met?"

"No. But you're the reason my boy wouldn't eat when he came sulking home."

Did everyone claim him as their own?

"That boy has been through more pain in his life than you can imagine. Everyone he loved as a child abandoned him. Discarded him like he was nothing. And you have some nerve coming to bang on my door, knowing you've done exactly the same thing to him."

"I didn't—"

She held a hand up to stop me. "He played his role well. Hiding the truth of you away. But a mother always knows. And I practically raised him. So, when he came moping in, refusing to eat before he left for war, plastering a fake smile on his face, I knew. He lasted three minutes before he spilled his guts. So don't come to me with a lie hot on that tongue. It will not work in your favor."

I took a step backward and bowed my head to a woman who reminded me so much of my own mother's fierce nature I had to steady my soul before I could pour it out for her.

"I love him."

"Of course you do. He's loveable."

"I won't pretend what I did wasn't awful. I know it was. I was desperate and wrong, and I wish I could take it back, but I can't. I need to get to him. To let him know how I feel."

"You'll get yourself killed long before you catch our army, girl." She held her breath, waiting for me to argue.

"Then I guess I'll deserve it."

"Just tell me what you're here for. I don't have time for the confessions of a young and stupid sea fae."

My heart jumped. "I need a horse or I'll never make it to him. Can you please help me?"

"I'm a cook, not a rancher, so no, I cannot help you." She turned on a heel, the ties of her apron whipping around as she grabbed the door handle, knuckles white.

"Thank you anyway," I mumbled, turning away.

"Get to the borderlands. You'll find scattered ranchers there. If you trek across this desert for Kaitalen, then perhaps a horse would be earned."

"Thank you."

I pushed and willed my body to run as fast as it could. I ran from my past. From all the shit I'd allowed myself to do behind the walls of a species. I'd thought I was allowed because I was a siren. Because I was of the sea, and I was ruthless and unrelenting, just as she was. But I was wrong, so wrong. I'd lost everything that mattered in the whole world because I'd let a veil of lies protect me, smother me, and break me.

Step by step—running—just as he had taught me. Small breaks, so my muscles wouldn't fail as I crossed the desert. As the sands pulled me deeper, as the sun beat down on me so harshly, each bead of sweat tantalizing my skin felt like my mind betraying me. As if it were his phantom fingers moving down my spine, lighting my skin on fire with his touch. The bond between us pulled so fiercely, I never once doubted where I was going; where he was.

His heartbreak throbbed through our bond so thoroughly it filled me with sorrow. Perhaps that was also my own guilt filling my veins; shredding my soul to frayed threads. I no longer felt my feet running below me, sheer will and determination pushed me forward, as I moved, hoping a single fae could outrun an army. Could somehow catch them.

The desert was unending. Brooding and relentless as I continued. As running faded into a walk and then nearly a crawl when I refused to stop. As I pushed my fae legs harder than they'd ever been pushed, I pictured him in my mind. His ocean eyes, his wild hair, that smile. The way he moved above me; gaze locked with mine. The way he laughed, the way he called my siren forward. How the world was happier when he was near. Every inch I moved was a tiny bit closer to the only fae in the world who had never betrayed me, never lied to me. Though I hadn't paid him the same courtesy.

The heat from the sun finally faded as day transitioned into night. I'd underestimated the dry chill that would fill the air as the moon replaced the sun, filling the sky with its entourage of glistening stars for as far as the eye could see. The stars were my only reminder that miracles still happened. But I was done. Everything hurt. From the worn arches of my feet to the pounding headache reminding me I hadn't drank nearly enough.

I'd stolen a pack from the city and for the first time in my life, guilt at that small action riddled my mind. I wasn't entitled to things just because I could take them. I'd always known that, but there was no longer a thrill pulsing through me at a job well done, only shame as I pulled the pack from my back. I took a long draw from the canteen and tried not to let the fear of emptying it overwhelm me as I huddled in the middle of the barren desert, compacted sand below me.

I'd hoped there would be a small blanket inside, but there wasn't. I had only a cloak and a headscarf, which would have to do. Curling into myself, I adjusted the scarf I'd wrapped around my face as I built a cocoon below the cloak. I hoped my breaths would help keep me warm, but as they became visible plumes of air in the bitter cold, I realized it was going to be a long night. My muscles, already aching, throbbed and seized up as I shivered. There would be no rest for them tonight. Nor tomorrow. They burned as my heart did, and it was no less than I deserved.

I was up before the sun and as it slowly rose into the sky, melting the chill deep within my bones, I stretched and continued to push my body. Walking for days, pausing only when I had to, until I saw the army. Far in the distance, a band of travelers, marching with packs, their voices slight murmurs, carrying over the expanse between us.

"Wait," I called, my voice scarcely above a whisper, the cracks in my dry lips splitting open as I reached my hand into the sky, muscles screaming. "Please."

And then he was there. So far away I could only make out the shape of him, his hair blowing in the warm breeze as he stood like a statue and waited for me. The muscles I thought would never work again began to move on their own. Tears filled my eyes, the only hydration I had left, as I pushed and pushed, yearning to reach him.

"I'm sorry, Kai. I love you, too. I'm sorry." I prayed the wind would carry my words as it did the sounds of the army behind him.

He blocked the sun with one hand as he reached for me with another, still so far away. No matter how hard I ran, how much I pushed past the pain, he remained the same distance away. So far. I sniffled, running until I collapsed, scraping my face across the coarse grains of red sand. I knew he'd come for me. In my heart, I knew as my heavy lids fell, I'd wake in the safety of his arms.

I woke, half-buried in the desert, shivering. He hadn't come back for me. Hadn't waited for me. Because he hadn't been real. The dehydration from the desert had altered my mind. And as I peeled myself from the ground, shaking the sand from my hair, I wasn't upset. Only grateful that I'd seen him. Even if it was just a mirage.

I surveyed my surroundings. Tiny pricks of grass blades poked through the sand. Blinking, I looked away, and then back again, refusing to trust my vision. But it hadn't altered, hadn't shifted in the dusky distance. A house. Not just a house, a homestead. It was dwarfed by the size of the old barn beside it.

Heart racing, I continued on, praying to the gods I'd be able to secure a horse. That I wouldn't be too late. Step by step, I trudged through the final bits of the desert landscape and toward the house. I knocked and waited.

Within minutes, the door swung open and a small boy with the most magical wings I'd ever seen looked up at me in awe. "I'm not supposed to answer the door," he said by way of greeting.

I knelt to his level, my eyes hardly able to leave the beautiful iridescent wings at his back. They appeared to be made of something resembling a spider's web, and held within it the twinkling stars of the night's sky. "Are your parents home?"

He nodded fervently. "Da's in the barn."

"Oh okay, thank you."

"Remi," a female's voice yelled from the kitchen.

He darted out of the door, and toward the barn as his mother came around the corner. One glance at me and she rushed forward. I stepped back, pointing at the boy flying toward his father.

"Who're you?" she snarled as she shut the door and started after the boy.

I followed. "My name is Lyra."

"What are you doing here? All abled bodies were to take up arms and join the fight. Don't you know how dangerous the border is right now?"

"Is the army fighting at the border?" I asked, trying to mask the hope that I was closer than I thought.

She stopped and looked over her shoulder, waiting for my reaction as she said, "No, but the dragons are."

"Oh, right. Those. I'd heard—" Sheer terror and panic rocked through the bond so ferociously I fell to a knee, sucking air in between my teeth in sharp pants.

"Good Grendle, are you okay?"

The female reached for me, lifting under my elbow. I stood on shaking legs as I rubbed my chest, hoping to somehow soothe the male on the other end of the bond. He'd done so well shielding his feelings from me, I hardly ever felt him. When I did, it was a subtle reminder that he was there. This was entirely different, though. Something was wrong and I was still so very far away.

"Please," I begged, grabbing the female's arm. "I need a horse. I'll never catch up to the army on foot."

"You can't be serious," she answered, shaking loose of my grasp. "The dragons aren't letting anyone through the border."

"It's my mate … I have to try."

Understanding shone on her face. "You'll have to ask Drayke."

Moments later, we stood in the musty barn. The boy sat on a bale of straw, his wings fluttering behind him, pushing clouds of dust around the fragments of warm light shining through the gaps in the walls. He looked at me and nodded as we waited for his father's decision.

"It's dangerous," the male said, brushing down a massive, black fae horse. "I'm not withholding my beasts from the king's battle, if that's what you're thinking. I'm charged with staying back and alerting the castle should the border be compromised. Even if I let you take a horse, the fastest must remain here. Ready at any moment."

I bowed and his wings, a match to those of his son, spread wide across his back. "Kaitalen's a friend of mine. If he is your mate, as you say, I'm torn. I know him. He wouldn't want his mate anywhere near that battlefield."

"It's like I said. I have information I have to get to him. Please."

It was a lie. One I had to tell. They'd never let me take a horse if they knew the truth. That I only wished to tell him I was sorry. Just in case. Sometimes lies were necessary.

"You're sure you know how to ride?"

"He taught me himself."

"All right. Saddle's there." He pointed. "You get the saddle on, you can take Hern."

"But Dad, that's my horse," the boy cried.

"And he will be the hero in this lady's story. Isn't that right, buddy?" the woman said, ruffling the hair on his tawny head.

"I guess." He pouted, crossing his arms over his chest as he tucked his chin.

"I promise to take extra special care of him."

The boy huffed and wrapped his wings around himself, effectively shutting out the world. I couldn't remember the last time I'd seen a child. No mother worth her salt would ever take a child to the Gulley and while there may have been some in the castle, they were hidden away.

I left the small family behind, acclimating my body to the feel of a fae horse as it carried me away. The female gave me a loaf of dry bread and a wool blanket, and it was more than I could have ever asked for. For all the hatred the Flame Court received, they showed only kindness in return.

It was not long before the beautiful beasts of nightmares came into view, pacing up and down a worn line in the ground below their mighty talons. The horse did not falter as we rode closer to a deep red dragon, his skin reminiscent of freshly drawn blood. At first, I thought he'd let us pass without incident, but as one of those great hands stamped down in front of us, Hern reared up, nearly sending me crashing to the ground. I gripped the reins tight and clenched my thighs to keep from falling.

The dragon's smoky voice was low and seductive. "Where might you be going, siren?"

I looked over my shoulder and back at the beast. How could he have known I was a siren in my fae form? "To the battle."

He chuckled, the scales on his back rippling as the beast moved. "Are you to race in and save the day?"

"I don't have time for this. Let me pass. Isn't it your job to keep outsiders from coming *into* the Flame Court?"

"You are of the Sea Court. Which brings all kinds of delicious questions to mind."

"The Sea Court belongs to the future queen of the Flame Court, does it not?"

The large horse fidgeted, pawing at the ground, and throwing his neck back as the dragon wrapped his tail behind us, lest we try to escape. "Tell me your name."

I jerked my head back. Dragons were ancient creatures of legend and lore. I'd sooner rip my arm off and feed it to Doriahs than give one my name. At least she'd tend to me afterward.

"I could just take the information from your mind, siren."

I smirked. "You could, but you haven't. I'll tell you mine if you tell me yours."

The red dragon's eyes lit with delight before narrowing as he wound tighter, the scales of his crimson body uncomfortably close. "A bargain?"

"Not even on my deathbed would I bargain with a dragon."

"It's been many, many years since I've spoken of a siren's bed; lain in one. But there was no talk of death on that day. Only pleasure as she screamed my name over and over again, writhing beneath me."

"I am disgusted for so many reasons."

"Do not let this form fool you. I have others. One similar to yours. But why take the shape of a small fae, when I can conquer as the beast I was born to be?"

I wracked my brain for information on dragons. There was nothing. Only the nightmarish stories my mother would tell at night, proclaiming at the end that they weren't real as she slipped away with an eerie smile. Yet here stood a dragon, every inch of him more real than the next.

"When you're done gawking…" the enormous beast said, a column of smoke snaking out of one giant nostril.

"Listen, I don't have time to banter back and forth with you. I must find my m—" I stopped myself, realizing giving information about Kai to an enemy could be used against me. Against him. And dragons seemed to fit the description of an enemy.

"I require a token. Something valuable for my treasure. That shall earn you a pass."

"You want me to pay you for moving ten paces to the left?"

He chuckled again and I could have sworn his scales shifted a shade darker. "Indeed. I'm a dragon. It is my nature to hoard treasure, just as it's your nature to lure males to their death."

I had nothing but the pack on my back and the horse I rode. I couldn't afford to give away either. He glanced down at my legs and I shuddered, well aware of what he implied. A different sort of treasure. One I would have bargained away in a second before. Before *him*.

The deep crimson scales reminded me of something I'd nearly forgotten. I reached into the pocket of my leathers and pulled out the only thing I had left, aside from the sea glass ring I wore. The dragon took several paces back, breathing low and deep as I held the jewel, warmed by my thigh in my outstretched hand.

"Your payment."

He swiped his paw so quickly, had I blinked, I might not have caught the motion at all. "Mine," he snarled, wrapping the jewel in both of his palms before backing away. It had seemed so large to me, but in his claws, it was merely a tiny pearl. "You have earned the first part of my name, siren. Should you find more treasure you wish to trade, find my horde and ask for Ash."

"Don't hold your breath."

I buried my heels deep into the horse's flanks and tore off, the ground becoming a blur beneath us as I crossed the final barrier between me and my mate. Now, I need only to close the gap.

CHAPTER 26

Though not as cold in the night, the Marsh Court was not much more comforting than the Flame Court. The ground was softer, but creatures called through the bleak darkness, hunting for prey. Surrounded by softly rolling hills, I was nowhere near safe. I tied the midnight black horse to a tree and hoped he fell into enough shadow to be undetected. He remained stoic and silent as I slipped the bit from his mouth, allowing him to graze on the overgrown grass.

I sat crossed-legged, breathing slowly as I closed my eyes and reached down the bond, hoping I could feel Kai. Hoping he could feel my love for him. Though I'd been rattled with emotion earlier, now only silence remained. Kai was so used to his walls there were moments when I wondered if he even realized they were there.

Too scared to keep my eyes closed any longer, I pulled the knife from my thigh and gripped it tightly in my hands. I had no idea if staying still or walking in the pure dark was the safest option, but I knew the horse needed a break and I needed him, so this was the only solution.

There'd been rivers and small ponds throughout the day, thankfully, so I drank deeply, nibbling on the bread. At some point in the night, I drifted to sleep, only to be woken by a haunting moan somewhere in the distance. I couldn't bear to sit still and silent. Couldn't bear to feel weak and scared. So, I gathered my things and we continued. The pull towards Kai was still taut even now, as his emotions vibrated along the line between us like a hum below water. His anxious feelings amplified my own as the sun rose, painting the sky in clashing reds and purples. The sun appeared above the horizon like a burning flame; like it was placing its vote for the victor of this battle. It stayed just as poignant and steadfast in the sky as it moved, guiding me the entire day, until once again, exhaustion took over.

At the snap of a twig close by, my knife was in my hand. I slid out of the saddle and landed softly on the ground. Holding Hern by the reins, I crept forward. On his back, I was an easier target. Here, he shielded half of me.

Another bite of a branch, closer. I held my breath, willing my heartbeat not to give me away. Instinctively, I reached for the empty cavern that was once my song. I hadn't done it in a while. Then I loosened my shoulders and slackened my grip slightly on the blade. I'd trained. I wasn't a warrior by any stretch of the imagination. But I wasn't weak, and I wasn't a victim. If I needed to fight, I'd fight, and that was that.

"Lyra?"

A desperate moan escaped my lips. "Kai?" I whipped around, searching for him in the darkness. Only shadows hiding from the moon lay behind me. "Where are you?"

"Why are you here?" He remained hidden. Unwilling to stand before me, though I couldn't blame him.

"To apologize. To get on my knees and beg you to forgive me. If you don't want to love me, I think I can accept that, but I can't accept hurting you. I can't accept the final look on your face as you walked out. Please come out of the shadows. Let me see you."

The faint sound of a careful footstep in front of me snapped my attention forward.

His voice crept down my spine. "I don't think I'll ever forgive you."

Tears welled, sliding heavily down my cheeks. I brushed them away.

"That's—I can accept that. But I'm sorry. If nothing else, I need you to know that. I never meant to hurt you."

"You didn't hurt me. You destroyed me."

He wielded his words as sharply as his weapons, and I deserved it. All of it.

"I know." My voice cracked. "I know and I'm sorry."

I ached for him so desperately, I dropped the reins of the horse and shifted forward into the open. "Why can't I see you?"

"Would you do anything for my forgiveness, Lyra? Anything I wished to be with me again?"

"Yes. Anything." The words stumbled from me before I could even consider them. Consider the odd conversation, the lack of emotion from him. Kai would never leave his army. His king. I'd been played for a fool and poured my heart out to a creature of the Marsh Court. Racing through the information in my mind, I vaguely remembered a creature that could pluck memories from your mind and imitate them. The crocotta. I couldn't see him, couldn't smell him. But the wolf-like creature was slowly closing in. Unable to overpower the beast, I'd have to outsmart him. I'd have to play a very dangerous game.

"Grovel. All the way to the ground. Beg me for that forgiveness."

"That's all?" I rotated the knife and slid it behind my wrist, hoping the moonlight would not shine brightly enough to reveal it. Then I stepped farther away from Hern and moved to the ground. My timing would have to be impeccable. My aim, even more so. "I am so very sorry."

A pair of yellow eyes grew from the darkness ahead, rushing toward me. The crocotta lunged, teeth gnashing. The coarse hair of a hound brushed my arm as I twisted to the side and plunged my knife deep into his ribs. A yelp filled the silence, followed by the whinny of my fae horse, still standing behind me. The creature came crashing down, his weight greater than I'd anticipated. An echo of a rasp rattled from the beast and then he was dead, flung atop me. I shoved his body away, suddenly aware of how chilly the night had become.

"If I had more time, I'd skin you and wear your coat as a trophy. Sick bastard."

Peeling myself from the ground, I snagged the reins and leaped back onto Hern. My adrenaline would never allow me to rest, so I kept going. Dawn eventually came and with it, a bit of relief. The tamped-down blades of grass before me were the sign I'd been begging for since I started this journey. I knew I was still in the wake of the army, but they had been here. *He* had been here. Somewhere. And that was all the indication I needed to push on.

Another day passed as I tracked the route of the army, noting where they had stopped in bigger clearings, where the hills had slowed them and pushed them closer together. I'd hoped I was getting close, but as time passed, I couldn't help but wonder if I'd chase them all the way to the Wind Court. It felt that way.

Stuck in my head, with only my thoughts for company, I spiraled down into my own grievous pity, hating myself more than I'd ever hated anyone. At one point, I drew the fae horse to a halt. I didn't deserve Kai. Not for all the treasures in the world would I deserve him. Crossing the desert didn't matter. Failure breeds failure, and I couldn't bring that to him.

My heart broke all over again. Pulling me off the horse and crashing into the army-trampled ground below me. I was fucking tired. And sore. Getting nowhere as I chased a male that didn't want me anymore. I'd given him absolute power over my heart, even though I'd crushed his.

The bond rattled to life, sending a straight line of sweet, golden love right through me. Wrapping me so thoroughly, I knew without a doubt the male was beckoning me. Wave after blissful wave of confidence fired into me as I mounted Hern once more and shot across the hilly landscape with renewed vigor. I hadn't felt an ounce of forgiveness, but he wanted me. I don't know what he'd seen, what had happened, but we flew onward.

The next morning, I found a small village of canvas tents scattered across the skyline. There were no sounds, no movements as I raced forward. They'd left their things behind. Perhaps the feeling from Kai had been a moment of weakness through his walls as he prepared for battle. I wove the horse through the Flame Court camp. My small knife would not be an adequate weapon. I needed a sword. I may not slay a thousand soldiers; but I was partially trained, thanks to my mate, and that would not be in vain.

Icy panic settled deep within my soul as silence transitioned into chaos in the distance. I tore frantically through the camp, searching for a sword. Remembering Kai's collection of weapons within his rooms in the Flame Court castle, I ripped through tent after tent, searching for his. I could feel him here, in this place, calling orders and marching around. I could nearly see the traces of his memory as he stalked through his soldiers' tents, ordering them to bed, or to rise and fight.

I spread apart another set of fabric doors and the world tilted below me as I realized I'd found it. He had been here, the space smothered in his scent. He'd kept it tidy, unlike his room at the castle. Ready to pack and leave at a moment's notice, likely. There wasn't much. A bag, a trunk, and furs lining the ground. I fell on my knees before the trunk and lifted the lid, finding the arsenal I'd been searching for within. My eyes fell on a pair of wrist bandoliers and the set of small knives to load into the weapon. I could wield a sword and use these as backup as I needed.

I didn't bother putting them on, nor shutting the trunk as I tore out of the tent and launched myself back onto the waiting horse, kicking his flanks and soaring toward the sounds of battle just beyond the next line of hills.

Making a swift decision regarding the workhorse that had been my only companion, I tied him to a tree. He wasn't mine. I couldn't ride him into battle. Step by step, I did what was needed in a mechanical effort to reach my mate. If not to pour my heart out, then to fight beside him and prove that there was something in me worthy of his love and adoration.

Cresting the final hill on foot, I looked down and nearly stumbled. A battle was only a word in your mind until you saw it with your eyes. Until each glance was watching the death of a fae. The ground wept with deep red blood. Screams and cries rang out as loud as the roars and clashes of weapons. I searched and searched the field below, so packed with fae I couldn't discern one foe from another. Magic wielders rattled the ground and built walls of water and fire. The sky was filled with cetani, the beasts of the draconian riders, darting in and out of the fight, dropping massive boulders as they roared and flew away.

A colony of giants swept their great arms through the sky and crashed their fists on the ground, capturing and smashing anything they could get their massive hands on. This looked more like an execution than a war. I couldn't force my feet to move. To step into that scene of pure rage and passion. Of bloodshed and ruin.

I could do nothing but watch and pray to the gods as a great shadow fell across the ground. A dragon. He screamed, great bolts of fire pouring from his maw as he moved across the field toward the giants and beasts. He swooped and swirled, his fire the change of the tide, it seemed. Until he, too, began to falter. No match against the overwhelming army of the Wind Court. He had flown close enough to the opposite side of the battle that a great lifted stage caught my eye. The occupants were too far to discern, though the long auburn hair of one figure looked familiar.

"Fen!"

I heard a familiar voice call, yanking my attention to the only male I cared to see. Before I could register my desperate movements, I was scrambling—doing all that I could to keep from rolling down the hill as I raced toward Kaitalen. He swung his broadsword in a perfect arc through the air, slaying the attacker before him as he fought beside the king of the Flame Court on the bloodied battlefield.

I wanted so desperately to call out to him, to feel his eyes on me. But I couldn't—wouldn't—distract him as he moved with such perfect precision and grace. He was the fiercest weapon I'd ever seen. I'd witnessed him fight encased in fiery rage, but this was different. His face remained trained into steady focus as he fought side by side with his friend.

The pair made it look easy. Too easy, as the rest of the world was immersed in terror and bloodletting. As the great yellow dragon went down in the distance, beaten and defeated. As the world imploded with such hatred and anger, nothing else mattered.

I stepped and stumbled as the ground shook again, rising just in time to hear the world-shattering cry of a male. It seemed to halt the battle, if only for a moment, before it surged back into motion. And then I was running.

Pulling the sword over my head, I slashed into an enemy. I rotated around him, wanting to jam my sharpened nails into the male beside him, and rip his beating heart from his chest. My nails had just begun to grow back, so I used the sword instead, though it wasn't nearly as satisfying. Two steps more and another fae attacked. I fought as I'd been taught, using the wrist contraption and sending a foe hurling backward, as I lunged with the sword, taking down another. Three steps closer to him and again I was attacked. I wasn't quick enough to dodge a strike and took a pommel to the head. The world spun and blurred and still I thrust that sword forward. Fighting for him. For me. For a future I so desperately needed.

I ran for Kai again, skirting around fallen bodies and severed limbs as I moved. Sheer luck laid a safe path before me as I sprinted. He was still so far. Racing toward that dais in the distance, burning flesh and the sharp bite of blood filled my nostrils. Taking a deep breath became a chore around the putrid smell. Fae roared and beasts howled, and though this world was undeniably broken, we, the faeries of Alewyn, were ignited with a passion I didn't think we'd had in a long time. It weighed as thick in the air as the promise of death.

Closer now, I surveyed the commander. Blood coated his left arm, and I couldn't tell if it was his or someone else's, but as a group of three harpies looped down from the sky, attacking him and the king, my entire life flashed before my eyes. I'd known it was dangerous, known he hadn't had a choice, but as I watched him falter, I wished on every fallen star, every wish the sea could grant that time would just stand still. That he could move away from that screeching bitch with her talons before her, attempting to shred him to pieces.

He shifted and it was King Fenlas that was pinned to the ground below one of the three harpies that swooped in. The king fought back, a sputter of flames flaring as he killed the harpy and leaped to his feet, moving toward Kai. He had pulled the other two harpies to himself to save his king. A male I didn't recognize tried to intervene, but failed. They were too strong; too vicious. A blur of talons and magic; it was a fight lost before it began.

As the harpies took Kai down, I fell to the sullied ground, his name tearing from my throat in a scream that echoed across the battlefield, the court, the entire world. They smothered him. He fought, thrashing and straining, as feathers dark as night scattered around him. And then, panic.

Mine. His. Ours.

A final caress of my mate through the bond before my entire fucking world shattered.

Our soul, pulsing and intertwined, loosened. Cracked.

"NO!"

I couldn't accept this. I wouldn't lose him. I crawled through the muck and mud. Over fallen bodies with vacant eyes.

"No. No. No." A begging, pleading prayer on my cracked lips. "It should be me. Take me."

Death seemed to answer as the pieces that fit so perfectly between him and I vanished. As his essence left me hollow.

A great, searing pain ripped through my chest, my mind, my soul. No longer ours, as he was taken from me. I screamed again and again and again as the only person I had in the entire world died on the bloodied battlefield, having protected his king one final time.

My chest caved in as memories taunted me. His arms wrapped around his friends the first time I'd seen him; glossy eyes as he drank in that tavern. A desperate ache filled me as the lump, so sharp in my throat, threatened to cut off my airway. Even in this place of bleakness, without a tangible grasp on the world, I remembered that moment in the road when a flash of who he truly was had come to the surface. The first time he'd touched my skin and I came alive for him. And now he was gone. And I was irrevocably broken.

The world went black.

I'd die here on this battlefield.

CHAPTER 27

"Hey there." A hand gripped my shoulder, and I lurched to consciousness, knife at the ready. "Woah. Easy."

A female knelt before me, palms up in surrender.

Reality came crashing back as I launched to my feet and backed away from the high fae female with cropped chestnut hair and a longbow strapped to her back.

"Stay away from me." The words were barely a whisper from my hoarse throat.

"Are you… Is your name Lyra?" Her words were soft, her eyes kind.

I looked over my shoulder at the spot where Kai was defeated, so numb, no tears would fall. "Yes."

"I thought I heard your scream. Come with me."

"No!" I barked, stepping closer to him.

"It wasn't a question. It was a command. No matter what your heart is telling you right now, listen to me and do not go to him. You cannot save him and you'll never unsee what has been done to him." Her voice cracked as she said those terrible words.

I jerked my head back to her and sneered. "What do you know of him? Or me?"

"He told me everything." Her chin dipped as she narrowed her gaze. "I've known that fae for most of his life. I've laughed with him, cried with him, and now I must mourn him, just as you will. We won. Barely. Now, the rest of the soldiers are leaving the battlefield." Pain slashed across her face as her eyes flickered to where his body lay. "You will too. I'm trying hard to keep myself together. Don't make me get the king."

Having no other choice, I dropped my shoulders, spun, and ran to Kai. I got three steps before I was tackled to the ground by a brute of a male. A well-placed kick and a punch to the throat of my assailant and I was up and running.

I was stopped again. The male, covered in slashes and different hues of dried blood, had seen the rough side of the battle, and without a doubt, he wasn't nearly as strong as he should have been. I guessed the injured, raven-feathered wing hanging limp at his back had something to do with it. Still, he wrapped his arms around me as I pushed off the ground, jumping, kicking, flailing until the fae female said softly, "Let her go, Rhog. Let her see him."

The male huffed and let me go. I launched away from him and tore through the expanse until I was close enough to see Kai fully. His chest did not rise, though I begged it. The lump in my throat hadn't wavered. I thought the tears would fall then, but they were trapped somewhere within me.

He was brutally mauled. My thrashing heart twisted as if my claws had reached inside the cavity of my chest and squeezed, nails gripping and piercing the sinew that held it together. Digging so deep, clenching, I could swear my heart left my body. There was nothing left. Not for me. The ringing in my ears grew louder as I beheld my Kaitalen. I couldn't breathe. Couldn't think. Couldn't anything. Everything, our entire story, had been for nothing but pain.

I swayed as reality darkened around me. A hand slipped into my own, anchoring me somehow; bringing me back down to this broken, bleeding world.

"I'm Wren."

Face slackened, I looked at her. Sorrow-filled eyes stared back at me as a single tear trekked down her flushed cheek. She pulled me away and step after numb step, I followed. The male lingered behind us as I twisted and twisted that ring on my finger. The only thing I had left of him.

All manner of injured fae crowded together as we collectively trudged back to the camp, the yellow dragon in tow. He'd made it out alive, though barely, it seemed. Our steps were as heavy as our hearts as we left the battlefield behind, an army adorned in golden armor fading over the horizon behind us. My mind was so numb, time seemed to blur. Somehow, I collected Hern and sent him with a stable master, then found myself standing inside Kai's tent.

"I won't tell the others about you if you don't want me to."

I turned to Wren, so exhausted I didn't even have the energy to respond.

She nodded once and opened the canvas flap to leave. "Half the soldiers will stay the night and pack the camp, following behind. It'll be safer for you to travel in one of the two groups." Her eyes darted around the tent as she swallowed heavily. "I'm sorry. I can't stay here."

She vanished without another word, the brute with the broken wing following silently behind her. Perhaps she'd wanted something from me. An apology for what I'd done to her friend. An explanation. But I didn't have the energy.

I collapsed on the bed and begged the tears to fall from my tired eyes. Begged for something to soothe my soul. I wished for the great open sea, so vast I could swim forever and ever, never stopping long enough to let myself dwell on these moments. But no gods would answer me, and as I curled up on his cot, placing my head in the last spot he'd rested his, I whispered a final wish. I wished for The Mists to swallow me whole.

Sadly, I woke the next morning. Sounds of the remaining army taking down tents and packing weapons filled the air. There was food being prepared somewhere but the thought only rolled my stomach. I'd seen horrible, traumatizing things during that battle. Severed limbs, final breaths, screams for help wailing from fae brought down by their adversaries. The images played through my mind in slow motion until I was gasping, crawling toward the door. I barely made it over the threshold before I was sick. Retching repeatedly, though nothing came to the surface.

"Here."

I glanced up to see the broken-winged male's boots and turned away. I didn't want his pity or anyone else's. Didn't deserve it. He dropped a canteen beside me and walked away.

Days later, I left Hern in the barn of the family I'd borrowed him from without seeing them at all. They'd find him. Eventually, they would hear of Kai's death and would understand. I marched the rest of the way back with the Flame Court soldiers. Though most were serious and mourning in their own way, a few bouts of scattered laughter left me bitter. How could they laugh? How could they feel anything but pain after something so wretched? How could they move on? How could I?

The castle became a beacon for the others. Seeming to grow from the ground as we trekked across the desert. I knew exactly where his bedroom was in the silhouette of the building. With each step closer, it became a challenge not to stare at that speck in the distance knowing he'd never be there again.

Even as we stood directly before the castle, shielded by the large shadow it cast across the sand, I refused to look up.

"I'm glad you made it home safely."

Wren stood before me, but kept her distance. Something I was used to.

"This isn't home." They were the first words I'd spoken in days.

Weak and weary from traveling, from that deep pit of emotional turmoil, I'd hardly seen the need. But she was his friend. He'd loved her. She understood. And maybe that's what I needed. Someone who understood how significant his loss was. Someone who treated that wound with tender caution.

She smiled and reached for my hand again. "There will be an honorary pyre tonight for all the fallen." She spoke the last word so softly, I nearly missed it. "He would want you to be there. To represent him."

The sight of him lying on the ground struck me out of nowhere, and I winced. "I don't think I can."

"You can." She linked her arm through mine and as the numbness threatened to take over again, I released a breath and let this stranger ground me once more. As if it were a magical power. "You'll come to my rooms at the castle and have a nice long bath. We'll find you something to wear, and you'll come."

"I can't—I can't face the rest of his family. Not yet. Maybe not ever."

"He swore me to secrecy, Lyra. I wouldn't break that promise. Not then and not now. Though I don't understand why you want to keep it a secret."

"Kai," speaking his name caused my heart to twist, "didn't like to reveal his vulnerabilities."

"A soldier through and through." She sighed. "But it's different now that—"

I shook my head. "I broke him, Wren. I wasn't worthy of him then, and certainly not now. I don't want anyone to know what we were."

She clenched her jaw but said nothing more as she led me to her room in the golden-domed castle. "Bath is through those doors. I'll find you something to wear."

"Thank you." I looked at the ground. "For your kindness. I know it must be incredibly hard for you to even look at me."

"No." She rested a hand on my arm. "Kai loved you. Even when he was miserable with the choice you made, that never changed. He was hurting, but not broken. He was my family. Whatever you're going through, just know you aren't alone."

She didn't know about his walls. Didn't understand how much he hid from them all, afraid to be the weakest among them. Afraid to be vulnerable. Still, it wasn't my place to teach them about the male they'd known. So, I padded into the bathing room and shut the door.

I turned on the water and let it fill to the brim, steaming hot. Slipping out of the clothes I never wanted to wear, or touch, or even see again, I sank into the bath. I stayed in my fae form, scrubbing every inch of my skin until it was burning, and even then it wasn't enough. Tears stung my eyes as I tried and failed to scrape the remnants of the battle from my body.

The walls started moving in on me and I couldn't seem to pull enough air into my lungs. I'd never known this level of sadness and heartache. Fully consumed, I crawled into the dark vacant hole in my soul and resolved to stay there forever.

"Lyra?" A hand shook me by the shoulder, and I peeled my eyes open to see Wren peering down at me through the surface of the still bathwater. "Are you okay?"

I wasn't. I didn't think I'd ever be okay again. I felt a defining moment weigh down on me as I curled in the bath. I shook my head slowly and the lump in my throat grew again. Something in that honest second, in hiding with my head underwater, nearly broke me again.

She reached in and pulled me up, water spilling over the edge of the bath. Without a word, she stood and moved to the counter, pouring soaps and oils into her hands. Deep amber and something sweeter filled the air as she crossed the room and buried her hands in my hair, massaging. Something about that touch, the kindness of a stranger, broke the dam. I began to sob. I hadn't since I'd seen his massacred body. The image threatened to suffocate me every time I closed my eyes and she'd known it would. Had tried to stop me. Even in her grief, this stranger had thought of me.

Tears fell like rain in an enraged storm. Mine and hers, as she rinsed my hair, taking extra care to work through to the ends. Sniffling, she helped me from the bath. As she wrapped a towel around me, she held her arms open. So weak, I crumbled into them, and we cried together.

Eventually, I pulled away, forever changed by this raw moment with a stranger. I dressed and brushed my hair, then crawled into her warm bed and slept as she snuck away.

Hours later, she woke me. Gently. "It's time." I opened my mouth to speak but she held out a hand. "I know you don't want to go. But you will do it, anyway. You will be respectful to his memory and the memories of all the others we lost. You aren't the only one mourning and you'll regret it if you don't."

"I only meant to ask what I could wear. My clothes … I can never wear them again."

"Oh. I'm sorry. I thought you'd fight me. I'm used to Ara." She handed me a glass of water and sat on the edge of the bed.

"I think I would have, once upon a time. Or I would have just ignored you. But not about this. Not about him."

"Friar brought several options for you to try on. They are in a pile over there." She pointed to the chair. "I already had your clothes thrown out. Your knife is on the dresser."

Hours later, after changing and trying to eat something, though I could only nibble before my stomach turned, we left. I stayed behind in the crowd, preferring to be alone. The weight of the hot desert air, mixed with the giant symbolic pyre, made my skin crawl. I didn't want to do this, I didn't want to be here, a face in a crowd of tens of thousands. Our collective heartache filled the night sky with so much grief, I wasn't sure any of us would recover. Hatred had broken the world before, and now it was shattered by heartache.

The king led the crowd in the farewell prayer and one by one, the mourners faded away. They'd said their final goodbyes and they were ready for life to move on. I wasn't. So, I stayed. Waiting for that feeling to come to me. With only a few hundred fae left lingering, I scooted closer to the hypnotic fire, studying the way the flames tossed and turned. The crackle of the wood, the shift of the pile, the way the glowing red embers flew from the pyre until they faded into nothing but ash on the wind.

Three more people left and I moved closer, sitting on the soft ground, only an arm's length from the fire. I hugged my knees to my chest and thought only of breathing. Of living. Existing in a world that he did not.

"I've learned over the years that it doesn't matter how long these pyres burn, the outcome is always the same. There's never healing here."

I looked away to find the old cook standing a few paces away, her eyes flickering in the firelight, an orange glow to her skin as she stood in a trance. "I don't need company. I'm fine."

"Only a selfish person would assume I'm standing before a funeral pyre for her benefit," she snapped, fisting her hands on her hips. "Are you so arrogant?"

"Depends on who you ask, I guess." I turned away and looked back to the fire.

"I'm sorry you've lost your mate. I know you're imagining standing in the middle of that pyre right now, wishing it would burn you to the ground too, but giving up isn't the way out of this. Kai isn't coming back but that doesn't mean your life ends with his. Get up, child. Dust the sand from your bottom and keep moving, because that's what we do. One day, one step at a time and no more."

"You lost your mate as well." It wasn't a question. I could tell by her tone and ability to read me so clearly. "I'm not sure what to do anymore. I don't know where I belong."

She stepped closer and held her hand out. "Welcome to the Flame Court, girl. Where no one belongs and somehow, we're all family, anyway."

I slipped my hand into hers and let her lead me back to the castle. Wren was waiting when I got back to her rooms.

She threw her hands on her hips and gave me a hard look. "I'm going to allow the sulking for now, but you have to work through this. I don't care how you do it. If you want to cry, cry. If you want to be pissed, go ahead. I draw the line at giving up. We never give up."

I took a step back. "You don't know me. You don't understand any of this."

Wren rubbed her temples. "You're right. I don't. Which is why I'm just trying to be here for you, because it doesn't look like anyone else gives a damn."

She could have punched me in the gut and it would have hurt less. I spun on my heel and stormed off. Not because she was wrong, but because she was absolutely right. So was the cook. And the hydra. Even Kai had been right to leave me on that ship and walk away.

Quiet steps turned to stomps in empty hallways as I tore through the colorful castle, praying to the gods I wouldn't run into the king as I tried to escape before breaking into a million pieces. I blinked and I was standing on the shoreline, the water crowding my feet as the tide came in, the ocean calling me home. But what was home? My father's ship? The castle? The rooms we'd shared? There was no home for me. Only vicious memories of a life that could have been.

I needed him. So desperately, I knew eventually I'd break altogether. I couldn't get in that water. The thought alone nearly took me to my knees. Instead, I went crawling back to the castle. Sneaking in through the cook's back door, I made my way to Kai's room and crawled into his bed. The seashell I'd given him sat on the nightstand. It was meant to be a lifeline between us. Something to remember me by when he was here, in these blankets. But now it was only a memory of him. And it fucking hurt. It was always going to hurt.

CHAPTER 28

"Get up."

For a moment, I'd forgotten the nightmare that was my life, but as I peeked out of the blankets enough to see the blond, one-winged warrior looming over me with the most annoying grimace slathered across his face, I remembered. My heart cracked a little more in response. He loomed over me, pure exasperation and irritation on his face. I wished I could feel that; feel anything.

"Get fucked." I threw the blanket back over my head, smelling every trace of Kai they held.

He practically growled as he gripped the edge of the blankets and whisked them away. "Get up, siren."

"Go. Away."

He leaned over me until I could hear the huff in his breath. "Of all the places and people in the world, you've fallen on Wren's radar. She cares about everyone. No matter how hard you push, she is just going to push back."

"I'm not interested in being her fucking charity project. Maybe she should focus on you instead. How's the wing hanging?"

Firm hands yanked me straight out of the bed, whipping me around until I was pinned against the wall with fingers digging into my shoulders. "You can say whatever the hell you want about me but you will not speak an ill word against the one person in this world that seems to care if you live or die."

I brought my arms up through his and cracked him in the nose with my elbow. He loosened his grip enough that I could twist away, desperate to crawl back into Kai's bed. The moment my back was to him, he grabbed my hair and yanked me backward. I stumbled to the ground, and he was on me in an instant. I gave up. Didn't fight back, didn't feel the rush of fear or boiling anger. I was numb.

He pulled his shaking fist back and I knew he'd hit me so hard it would break something. I could see the urge in his eyes. The fury I wish I could feel.

"Do it."

"I should," he roared.

"Do it!" I screamed, begging to feel anything but sadness.

Instead, he shoved off me, the black feathers on his single wing rustling against the ground as he moved. His shoulders heaved as he looked at me with disgust and clenched his teeth. "We do not give up. Get up."

Face blank, I crawled back into the bed and pulled the blankets over my head. "Fuck off."

The door clicked shut and I knew I'd won. I saw something then. The framed photo of the mysterious young woman on his bedside table. I hadn't looked hard enough before. But now, having memorized those lips that were so clearly his, the eyes that haunted me, I knew. Even after she'd abandoned him, he'd still loved his mother. Maybe Wren was right.

Closing my eyes, I waited for sleep. Kai would be there, in my dreams, waiting for me. If that was the only way I could be with him, then that's where I wanted to be.

Sometime later, muffled voices outside the door turned to heated words.

"She needs time."

I recognized the voice. Loti, the cook.

"If she's going to be staying, we have to tell Fen and Ara." Wren's voice was full of worry.

I had no intention of staying in the castle. Maybe I wasn't planning on going back to the sea, but this wasn't right for me either. I only wished they'd let me take the bedsheets with me. Wherever I was going. I drifted back to sleep, taking slow, deep breaths until he was standing before me. Every inch of tall, tan, wild-haired Kai. So beautiful it hurt.

I reached for him. Moving a thumb down his cheek as he smiled. "I miss you so much. I'm sorry."

He didn't answer. He never did. But he was there and that was enough. Until the world came jolting back to me as the blankets were ripped town and a pissed-off Wren stood over me with her arms crossed again, cropped brown hair tucked neatly behind her pointed ears.

"Get up."

I moaned and rolled back over.

"Get. Up. Fen comes in here. It's where he feels close to him, too. If you don't want to explain who you are, then get up." With the voice of a haughty mother, her words had me moving before I'd made a conscious decision.

I didn't want to face the king. The one whose life had taken the place of my mate's. So, I swung a wobbly foot over the edge of the bed, gripped the sheets in my hands one final time, and stood. It was so much easier to do nothing. To sleep. To give up. Standing here now, I had no idea what I should do. Where I should go. I let my feet guide me until once again, the water lapped around them.

The ocean had always been a soothing balm to me. Comforting as it rushed over my skin and between the gaps of my scales. A siren. That's what I had been. Once. Irresistible and alluring. The world would fall before me, and I would let it. Because I could. But now? I dropped to the sandy shore, gripping my knees as I dwelled in that emptiness I had inside of me.

"You are a sad, sad little being, you know that?"

I looked over my shoulder and glared at the massive, one-winged male sitting down beside me. "Why can't you just leave me alone?"

He pointed to the castle where I could just make out Wren, standing with her arms around herself, hair blowing in the desert wind. "She cares. She cares about literally everything."

"And you're just her servant?"

"I'm anything she wants me to be, whenever she wants me to be." He brushed a hand through his long, blond hair, so close to mine in color it was jarring.

I dusted the sand from my palms as I looked back to the tumbling ocean. "What does she want from me?"

"Why don't you get up and come find out for yourself, rather than sitting here wallowing in self-pity."

"I prefer to be left alone."

"I prefer subordinates to fall in line. Yet, here we are."

A ripple of familiarity in those words washed over me. "I'm not your subordinate. I don't even know you."

He stood, dusting himself off. "I'm Rhogan."

"I don't care. The Elder King lost his mate and hid in his castle, grieving on his terms. Why am I not allowed the same courtesy?"

"If you want to do shit on your own terms, go back to the sea. It's right there."

I stood, glaring at him. "You're an asshole."

His answering smile was so obnoxious, I balled my hands into fists as I stomped into the water. Locking eyes with him, I pushed at my fae form, calling the siren forward. But nothing happened. I looked down, finding only fae legs standing knee-deep in the sea. Panic set in as I looked back up at the cocky male and then back down to my feet. I tried again. Nothing.

I turned my back to him, taking short shallow breaths as I tried to focus my mind. But I couldn't. If I closed my eyes, I saw his fallen body. My hands fluttered. I shook them at my sides, desperately holding onto my stance as the ocean pushed and pushed against me, as if sending me back to land. Not even she wanted me anymore.

Overwhelming dread coalesced with my panic and sorrow until I was walking, defeated, back to the shoreline; toward Rhogan, staring at me with the question on his lips. I shook my head and shoved past him, making my way to the fae standing in the shade of the castle, completely unaware of what had just happened.

"You don't have to go," she said, putting her hand up to block the sun as she peeked at the brooding male behind me.

I swallowed, reality flooding my ears. "What am I going to do here? I can't be still. If I'm not moving, my mind is, and it never stops in a good place. I have nothing but a ship anchored in an ocean that just refused me."

"Can you work? Do you have any skills? You could stay with the refugees."

I pulled back, remembering the conversation with Kai when he'd asked if I had skills. *I can pick any lock, steal anything I want, and rip your heart out, Commander, so don't tempt me.* I had ripped his heart out. And he'd taken mine with him when he left.

"Lyra?" Wren reached for my arm.

"I'm sorry." I shook my head. "I have no skills."

"Anyone with two brain cells to rub together can learn. All you have to do is want to." Rhogan stalked past us and into the castle. "Meet me in the courtyard at sunrise. And work on that other brain cell so we have something to start with."

"He's usually not so moody. He can't fly anymore. It's making him grumpy."

I kept my tone flat. "I hadn't noticed."

"I'm not here to babysit you. I'll teach you what we're doing and it's your job to decide what you want to do with that. You want to keep your mind busy? This will do it. The minute you stop making excuses for yourself, it will become easier."

My world stopped. Kai had said those words to me during my first training session at the lists. Those vibrant memories of him hurt the most. Destroyed me with no shame. A lump grew sharp in my throat, but I swallowed, pushing it away. No excuses.

With a fresh wound, wrought by words meant to be helpful, I ran behind Rhogan as he strode through the city toward a home we would be working on. With all the casualties from the battle, several homes were vacant. Wren had informed me this morning that Rhogan would be working with a team to fix up the ones that needed it before the refugees moved in.

The dry air was already hot, and the sun was only just rising, filling the sky with a myriad of desert reds and fiery oranges. We rounded a sharp corner, and I kept my mouth shut as Rhogan led the team to a building that was standing by miracle alone.

"Don't lean on this one," someone murmured. "It'll fall to pieces."

"Correct, Briggs." Rhogan halted, turning to face the five of us. "We will have to brace the walls from the south side and adjust them, or we tear it down and build new."

A fae with hair nearly the same as Kai's stepped forward and raised his hand.

"This isn't a classroom, Cru. What is it?"

"Sorry, Sir." He dropped his hand and jutted his chin forward. "I vote we take it down."

"We'll take a closer look first, then decide."

"Yes, sir."

Rhogan's eyes flashed towards me, but a second later his boot crunched the compacted sand and he walked away, surveying the leaning house with his arms folded across his chest. We followed. I wasn't sure what I was doing there. I knew nothing about building or rebuilding. I just wanted something to keep me busy. Something that gave me a sense of purpose. Because as I laid on Wren's couch last night, I'd realized I was nothing. I wasn't a siren. The thought of trying to beguile a male made me sick. My siren form was gone, my song was gone, my mate was gone. Whoever I was months ago, was gone.

"Lyra?" Rhogan barked.

I looked down to find a tool in my hands and the others spreading out around the house. The fog over my brain was resettling. Blinking slowly, I shook my head. "I'm sorry. What?"

He marched in close. "This job can be dangerous. You need to stay focused or you're going to end up needing a healer. Two brain cells. Do you know how to use that thing?"

I looked down at the tool and back to him. I saw only hardness in his eyes as he took it from me and held it up. "This is a hammer. These prongs will pull nails, this tip will drive them. Basically, you use it to bang on shit and try not to hurt yourself. Got it?"

The morning was a blur. Scattered moments of barked orders and trying not to get in the way as the others decided the structure could stand if adjusted. I leaned against a sturdy wall and wiped sweat from my eyes as Rhogan came around the corner.

"What have you accomplished today? Give me a list."

I opened my mouth. Then shut it. I wasn't sure.

"You've gotten out of bed. You've stood on a job site. You've held that hammer for three hours without complaining."

I nodded. Maybe once I would have had a snarky comment. No longer.

He stepped in closer, taking the hammer. "You got out of bed. That's enough for today. Tomorrow, you do more, and the next day, more. That's all you can do. You keep going. No matter how empty you feel, you keep going."

I nodded again, still numb.

"Wren's waiting at the refugee center. Briggs will take you there, she'll get you settled. We'll do a week of mornings and then double shifts, taking off the hottest part of the day. You should bring water with you. And try to make a friend."

I drew back a step but kept my face neutral. "I'm not a kip. I don't need to be coddled."

"You've barely moved from that spot all day. You've just been standing here."

I let out an exasperated breath. "I'm trying."

He tucked the hammer into his belt and stepped away. "Those words will only get you so far."

"Here." Wren handed me a bowl with thick roasted meats drowning in stew sauce.

It was the first time in days I'd felt like eating. We sat together in the refugee eating hall in silence until Rhogan pulled up a chair. He bumped his shoulder against Wren and devoured his meal in five seconds before wiping the back of his arm across his mouth. Wren was wide-eyed as she stared at him, her mouth agape.

"What? I had to pick up someone's slack today." He tilted his head toward me as if I wouldn't notice.

"How was it?" she finally asked. The question seemed to have been brewing since she'd helped me find an open cot.

I shrugged.

Rhogan cleared his throat. "Tomorrow we'll try *swinging* the hammer and see how that goes."

Wren bit her bottom lip to hide her smile. She pushed away from the table, grabbing the empty dishes, and walked off.

"She wants to be your friend, you know." Rhogan leaned back in his reversed chair, the feathers of his wing stretching along the floor.

"I'm a shitty friend."

With that, I stood and walked out, remembering my way back to the sleeping quarters. I pulled the dinner roll I'd swiped out of my pocket and handed it to the only fae child I'd seen. She smiled eagerly and though I tried to return one, it just didn't work.

I didn't know why I'd taken it. Maybe just to remind myself that no matter how much had changed, a tiny seed of who I was remained, though buried. After showering, I fell asleep with that thought circling my mind.

I woke to the sun heating my face and leaped out of bed, knocking over the uncomfortable cot as I rushed out of the door. An hour. I was an hour late, if not more, judging by the sun. I couldn't stop for breakfast, or even water, as I rushed through Halemi.

"I'm sorry I'm late," I panted, hands on my knees as I drew in breaths. "No one woke me up."

Rhogan didn't look up from the nail he was driving into a board. "Did you ask someone to?"

"I… no."

"Then why would they?"

I turned to walk away. Fuck this. I didn't have to be here. I could find a way back to my ship and live out my days alone. I didn't even know what I was doing. Wasting time? Digging my feet into the ground as I stomped away, I got all of four paces before he shouted from behind me.

"I knew you didn't have it in you. You're going to let his death destroy you and it's going to be no one's fault but your own. He died and took you with him."

I rounded, gritting my teeth, and before I knew what I was doing, I was running—flying into that mouthy fucker at full force and pounding my fist into him over and over again.

"Shut your gods damned mouth!" I screamed. "You don't know me." *Punch.* "You don't know what this feels like." *Punch.*

My veins pulsed, roaring to life with more anger than I'd felt since I'd seen my father. I ground my teeth as I continued to swing, heat rushing through my body in the form of red-hot rage. He lay there and took it as I struck again and again. All of my thoughts, all of my feelings, came boiling to the surface, and I roared to the sky as I beat the daylights out of Rhogan and the shitty grin on his stupid face. I hated him. Absolutely hated him. And yet he smiled. He fucking smiled as my strength fell away and angry tears slid down my cheeks.

He stood, reaching out a hand for me. "Feel better?"

"No." I took it and let him help me up.

"Anger is better than numbness. Grab your hammer, let me show you what we're working on."

"I'm not staying here. There's no point."

He eyed me carefully. "Are you a quitter?"

"I guess." I threw my sore hands in the air.

"Unacceptable. You can be an asshole, Lyra. But you agreed to help with this, and you'll see it through. Pick up the hammer."

"I hate you." I picked up the hammer.

His obnoxious smile warranted another punch to the gut. "We're going to build the frame for the brace and then bring in some fae horses to fix the angle on the house. Nails are there." He pointed to a cloth bag. "Hold the nail like this," he said, gripping it firmly between two fingers, "and beat it in with the hammer. Drive them straight and all the way through the boards. I'll get the frame started and you'll follow, securing with more nails. Got it."

"I guess," I mumbled.

It was mindless work once we began. He started by showing me where to place the nails into each piece until I realized the pattern and set off on my own. I drove in nail after nail, letting my aggression and anger pour from me as I spent the day moving one nail at a time. The sun grew so hot, salty sweat poured into my eyes, stinging. I deserved it, though. All of the pain. All of the suffering. So, I just kept moving. Focusing my mind on nothing but the task before me.

"Drink," Rhogan barked for the third time.

"I said I'm fine."

"Yeah. You're fine until you pass out. Drink. Or go back to the compound."

I took the canteen from his offered hand and swallowed, then gulped until my chest hurt and I was coughing.

"That's your body trying to tell you to take better care of it. You can't sit out here in the sun without water."

"Fine." I took another drink as I caught a glimpse of Wren coming around the corner of the house.

"Almost done for the day?"

"Not my call," Rhogan answered, looking at me. I knew what he wanted. He wanted me to make friends with Wren. And if I was being honest with myself, I probably needed someone. Just one person in the whole fucking world, as he liked to remind me.

I nodded. "Rhogan offered to buy me some clothes since this is all I have. Do you think you could show me around?"

Her face lit with delight and she pulled Rhogan into a hug. "I knew you were just a big old softy."

"Oh yes. You know me. Soft." He glared at me over her shoulder, and I flashed him the first genuine smile I'd had in what seemed like forever.

She pulled away, and I untied the apron I'd put on to hold the nails and passed it to the moody brute. "Wake me up tomorrow?"

He dipped his chin and turned back to the project. As Wren and I were just about to round the corner, I saw him kneel over my work and start pulling out the nails. I'd done a shitty job. Each nail took far too many swings; I'd put them in crooked, I'd broken some of them, I'd even left a few halfway in, trying to keep up with him. But he'd never stopped me. Never corrected me. Just let me go. He'd be there for even longer, just fixing everything I'd messed up. Rhogan was a stubborn asshole, but at least he hadn't given up on me.

"What's his story?" I asked as we walked.

"Rhog's? Well, it's really not my place to say, but he's from the Wind Court. Fought in the Iron Wars. Traveled south with the rebels. He's been here a few months now. He's friends with Tem, our newest family member— a healer."

"And you two are…?"

"Yeah, that's complicated." She cast her eyes down, biting her lip.

I picked at the hem of my shirt as she moved toward a shop with clothing hanging in the giant picture window. "He seems to like you. Too moody?"

She pushed the door open. "No. He's… it's like I said. Complicated."

We picked through the shop and Wren laughed at a few pieces she found atrocious, but my heart just wasn't into shopping. Maybe I wasn't ready to try. I wasn't ready to be a person that shopped with friends and had tea with the ladies. Honestly, I just wanted to crawl back in a hole somewhere. I think the darkness within me started to show because Wren pulled me outside and patted my hand as she took me to another shop.

"This one will be more appropriate for the work you're doing. Simple shirts and lightweight pants. Nothing fancy or flashy and they have boots."

Within minutes, we had a few things picked out and Wren asked the shopkeeper to put it on Rhogan's tab. That was enough people time for me. An hour of socializing and I was exhausted.

"I think I'm going to head back to the compound. Try to find a way to make that cot more comfortable."

She winced. "I'm sorry. I know they aren't great. But we are slowly making homes available. As you know."

"It'll work for now. See ya around?"

"I could walk you back?"

I shook my head. "It's on the other end of the city. Maybe we could get dinner together sometime soon."

Her eyes fell. "Oh. Okay, yeah. That will work."

I pushed the dejected tone from my mind and left her standing in the street as I walked away. I got out of bed today. I worked. I talked to another person. Progress. But as I crawled onto my cot and pulled the woolen blanket up to my chin, silent tears slipped from my eyes as I thought of telling Kai about my day. I'd never be able to tell him anything ever again and it was so unfair.

"Rise and shine, fishy. Time to earn those new boots." Rhogan's voice was chipper. Too chipper.

I groaned and pulled the blanket down, unsure if I'd even slept. I wiped the sleep from my eyes and nearly tipped the cot as I got out of bed. "I hate mornings."

"Get dressed, we'll stop for breakfast before we head out. I'll round up the other guys and meet you there."

"The other guys are here at the compound?"

"Yeah. You should introduce yourself today."

I cut him a hard look. "I'm doing my best. Don't push me."

"Sometimes we need to be pushed." He surveyed me from head to toe. "Sometimes we need shoved."

Rhogan had pulled and replaced every single nail I'd put in the brace we built the day before. He didn't say a word about it as he handed me the apron full of nails and the hammer I'd had the day before. "A few more hours and this part will be done. The rest of the team have been gutting the inside. We'll be ready for harder stuff tomorrow."

"You sure you want me helping with this?"

"Swing straight."

CHAPTER 29

"I hope you know what you're doing." Wren called up to Rhogan, who stood on top of the crooked house, directing the team with low shouts and sharp hand signals.

Though the project had taken weeks, she'd come the last few days to lend a hand and mostly chat with me while she eyed a sweaty Rhogan from afar. He was extra obnoxious when she was watching, but there was something comforting in being around them. Wren was clearly fighting her feelings for Rhogan, but nowhere near enough if she really didn't want to be with him.

The crooked house sat on a corner in the desert city. Every passing fae stopped to watch as our project house became strapped to four massive fae horses. They would take it slow, one step at a time, pulling the little home back into its proper position before it was secured by the brave team inside.

"The braces are set," Cru called from the doorway.

"All right, boys, slow and steady now. One step forward and let it settle. Wait for my call." Rhogan signaled the riders atop the fae horses to move.

Wren slipped her hand into mine as we waited and watched. The gathered crowd seemed to move in closer as they each held their breaths, watching out of curiosity and likely to see if we'd mess up. A sharp creaking sound filled the silence as the beasts started forward.

"Hold," Cru called, racing from the doorway to adjust something inside.

I bumped Wren with my shoulder. "You realize he's only riding the top of the house to impress you, right?"

"I know." She beamed, blocking the sun with her hand as she stared at him.

"Lyra, get your ass inside and see what's taking so long," he barked.

Wren giggled as I tore away from her and bounded into the leaning house.

"Bolt came loose from the brace." Cru strained with his tool, veins showing in his thick arms as he held it firmly. "Tell him two minutes and we go."

I turned to deliver the message when Cru's tool went shooting out of his hand and cracked Briggs on the forehead. He went down immediately.

"Woah! Woah." Rhogan shouted from the roof and I realized then that Briggs had been holding the brace steady while Cru tightened it.

As soon as Briggs had let go, falling to the floor, the pressure had reversed, the house creeping in the opposite direction it needed to. No one was safe as it edged the wrong way. The horses began to snort and squeal in protest from outside, just as the crowd starting screaming.

I dashed forward, snatching the tool from the floor where it had landed beside an unconscious and bleeding Briggs. I tried handing Cru his tool, but his face had gone pale and, though he looked at me, he was completely still as panic set in.

"Cru!" I shrieked, trying to get his attention, but it didn't register.

I did the only thing I could think to do and jammed his wrench over the bolt and twisted to try to keep the crossbar from slipping through any farther. Sweat began to bead on my forehead as I shoved to tighten the bolt, putting all my weight and strength onto the wrench, just to try to keep it from slipping. Two other members of our team, Hagan and Mav, held the opposite wall, but I was on my own.

"Rhogan!" I screamed.

He and Wren ran through the doorway. She instantly headed to Briggs while Rhogan came for me, taking the wrench and throwing all of his body weight against it to hold.

"Wren, get Briggs out of here, now. Lyra, grab that other pipe and see if you can get it back into place." He leaned toward the door, shouting, "Hold the horses in place, Frei!"

The other two on the opposite wall were grunting, using all of their strength and a prayer to keep the small house from collapsing on us. The brace Rhogan and I had built pushed from behind, and that might have been our saving grace as we struggled to keep it from going in that direction.

I almost had the pole in place, I just had to line up the bolt holes to the frame of the house and pray Rhogan could hold on while I shoved the other bolt back in and tightened it. My nails had been slowly growing back and although this strain was a painful process, I pushed through.

"Come on, Lyra." His forced calmness worried me more than if he would have shown alarm.

I pushed and pulled and threw myself into that fucking pole, and by luck alone, I hit the right spot, jamming the bolt into place. I gave one massive, full-body weight rotation on it and a crash behind us proved we'd secured the frame just in the nick of time.

"I'm sorry," Hagan moaned from a heap on the floor. "My hands were too sweaty. I couldn't hold it any longer."

Rhogan's big hand landed on my aching shoulder. "No problem, Hag. Lyra's our lucky charm." The horses whinnied, reminding us that we were still standing in a crooked house, albeit far more secure now. "Let's get this done. Drinks are on me tonight."

The rest of the job went off without a hitch. The horses pulled the house forward, the braces held, and they were able to tighten them from within to hold it. It was strange. Working on something and seeing it finished. The pride in a completed job, doing something to help someone else, cleared a bit more of the fog obscuring my mind. Stealing something came with its own dark rewards, but earning it? Putting in the time and seeing it through completion? It felt different.

"Are there no other taverns in this city?" I dug my feet into the sand, jerking Wren to an abrupt stop.

"This is where we always go."

She started to move again, trying to pull me, but I couldn't do it. Couldn't force myself into that bar where he'd stumbled toward me and insisted he didn't pay for sex.

"You came here? With … him?"

There were days when Wren couldn't bring herself to say his name and I loved her most for those times. When her grieving aligned with mine and I didn't feel so lost and alone.

"We spoke here first, actually." I looked down at the road. The spot where I was standing. "I thought he'd kiss me right here." I closed my eyes, a lump forming in my throat. "I'll never be okay, Wren. I'm never going to be okay again."

She pulled me into her arms. "The best things in life are flawed and not perfect. The imperfections make them that much more special. I know you're hurting. I'm sorry. But it doesn't mean you're not going to be okay."

"I don't know who I am anymore. I'm not this person. Who cries. Who stands hugging her friend in the street. I have walls. Loads of walls. I just can't find the strength to hold them up."

"Then let them fall." She rubbed my back as her voice broke. "It's okay to be vulnerable."

I pulled away, wiping the tears. "You have no idea how defenseless I really am."

"I'm trying to learn, though. You just have to trust me."

"I'm trying too." I lifted my chin, swallowing before I took her hand. "Let's go."

We stepped over the threshold of the tavern and the world tilted as I was sucked back in time. Watching him pickpocket a thief. He'd won me over then. Even if I wasn't ready to admit it. That was back when he was just a mark. Just the commander.

"One step in front of the other," Wren whispered, pulling me toward a large table where the others were laughing and drinking as if their worlds all made sense. I resented them for that blanket of happiness. For the ease in which they smiled.

Wren cleared her throat and all heads swung to us. Cheers erupted as they chanted my name and threw their mugs up, beer and froth spilling over the edges and soaking the dark wooden table below them.

"Our lucky charm," Rhogan shouted, showing his biggest smile as he shuffled seats so Wren could sit next to him.

I took her other side, with Cru beside me.

He leaned in. "Thanks for taking over today. Sorry I clammed up. Get it? Clammed? Because you're a sea fae?"

The table went silent as everyone watched me for a reaction. Probably not sure if I'd explode or run away. Instead, I forced a laugh and rolled my eyes. "Thank the gods we never marked you for the clever one."

The others laughed and I let the moment pass, but as Cru swung his arm over my shoulder, rubbing my neck with his fingertips, my skin began to crawl. *Wrong.* This was wrong. He was too close. The walls started moving in and I could feel the panic clawing its way up my throat.

Wren laid her hand on my arm. "Come with me to get drinks?"

I nodded frantically and leaped from the chair in such a rush, it flew backward, crashing to the floor. I didn't bother picking it up as we scurried away, weaving through drunken fae with wandering hands that made the panic near suffocating until we got to the bar.

"Breathe," she said.

I could do nothing but obey as I drew shallow breaths in and out. "I'm sorry. It's just worse here, I think. This place reminds me of him."

"Don't be sorry. Cru made you uncomfortable. Don't apologize for his actions." Her eyes were fierce as she scowled at the table. "You get to set your own boundaries, Lyra. Always. Just because you're beautiful doesn't give them a right to take liberties with you. Not one."

I nodded. "I don't think he meant anything by it."

"Maybe not, but if I could tell you were uncomfortable, so could he."

I glanced over my shoulder at the males laughing as if nothing had happened. For a split second, it was Kai sitting in that empty chair next to Rhogan, his laughter filling the air, and then it went back to just an empty chair.

"I should go."

"No. Please don't leave. We can make them all move. You can sit between Rhogan and me. You know we're safe."

I bit my lip. I wanted so badly to heal. To stop hurting. To not be the sad story in the room. So, I agreed. Because growth wouldn't come without challenging myself. Wren ordered enough drinks to fill the whole table and Rhogan had to come help us carry them. Wren and I switched seats, planting me between her and Rhog. Cru's face fell when he realized I'd be moving seats, but only for a second. There was no mistaking Rhogan's though, who scowled like he might throw a tantrum.

Wren and I sipped on decent wine while the others chugged and sloshed their ale all over the place. The tavern, with walls lined in wooden planks, could have been found in the hull of a ship, and as the final rays of the day's light peered in through the windows, my mind slipped away into that sky and perfect orange sunset. I'd see him again someday. Where the sea met the sky. On the perfectly painted horizon, within the depths of the Ether.

"It feels like we're sitting with a pack of wild animals," Wren said, leaning into me with her shoulder as she yanked me from my lonely thoughts.

"Half-wild," Rhogan roared, letting his single wing lift into the air before he wiggled his brows at her.

"Oh, I'm full wild. I'd be happy to take you out back and show you." Briggs leaned across the table, soaking the sleeves of his shirt as he took her hand and planted a big sloppy kiss onto it.

Wren pulled away, curling her lip in disgust. "It'd be a lot easier to take you seriously if you didn't have that giant lump on your forehead."

"Come on," he goaded. "You should smile more."

Rhogan must have swept his foot behind Briggs' chair because one minute he was smiling behind dazed eyes and the next he was on his ass.

The tavern jerked to silence as everyone turned to see if a fight would start. But Briggs merely stood and leaned down on the table with his elbows again, staring Wren in the face. "Meant to do that, beautiful."

Wren vanished and my heart stopped. She'd said she had magic, but I'd never asked to see it. Invisible hands shoved Briggs forward, holding him flat against the table, and Rhogan leaned back in his chair, flexing his arms behind his head.

He turned to me. "I love it when she gets feisty."

Wren must have bent Briggs' arm behind his back. It looked as if he slammed himself against the wall, his arm still twisted behind him. I'm not sure the patrons realized Wren was there as they watched the crazy male getting cozy with the wall, nodding frantically as she must have been whispering in his ear.

Briggs stayed put, but Wren reappeared at my side, beaming as she watched her prey pull away and turn to face the crowd. He grinned as he stumbled back to the table and bowed low to the ground before taking his seat.

"Say it." Wren rested her chin on her hand as she watched him.

"I uh …" His voice faded away as he tried to get away with a quiet mumble.

"Louder," Rhogan said, his eyes glued on Wren as she grinned.

"I use my personality to overcompensate for my micro penis."

If the tavern could have gotten any louder from the roars of laughter, the windows would have broken. Rhogan and Cru fell out of their chairs laughing so hard and a female from the other side of the bar walked over, dropped a glass of wine in front of Wren, and walked away without saying a word. It occurred to me then that maybe Wren had a little siren in her. She didn't take shit from anyone, and she didn't fall over herself for the male trying his darndest to win her over.

It was a little easier after that. Her power seeped into me, and I found I could sit there and smile—join the others without that heavy cloud of guilt. It wasn't gone, just manageable. I had a whole life ahead of me to live, and as long as I woke up every single day and put one foot in front of the other, maybe I'd figure out how to survive.

Later, the others crawled out of the tavern, singing, laughing and soaked in spirits, having the time of their lives. I stood, ready to leave, when Wren grabbed my hand.

"Come back to the castle tonight. We can invite Ara over for a girl's night. We don't even have to tell her who you are. You can just be my friend."

I opened my mouth to answer, but Rhogan gave me a look. He wanted her. And I'd be in the way of that. She was fighting the urge to want him, and maybe she needed me to be an excuse. I was stuck right in the middle of them, and I hated it. Though we'd started off rocky, I'd grown fond of both of them.

"Why don't you tell me what's going on between you two, first?" I answered, slumping back into my chair.

"Yes. I'd very much like to hear the answer to that as well." Rhogan mirrored my position, crossing his arms over his chest.

I hadn't meant to put Wren on the spot, but I guess I'd done just that as the hurt on her face went straight to my heart.

"Don't do this," she whispered to Rhogan.

I meant to stop it. To stand and just agree to go back with her to the castle, but instead, Rhogan turned to me, face blank as he said, "My mate died too."

He might as well have blown me over with those words. He'd

known. When he'd been so hard on me. He'd known it was the only thing that would push me to keep breathing. To get out of bed.

"Why didn't you tell me?" I felt betrayed in a way. As if I was owed that information. As if that would have changed things somehow.

"It's not the same, Lyra," Wren said, eyes full of unshed tears.

"How is it not the same. What aren't you saying?"

"We were children," Rhogan said, staring into the empty space between us. "It never happens like that, you know? It takes forever to find your mate. But Jarin was the only other child in my village, and we knew right away." He paused for a moment as if living in a memory. I didn't dare look at Wren and wonder how this made her feel. "It wasn't like an adult mating bond. It was platonic, but even then, my heart called to hers. We were inseparable. Our parents tried to keep us apart, afraid of what a bond formed so young would do to our hearts and our lives."

Wren shifted in her chair, but still, I stared at Rhogan.

"We would sneak off just to play together. To build snow forts and have snowball fights." He smiled sadly. "I learned to fly and she couldn't. So, she would sit and watch me circle through the sky and cheer for me. One day," he cleared his throat, and I knew what was coming. "One day, I thought I'd bring her with me. I thought I was strong enough to carry her. I was nine."

"Oh no." The words left my mouth before I realized. And then I was right there with him. His pain was the same as mine. I couldn't breathe, couldn't feel my limbs as he continued, sweeping me away into his tragedy.

"It was fine at first. She squealed and laughed, and that sound filled me with so much pride, I never wanted anything else from her but that level of happiness. She begged me to go higher, and so I did, swooping as I carried her in my arms. The moment I felt my hold loosen, I started to go down. But she said it was fine and to keep going. Before I knew it, my muscles were screaming and I was diving for the ground, trying to get as low as possible before she fell."

His voice cracked as the final words left him. "I'll never forget the sound her small body made as she hit the ground, shattering all of her tiny bones as our soul ripped in two."

He stood from the table and walked out.

"That's what's going on between us," Wren whispered, pulling me from the devastating trance Rhogan had left me in.

"I'm so sorry, Wren. I didn't know. I thought it was just petty stuff."

"To him, it is. I can't be with him."

I snapped my head to her, noting the tears staining her cheeks. "Why? He clearly loves you."

"You can't have two mates. He's already lost his."

I took another drink, though it turned my stomach. "I'm not following."

"Time to call it a night, ladies."

"Right. Sorry, Gil," Wren said, standing from the table.

We left the tavern and stood just outside, lit by a full moon and sea of stars. She fidgeted with her clothes for a few minutes as I stood waiting, unsure if she'd explain.

"I have a sister."

"You do?" The rarity of that was powerful.

"Yes. And my mother and father were blissfully in love. Until my mother's mate showed up. She left us. I was so young. And she just abandoned her whole family for a mate that wanted nothing to do with us. He thought he owned her, and she just let him, stealing away in the night.

Realization dawned on me. "So, you're afraid to fall in love with Rhogan and have a family because you know he can never be your mate since he's already had one."

She nodded.

"Wren, he loves you. Absolutely adores you and that's after he's had a mate." Some kind of fury built within me as I realized Rhogan and I were so similar and maybe I was fighting for myself as well. "I'm never going to have that. Kai loved me so deeply, no one will ever come close to replacing him. I'll never love again. That part of my life is over. But Rhogan, though he doesn't see it and it's hard to say, he was blessed. He was a child. He fought in the Iron Wars over five hundred years ago. It's been a really long time since he lost the love of a friend. Why would you deny yourself happiness? Why would you settle when it's so rare to find your mate?"

"You don't understand because you found yours."

"Found and lost him in such a short time. I was robbed. Not just of him, but of the ability to love again. You know this. You know how it works. But you're suffering for no reason, and you need to get the hell over it."

"Get over it? Just like you're getting over Kai?"

She might as well have slapped me in the face. I stumbled backward. "You know the difference between you and me? I'm telling you something that you already know. But you're just being a bitch."

I could think of nothing else to do but run. Shoving my walls back into place with ease as I darted for the sea. This life wasn't for me. It wasn't who I was. I wanted to live *my* life. I wanted my song back. I didn't want to be fragile anymore.

The sea called to me more strongly than it ever had before. I was meant to live in those waters, to drown enemies in them. I was meant to be ruthless and unforgiving as I brought my rivals down. I was powerful. I was a siren. Maybe I didn't have a song, but my nails were a sign that they couldn't take that identity from me. I stomped into the water and commanded the change from within me, shoving the siren until she listened. My strong, beautiful tail took shape below me, mirroring the sparkling night sky.

"Lyra, wait." Wren stood on the shoreline as she called to me over the waves. "Come back."

"I can't stay here. There's so much about me you don't even understand. I'm not a great person. I'm not even a decent person, and the more I sit around here and play the role, the worse it feels."

"Then tell me who you are. I told you my secret. Tell me yours. I didn't mean what I said. I'm sorry. I was just mad and I hate hurting Rhogan. I just can't help my heart."

I changed forms with ease and moved back to the shore, but never leaving the water entirely, drawing strength from the tide that pushed and pulled against my fae legs as I resolved to tell Wren everything. To finally let all the words I'd never gotten to say out.

"I met Kai as a mark. I was supposed to steal a key from him to free Morwena from the prisons here. I am half siren and half fae. That means I can stand on land with legs or swim in the ocean with a tail. I don't need a pearl. It happens by will alone. I trained my whole life to do my father's bidding, following the lessons my mother taught me before she was killed.

"Like all sirens, I had a song. A perfect melody gifted from the sea to twist the mind, to bring fae to my beck and call, should I desire it. My mother warned me not to use it unless I absolutely had to. But I didn't listen. I came here, and it didn't work on Kai. Because he was my mate, the universe wouldn't give me that power over him. I didn't know that. I couldn't figure out why it didn't work. It became an obsession. I never got the keys. My father was angry and the next thing I knew, my song was stolen." I rubbed my chest, willing the ache of saying the words allowed to subside.

"Morwena died and my father was captured. He claimed he knew where my song was, so I had to help him escape to get it back. But what happened with Kai, what I felt for him, it was real." I paused, realizing I was saying the words I wanted so desperately to say to him. I pictured him standing there instead of her. "I loved him. I loved him so hard, I would have drowned the world for him. But I was selfish. I wanted my song back. I wanted to stop feeling like a part of me, a part of who I was, was missing. So, I betrayed Kai to get the information, only to find out that my father was the one who had my mother killed. He'd sold me to a vile male, and Kai rescued me, even after I'd broken his heart."

I could see his face then. The look he'd given me as he set his jaw and realized he could never trust me again. It destroyed me all over again.

Wren was standing in front of me now, placing her hands on my arms. I hadn't even seen her move into the water. "You should have told him. From the very beginning, you should have told him. He would have helped you. He would have ripped the information from your father without a second thought the moment he found out."

"I know that now. But you have to understand, I didn't know it then. I couldn't even trust my father. I didn't know how to trust other people. And by the time I realized that? I was in too deep, and I knew I was going to hurt him no matter what." I swallowed the lump in my throat. It felt so good to say the words and let them go. To confess how terrible I was.

"What are you going to do now?" The moon lit her eyes, and I could see the genuine concern deep within them.

"I have to get my song back. I need something, Wren. One thing from my former life to remind me of who I am. It was mine. I'll probably never use it the way I did before, but shouldn't that be my choice? No one had the right to take that away from me.

"Maybe I don't want to be a shitty person. Maybe I don't want to be a liar and a thief forever. But that's the only part of me that's left, and I'll hunt whoever took it to ends of this world before I accept that it's gone."

She took my hand, setting her jaw. "Let me come with you."

CHAPTER 30

It took Wren only moments before she was back with an evada pearl. I twisted it into the back of her hair so it was less noticeable than her ear and harder to take from her.

And then we swam.

The ocean, my ocean, called me home. The moment I was below the water, the salt of the sea moved over crevices of my tail and there was joy there. Pure joy as I got a little of myself back. I held Wren's hand tightly as we swam to the castle. No longer on lockdown, a lot of the sea fae from the castle had gone, but there were still Flame Court soldiers Wren waved to and it didn't take long until we found Doriahs. Surprising us both, she addressed Wren first.

"We missed you last week at girl's night."

"I've been busy helping a friend." She nudged me with a shoulder.

Doriahs' heads swung to me. "You have other friends now?"

I winked. "Don't worry, D. You're still my best girl."

She smiled what I thought might be a wicked and terrible smile, but it was hard to tell behind those razor-sharp teeth. "Obviously."

I rose in the water, stealing the light heartedness from the room. "I'm going to get my song back. I'm assuming you heard about Kai."

Her heads dropped in unison. "And Gaea. They were terrible losses." She shuddered, tremors rippling down her massive body, filling the halls behind her. "What do you need from me?"

"We're going to have to do some recon work, so I'm not sure a hydra on the team works this time. But I do need that key I left with you."

"I put it in his room."

"I don't … I'm not sure I can go in there."

"It's okay. I'll go," Wren said. "Do you want to show me where it is, Doriahs?"

"Sure, baby bird. It's just this way."

"I asked you to stop calling me that over a month ago," Wren said as they moved together down the hall.

"Oh right, sorry. Forgot," the hydra said innocently, but one of her heads looked back to me and smiled.

So fucking creepy.

Within a couple of hours, Wren and I stood on the deck of my father's anchored ship. We decided to sleep until morning and then call a meeting with everyone still on board. Sleeping in my bed with Wren softly snoring beside me didn't bring me an ounce of comfort as I considered the dead-end we'd likely face the next day. I knew finding my song would be like finding a single shell amongst a million, but I had to try.

The sun beat down on us, relentlessly. It would be a scorcher and the only thing I wanted was to be in the water. A welcome change from what I'd been feeling only days ago.

Every fae that worked on my father's ship—who had done his bidding, cooked his meals, cleaned his sheets—now stood before me. I'd never addressed them. My whole life, I'd been taught to avoid and pay them no mind. Perhaps that's when I learned to hate anyone that wasn't in my circle.

Some pulled hats from their heads, working their hands as they swayed from foot to foot, all curious and worried about what I might need of them. A nervous silence hung thickly in the sea salt air as I stood among them, looking them each in the eye for the first time in my life. They were just fae, something I'd never grasped before.

"Is this everyone?" I asked my father's quartermaster.

"It is, my lady. Right down to the deckhands." He tilted his head in reverence, though none was due to me.

"My father is dead." I let the words settle upon them. Let them realize what they meant. "You are not lesser fae. You are simply fae. Born into the world as equally as my mother, father, and myself. You're all due a wage, which I will pay out right now, and then you are excused."

Several of them gasped in response. A few outwardly protested.

"I'll hear nothing else of this. You were loyal, good fae to my father, and I thank you for that, but your services are no longer required."

"But where will we go? I've lived half my life on this ship." The cook slipped his hat off, pressing it to his chest, worry heavy on his face.

"There's a sea fae named Leora working in the castle. There are no royals there anymore, but she's still feeding the masses. I'm quite sure she'd be happy for the company and the Flame Court prince pays a fair wage."

"Wage, my lady?"

"I am no longer your lady." I leaned against the railing of the ship, letting them feel however they needed to feel.

"If you need somewhere to go, the Flame Court has a refugee compound," Wren explained. "We're working on getting everyone homes and jobs as they start new lives. If you go to Halemi and ask for my sister, Sabra, she will take care of you. Or you can stay in the sea castle and be provided with the same efforts. King Fenlas' council will be establishing the same order as soon as a leader can be appointed there. As an extension of the Flame Court, which is technically no more."

I hadn't thought about the world-changing so much. I'd been so lost in my own sorrow, it hadn't occurred to me that the four courts would have been nullified. With only one set of royals left, they would become the high king and queen of Alewyn. What a terrible burden.

"Are we allowed to take our things?"

"Your personal belongings are your own." I kicked open the chest I'd had brought to the top deck. "As well as a bit more." They gasped and drew back at the chest full of gold coins and jewels. "Please sort this out among the crew in equal amounts," I told the quartermaster.

As they moved in, Wren and I stepped away, letting them take their fill. We used it as the distraction we needed to go below deck and start searching. Half of these fae would still be loyal to my father. If he'd given them orders to hide something from me, they would, even in his death. If not from loyalty, then fear alone. I went directly to his room while Wren turned invisible, set on watching the crew to see if anyone would lead us to something.

I'd expected his room to still smell of my mother. To see her blankets across the foot of the bed. Nearly forgetting he made us get rid of all of it, it pained me to see how this was no longer a memory of her, but of him. Full of his things, strewn about as if he hadn't a care. It was curious that the crew hadn't come in to tidy, but then I'd bet there was a charm somewhere preventing them from doing so, or a well-placed threat.

I needed to get into his treasure room. It was the last place I could look for his secrets, since they wouldn't be spilling from dead lips. Knowing it was warded created many problems. That magic was so rare, the knowledge of breaking those barriers so sparse, I had no idea where to start. That's why he'd used that magic, naturally. I wondered if there was a key.

Lifting the mattress, I'd almost found nothing had my eye caught a tiny tear in the stitching along the underside. I ripped into it and pulled out an emerald larger than Isla's Eye and a few handwritten letters. I stacked them in a pile for later reading and continued to search. He had a few ledgers filled with secrets and treachery. I put those on the pile as well. If not for me, then to turn over to the king for his purposes.

I crossed the room one final time and noticed a hollowness in the boards below my feet. Thinking I'd finally found something worthy, I began prying them up, one by one. More treasure. Most were things I'd stolen over the years and turned into Vexyr, as well as a few maps that seemed foreign to me, and a small book with emblems of the gods scratched into the cover. Nothing seemed to trigger the door, though. I gathered it all into a pile and took it to my rooms.

I'd planned next to visit the final room that might be of significance, but before I got there, Wren stopped me. Holding one of the shipmates by the collar, though he squirmed and scowled.

"This one was in that room, shoving things down his pants," she said, tilting her head toward the small library. "Says his name is Rual."

"Drop 'em."

"I most certainly will no—"

Stepping forward, I had my knife to his throat before he could finish. "I said drop 'em."

He put his hands to his waist and trembled as he hooked the top with stubby thumbs and shoved his pants down. Several scrolls, tightly rolled and tied with red ribbons, fell to the ship's hallway floor.

"What are they?"

Rual, who'd watch me grow on the planks of this ship, let his eyes fall to the ground. "They are your freedom."

"I should kill you. Right here and now."

"I should return the favor," he spat. "Always coming and going, never appreciating this ship as the vessel it is. Never listening to your father. He hated you, you know. Told me so several times."

"The feeling was mutual." I grabbed him from Wren and yanked him up on deck. He screeched and hollered until I threw him overboard.

"We're in the middle of the ocean," he protested, wading frantically in the water. "I'm not a sea fae!"

"Oh darn. I hadn't considered that thoroughly. At least you get to live … until the Kraken finds you." I turned away, confident the vicious ocean would serve his karma as thoroughly as he deserved.

Wren stood behind me and held the scrolls out, though she twisted her face in disgust. I gave her a look and she shrugged. "They were *down his pants*, Lyra. Gross."

"My lady?"

"What?" I snapped, spinning.

A short fae with white wings and even whiter bushy eyebrows looked up to me.

"I won't say I'm sad to hear your father has died. But do you really mean to leave again, and abandon the ship at sea?"

I paused. That was my plan. I didn't have a babysitter and wasn't willing to trust the fae on board.

"What I do with this ship is my own choice."

He nodded. "It is your choice. Of course, of course." He worked his fingers in front of him, drawing the courage to continue.

"We're not going to harm you. If you have something to say, say it."

"It's just… My name is Binsin. Your mother is the one who brought me on board. She hid me amongst the crew, knowing your father wouldn't notice. I worked for her. Smuggling letters on and off the ship. I've even placed some in your room."

I jerked back. "For whom?"

"I… I don't know, my lady. There's a messenger that leaves the letters and I've always just delivered them. Discreetly, of course."

"Why are you telling me this now?"

"Because I'd like to stay. You can't leave the ship abandoned. It'll be stolen or plundered. I could make it look like there's a full crew, I could keep it clean. I could work for you. An honest job."

"Why should I trust you?"

He reached into his pocket, pulling out a silken sash. I recognized the print. It was my mother's favorite.

"Because she did. I swore to her I would help you, should the time come."

Wren pulled me to the side, mumbling. "What's the worst that could happen? He stays on the ship and robs you, or pirates pass and rob you. Either way, if there's a chance he's telling the truth, you should give him a shot."

"I was already going to," I answered, turning back.

"You can stay. But don't get in my way. And if one day, I don't return, the ship is yours. Just rename it Kaitalen, for me."

I didn't care. The ship was just a vessel my father had traded for. He'd worshipped it, claimed it his most prized possession. But we were not the same.

The contents of the letters were disturbing. Not only did they discuss my father selling me to Vexyr for permanent amnesty from his tithe, they pointed me right to the one fae I should have known was involved. The one I'd burned so thoroughly, he was destined to seek revenge. *Hollis.*

"What's the matter love? Jealous that your friend doesn't have to use magical powers to take someone to bed?"

The fact that his balls were big enough to stand before me and speak those words, his mere presence the day I'd come back from being attacked, should have been obvious. I should have known. Especially because I hadn't seen him since.

His name came up in several of the messages between my father and Vexyr, and one even alluded to the two bastards that drugged me the night my song was stolen.

Jumping back into the frigid water, I led Wren to the Gulley. Halfway there, my senses were overwhelmed and for a moment, I'd stopped. My body was not my own as a song moved through the water, luring me in. Wren jerked on my arm and snapped me back to reality.

"What are you doing?" she asked, looking around.

"Didn't you hear it? The melody?"

She shook her head.

"It's happened before. Like someone is pulling me."

"Do you think it could be your song?" she asked, hope lining the edges of her voice.

"No. It's not mine. It's different and it feels dangerous. Powerful too."

She pulled me back the way we'd been going. "Okay, let's avoid the creepy singing voice only you can hear. Are you sure we have to go to asshole pirate town?"

"Yes, and you're going to have to get comfy because most of the Gulley's villains don't come out to play until night. With Vex gone, I have no idea what that means for hierarchy, so keep your guard up. We get there, we take no shit. Got it? It's not going to be pretty."

"I think you and Ara would get along so well."

"Or not at all," I countered as we swam ahead, remembering the swell of power buried within the king's mate.

The looming guards that worked for Vex, swimming below the Gulley, were gone. The water was eerily still, save a few passing fish weaving through the sunken ships. I jumped from the water, transforming in the air and landing on my feet, before pulling Wren onto the sun-dried dock.

"No one likes a showoff." She grinned, throwing her hands out to steady herself. "Such a weird feeling switching between the two."

"Ready?" I held my hand out and she took it.

We vanished, stealing away onto a ship where we swiped two long cloaks. I left three coins in place of them for the trouble.

"You'd have made the best partner in crime when I was a thief," I said.

"I'm still a pretty good partner in crime. Just with morals."

I dropped her hand and threw the cloak on. "Sort of defeats the purpose."

We crossed the bridges, though Wren moved slower than I would have liked, looking over the edge of the bridges and cautiously tapping her feet on the questionable planks before she stepped. I tried not to rush her, but I also didn't want to draw any unnecessary attention. Slipping into Merk's tavern, I found a spot close to the sleeping lump that hid in the back of the room rather than my usual spot near the door.

"What'll ya have?" Adair asked as she stepped to our table. I pulled my hood back far enough for her to see me, and she dipped her chin once in understanding before turning to Wren. "Got ale, wine, and rum. Merk's got eggs on, side of orange fin."

"Pass on the fish." She scrunched her nose. "I'll have wine and bread if you've got some."

"Sure thing." She walked away, not bothering to look back at me. She knew I'd only have the wine.

"This a favorite spot of yours?" Wren asked, thrumming her hands on the table.

"Something like that," I answered, considering my next move.

CHAPTER 31

"Tell me about the lurker," I asked Adair, slipping onto a bar stool and jutting my chin toward the being hunched in a corner, hiding under a black cloak.

Wren had excused herself to use the restroom and was hopefully in place for the next part of our plan.

Adair shook her head and turned her back to me.

I whispered, "I need to know why Merk lets that lump come and sit in the tavern every single day from sunup to sundown."

"I'll check with the cook, but I think stew's on for dinner," she answered, sliding a glass of wine over the bar.

I lifted the glass to find a small piece of paper with the word *seer* scrawled on it. Crumpling the note, I slid it into my pocket and strode back across the tavern. I was half tempted to bail on the plan, but Wren stood close to the seer with a knife ready and I couldn't let her risk herself. I got almost to the table when I feigned a trip and lurched forward, my glass of wine in my hand. The seer leaped from the seat, her hood falling around her shoulders as she avoided every last drop while I crashed into the wall beside her chair.

She was beautiful. Hair fell around her face in luscious waves of chocolate and violet eyes met mine as she pursed her lips and scowled. "Tell your friend to show herself."

"I'm not her keeper."

The woman moved as quick as a marlin, snatching Wren as though she wasn't invisible. "I'll not harm you if you agree to the same. Otherwise, I will speak your deaths before you can get out that door. You'll know exactly how they will happen and when, and spend your life watching the grains of time slip away from you."

Wren appeared, shaking herself free from the seer's grasp. "That's actually a really creepy threat. Hard pass, though. We mean you no harm."

The seer didn't take her eyes from me. "And you?"

I dropped my shoulders and dipped my chin. "I will not harm you, seer."

She nodded once and helped herself to our table. Adair watched carefully from the bar, but never approached.

"I'm Lyra and this is Wren."

"I know." She swiped Wren's glass of wine and swallowed it in one gulp.

"Oh right. Because of the…" I pointed back and forth between my own eyes.

"No," she answered. "Because you've been sitting three feet from me and used your names in conversation."

"Why do you sit here all day, every day?"

"The world is loud, Merk's is quiet. And I gain all the information I need from this spot."

"But why do you hide?" I asked, sitting back in my chair.

"Tell me, siren, what happened to you the louder you were with your song?" She smirked, pulling her lips into a perfect pucker as she watched me carefully with her haunting eyes.

"You were here. You know what happened."

"And if people knew of my talents? Would they not hunt me just the same? To learn of futures and good fortunes. To try to change their fate?"

"So, you think this is the safest place?"

She leaned in, holding her hands in a fist as she held my stare. "How many times have you paid me more than a passing glance when you've entered this tavern?"

"But you could just stay at home."

"You know nothing of seers. We must be around people. If we shut ourselves off from the visions, from the proximity of others, we lose control, which often leads to the loss of our lives."

"Holy gods." Wren gasped. "I know you. You're the seer that delivered Ara's fate to Efi. You told others. You let the secret out." She scrunched her face. "I thought you were killed."

"I was tricked into the sea queen's hands and enchanted. I had no control. I did what I could to save the girl. Just as I did what I had to, to save my own life. I have seen my death. Many, many times. I do prefer others to think me dead, though. It makes hiding much easier."

"But perhaps if you told Fenlas—"

"Can we please get to the point of this bombardment? I have three pieces of information. I will share only two. One is about you," she said, gazing at Wren, "and two for you," she said, looking to me. "Two of the three truths are regarding mates, and one is relevant to the actual reason you've come today. Decide which you prefer to hear. And don't bother trying to get all three. I'll only take one away."

I looked at Wren. There was no question what her truth was. Could she freely love Rhogan, or did she have a mate she was yet to find?

"We came here for you," she said, taking my hand. "Learn your truths, Lyra."

"Give Wren the information she needs."

"Lyra, no. You could learn about your song and something about Kai. It could mean closure for you."

I shook my head and looked at the seer. "I've spent my life being selfish and it's gotten me nowhere. Tell her."

The seer shifted, tracing a finger up Wren's arm as she tilted her head to speak. "There were two options for your future, as most have.

Your mate lived in this world at the same time you did, but he died before your paths could cross."

Wren smiled, tears filling her eyes, as she realized what the seer had given her: a chance at love. She leaped from her seat and hugged the female, who stiffened, but allowed it.

"Sorry. Sorry," Wren said, wiping her eyes. "I just didn't think I'd ever have the right answer for him."

"I'm so happy for you." I nudged her.

Wren shook her head. "You could have had both of your truths, Lyra. Why did you do that?"

"Rhogan loves you. You deserve each other. It was worth it."

The seer straightened her black cloak and cleared her throat. "What will it be now, girl? Learn something you might not have known about your mate or learn something about your song?"

Wren studied me carefully as both options weighed my shoulders down. If I chose my song, I'd have something I needed desperately, but if there was anything she could tell me about Kai… How he was feeling before he died. Whether he forgave me. I needed to know. I needed that information to finally close that door. And though I still had a chance to find my song on my own, I'd never again have the chance to learn that.

"I want to know what you know about Kaitalen."

"His life had two paths only. Two very long paths and he followed neither."

I shook my head, trying to clear the fog of her words. What could she possibly have meant by that? "That just sounds like him choosing me was never the plan, but now I'm to blame for his shortened life."

"Does it?" she asked, a smile spreading across her face as her features turned from kindness to something far more terrifying. "Best keep that key, girl. You're going to need it."

She stood from the table and walked away, stunning me with the reality of her words.

"It was my fault," I whispered. "I truly am the reason he died."

"That's not what she said. Don't read too far into it."

I nodded, but felt numbness threatening to take over. "I should have stayed away from him the moment we met."

Wren pushed her chestnut hair behind her ear and tilted her head. "You would take away what you had?"

"If it meant he lived, I would do anything."

We sat in contemplative silence for a long time. I knew Wren was thinking about Rhogan and feeling guilty over the choices she'd made with him, and I was lost in thoughts of what could have been and the decisions I'd made.

"You know," Wren said, breaking the silence. "When I was a kid, this boy threw a rock at me. I cried, went home and told my father, who insisted I tell him who it was. I feared what my father would do to the boy, who seemed to have a troubled life. I chose to keep the name of that boy from my father. I told him I didn't get a good look at him."

"I'm sure this has a point; I just don't know what it is."

"Well, the boy was a wild little thing with crazy blond curls and a penchant for the ocean. Had I told my father, he would have never let me be friends with Kai. But, the next day, I sought him out and demanded my own apology. It took me three days to get it, but we became fast friends after that." She swiped at her eyes and forced a smile. "Had I made a different choice, my entire life would be different. My friends would be. Everyone has choices every single day. There are a million paths for what could have been." She gripped my hand and squeezed. "We know Hollis is involved. Let's find him. Someone must know something. We're just going to have to listen."

I sighed heavily and agreed. "I guess we won't get anywhere by wallowing."

"I'm going to use the restroom again." Wren tilted her head toward a table of patrons who'd entered just after the seer left. With a conspiratorial wink, she left me waiting as she eavesdropped on the table of questionable males devouring breakfast.

So much time passed, I'd begun to worry, but by the look on her face when she returned, she had news.

"Let's go, right now."

I threw my cloak over my shoulders and headed for the door. The moment we were out of Merk's tavern, she clasped my hand and we vanished.

"There's a big uprising happening," she whispered. "Apparently the old boss, Vex, was replaced by our guy, Hollis. Only those scary fuckers don't like him. There's going to be a meeting somewhere called the Feral Boar. Heard of it?"

"Yeah. It's dangerous. There are three taverns in the Gulley. Merk's is where you go for gossip because people tend to eat there and it's relatively safe. Rogues is where most go after they leave Merk's, already drunk and looking for someone to fuck or fight."

"And the last?" she whispered, as we carefully huddled together, letting a pirate with a red beard hanging down to his navel slip by.

"The Feral Boar is the worst of the worst. There's a bone graveyard beneath the south side of this town. It's where the bodies from that tavern are dumped in the morning. The floors are stained with blood, and even though there are guards commandeering weapons, they somehow always make it in."

"Sounds lovely."

"Welcome to the Gulley." I led the way, taking several questionable bridges to avoid bumping into others. "There's definitely something going on. Look at the traffic moving around the paths."

The fae were trying to be inconspicuous, but there was no mistaking the band of bulky pirates, male and female alike, working their way toward the Feral Boar. As we got closer, I noted the extra guards, and we fell in line behind the bunch that had been in Merk's watching as they were patted down. All weapons were confiscated and dumped into a barrel sitting outside the door. Two sat full to the brim already.

Wren and I were silent as we snuck in, still invisible. We stepped around the guards and shuffled along a wall. The whole place stank, and only four candles lit the entire ship's belly. Three rows of long tables with bench seats filled the room. They faced a slightly raised platform holding a couple of chairs that barely contained two burly males with unruly beards and more tattoos than bare skin.

"See that one there?" I breathed in Wren's direction.

"I can't see you pointing."

"Oh right, sorry. The biggest one on the stage, with the eye patch."

"Yeah?"

I leaned closer to her, afraid to be overheard. "That's Bregand. He's on the sea more than land and used to be a runner for Vex. I've seen him obliterate a ship in minutes for skipping tithe. He's very dangerous and probably really pissed if Hollis is trying to take over the hierarchy on the seas."

"Shh." She tugged on my arm and my head snapped back to see a few males at the table nearby looking in our direction.

We might have been caught had the other male on the stage not stood and clapped his hands together, calling everyone's attention.

"This is gonna be real short and sweet. If someone starts fightin' in the meeting, yer ship's flagged for target practice. This inna joke and I don't have the time to deal wit' yer petty bickerin' today. Shut yer traps and listen." He looked over his shoulder. "Bregand."

The pirates traded places, and Bregand began pacing, stroking his beard while the room grew more and more silent with each thump of his wooden leg across the stage. "We have a problem, boys. And when I say we, I mean all of us. Hollis' got to be taken down."

The room erupted in a chorus of outraged voices, protesting, agreeing, and all around voicing every opinion as loudly as they could. Bregand held his hand up, but no one was listening. I pulled Wren tightly against the wall as he strode across the stage, grabbed his wooden chair, and flung it into the wall opposite us, shattering it to pieces.

"Shut the fuck up and listen!" The room fell silent once more. "We'll be here all day if I have to wait for your opinions. This isn't a matter of choice. We either shut that ship down, or he takes over the sea.

"But he's got an army on his ship," some brave soul from the audience called out.

"One ship can be sunk. Sink the ship, sink the problem."

"No." Someone stood and pulled his hat to his chest, trembling. "He's got a brigade now. They say he's using siren songs."

The volume rose again as they started yelling. Each with their theories and ideas. Pulling on Wren's arm, we snuck back along the wall and out of the tavern. I held her hand as we ran, still invisible.

"Lyra, stop."

"No. You heard what he said. He's using siren songs. He is definitely the one that has mine. We have to find him."

"Did you hear what else he said? He has a full band of ships. What are we going to do? Sneak up on them and take them all out."

"I'm a thief. I'm going to do what I do best and steal back my song."

She pulled her hand from mine and we both appeared as she threw her hands on her hips and leveled her stare. "Would you just listen to me for a second?"

"Every second wasted is a second too long."

"We have to go back to the Flame Court. We need help. This doesn't just concern the sea. What do siren songs do in the hands of someone that isn't a siren?"

"I'm not sure. But how can we find out? And why take the time? If those pirates get there before I do, everything will be destroyed anyway. Maybe Doriahs could help? I don't know. But if we take the song back, he can't use it anymore."

"For fuck's sake, Lyra. He said *songs*. Multiple. There's got to be power in that. There's no way we're sneaking on a ship and stealing his most valued treasure. We need help. One day. Give me one day. Let's go back to the Flame Court and get help. We can pick Doriahs up on the way. Think of the choice you're making and the path you're choosing."

I took a deep breath and let her words settle over me. She had to hit me where it hurt. "Okay, fine. You're right. If we don't have to do it alone, we shouldn't."

"Wait here."

Before I could protest, she was stomping past me. Naturally, I followed as she stormed back into the Feral Boar, grabbing a sword from the barrel on her way. The guards moved to block her way, but she used the king's name to get past. Based on the determined look on her face, they weren't going to stop her, anyway.

I pushed the doors open just as she was leaping onto a table in the middle of the room, screaming for them all to shut the fuck up.

"You have one day to get your ships in order. I'll be back here tomorrow with coordinates, unless anyone knows where Hollis is right now?" The room was silent, though a hand crept toward her on the table, and she didn't hesitate to swing the sword, stopping an inch from a male's neck. "Unless you have my permission, you do not touch me."

A laugh came from the stage and she whirled to see Bregand sharing a ruthless smile. "Say what you came to say."

"The Flame Court king will help you with this enemy. If you want to join this fight, be ready to ship out tomorrow. And try not to piss off the hydra during the battle. She's moody as fuck."

With that, she jumped off the table and walked out, leaving a room of open mouths and wide eyes following her.

"Ready?" she asked, holding a hand out to me.

"Ready." I shook my head, beaming at her as we vanished once more.

CHAPTER 32

"Trust me, they just got married. Ara probably hasn't been in a good fight for a while."

Wren let herself into the dining room and though I was expecting it to be full of court lords and ladies, it was mostly empty, save the king and queen at the head of the table and a couple of others close by. One had deer antlers so big, I wondered how he kept his head upright, and the one next to him had beautiful curly red hair. I thought for sure the draconian would be there, since Kai spoke of him so often, but he wasn't.

As we walked down the length of the table Wren didn't bother with formal bowing or even niceties. "What do you know about siren songs, Fen?"

"A bit. Not an abundance though. Who's your friend?"

He looked me over and I felt a wave of jealousy drown in a pit of rage at his mere acknowledgement. He had lived and Kai had died. No matter who he was, I'd never forgive him for that. I guessed I'd never forgive myself either, so maybe we were even. I curtsied despite my feelings.

"This is Lyra. She was a friend of Kai's."

"Siren?" the queen asked, tilting her head one way and then another as she picked up a dinner knife and moved it casually between her fingers. "We've seen you before."

"Half," I answered, matching that cool tone of hers. "And yes, I was there the day you nearly drowned an entire island."

Her mouth quirked into a smile. "Nearly."

Wren cleared her throat. "Do you know about the Gulley?"

"Vaguely." King Fenlas looked away, searching his thoughts before something came to him. "Kai mentioned it. Said he took care of the tyrant lording over it, though. Morwena didn't deign the place worthy of rule, it seems."

Wren pulled out two chairs and gestured for me to sit. She started loading fruit onto a plate in front of me.

"I don't think Morwena really cared about the Gulley, to be honest," I said. "She had to have known about the pirate lords and their dominance over her waters, but most, like my father, did her bidding just as they did for Vex before Kai killed him."

"And why did Kai kill him?" Ara asked, her eyes never once leaving me.

"Because my father sold me to him, and he tried to keep me as a prisoner."

She narrowed her eyes. "And what happened to your father?"

"He's dead."

"Good." She folded her hands on top of the table. "What can we do for you?"

"Well." Wren cut me a glance and I nodded, taking a deep breath. "Lyra is Kai's mate."

The room went still. Too still, as every head whipped in my direction. Each stare filled with pity.

"That's impossible," the king whispered.

I kept facing forward, refusing to look him in the eye, even as my cheeks heated, and a sharp lump grew in my throat. He should have been here. He should have been the one to tell his family.

"It's true," Wren answered, taking my hand under the table and squeezing. The sea glass ring on my hand pressed into the sides of my fingers. "He told me himself the day we left for the battle."

"Why didn't he tell us?" Ara asked, her lips pressed into a firm line.

I opened my mouth to tell them it was because I'd broken him, but Wren cut in.

"Because there were bigger things happening, and Kai was worried about you, Fen. He wanted to. After we got back. He just never got the chance."

The king rose from his seat, the legs screeching as the chair slid backward across the marbled floor. "Give us a moment, would you?" he asked the room.

As one, those scattered around the table left, leaving only Wren, Ara, and myself. The room became far too small, closing in as King Fenlas walked around the table and moved behind me, holding his hand out until I turned and placed mine onto it. I couldn't breathe, wanting so badly to lash out at him, even though his heart was broken too.

As I stood, he took a knee before me and brought my hand to his forehead, speaking quietly.

"Every second since he's been gone, I've missed him. I've mourned him. I've thought of him." His voice shook with the words. "Kai was my friend. He was my brother. He was the laughter in the darkest moments, the sword in the dangerous moments, and the shield in the quiet ones. I know what happened on that field. I heard your scream. I know you saw. He gave his life for mine a final time."

I swallowed, a hot tear slipping down my cheek as the king spoke the words sitting heavily on my heart.

"I'm sorry." A tear splashed onto the marble floor though I couldn't see his face. "You don't know me. You have no reason to trust me. But know that I'd do anything to help protect you, because Kai would expect no less, and even in death, I'll never let him down."

A sniffle from Wren as she hid her eyes distracted me enough to push back the sorrow threatening to suffocate me.

Rising, the king looked at me—really looked at me—and in that moment of vulnerability, I stepped forward letting him wrap me in an embrace. There was so much room for hatred in the world but how could I fault someone that had simply lived? Someone Kai thought was worth dying for.

Wren pushed away from the table, taking over the conversation so I could let the resurrected pain resettle. "A fae named Hollis has taken over for Vexyr. We heard he has stolen siren songs and is using them somehow."

"Songs? As in multiple?" Fen stumbled backward.

"Yes, but what does that mean?"

He looked to Ara and they stared back and forth for several minutes.

Wren leaned over. "They are Ameriala. They can speak in their minds to each other. Super annoying."

"I'm guessing it means he's amassing an army," the king finally said. "The songs, collectively, can be used much like enchantment used to be. Since the former rulers are all dead, that ability should be, aside from the bit that remains with me and one other up north. Stacking the power will make it more and more powerful, but he would have to know how to steal the songs."

"Would Morwena have had that information?" I asked.

He shrugged. "It's possible, but there's no way to know for sure."

"Wait." I looked to Wren. "Hollis' new girlfriend used to be very close to the queen before she moved to the Gulley." I turned away from everyone, letting the dots connect in my mind. "She was there that night when my song was stolen. We were friends. She absolutely knew. She was part of the plan." I turned to the king. "Hollis has somehow found a way to steal siren's songs and I'm guessing he's hunting them. That's why no one can find him."

Ara snorted. "I bet the hydra can."

I nodded. "Doriahs. Yes. But how fast? That's the question."

"There's more," Wren said, grabbing a crisp red gaura fruit from the table before walking over to me. "Hollis has a fleet of ships he's commanding. He's obviously using the stolen siren songs to do it. The pirates from the gulley don't care for him taking over though, so they've agreed to help us. I'm to give them coordinates tomorrow."

Ara stood. "Well, that doesn't give us much time."

Fen walked to the door. "Let me see what I can find on siren's songs in the library." He held his hand out to his queen. "Join me?"

A blush spread across her cheeks, and I envied their happiness as they swept out of the room.

"I've got to go and find Rhogan. I'm guessing he's in the lists. Come with me?"

I stole a piece of bread and followed her out of the castle. Once we were close, I stopped her.

"I'm going back to the sea. Whatever it is you need to work out with Rhog, do it, but that's between you two. I have to get Doriahs started and check in with a friend. I'll meet you on the shoreline in the morning."

"Don't do anything stupid. Stick to the plan."

"Yes, mother."

A shadow crossed her face at those words, but she turned and ran off before I could ask why.

Within an hour, I was racing through the familiar winding halls of the sea castle searching for Jof, who I hadn't seen since he'd left with Kai. I was also keeping an eye out for the hydra, and Narina.

Doriahs was the easiest to find, so I started with her, telling her of the king's involvement and what she needed to look for. She left the castle to rip through the ocean on the hunt and I thanked my lucky stars I wasn't on the receiving end of the hungry look in her eyes.

I checked Narina's room but didn't find her, and none of the patrolling soldiers seemed to know where she or Jof was. I finally had to give in and find Leora, even though I knew I wasn't on her good side. Especially now that everyone knew Kai had died.

As I drew near, trills of laughter made their way to me. I crept slowly closer to see Leora glowing so brightly I nearly had to shield my eyes as she giggled and offered food to the cook from my ship. If it hadn't been absolutely necessary, I probably wouldn't have interrupted.

Clearing my throat, I swam into the kitchen. "Leora?"

She dropped whatever she was trying to feed to the cook and then her light dimmed with embarrassment. I flew forward and picked it up off the floor.

"I'm so sorry. I didn't mean to intrude. I just need to find Jof and Narina and they both seem to be out. Do you have any idea where they might be?"

She wiped her hands on an apron, not unlike the one the cook from the castle wore. "Perhaps you could not find them apart because they are together."

"Together?"

She giggled and then covered her mouth, her glow returning. "They've been spending a lot of time together recently. Have you checked his room?"

"I don't know where his room is."

"I can take you."

Giving the cook a glance, I lifted a brow. "Are you sure? I can wait if you're busy."

"No. I'm sure. You sent me a friend." She peeked at him behind heavy lashes. "I can spare a moment."

She sped through the castle, winding this way and that, faster than I knew she could move. Within minutes we were floating in front of a lone door at the end of a long hallway.

"Why is his room all the way over here?"

"The commander insisted he take this room after seeing the rooms the old queen allotted for the lesser fae. You'll see."

She was gone before I could knock. It took three tries before Narina, flushed and sporting wild bedhead, opened the door wrapped in a blanket. The heavy smile on her lips did not fade as she swam aside and let me enter Jof's room. Which was apparently Morwena's old room.

A grid of a thousand crowns filled one wall, and the bed was bigger than any I'd ever seen. Jof was lost somewhere in the middle of it, and though he shied away, I only turned to Narina with a questioning gaze as she crossed the room and plopped onto a chaise in the corner.

"Nice place."

"It certainly has its perks." She smiled. "Jof, my darling, could you give us a moment?"

He was up and across the room in an instant. At first, I thought this might be another of her games but as she watched that male swim to the door, a genuine smile on her face as he did, I knew it was real. A pang of jealousy shot through me.

"Wait. I need to talk to you too, Jof. You might as well stay."

I told them everything. About losing Kai and finding a kernel of healing in the Flame Court. About going to the Gulley and the seer. And then I told them about my song, watching Narina carefully as I explained that I suspected her sister to be involved. True hatred shone on her face, but I still had my doubts.

"I need to be sure I can trust you. And that starts today. I need to know how close your family really was to Morwena."

She bristled, sitting upright as she contemplated her place now. She looked at Jof and then back at me and nodded slowly, letting her shoulders drop and then her gaze. "You know what happened to my parents. Both were killed working in Autus' court. Before that, when Ori and I were the only kips swimming around here, Morwena took a liking to Ori. She would con her into playing tricks on me and watch from the shadows as she became hateful. I truly think Morwena was the root of"—she picked at her fingers—"you know."

Jof hardened his jaw, a clear indication that she'd told him. Which meant this was real between them. He reached for her hand and squeezed.

"You think Morwena talked Ori into sleeping with your betrothed? For what? Spite?"

"I know it sounds absurd." She swam away from the chaise and started moving in circles. "Morwena would invite her to lunches and specifically state on the invitations that I wasn't invited. She would give Ori gifts for spying for her and she would whisper poison in her ear for sport."

"It's not absurd. It makes perfect sense. Morwena despised happiness, and families more so. Look at what she did to her own parents. What I don't understand is why she would allow you to stay and Ori to go. Ori hates the castle."

"I was allowed to stay because my father bargained for us to always have a home here. He assisted Morwena ages ago and she agreed to the bargain. Once struck, she wouldn't go back on it. Even though she hated me. Ori left because I refused. And it was either going to be her or I. But she was always the stronger one. More cunning and persuasive. I would have never made it out there on my own. Plus, it's possible she's still doing Morwena's bidding. I have no idea."

"Of course." I pressed my thumbs into my temples. "Of course. Morwena told Ori about the magic of the sirens because she knew I came to play here. She didn't have a family… she was training Ori to take her place. But since she couldn't pass down her magic, she showed her how to replace it. With siren songs. And then Ori gave the information to Hollis, and he's using it to take over the sea."

"Maybe my mother and father knew that and found her favoritism unfair. Perhaps that's why they were shipped off unexpectedly to the Wind Court and never returned. What if they never even made it that far? What if she killed them?" Narina covered her face and sank to the floor. "What if they died because they wanted better for me?"

I swam to her, pulling her into my arms. "Then they died for a far more valiant reason than my father."

She hugged me so tight I wasn't sure she'd ever let go, but eventually she did and when she rose, the vulnerable mermaid was gone. Replaced by a true queen with a score to settle. "If Ori has anything do to with this, I want in. What's the plan?"

"Right now, it's all speculation that she is involved. We will know for sure tomorrow, assuming Doriahs finds Hollis and his fleet."

"What can we do?" Jof asked, moving forward to take Narina's hand.

"I need a crew for my ship. I don't know what numbers Hollis has for fighters, but if the pirates don't show up, we are setting ourselves up for a tough battle. I'm leaving soon. Can you find troops?"

"We will meet you at the front of the castle in an hour."

With that, I left and swam to Kai's room. Placing my palm on the door, I let the memories wash over me. I prayed he'd be with me tomorrow. Looking down on his friends and smiling, though he couldn't be there to stand with us. I hoped somewhere he could see that in the end, we'd all come together anyway. And even though he wasn't here, he was still the link.

Unable to open the door, no matter how much my heart wanted to crawl into that bed, I left the halls behind. A busy ship was a better companion than a bedroom full of sadness. It came in waves. The severity of grieving. It consumed me in random moments and was only a constant ache in others. Still, not a moment passed that he wasn't there, in my mind. Reminding me that I'd never be whole again.

Jof was a male of his word. With Narina in tow, about thirty sea fae set out with us toward an anchored ship, practically abandoned. Save one little fae with bushy white eyebrows, Binsin.

They followed silently, flying through the water behind me. A sea of fins, tails and flowing hair, mostly merfae, but a few mermaids with weapons had joined. Kai had changed the mindset of the females in Morwena's castle. No longer just pretty faces, most had taken his training seriously. He'd empowered them all and as they swam behind me, I remembered what the seer had said. I had to believe he would have been proud of the choice he'd made, seeing them now.

Beneath the full moon, the vast sea was endless but ever enchanting. That phantom song haunted me, pulling me, though I could feel the knife on the other end. The looming danger encompassing the beautiful, mysterious notes. I reminded myself not to be weak. Not to forget my journey to get here. A journey built of love and heartache, of loss and healing and discovery. Maybe this wasn't entirely my fight and maybe I would have tried to do it on my own before, or not bothered at all, but I was not the same. I couldn't go back to who I was before I met the male who changed the core of my world.

I didn't make it to my bed that night. After getting everyone settled in, touching base with the loyal fae that had kept the decks cleaned and the food fresh, I lay on the wooden planks of the deck and watched the stars follow their chosen path across the sky. I was permanently scarred from the trauma of the last battle I'd witnessed. Fae would die once again for a selfish reason. There would be no way around it.

As planned, with a full crew manning the sails and myself at the wheel, a place I'd once dreamed of standing, though now it made me feel sick, we soared across the waters, toward the Flame Court.

On the shore stood a team of fae, ready to join us. Wren held Rhogan's hand and the king and queen stood side by side. The draconian, Greeve, was there, as well as the fae with stag horns. A few more lined the shore but I didn't recognize them. Doriahs' great figure filled the deep waters below us.

As the draconian carried the land dwellers to the ship with his magic, Jof and I jumped into the water to see what the hydra had found.

"They are far. The waters are colder and more treacherous, but I found them. It will take two days to get there.

"We have to go to the Gulley first and see if any of the pirates will join. As soon as all of our extra passengers are—"

"Hydra," a voice drawled from behind me.

"Queen," the voices sang in unison.

Ara swam past me until she was inches from Doriahs' center face. "You're doing cool shit down in the sea and didn't even fucking invite me?"

"You're here now."

"I'll forgive you if you promise to snap at least one ship in half. We're talking arm tentacle things out of the water, reaching around and just crushing it."

Three wicked smiles stretched easily across her faces. "As you wish."

"Hollis will be on a ship with red sails. Just avoid that one, would you?" I asked.

"To start." She smirked.

We loaded back onto the ship and most of the newcomers stood with me on the main deck as Jof led us to the Gulley. A line of pirates, flags raised on their vessels, waited in the harbor. Greeve took Wren to the docks so she could give them the plan and they were back within minutes.

The king would use his wind magic to push the ships faster. We wouldn't need two full days, but he would have to rest because we needed him ready for battle. He and Ara moved to the starboard bow; Rhogan and Wren found their way into the crow's nest. Rhogan whooped, spreading his arms out wide and I'm sure it was the closest he'd been to flying in a long time. With Wren beaming up at him, I'm not sure I'd ever seen him so happy.

"Sucks, doesn't it?"

I spun, coming face to face with the draconian. He stood much taller than I did, covered in dark tattoos that matched his hair and eyes. Beautiful, but hauntingly sad. "I don't know what you mean."

"We get to sit back and watch everyone else be in love while we question ourselves daily. Chased by the what-ifs and the memories of our mates."

I opened my mouth to protest but I had nothing to hide. No reason to deny what Kai meant to me. What we had once meant to each other. "How did you know?"

"Broken recognizes broken."

I nodded and let the sound and spray of the sea take me away again. The wind grew colder and the clouds darker. It wasn't long until we were below deck, sitting in the small dining room discussing battle plans. Greeve had retrieved Bregand and before he was allowed below deck, he was given a truth serum the healer had brought with him. Apparently passing his test, he sat sandwiched between Rhogan and Greeve. Anyone else would have been dwarfed in comparison to those two massive armed fae, but not this one-legged pirate.

"Just let me and my crew take care of it," the pirate growled, clearly irritated by the vetting.

"Destruction is not the first answer here," King Fenlas answered.

Ara scoffed. "Destruction is always the answer with wayward pirates."

"Bah." Bregand stomped the floor with his peg. "What do you know of wayward pirates?"

She picked below her nails with a dagger. "I'm getting a full education just sitting in your presence."

The pirate leaned in, baring his yellowed teeth.

Greeve cleared his throat. "Enough."

I stood. "We can't parlay. They aren't going to listen; they aren't going to bargain. I say we send the pirates forward as a distraction with Doriahs. The *Talea* hangs back with the healer and does not engage. The sea fae on this ship can take to the waters and I'll sneak onto Hollis' ship and find the songs. And Hollis. Though I can't promise he will live."

"Two things," Ara said, also standing. "One, it's creepy when you call the hydra by her name. Two, I don't want to be on a ship that does not engage. I'd rather wear an evada pearl and head to the ship I can fight on."

I shrugged. "That's fine with me. You might want to take that up with him, though."

The king pinned her with a stare, but she didn't even glance in his direction. "It'll be fine. This is a fun game we like to play."

"I think you're the only one that likes it." Wren laughed.

"Take me back to my ship so I can take the lead," Bregand said. "I'll follow the big, scary bitch the rest of the way."

I don't know what came over me. Maybe my pent-up emotions, maybe my fear of what could happen, maybe losing my entire sense of self. But I had the pirate slammed up against the door before he ever saw me moving. "Call her that again and I'll peel your heart from your chest while it's still beating and shove it down your gods damned throat."

"Finally, the siren comes out to play," he answered, shoving me away.

Rhogan was between us in an instant, saying nothing as he stared down the pirate, daring him to say another word. Greeve moved in and whisked him away.

"Well, that was fun," Ara said, sharing a genuine smile. "I might like you one day, siren. If we all live through this."

CHAPTER 33

Rain so cold it bit into my skin and rattled my bones fell in sheets from the angry gray sky. Icy wind ripped through the taut sails, shifting direction as we tried to maintain a distance from the band of pirates surging across the tumbling water. Jof's crew remained calm, tying themselves to the ship like they'd been sailing their whole lives as we weathered the storm. Somewhere ahead of us, Doriahs led; her great body likely stretched to full size as she did what she did best. Hunted.

"I can't believe the king's magic is strong enough to fight this storm," I yelled to Wren, holding onto the water-slicked railing of the ship, watching the king as he pushed his magic into the sails, staring directly ahead.

"It's personal," Wren said with a shrug. "He wasn't expecting to hear about you being Kai's mate. Now he'll do anything to protect you, just like Kai did anything to protect him. They really were like brothers."

A great wave tilted the boat and Wren crashed into Rhogan beside her.

"Gotta work on those sea legs." He nuzzled into her ear.

A swell of sadness struck me, and I slipped away, giving the excuse of checking on Jof. If the estimated times were right, we wouldn't come upon our mark until tomorrow, but the closer we got to battle, the more panic set in. The trauma from the last one settled into my gut like a boulder. Each step I took weighed more and more as the tension became a palpable entity, sinking into my heart.

I had to get away. I couldn't do this. I thought I could, but I was wrong. I closed my eyes, and he was there, lying on the ground. Unmoving. I blinked and it was Wren's body there. The walls of the world moved in as I began to run.

Sliding on the deck, I nearly crashed into a mermaid gripping the railing with white knuckles. The rain beating on the top of the water grew louder. The shouting of the makeshift crew trying not to toss the rest of us overboard filled my ears. The wind howled and the waves crashed. I met eyes with the draconian watching from across the ship mere seconds before I jumped overboard and plunged into the freezing sea. The silent sea.

Sinking to the bottom, I pushed my tail across the sand, doing anything I could to clear my mind. The cold from the water slowed my heart. Once thundering, it now beat in time with the ocean waves. The panic that threatened to end me subsided, if only a little. Still, I closed my eyes, and he was there again.

Difficult does not mean impossible. One day, there will be a line drawn in the sand and you'll be faced with the impossible. Impossible is where heroes are made. Where dreams are answered. Impossible is where my passion for you comes from because nothing is perfect, except for this..

His lips always burned. So much desire and so much heat between us. I needed that passion. I needed to remember the impossible.

"Lyra?"

Jerking upright, I tensed as Rhogan swam for me, two great iridescent wings moving through the water behind him like that of a butterfly and jellyfish mixed together. The soft purple glow provided just enough light to show the awe on his face.

"Rhogan? What happened?"

He shook his head, spinning in the water as he tried to see the wings behind him. "I don't know. I put the evada pearl in my ear and then I was gasping for water. I leaped in after you and these wings appeared." He paused, audibly swallowing. "Wings. Two."

I let the moment hang between us as he worked through his emotions. Eventually, he turned back to me.

"What are you doing here?"

"Greeve said he saw you jump. Thought I better check on you."

I sat with my tail hugged to my chest. "I'm fine."

"That's female code for 'the world is burning.'"

I nodded. He knew me better than I'd ever known him. "What if someone dies? What if we brought all these fae out here to their deathbeds? It'll be my fault. Just like his death was."

"Woah. Woah. Woah. Kai's death was not your fault. That battle was fated way before either of us were born."

I shook my head. "You don't understand."

"Then explain it," he said, darting through the water, propelled by foreign wings, until he nestled in beside me.

"If Kai hadn't chosen to stay in the sea, if we hadn't decided to get closer, maybe his life would have taken a different route. The seer said he had two options at life, and both were long. Yet he chose neither." I spun the ring on my finger and pushed away the memory of the night he gave it to me.

"Have you ever spoken to a seer? Before her?"

"No."

"Well, then how you do know exactly what she meant? What if she's telling you Kai had two long lives ahead of him and neither path was something he could choose? It would only be based on what happened to him."

"That doesn't make sense, because either way, he didn't get a long life."

"It doesn't mean you're responsible for the life he did have. He stepped onto that battlefield knowing the dangers. That had nothing to do with you. Had he not met you in the sea, he still would have been on those hills. Still would have fought beside the king. But that is in the past." He moved, pushing off the seafloor, and holding out a hand. "That pirate stole something from you. He violated you. We don't let him get away with that. We do not give up. We do not stop fighting."

I rose and instead of taking his hand, I hugged him. "We do not stop fighting."

"Atta girl. Now, let's go kick some pirate ass."

Smiling, I shoved him, his blond hair rippling through the water in beautiful waves around him. "I can't take you seriously as a half jelly-fish-winged male. They are too pretty for you."

He quirked a brow. "Wanna race?"

"You sure you can handle those things?"

"I was born to fly," he said and darted away.

I slept better that night than I had in days. I woke before the rest of the ship, except for a few tired workers and the king, who stood behind the wheel, his hands holding steady as he stared off into the distance. Eerie fog settled over the water, so still we seemed to glide across a mirror, moving slowly but still following a perfect flock of ships into a wide cove, formed by a massive, snow-covered island.

I shivered and ran my hands up and down my arms in an attempt to push away the harsh cold nestling in my bones. A blanket of heat-laced magic wrapped around my body. Stiffening, I nodded my thanks to the king before turning back to survey the hazy water. Great red sails waved in the distance, as if calling forth the bloodshed that would soon follow. The last time I'd seen that ship, before Hollis claimed it for himself, had been the last time I'd seen Kai alive.

It was time for me to pull off the greatest heist of my life, in the middle of a battle on the sea, led by a hydra and a band of questionable pirates.

As the ship crept forward, the deck grew full with our improvised crew. Rhogan took the crow's nest, observing as he signaled to Jof, now standing comfortably at the helm. Greeve took his place at the front of the ship with the king and queen. Wren and Narina remained at my side as we hung back. Watching. Listening to the eerie silence.

We moved in closer, though we kept the line of pirates between us and the band of nearly thirty ships we faced. Screams from the distance rang out as one of Hollis' ships surged forward, clearly pushed by another fae with wind magic, and crashed right into the left side of our tiny fleet.

They didn't want to hear what we had to say, just as I'd predicted. Both ships took damage as wood splintered and fae began to yell. Battle cries and howls of fear rang out as they realized bailing would mean jumping into the dangerous, hydra-filled waters below.

As if on cue, three great tentacles shot out of the water, wrapping around the middle of a few ships, and snapping them in half, dragging them and all occupants into the freezing ocean water. Ara clapped her hands as loud as she could at the fulfilled promise.

My family's ship wasn't made for war, but we did keep weaponry on board for protection. Still, the pirate ships came for blood, releasing spring loaded ballistae that launched massive rocks into the opposing ships, causing instant, catastrophic damage. Our king held his arms out and a ship far away from the hydra burst into flames. I strapped on the wrist bandolier and loaded it carefully. Narina slipped a spear into a strap across her back. Wren already had her sword ready to go.

"Now or never," Wren said, taking my hand.

"I'm ready," Narina added.

"Me too." Ara took Wren's other hand.

Ignoring the king's grunt, I dropped Wren's hand and leaped into the water. Narina followed. One by one, the fighters from our ship joined me. Mermaids equipped with weapons Kaitalen had taught them to use. Guards that used to work for a tyrant queen with a penchant for murder. Slaves, freed at the hands of my mate and his friends. This was my fight. My single purpose. I wanted my song back. Everything I'd been through was for this moment, and I was not alone. Even in death, my mate had given me a friendship I hadn't deserved. Wren.

Long tentacles surged through the water in front of us, plucking Hollis' fighters as they fell from their battleships. Ara zipped through the water just as gracefully as she fought on land and Wren vanished, jabbing unsuspecting foe as she attacked. Blood-colored water filled the cove as we swam toward the ship with limp, red sails. If our guesses were right, my song was somewhere on board.

I gripped my hand into a fist, feeling the cold metal of the ring on my finger as I twisted my wrist and let a knife dart through the water, nailing a male from a distance. It didn't take him down though, just seemed to piss him off as he turned, his amber tail flourishing behind him as he came for me. Glossed-over eyes met mine as he gripped his half-moon shaped blade and sliced through the water. I jerked to the side, narrowly avoiding another set of fighters as I engaged my weapon and shot again. This time aiming straight for the chest.

The merfae died on impact, my blade piercing his heart as he froze, a look of shock his last expression as he sank to the shallow bottom of the cove. I pressed on, surging through the red water, fighting only when necessary to get to the ship on the back row. Another fae, a female with hair so dark it matched the purple tones in my tail, launched a spear at me, but she was too weak to reach me from so far away. I grabbed the weapon from its descent and held it in front of me. She was within arm's reach in seconds. I nearly missed the hook she had until Narina shouted from my side. She whipped that giant hook through the water in perfect form, and it would have snagged me had Wren not shot in from seemingly nowhere, shoving us both aside as a dagger zipped past.

I'd never been in the thick of a fight before. Even when I'd fought to get to Kai, I'd stuck to the outskirts of the battle. My heart rattled against my ribcage as I pushed forward. Danger seeped into every inch of the water, reminding me that no one was safe. Not me, not the king, not even invisible Wren. I swallowed as Kai's body flashed through my mind again, but this was not the time to be haunted by that image.

The blood in the water made it hard to see anything, but the muffled sounds of fighting, of discharged weaponry above, and screaming fae, kept my mind clear as we moved closer to Hollis' ship.

A yawling cry, louder than anything I'd ever heard, came from atop the water. *Doriahs*. An inky black substance clouded the area surrounding her within seconds. She thrashed about, sending wave after wave of fae away from her. I turned, swimming in her direction, but an arm gripped me. I swung to fight but stopped at the last minute as I looked into Narina's eyes.

"You can't help her. You have to keep going."

"She's my friend."

She nodded, pulling me. "Exactly. She needs you to live through this. Keep going."

I fought the sadness and continued forward, praying to all seven gods and even the fallen god of the sea that she would still be alive at the end of this. Approaching Hollis' notorious ship, I shot out of the water and landed on board, kicking a rolled ladder down as I fought between staying hidden and checking on the hydra. Ara was the first up the ladder; she had her weapons out and led us forward quicker than the others could board. Greeve landed beside us with Fen and, before the deck crew even knew what was happening, we rained hell down upon them.

The Flame Court warriors fought with such deadly accuracy; if the circumstances hadn't been so serious, the smile on Ara's face would have been comical. Greeve dashed through the air, slicing with great curved swords as he raced from this ship to the next.

One of Hollis' crew members came barreling for me, the familiar blank look on his face exposing his enchantment. With wide shoulders and rippling muscles, he was a brute, slashing a sword through the air so quickly it sang before crashing into the railing behind me as I dodged. I stayed low, forcing him to swing, as I twisted my wrist and shot him in the neck with a small knife from my bandolier. He slowed only slightly, but it was enough of an edge to get an opening, so I slammed my fist through his chest and ripped out that warm, beating heart.

Having experienced the other side of mourning so strongly, I wanted to feel guilty for yet another murder, but there was no time. One moment I was standing and the next a searing pain ripped through my arm, and I was on the ground. A spear tore through the flesh on my bicep, pinning me to the splintered deck. With little strength and afraid to turn and do more damage, I lay there, bleeding out until the king ripped the weapon from the deck and jammed it into the pirate coming for both of us before helping me up.

"Greeve," he shouted. "Take her to Tem."

"No." I shook my head, staring at the deep red trail of blood cascading down my shredded arm. "I can't leave. I have to get to Hollis. I have to find my song."

He grabbed me by the collar, yanking me forward until we were nose to nose. "I'll see you back here in five minutes. The healer is quick. Then you can go below."

Fiery tears filled my eyes as I nodded and the draconian gripped my good arm. A gale-force wind zipped through my body, and I felt more than saw us leave the ship and land back on mine. Temir was on the deck, waiting. The moment he placed his hand on my arm, I fell to my knees. The pain of his touch was like being burned, but as if he understood, it was followed by a wave of numbness until he released me. The wound was gone.

The world paused. I moved my hand over the smooth skin and looked into his calm eyes for the first time. It wasn't a patch. It wasn't stitched. The hole in my arm was just… gone.

"Thank you." I could barely get the words out before Greeve held his hand out and we were riding the wind back to Hollis' ship.

"Don't die, siren." The draconian's words were nearly a warning.

Only bodies filled the deck and more blood stained the water as ships burned and pirates battled before us. Then I remembered the hydra's scream and before I could do anything else, I ran to the edge and looked over, panicking when I didn't see her shadow below.

"She's there." Narina pointed.

Far in the distance, a river of black trailing her, the hydra's body was still. The water was still. A lance the size of a mast pierced her. My heart stopped as I realized I was the cause of her death. The first friend to claim me after I'd betrayed Kai had died. She'd followed me into battle to meet the same fate that seemed to haunt those that got too close to me. Tears filled my eyes, and I clutched my arms to my chest, caving inward. I could nearly feel my heartbeat slow as the world around me became that much more painful. *Failure breeds failure.* There wasn't time. Not to think about her kindness, not to remember her fierce loyalty to us. Nothing.

I struggled to take in air until a gasp pulled me back to the deadly ship. I spun in time to see the queen running at full speed before leaping into the air and into the water, not bothering with a pearl as she swam like both their lives depended on it, screaming for the healer. Greeve and the king were gone an instant later and, while I would have followed next, Wren slipped her hand into mine and we vanished. We had a job to do. This couldn't have all been in vain.

CHAPTER 34

"It's time," Wren said, pulling me away from my heartache. "If Hollis is on this ship, he's below deck. We have to go. Don't forget our purpose."

Stiffening my shoulders, I closed my eyes and forced myself to accept what I couldn't control. I led Wren into the hull of the ship, stepping over fallen bodies as we tried not to slip on the bloodied deck, nor leave footprints down the hall. The sweep of familiarity took hold and for a moment I froze, remembering the last place I'd spoken to Kai. The place he'd fought for me and the place he'd let me go. Remorse gripped me as we began breaking into locked rooms, searching.

With soft, careful footing, we crept along the dark-paneled corridor. We entered an empty room and shivers surged down my body. Though I knew it wasn't the same, it was identical to the tithe collecting room on Vex's ship in the Gulley. Even the gaudy paintings with gold trim and the obnoxiously large desk were the same. I imagined this was where he conducted much more nefarious business deals, like selling those he considered lesser.

"I still have Vex's skeleton key," I said, patting my chest where it hung beneath my clothing. "If we find a lock we can't open, the key will."

We wandered around the room, invisible. The desk had already been cleared out except for a small hidden compartment below the false bottom of a drawer they wouldn't have known to look for. I pulled out a dagger with golden snakes twisted into the handle, circling a perfect ruby on the hilt.

"Do you need a knife?" I whispered.

"I've got mine still."

"Does it have a giant ruby on it?" I asked with a smile, though she couldn't see it.

"Good point. Hand it over."

I snorted, but complied.

"Here," Wren whispered, tugging my hand toward a wall. "This map doesn't sit flat against the wall."

She lifted the oversized map from the bottom, ripping at the tacked corners until it revealed the safe behind it. Though nearly flush, it wasn't quite.

"Good eye." I placed my hand flat against the safe and could feel a thrumming, soft, but present, coming from within. My heart began to race. "There are songs in here."

"I'll watch the door."

Wren released my hand and I popped into view, the sight of my arm surprising me. I worked quickly, closing my eyes as I attempted to shut out the chaotic world. *One number at a time*, as my mother would say. *Feel the click as you would a single beat of your heart.* Holding my breath, I moved the dial smoothly, waiting for the catch of the gears within. A tiny prick and I knew I'd caught it, so I reversed the dial and followed the same process backward until again it clicked.

Wren gasped and crossed the room, grabbing my hand. If I let go, I might have to start over, but if someone saw the map held up by invisible forces, we'd be caught for sure. I wanted my song, but we couldn't risk being caught. Stepping away, I let the map go just as the door slammed open.

My heart sank into my stomach as Ori walked into the room and I was glad Narina hadn't insisted on coming. Wisps of her blue hair showed from under the bandanna tied around her head. Wearing head to toe brown leather with gold buckles, she looked every bit the pirate wench.

She ripped the map from the wall and began turning the dial on the safe as if she'd done it a thousand times. Opening the iron door with a squeak, she reached in and scooped out an arm full of softly glowing vials. She looked over her shoulder, drenched in paranoia. Somehow she'd managed to escape Hollis' control and now she would free them or return them. Guilt crept over me as I realized how quickly I'd turned my back on her.

She ran from the room, and I tried to follow until a voice echoed from down the hall.

"Ori, wait," Hollis called.

Wren squeezed my hand in warning as I halted. I'd kill him. He was responsible for so many things. Seeing the plethora of captured siren's songs, it was only then I realized the depth of his disgusting nature. I had no idea there were so... *many* of us. The army of mindless fae that fought above us was only the beginning.

"Lyra," Wren whispered. "She didn't clear the safe. Look."

Four vials. I pulled them out one by one, handing two to Wren and taking two for myself. The moment my hand wrapped around the final vial, it nearly brought me to my knees. Rage surged through my veins, and it took all my power not to cry out. I hadn't found my own song, but my heart recognized my mother's. It was pure and powerful, and she'd died without it. The same would not happen to me.

"My song isn't here. We have to follow them."

Moving carefully down the hall, we crept to the final room, sliding through the door that had been left open in their argument. I planned to sneak behind Hollis and kill him before he saw it coming. He stood on one side of the storeroom, Ori on the other.

Lit only by sconces, there was hardly room for us to stand in the small room. Wooden shelves lined the wall, stacked high with provisions.

Loaves of breads wrapped in cloth and sacks filled with dried beans nearly filled the space. Sealed barrels covered most of the floor.

My eyes flicked to the ring on Hollis' finger, protecting him from the siren songs. Vexyr's. Had he nothing of his own? Stealing was once a job for me, a thrill even, but it was clearly a lifestyle for him.

"They will kill us both, regardless of fault." The worry in Ori's shaken voice was unmistakable.

Hollis turned red as his fists clenched at his sides. "Are you planning to refuse your guilt?"

Ori turned with a dancer's grace, pinning the male with a glare so fierce he stumbled backward. "I wouldn't dream of taking the title you've given yourself away from you. You took this ship. You wanted everyone to know you were the new Lord of the Sea, didn't you? Did you not get exactly what you asked for?"

"This isn't what I meant when we made that bargain, and you know it."

"We must always be careful what we wish for." A wicked smile spread across Ori's face as the pieces began to fall into place for me. She set the stolen songs down on the barrel before her. "You agreed to a bargain, did you not?"

"I agreed to help you steal that song in exchange for this ship. That was it. You took it too far, Ori. Everyone thinks I'm to blame for the army of mindless fae up there."

"I convinced Vex to take what was already promised to him. You saw Lyra and that Flame Court brute together in the Gulley. You knew he'd come for her at whatever cost. You got your ship, I got the songs. That's all that matters."

"You had nothing to do with that. It accidentally worked out in your favor. That's all."

She pulled a glowing gemstone shaped like a seashell from beneath her shirt and a wave of nausea washed over me. Uncorking the vials, she poured them into the hollowed center one by one as she continued. "There are no accidents."

"Just tell me why, then? If I'm going to die no matter what, what was it for?"

She sidestepped a barrel and moved to the wall, lifting a loaf of bread. Sniffing it, she placed it back, clearly deciding if she wanted to tell him or not.

"Lyra's mother's song was stolen as an experiment using a stone she'd been trying to keep hidden away. Morwena knew she had it." She lifted the gem toward him. "Lyra's father was only bait essentially, luring her mother to her own eventual demise. It's surprising, really. You'd think after centuries of hunting sea fae, she would have seen it coming. But, when he got her on the ship, he seduced and drugged her, stealing the gem and then using it against her to take her song, as per the queen's orders. He kept the song, and her mother never discovered the queen's involvement. Here's the catch; her mother stayed. Do you know why?"

"Don't treat me like a child, Ori. I know how it works. If you have the song, you control the siren. They'll stop at nothing to retrieve it."

"Precisely," she said, holding the gem between her hands as it glowed brighter and brighter. "They cannot resist the urge. Which is why we kill them now. It's all falling into place. I would mind your manners before I snatch that ring from your finger while you sleep and bury my knife in your heart."

"Falling into place? Have you not heard the battle? It's a miracle we've not been infiltrated below. And also, a problem. Something's happening and you're too blind to see it."

"Relax. We can leave this ship behind now," she said, gesturing to the vials. "I just need to find Zariya and I'll have everything I need to build my power and control the sea. This was always the plan."

I dropped Wren's hand, fire rolling through me. "This whole fucking time? You've been scheming since we were kips? You knew about my mother's murder? You watched me cry! You were the only one that was there for me. How could you?"

She stumbled backward a step before turning her face neutral once more. "Where did you come from?"

"Answer the fucking question, Ori."

Hollis moved toward me but stopped mid-step, his back rigid. Wren must have had a knife jabbed into his spine.

"Not that I have to answer to you, Lyra, but this was always my fate. You paraded around like you were so much better than everyone. But you never were. I always had the upper hand."

"I'm guessing you haven't been above. The king and queen would likely disagree."

"For now. But once I find Zariya, they won't have a chance. But then, you have no idea about that, do you?" She tsked, shaking her head. "So sheltered."

I surged forward, leaning into the rum barrel that separated us. "Zariya is a fable."

"It's real. It's the land of your people," Hollis rushed out. "There's a whole colony of sirens. She wants to—"

A knife landed in his chest before he could finish. He gasped, spinning his head to Ori before he fell backward to the floor.

"I'm glad you're here, dear." Ori stepped around the drum. "I'll need bait to draw the siren leader from hiding."

I took a step back. "I'm not going anywhere with you."

She closed her eyes. The air in the room became thick, haunting, as it filled with smooth vibrations. A small glow from below her shirt grew into a beaming light as she drew upon the song of the sirens she'd been commanding. I realized too late that I was not safe.

"Sit," she sang.

A sensation grew from the tips of my fingers through my hands, down my body and into my feet as I moved, grasping for the first time how uniquely beautiful Ori was. Cropped blue hair brushed her shoulder as she tilted her head and studied me.

I sat.

"Good girl."

Those words were so powerful. I wanted nothing more than to hear them from her. To let her eyes move over me as she rounded the desk, standing directly in front of me. Desire lit my skin on fire as I clenched the arms of the chair, wishing she'd release me from her command so I could touch her.

But there was something wrong with that. I was only to touch one person. I squeezed my eyes shut, trying to see his face. Trying to remember why the thought of him made me so sad. When I opened them again, the tip of a knife pressed into my throat. Warning bells sounded and slowly I fought against the magic.

"Don't move." Her song was so melodic and beautiful. Perfectly tuned as it rang peacefully through the air.

Sheer defiance caused me to swipe the knife away and stand from the chair. Her eyes doubled in size as she grabbed at the collection of siren songs she'd hoarded below her clothing. "I will take your heart, just like you've taken the hearts of those before you. I've started a collection. Trophies."

I reached for her hair, so soft and delicate between my fingers. She gripped my face, pulling me closer until I couldn't decide if I wanted to kill her or kiss her soundly. Again, I pushed. "How are you hunting them?"

"We are so alike, you know."

"I'm nothing like you."

"You are the most selfish person I've ever met. I heard you betrayed your mate to free your father, just to get your song back. Couldn't resist it, could you?" She shoved me away, crossing her arms over her chest. "Oh, that's gone by the way."

My ears began to ring, panic rising in my throat so violently, had it not been for her magical hold over me, I might have been sick. This world had a way of punishing me. Of beating me so far down, the will to rise was easily slipping away. Forced to breathe, to think, to focus, I swallowed the final piece of knowledge as she continued.

"At first, we weren't sure how to use your power," Ori continued, oblivious to my devastation. "We practiced with a few, but they ran dry. Apparently, we need a well of them. Hence the reason for going to Zariya. The queen found another siren. She didn't want to use your mother's song in case we needed it to lure you in. There was a lesser fae she recruited to work for us, who used this priceless jewel to steal a song from an exiled siren. He was to meet with me that night, you know. You cut off his fucking tail and stole it back."

"So, I became your next target. Your only target because the rest of the sirens are hiding in some glorious, gilded city no one has ever been to."

"Plenty have been. None can return. But not for long. I will find Zariya, and one by one, I will kill them all, just as your father had your mother killed. Vex did that, you know? With his bare hands around her neck, or so I heard."

My pause at the mental picture her words created was just enough for her to draw on that power she'd been building. "Pull that knife from Hollis' chest, Lyra."

I was slow, but still moving. As if I were numb and she commanded my legs. Ripping the knife from the dead pirate on the floor, I heard those words he'd spoken to me. *I thought we were friends.* I'd betrayed him for my own selfish reasons, and here Ori was doing the same to me. Perhaps we *were* the same.

The numbness faded away as a choking sound came from the mermaid. I whipped around to see Wren, holding a broken chain and the Bloodstone in one hand, and Ori by the throat in the other. I surged forward with the knife I'd freed just as Ori shoved another she'd been hiding into Wren's side.

Falling to the ground, she still held the necklace, wrapping her body around it as she began to bleed out. I threw the knife in my hand as hard and precise as I could, knowing I'd have one shot. Ori kept her blade. Given the chance, she'd stab Wren again and though she might live through one, she certainly wouldn't survive another if aimed correctly.

Unfortunately, Ori dodged my knife and, as predicted, made a move toward Wren. She needed that magic desperately. I didn't hesitate, launching myself over Wren as the knife came down again. Fire burned through my back as the weapon sank deep into my flesh, but as she ripped it out and slammed it back in, shoving so hard I was sure it went through my body and into Wren, I whispered into her ear. "Hold on."

The pain of the knife was severe, but not the worst pain of my life. I'd suffered far worse losing my mate. I pictured Rhogan and what losing Wren would do to him and found the strength to turn, if only slightly, so my arm was free.

Ori screamed, face covered in splatters of my blood as she arched her arm up, staring me right in the eyes as she brought that knife down again. Only this time, I caught her. My nails still a permanent weapon as I put the last of my strength into piercing her skin. Though it happened in a split second, I felt each layer of her lacerated skin as my hand slipped into her body, grabbed her warm, beating heart, and squeezed as I ripped it from her chest, still holding her stare.

And then the world went dark, as I bled out on top of Wren, who hadn't moved an inch since the moment I landed on top of her.

CHAPTER 35

Unruly sandy blond hair and ocean blue eyes met me. A male with a smile that melted me stood haloed in pure golden light. He was absolute perfection, with tanned skin and enough charm to eviscerate the world. "Hello, little vixen."

"Is this… are you real?"

He didn't answer, only held his arms open. I sank against him, wrapped in a place I thought I'd never feel again. Slipping my hands around his waist, I looked up, resting my chin on his chest.

"I'm sorry, Kai. For everything. I was never the person you thought you loved, but you were always the male I knew you to be. I've spent every day wishing I could take it all back."

"I know."

He put his cheek on my head and held me as I listened to his heartbeat. As tears began to fall. As I realized I'd died on top of Wren, and Kai had waited to greet me. He was whole beneath the fingers I stroked up and down his muscled back. I pulled away, only to look into his face as he smiled down at me, tucking my hair behind my ear.

"One day, I'll tell you how much I missed you. I'll spend that day whispering into your ear how my heart ached. How I've waited right here, so we could go on into the Ether together."

"Not today?"

He stroked his thumb over my cheek, wiping away a tear. "Our soul's journey is not complete, my love."

"Yes, it is," I breathed. "I'm here with you. There's nothing else to be done." His form wavered. I shook my head, gripping his arms as if I could hold him in place. As if I could anchor myself to him.

"Lyra." My name on his lips felt like a prayer. A wish. A stroke of luck he had to let free.

"Kai. Please don't leave me. I'm done. There's nothing there for me."

"Lyra." His voice faded into my mind, though his mouth didn't move. "Find Zariya."

The purity of the dream faded in a gasp as I shot upright in my bed, drenched in sweat. Rhogan sat beside me, eyes wide as he searched the room, unsure of what to do.

"Wren?" I croaked, heart racing from the vivid dream still clouding the edges of my mind.

"She's okay. Temir is with her now. They kicked me out."

I touched my body, searching for wounds that were not there. The only thing I felt was pure exhaustion as I buried my face in my hands. I could have leaped out of my own skin in frustration. "I thought I'd died. He was there, and it was perfect. It was so real, Rhogan. I could feel him."

He moved from his chair and sat on the bed beside me. Only then did I realize I knew the bed below me, the room around me. We were back on the *Talea* and I honestly had no idea what had happened with everyone else or the battle I'd dragged them to.

"I'm supposed to tell you the minute you wake up, you have to report to the king."

I groaned. "Help me think of a way out of it?"

"I don't think you want to miss this, plus they say Wren's been asking for you." He looped an arm over my shoulder. "So, what do we do?"

Find Zariya. "We get out of bed."

The king stood alone at the wheel of my ship, anchored in a sea of blood. I turned to the right, expecting to see the fallen body of Doriahs, but only the open ocean greeted me amidst scattered planks of shattered wood, and the ships that had made it out of the battle. None were unscathed. Including the one with blood-red sails.

"Why do you think Ara was promised to this world?" he asked by way of greeting.

I knelt, then rose slowly as he watched me. "They say it's because she was to be the change when the world needed it most."

He smiled sadly. "Indeed. Though had she come sooner, it would have still been needed. With her prophecy fulfilled, the ability to enchant the mind has nearly faded away. I can still do it, in small ways; another descendent can as well but, I think the point was to remove that power."

"I'm sure you're right."

He ran his fingers through his dark hair. "Fae died today."

"I know. And I'm sorry. That was never my wish. I tried to handle it alone, but Wren—"

"You were right to include us. From what I've gathered, the mermaid was still carrying out the wishes of a dead queen. Dangerous wishes that would cause the world to move backwards. Her death cleared the minds of those she'd used that stolen power on. You did the right thing. I'm not here to reprimand you."

I thought back to the comment Ori had made about killing the sirens. "I'd just wished I'd known sooner. I wish I could have retrieved my own song without all the trouble. And now it's gone. Drained."

The frenzy that had driven me so far, irrationally so, was quiet within me. As if something inside of me had finally accepted the truth of my lost power. Or maybe that was just the numbness creeping back in.

The wind blew through his dark hair as he dipped his chin. "I'm sorry. I wish we could have done something sooner."

"I've spent this whole time trying to get it back. Thinking it made me who I was. But the only thing I've gotten is a sea's worth of heartache. Nothing went to plan." I leaned against the railing and sighed. "I guess it doesn't matter now, does it?"

The king turned to face me, his green eyes piercing the tension. "It never gets easier. The death. Knowing that the decisions we make affect so many other lives. Yet we must do these things. *He* knew that. That's the only reconciliation I've found with his death. He knew every day what he'd signed up for."

I made peace with the young king at that moment. I knew what he was trying to say. That Kai's death was not in vain and though he struggled to move on, just as I did, there was comfort in the memories.

"Thanks for coming. I know it's no small thing."

"It is a small thing for the mate of my brother. I will always come. I promise you that."

I nodded and walked away, finding my way to Wren's crowded room—my father's old room.

No words were exchanged as she leaped from the bed, around the healer and the queen, and into my arms. "You saved my life, you crazy siren. You could have died."

I squeezed her back, remembering the way her unmoving body felt below mine. "I thought you did," I whispered into her ear.

"I thought *you* died."

"The hydra lived, in case you were wondering." The queen patted me once on the back and stepped out of the room, looking back between Wren and me once before slipping away.

I caught the sadness in her eyes but didn't think it my place to ask.

Still Wren whispered, "Gaea."

I pulled away from Wren and stood in front of the healer. "Thank you, Temir. I know you saved me."

"We had to change your clothing as I'm sure you've noticed." He said, scratching his head near the base of an antler. "We saved the songs, apart from one. The vial shattered during your fight with the mermaid, and you've still got your key."

"Did I die? Did I die and you brought me back? Or did I live and only dream?"

"I cannot resurrect the fallen. You did not die. But nearly. It took a massive amount of power. That's why Wren is still supposed to be in bed. She isn't fully healed."

My head snapped to Wren, and she pursed her lips. "I've already got forty-two people yelling at me, don't you start."

"I wouldn't dream of it."

Rhogan moved from the corner of the room. "We've got a hoard of moody pirates out there fighting over the ship with the red sails. I asked Fen if he wanted to handle it and he said you might be able to provide some advice."

"Why don't you keep it?"

He snorted. "I'm no pirate."

"No, but you did look awfully pretty with those jellyfish wings."

"I'm not pretty. I'm ruggedly handsome. It's not the same," he said, stroking the light stubble on his chin.

"Do you want the ship, or should I push it off onto Brigand?"

"I suppose I could look after it for a while." He winked at Wren, and she nodded.

"What are you going to do?" she asked.

"I think I'm going to find the sirens."

She gasped. "You are? Alone?"

I smiled at her concern. "Yes. It's something I have to do, but first, I have to get into my father's warded room. Maybe it's full of secrets and maybe it's not, but I need to know."

"Greeve's up top. He knows all about wards. You could ask him."

I trotted up the stairs seeking the draconian. He stood with his back to me, staring out over the carnage of the battle. I knew exactly where his mind was.

"It's never going to get easier for us, is it?" I asked, sliding up next to him.

"I hope it doesn't. I hope I never stop wanting her."

"I dreamed of him," I whispered. "It was so real. So vivid, I could have stayed there forever."

"At least you dream."

"You don't?"

He shook his head. "I barely sleep. And when I do, it's only darkness."

I nodded slowly. "Maybe that would be better. Maybe then I wouldn't wake up wishing I never had."

A long silence stretched between us. There was peace with the draconian. I didn't have to explain. Pretend. Force a smile. He was just there. And so was I.

"What do you need, siren?"

I took a long breath, switching gears. He was ready to change the subject and so was I. "There's a warded room on this ship and I need in there. Can you help?"

He swept a hand toward the stairs. "Lead the way."

I'd spent my whole life wondering about the room Greeve had gotten into in less than a minute. Perhaps that's why wards weren't used as much as they used to be. Or maybe he was just that powerful. Still, as everyone gave me the space to see what was so important it was worth hiding, I somehow felt like I was still going to get caught.

It wasn't what I had expected. There weren't chests of gold, or piles of treasure. There were a few solid items, but mostly… the walls were lined by the biggest map I'd ever seen, filled with pins and notes. Strings were tied carefully between some of the markers, others color coded. Stacks of books, ledgers and journals filled the space on the floor and solitary shelf.

Pouring myself into that room as the ship lurched forward, carrying us back to the Flame Court, I began. So many favors owed to my father were tied up in here. They meant nothing now. Whatever he'd been hoping to cash in on, he'd never gotten the opportunity.

One very worn, carefully bound journal sat separate from the others. The most familiar of them all as I remembered his attachment to it. The way he'd devoured the pages.

I sat on the crowded floor and opened it carefully. Though charmed so water wouldn't ruin the pages, apparently blood didn't count. Several pages were stuck together, some faded beyond recognition, but there were more than a few with beautiful handwriting that felt like home. Maybe she'd had this one with her when she was killed.

I saw that male again today. It's as if he can't see Zariya, but he knows we're here. He bathed in the sea and lazed in the sun. I wanted to touch his bronzed skin. I wanted to lure him into the city and show him to the others. But then I'd have to kill him. And he was so pretty to look at. Today was the first day I considered leaving. But I could never come home. No male is worth that.

I turned the page.

Talea saw him. His ship remains anchored around Stoneshell. The sea witch says the ocean sprites likely won't let him stay much longer. The little demons. Talea forbade me from going back. She might be the leader, but I have a choice. I could leave. I could take the Bloodstone with me. I'd still be fulfilling my duties if I protected it.

"Anything good?" Wren asked as I joined the others on the ship deck.

"Just my mother, deciding to leave for my father." I handed the book to her so she could flip the pages. "It's so crazy." I glanced at Rhogan, who hadn't left her side. "How many times have you heard of Zariya?"

He shrugged. "I can't say I've ever heard of it."

"Must be a sea thing."

Temir cleared his throat. "I've heard of it before. A fabled city below the sea, built of stolen gold."

"Yes. Essentially. But I never knew it was a real place. My mother never mentioned it more than a figure of speech. As if she kept it from my father, even though he'd gotten everything else from her. She could have gone back. She could have taken me."

"I wish I had answers," Wren said, folding the book shut. "Maybe someone there will. Whoever Talea is. Or the sea witch she talked about."

I scrunched my nose, shaking my head as I took the book from her. "Isn't that weird too? Why was the sea witch in the siren's city? Why would… Holy gods." I launched myself into a full run, back down to my father's warded room, running my fingers along the strings, studying the pins colors and locations. "The Kraken."

"The Kraken?" Wren asked, catching up.

"Since my mother died, my father seemed to have mourned her loss." I began to pace, taking small steps as all the pieces fell into place. "When I went to free him, the only thing he wanted from Vexyr was a book he'd traded long ago. My mother's journal. Not because he'd missed her. He was looking for someone. This book confirmed the sea witch was in the hidden city my mother had come from. The gods damned sea witch."

Rhogan rubbed the stubble on his chin. "Am I the only one still confused?"

"Sorry," I said, shaking my head. "My father wanted one thing. The Kraken's treasure. He must have thought the sea witch could help him find it. I'd bet my life on it. And since he didn't get hold of my mother's journals until after she died, he didn't know she already knew how to find her. That's why he coveted them so dearly. He was trying to piece together her memories to find the truth. When she left Zariya, she brought this journal with her. She must have been writing in this one at the time she left. Because someone else has her childhood pages."

"Who?" Wren asked.

"Before I met Kai, I was getting these gold-trimmed letters. Gold. I feel so foolish. A. T. It was her. Talea. I just know it. She and my mother have a deep-rooted history. She named this ship after her. The last letter I received had a journal page from my mother attached to it with a warning." I walked to the edge of the room and took Wren's hands into mine. "I know this is going to sound crazy, but Kai told me to go to

Zariya. I thought I had died, and he was there. He told me to go. He said our soul's journey wasn't complete."

"Then go. Maybe you can find a way to get a new song." She stood and dragged me into a hug.

"There has to be something. I refuse to let all of this be for nothing. Our hopeless paths crossed for a reason, and not just because he was my mate. Maybe it's nothing. Maybe I'm desperate because I'm afraid. Maybe I'll live the rest of my life chasing fading hope through the sea. But it's worth it."

"The siren city?" Ara asked, rubbing her temples. Her auburn hair blew in the wind as she stood beside me on the deck.

"You've heard of it?"

Standing at the helm, steering my ship through a freezing ocean, I'd told the king and queen everything I suspected, everything I'd learned of my father, of Vexyr, of Morwena, the diaries, the letters. All of it.

"It's a long story about my childhood. Not important." Ara gripped the railing in front of me as she searched her memory. "I can't think of anything that would provide a location, but I think I know why your mother never took you back."

The wheel slipped from my fingers. "Why?"

"She couldn't. Once someone leaves the city, its location fades from their memory. It's like a mental ward. There's enough gems, gold, and hidden power there to keep it a secret. That's all I know." She turned and pinned me with a look that reminded me of Doriahs. "Try not to get yourself killed. The sirens can be vicious."

"Now that, I did know."

"You should return this." King Fenlas held the Bloodstone between us.

Though not glowing, the memory of it wrapped around Ori's neck still made my skin crawl.

"Part of me wants to keep it, to make sure this never happens again," he said, frowning at the hollowed gem. "I think it's better off in a hidden city, protected by those who covet it most."

I pulled a slow breath into my lungs and reached for the hollowed-out gemstone. The power of the songs within vibrated against my fingers. There was only a trace of mine left, like fragments of invisible dust flecks embedded into the gem itself, as if they'd left an imprint. It didn't matter anymore. If I couldn't find a replacement in Zariya, then someday, I'd have to find peace without it. Which felt a lot simpler than finding peace in a lonely life. Now I just had to locate a hidden city that had always been nothing more than a fable. A city that even my father couldn't find again.

CHAPTER 36

After swearing to Wren I'd check in as soon as I could, I leaped from my ship and did the only thing I could think of. I listened for that song in the water. The one that had pulled me for so long; had haunted me. The shallow swells outside Efi's Isle carried nothing more than chittering dolphins and the deep, faraway moans of a whale. The half-moon lit a shadowed path for me as I swam south, leaving everything I'd ever known behind.

As I swam, I let the memories wash over me until my emotions were the only thing guiding me. I thought of Kai first. Always. His firm hands on the small of my back, his laugh that carried through a room effortlessly. The pin of his gaze. The sound of his heart when I laid my head on his chest. That look he gave me when he first woke, sleepy and blissful. I thought of him until my heart ached. Until I couldn't do it anymore. Living life without him was the cruelest form of torture.

Pushing blindly through the warm water, I thought of my father and how much time I'd spent believing he was mourning my mother. My severed soul was far greater than any wound my father had ever experienced. I'd been so blind. So wrapped up in my own world, my selfish hatred for everything and everyone around me, I had no real idea how hazy everything was until I got away.

Swimming through a familiar shipwreck at the bottom of the ocean, I pictured my mother's beautiful face. In so many ways, I was just like her. Willing to do anything, including sacrificing my happiness, just to try to get my song back. At first, I hadn't understood it. How could she stay? Now, knowing my father had stolen her song and used it to control her, I was better off asking how could she have left. I thought of her golden eyes and her hair the same light tone as my own. The way she'd always seemed to glisten in the sunlight, always exotic. Always so beautiful.

Wishing I'd heard her song at least once in my life at full power, I was still grateful for the few we were able to retrieve, including hers. I doubted they would ever be reunited with the sirens that had likely been killed, but nevertheless I felt a duty to deliver them to Zariya along with the dimmed Bloodstone secured within a pocket of my fae form. Should I fall, it would never be found, and perhaps that would be the greatest gift I could give the sirens who seemed to have abandoned my mother. Or perhaps it was as it looked, and she had abandoned them. The path of betrayal that had brought me to this point convinced me to question everything I knew.

Maybe finding the lost city was not my fate. Every time I'd entered the water, that eerie song had been there. Like a companion, the danger emanating from the height of the notes within the melody like a warning. As if my subconscious knew better than to trust it.

Though odd that I sought a place I thought to be a fable, the moment that foreign melody vibrated through the water, I latched onto it, jerking to the side as it beckoned me. Steeling my nerves, I worked every muscle in my body as I chased that sound. Although it felt as if it carried me, I'd already swam so far, and I wondered if I'd tire before I made it. The sea was a dangerous entity, and I was alone in a great valley of fluid death and peril.

Darker and darker the sea became, as even the faint light from the moon above began to fade. No longer in familiar territory, I questioned every turn, every inch of my path, wondering what lurked within the darkness. There were times when, even along the bottom of the ocean, through the chilled waters, creatures moved with enough force to knock me astray. I began to miss the comfortable wails of sea life as near silence, aside from the faintest notes of that haunting song, filled the ocean.

Eventually, I was sure the sun had risen high above, but nothing changed this far down. A tiny glowing light zoomed past me, or perhaps I flew by it, and though I wanted to stop and investigate, the siren's call had grown louder, and I could feel the urgency within the tones. Another lighted object moved by, and then several more, before I realized I was swimming through scattered sea sprites. Remembering my mother's journal entry, I sped up, confident I was getting closer to the hidden city Kai had urged me to find. There would be something there. Someone that could help me. And that was worth everything.

Still nearly blind, I slammed directly into a solid figure with leathery skin. No scales. I pulled back just in time to avoid rows of jagged teeth. A jaw snapped closed behind me and I could do nothing but swim far and fast away, sometimes moving in the wrong direction as I avoided whatever chased me.

I was so tired, and my muscles ached more than they had after hours of working on that home with Rhogan, or hours in bed with Kai. The beast was so close, I felt it brush against the fan of my tail. The song grew louder, but it didn't matter. I could do nothing more than search the deepest shadows, looking for a place to outsmart a monster I couldn't even see. Another sea sprite passed me, and then a swarm of them, glowing a soft amber color, moved in. I dared a look over my shoulder, only to see the sea sprites dashing in and out toward my assailant. They provided enough light to show the rugged face of a rubelas.

I'd only ever heard of the beasts through my father's warnings. With the body of a shark and the head of a goblin, I didn't stick around to test my luck against one. Blood in the water was a guarantee of death at these depths. I relied on the sprites that continued to distract the creature as a wave of panic sent me racing toward the urgent siren song.

Afraid of what else I might find in the depths, I pushed to the surface. After so long in pure darkness, the sun threatened to blind me as I adjusted to the strength of the golden sunlight glinting off the water. I brought a hand to my eyes to shield the gleam, only to realize, though it did reflect off the water, the blinding light came instead from a pure gold crescent moon that appeared to sit just atop the water's surface.

"Come closer, child. I am not your enemy. At least not today."

I recognized the tone of the voice that called me.

Swimming toward the gilded moon, I noticed more and more of the sea sprites glowing within the water, along with the beautiful siren sunning atop it. Their tiny water wings were twins to the ones Rhogan had grown when he'd worn his evada pearl.

My eyes blurred and my heart stopped. I looked away and back again. Though I knew it couldn't be, the siren was identical to my mother. I swam closer. The color of her hair matched mine. Her golden skin a mirror of my own. High cheekbones and full lips. It was too uncanny to be a coincidence.

"Close your jaw, child." The siren slipped from the moon and into the water without a splash, appearing before me within seconds. "We've been waiting."

I moved backward. "How did you know I'd come?"

Reaching for my hands, the siren squeezed them tightly as a cunning smile crossed her face. "We are family, Lyra. You are meant to be here. To live among our people. Perhaps your mother learned her lesson the hard way, but now you know."

"Know what exactly?"

She tsked, shaking her head as she watched me with the same cruel look my mother would give my father. "The world out there is dangerous and brutal. Here, within our golden city, you are safe."

I pulled my hands from hers. "Who are you?"

With the quirk of an eyebrow and an instant look of disdain, she scoffed. I didn't trust her. I'd been burned so many times. So many lies had been hidden from me, I'd be a fool to put any faith into this stranger. Rather than speak words, she pulled me below the water and the shock that wracked me caused her to chuckle.

The legends hadn't done it justice. A great city spread before us as if Halemi had been dipped in gold and sunk into the ocean. Buildings encrusted with jewels, pathways paved in gold, and sirens of every color filled my view. I'd nearly forgotten my hand was being tugged until I looked into beautiful, dangerous eyes.

"This is your new home, Lyra. I am your aunt Talea and I'm going to watch over you from now on."

I jerked, narrowing my eyes. "I don't need a keeper."

Looking down her nose at me, she argued, "Of course you do. You've lost your mother, your song, and your way. Who knows what kind of poison your father has slipped into your mind. I'm afraid you need me more than ever. Come."

As I followed her vibrant orange tail into the golden city, I reminded myself that Kai told me to come here. It wasn't just a dream. There was something here that could help me, and I meant to find it, regardless of Talea's thoughts. I could play along. Play the part. It was the one thing I was good at.

"It's beautiful." I reached out a hand, gliding it across the gleaming roof of a building as we descended.

"Isn't it? It's a thousand years in the making. Desirable and sought after by every living soul in the world, and yet here you are, so blessed. Remember that."

"I'm not sure it's as popular as you think it is, but it is magnificent."

"You don't know the minds of the world like we do. You've lived a very tainted life."

I bit my tongue to keep from returning the insult, and as we continued through the golden city, all eyes were on us. Some sirens whispered, some glared, few smiled. Eventually, we entered the largest building on the far side. Not quite a castle, but certainly larger than any home I'd ever seen.

"You'll stay here," she said, leading me into a small room with jeweled walls and odd furnishings. "I'll come and get you for dinner."

"Wait," I stopped her just before she slipped out. "It was your song that called me here, wasn't it?"

She dipped her chin, her blonde hair fanning around her with the movement. "It was."

"Why?"

Talea leaned against the arched door frame with her shoulder, crossing her arms as she contemplated. Hesitation shaped her features as she pursed her lips and tapped her fingers along her arms. "I thought you'd get here and trust me right away since you followed my song across the ocean. I can see it will take more than that, and I commend you for your cautious nature. I can assure you, though, as long as you remain respectful and follow the few rules within our city, you are perfectly safe. I've called you here because this is the city of sirens and quite simply, it's where you belong."

"Why did you send the letters? Why me?"

"Did you not think it odd they began as soon as my sister died?"

Hearing my mother referenced as a sister was jarring. There were so few siblings in our world. "I had no idea my mother had a sister. Why go through all of this? Why wouldn't she have told me? Or you, within the letters?" I began to swim back and forth, working a thousand questions through my mind as quickly as they poured from me. "Why did she leave here and never come back? How did you manage to send me the letters?"

"Gods child, must we discuss it all in one go?" She gestured to the giant clamshell, bidding me to rest.

As she worked through what she'd be willing to share with me, I took in the room. The sirens were different than the sea queen. Morwena had preferred her high fae form and her castle used magic to emanate life above water. Things didn't float around there; they used beds and tables and things you'd find in the other courts. Not here.

There were no windows through the building, only openings in the walls to let the sea current float through. The bedroom I was assigned had no bed. Instead, a thick, blue netted grass drifted from the ceiling. A hammock? Rather than shelves or framed artwork, the walls were painted in intricate murals depicting scenes of sirens and forlorn pirates.

"Your mother was always a free spirit. Since she was a kip. Our mother died giving birth to her and because I was quite a bit older, I transitioned into my mother's role as the leader, but I also helped to raise her. We are not allowed to leave Zariya. If we do, we cannot return. You must remember that above all else. If you should sneak off tonight, you'll never find your way back." She smiled sadly. "Your mother knew what she was doing when she left. She stole the Bloodstone. I think she thought if she had the gem with her, it would somehow allow her to find her way back. But now we're being hunted. That stone was created and kept for punishment, should we see fit to do so. Now it's caused nothing but heartache.

"I thought if I sent you the letters, with tasks you were used to doing, you would learn to trust me. I have a messenger, you've met him, given him that song? He does my bidding. It's safer for him, as a male, to run errands. He was almost always successful in delivering letters."

I bit my bottom lip, considering what she'd said. "A.T... *Aunt Talea.* But how was he able to make it back into the city?"

The sharp trill of her laugh caught me off guard. I cocked my head to the side, waiting for her to collect herself. Perhaps she was losing her sanity.

"Males are not allowed within this city." She pressed her palms into her forehead. "That should have been the first rule I told you. I thought it would be obvious. Such an innocent thing. I meet him at our borders, and he does what I ask because he thinks one day I'll grant him passage here."

Lying must have come naturally for our kind. I considered telling her about the songs and the Bloodstone I had brought, but I decided to wait, hoping an advantageous time would present itself.

She eyed me carefully. "Tell me what you know about your mother and father's relationship. And of her death."

I looked away, again considering what I should say. More than anything, this felt like a test. "I knew my father was just like every other male on this planet. Cunning and disgusting. And sadly, my mother fell for his trap. He stole the gem, then stole her song."

"Your mother and I exchanged letters as often as we could without him knowing. It's how my messenger has always been able to find you. She was going to tell you everything the night your father had her killed. She'd decided she didn't care what it meant for her own life. He got to her first and when he realized her plan, that was it." She rose in the water, hardening her face as she reached for my own. "We will never speak of your father again. What's done is done."

I pulled away from her grip. "My father was chasing down the sea witch. He learned my mother knew of her existence and I'm sure he wanted to use her to find the Kraken's treasure."

"Your father was a gods damned fool. The sea witch has the power to move mountains, to resurrect the dead, to build cities, and bury them. To use her for a futile hunt would be such a waste of time." She moved to the door once more. "Now I mean it, I never want to hear you speak of that vile creature again. Let his memory die with him. He deserves nothing more."

My heart was beating so fast I needed to move. To swim far and fast just to expel the speed at which my mind raced. Sheer will power held me in that spot as she finally left the room. I sped across the small bedroom and shut the door behind her, then swam around and around and around as I let my mind repeat those words over again. *Resurrect the dead.*

This was why Kai wanted me to come. I'd never been so sure of anything in my entire life. Even the seer had confirmed his life was meant to be long. I just needed to do the impossible. Find the sea witch. I had to believe I was a lot closer than my father had ever come. My mother had known her, so I had to believe that meant my aunt also had.

I settled down into the netted grass bed and let my mind wander, building a plan to coax the information from her. I'd tell her everything. About my fallen mate and my broken heart, my severed soul. My stolen song and how I'd betrayed him. Of how I wanted nothing more than to bring back the single fae I loved more than my own life. The real question was, would she listen?

CHAPTER 37

A young siren, with bright green hair that matched the colorful tones of her tail, came to get me for dinner hours later. I'd hoped for a private audience with Talea so I could explain everything that had happened and what I needed most from her, but instead, we entered a great hall with dim lighting and warm waters. Every siren from the city must have come for dinner and, judging by their actions, quite a bit more.

Hardly any of them wore covers around their breasts. Most were exposed and there was no question why. Though they simply floated around the room, no tables of course, many were lost in the throes of passion as they waited for food to arrive. Music pumped through the room with deep bass notes and even the water moved to the rich tones.

I was escorted to my aunt. She sat at the front of the room atop a tall stone pillar with another siren on her lap. Holding the siren's hair twisted in her fingers, she moaned as she kissed her deeply. I floated there, waiting for her to acknowledge me, but instead, she dragged her tongue down her guest's chest, pulling a perked nipple into her mouth. The siren groaned as she writhed in my aunt's lap, living solely for the pleasure.

I turned. Though most fae were open sexual beings, especially at social gatherings, I was not. Not anymore. A memory of the person I used to be flashed through my mind. Once upon a time, I would have loved this. But now? The thought of hands on me that did not belong to Kai made my stomach roll.

There was not a male in sight, just as my aunt had explained. They were simply for breeding. Here, the females provided the pleasure, the pain, the entirety of camaraderie. It was then that I realized I could never tell my aunt my plan. My desires would not matter when it came to having a mate. They simply did not exist in this place, where they thought they knew everything about the world, and yet had no idea.

A brooding siren with blue hair rested her hand upon her chin as she lingered unamused nearby, waiting for food. I thought I might join her until she cut a cold glare in my direction and turned away. Another across from her waved a couple of fingers at me, but she also turned. I was not welcome here. Be it for the mistakes my mother made in stealing the Bloodstone, or my own tainted background, full of males, I had no idea. The sooner I could leave, the better.

I gave up waiting for my aunt's acknowledgment and backed away, listening to the sexual sounds she and her partner made as we waited for dinner to be served. I didn't know what I'd expected. Mindless sea fae serving the dishes, maybe. But when a line of sirens came through, releasing nets of captured fish, I had to commend the sirens for at least one thing. They hadn't taken slaves. That might have been their only redeeming quality, making them better than Morwena.

The sirens attacked. Snatching the schools of silvered fish from the room as they dined with sharpened claws and even sharper teeth.

A throat was cleared near me, pulling the squirming room to a silent halt as my aunt rose from her pillar.

"In honor of my niece finally coming home, I'd like to say a few words. It is quite unconventional, bringing an outsider into our city, but you all remember my sister. Loved her once, before she betrayed us all. Let us not pin the sins of my sister onto her daughter, but instead teach her the way of the siren. I implore you all to keep an eye on her as she learns what it means to live among the greatest species to inhabit this world. Where we love openly," she looked down to the female she'd been pleasuring, "where we celebrate the roles of females. Each of the gods gave a drop of their power to the ocean and thus we were created. Let us not forget that. Every siren"—she narrowed her eyes on me—"even those that are half land dweller are still priceless."

She sat on her pillar once more and, without any acknowledgment of her words, the swarm of sirens began to feast. Be it on each other or the meal, all became occupied yet again. Except for the blue-haired siren and my aunt, who both stared at me as if they waited for me to crawl on the ocean floor, thanking them for taking me in, as though I was not worthy. Sirens were assholes.

Uninterested in eating, I swam back to my room. They could look down on me all they wanted. I wouldn't be there long, and gods knew I wouldn't return, even if it were possible. Sitting on the edge of a sealed clamshell, I fanned my tail through the water as I considered my next move. I needed to figure out how my mother knew the sea witch. If she was here somewhere, I would have to find her quickly.

A firm knock at the door startled me and I leaped up as if I needed to hide the thoughts within my mind. Realizing how ridiculous that was, I allowed my shoulders to relax, taking on the role of the poor half-siren that needed rescued. "Come in."

The blue-haired siren entered, pert nose high in the air. "Talea sent me to make sure you hadn't run off like your mother on the first night. I assured her you hadn't been exposed to enough treasure to find something to steal yet, but she insisted."

I grazed my nails along my palm to keep from lashing out. "Still here." I kept my voice calm and sweet as I pictured murdering her in this borrowed room.

"For now," she said over her shoulder as she swam out. The click of the lock amused and infuriated me at the same time. It would never keep me in, but the audacity to treat me as a prisoner made my blood boil.

"Mirin will take you to tour the city. You're to be back by lunch for etiquette classes and I expect you to stay for dinner tonight, instead of scampering off." My aunt loomed in the doorway; arms crossed as they always were.

"You do realize I am not a kip. I don't need a chaperone, nor do you need to lock me into a room like a prisoner. I came here of my own free will."

"You do not know right from wrong yet, Lyra. You will do as you're told until I'm confident you do. Your mother left me alone. I miss her more than there are words. I'll not have the same repeated. You're to learn to rule over the sirens, just as I do. Unless a pregnancy happens before I'm returned to the salt, you'll be next to lead. And right now, not a soul trusts you."

I jerked at her words. "I don't want to lead these sirens. I just want to be left alone."

She moved in until she was inches from my face. "I didn't want to lead these sirens either. I wanted to be free with my sister. But that didn't happen, and such is life. She's not coming back, so you're all I have."

I lurched back in response. "What if she could come back? You said yourself the sea witch can resurrect people. Where is she? Can't we ask her to fix this? To bring my mother back?"

She eyed me carefully before answering. "The sea witch hates me. She may hate us all, in fact. She'd never agree to it."

"Why does she hate you?"

Talea lifted her chin as she rose in the water to stare down at me. "She used to live here and I teased her endlessly. We were just kips when she found us, choosing to grow up here. That's why your mother spoke of her in her journal entries, and that's likely why your father became obsessed with her after your mother's death."

"She hates you, but I'm different, right? Not full siren, not full fae. Maybe she wouldn't hate me."

My aunt shook her head. "Remove this from your mind, girl. It would never be worth the price that wicked thing would ask. What's done is done. You are here now."

She left the room without another word.

Within minutes, the blue-haired siren appeared. "I'm supposed to take you on a tour, but I can think of at least a thousand other things I'd rather be doing than parading a leech around the city. Be a doll and tell your aunt we had a great time." She pulled the door shut and the lock clicked once more.

Something told me Marin had more to gain from my absence than presence. I unlocked the door and followed her out. "Wait."

She spun around, looking over my shoulder to the door and down to the key in her hand before tucking it away. "I guess escaping does run in the family."

"Apparently. Look, I don't need your tour, but could you point me to where my mother's things might be stored?"

She scrunched her nose. "What makes you think we kept anything from that traitor?"

"I'm going to need you to shut the fuck up about my mother. She's not here to defend herself and I'm trying really hard not to hit you in the face. Don't push me." I waited for a retort, but she kept her shock to a minimum and let me continue. "My aunt is still obsessed with her, otherwise I probably wouldn't be here. Also, I know enough about sirens to know you're hoarders. Anything of value is kept."

She pointed down the hall. "Her room hasn't been touched since she left. Go to the end, turn right, go again to the end. It will be the final door on the left, just beside a giant ruby painted on the wall. I won't cover for you. If your aunt finds out you've broken in, I'll tell her you hit me and ran off on your own."

"That actually sounds like something I'd do."

As her eyes widened, I raced away, following the directions she'd given me. There had to be more. Talea had sent me a page from my mother's journal with her name on it, hoping I'd seek her out. But that journal had to have come from somewhere. Hopefully somewhere that had more information on the sea witch.

I opened the door carefully, watching over my shoulder as if I were being watched. The room was dark, with only a soft glow of light coming from a light blue rock embedded into the wall. Heavy trunks lined with gold covered the entire floor. A worn hammock hung in front of a mirrored wall. That was it. Nothing floated in the room, nothing more covered the walls.

I closed my eyes and tried to imagine my mother sleeping in the small net. Or packing her treasure chests. Or brushing her long, beautiful hair in front of that mirror.

She was never overly loving, but she had been mine, and the loss of her hit all over again as I moved through her childhood room. Losing my mother had been the catalyst to losing my mate, and both losses had changed the way I saw the world. They had changed the way I saw myself.

A small pile of charmed books lay in the corner atop a chest. I opened them, thumbing through the stories of siren heroines and brooding pirates. Apparently, my mother had been a dreamer and a romantic. I wouldn't have guessed, but then maybe my father sucked the life out of her. I pulled the heavy lids of the chests open one by one, finding mostly sashes and more books. Nothing handwritten, though. A few trinkets were tucked into the lid of one chest. To the untrained eye, that was all this room would offer. A glimpse of the past.

But I had eyes educated by the previous occupant of this room, and she had always taught me that few things worth finding were hidden in plain sight. Searching for disturbances in the ordinary, I moved my hands along the walls. Behind the mirror was a successful spot, as was the false bottom of a chest. She wouldn't have hidden something tied into her bed, but she would consider hollowing out a book or two.

Overall, I acquired two journals and a few small notes. They must have meant something to her. I hurried back to my room and, taking inspiration from Kai, flashed into my fae form. Switching below the surface was not pleasant this far down, but it was necessary. I stuffed my pockets as if my life depended on it. Because it was beginning to feel as though my freedom absolutely did.

The first journal was nearly useless, aside from confirming the presence of the sea witch, to which my mother described as unnerving when she arrived. Other than that, her journal was filled with memories of playing with Talea and a general disdain for the siren community.

The notes were only wishes my mother had tucked away, dreaming of a different life. While it told me something about her I'd never known, they were of no use now. The second book proved to be far more useful. Not on the whereabouts of the sea witch, but more so on Talea and her obsession with the Bloodstone. She'd begged my mother for it when they were younger. Though it was strange that my grandmother would leave it to my mother and not her eldest daughter.

My room remained silent for the rest of the night. No one came to bring me to a meal, which was fine. I settled into a vivid dream, staring into deep ocean eyes.

"I have a plan, I think," I told him as he caressed my cheek. "I just have to make sure it's the right move."

"It is," he mumbled into my ear, the vibration of his deep voice sending shivers down my spine.

I turned into his palm, knowing the tears falling down my cheeks would be lost to the sea when I woke. "I wish this was real, Kai. I wish more than anything that I could have this with you again. I'll do everything, give everything if that's what it takes. I don't care about my song anymore. That hole within me is so much smaller than the void you left."

"No more nightmares?"

"When Ori told me they'd destroyed my song, something snapped. I was devastated. But now that it's final? Knowing it's gone? I think I'm just accepting that. The pursuit of my song has been a one-way path to misery."

He crushed me in his arms, holding me tight. We stayed there in silence for so long, I worried this was goodbye. As if my mind would no longer conjure these dreams. The thought terrified me. But dream Kai must have known.

"You know, if I'm only going to meet you in your dreams, you could at least sleep naked," he purred into my ear.

I laughed and that was enough to soothe my soul for now. He held me close, his arms the only security I'd felt in so long, and I wished I could lie there forever, never waking again.

"You've been in this room since yesterday and slept the entire day away."

I jolted awake, immediately missing the phantom arms wrapped around me, though his touch lingered on my skin. "The door was locked. I couldn't leave."

Talea ignored my easy lie. "How was your tour? Did you learn the basics?"

"Yes. It was quite enlightening."

"Good."

"Will it be just you and I for dinner?" I asked, yawning as I stretched my hands above my head.

"No. Of course not. We never dine alone. You have one hour." She whipped around and swam away without another word.

I moved from the bed, retying the red sash around my chest as I went over the plan in my mind. If this didn't work, I'd just fight my way out and try to find another way. The siren's golden city was yet another place in this world that wasn't for me.

Making my way through my aunt's home, I found the dining hall packed with sirens, exactly how it was before. The pulse of the music and comfort of the warm water created a lethargic atmosphere as I swam through the room full of famished females and waited in front of my aunt as she caressed her lover.

I pinned her with a look, dragging her attention to me as I twirled Kai's ring on my finger, wishing it could give me the luck I'd need for this.

"Go away. Don't be a nuisance."

"I've had about enough of you treating me like a kip. I'm not your sister and I'm not your pet project. I came here because you called me, but I refuse to be a prisoner in your city. Perhaps the rest of the sirens don't mind your walls, but I sure as hell do."

She shoved the siren from her lap and rose, swimming until she was inches from me. As she so loved to do. I flicked my tail until I was higher and kept my voice low so only she could hear me.

"You are no better than the males of this world, controlling these females under the guise of protection and superiority. I have something I think you'll want, and I believe you have something that I want."

Narrowing her eyes, she matched my volume as she realized I'd come to bargain. "I doubt you have anything I want."

I switched to my fae form. The room stilled as I pointed to the songs and the Bloodstone I'd tied onto the pockets, then switched back before she could grab them. "I want to bring my mother back, and the only way that happens is if you tell me where the sea witch is."

She threw her head back and laughed so hard it filled the room. "You are just like your mother."

"I will take that as a compliment. I will return these items to you if you tell me where she is." She would never comply if I gave her the real reason, so I heightened my chances by using her weakness. My mother.

"What makes you think I know where she is?"

"I've been reading up on your history with my mother. Before I came, I read almost every journal. Even locked in this city, you chased my mother around the world, writing secret letters to her. She wrote about them in her journals. My father knew, but he hoped one day to find this city and deliver you all to the queen. So, it didn't bother him. Until my mother told you she was ready to tell me the truth. And then she was killed.

"But you knew that because then you pursued me. Which makes me believe you have more tabs on the outside world than you let on." I brushed my hair over my shoulder, watching her carefully. "A siren's greatest pleasure is the treasure she covets. The sea witch was here, in your grasp, and you let her get away. My mother believed you were cruel to her as a kip because you wanted her to fear you. To work under you. She wasn't interested in being your minion, so she left. Just as I will. I'd bet my father's treasure you've kept tabs on her, too. She's too valuable not to. And too dangerous now that you've made an enemy of her."

"Clever girl," she said, moving her nails across her bottom lip. "I do hope you'll tell my sister hello for me if you can pay the witch's price. You'll find her nestled somewhere within the Cliffs of Mar." She held out a hand. "Now give me my treasure and be gone, you wretched thing."

CHAPTER 38

There was nothing within me that felt a trace of remorse as I left the siren's golden city behind, knowing I'd never find it again. Males were tools for breeding there. Lured into their city, bred, and killed. Perhaps that was a siren's prerogative, but it wasn't mine. I had no idea who I was anymore, but it wasn't a siren. I wasn't a land dweller. I wasn't helpless. I wasn't free. Not hateful. Certainly not happy. I just… was. But this moment in my life mattered. Within this frame of mind, I realized I'd sacrifice every last piece of who I was for Kaitalen. Maybe I was selfish, but not when it came to him.

As I crossed the treacherous waters toward the Cliffs of Mar, I stayed closer to the surface, bathing in the warm sunlight as I swam for hours and hours. The moon rising reminded me of my dream and with it, my desperate need to right my wrongs. To bring him back, if only to tell him the full truth and apologize. To make him see that I never meant for any of this to happen and I certainly never planned for him to die angry and heartbroken on a battlefield.

I thought back to the day he rescued me, the look of utter betrayal on his face causing the growing lump in my throat to sharpen. The shock and guilt of my own body rose to a breaking point as I recalled those final words to me. *I never want to be reminded of the sea again.*

Farther south than I'd realized, I knocked my tail on a jagged rock protruding from the murky ocean. Black sands on a foreign land in the distance encompassed the Cliffs of Mar. I'd have to be extremely careful as I moved forward. The dark sand on the ocean bed, camouflaging the deadly rocks leading to the Cliffs, made me nearly blind. A hiding place well-chosen.

I slowed my pace to only two or three thrusts of my tail at a time, my hands before me as I felt myself being pulled lower into the water. My vision, though faint, blurred. I went from moving in slow motion to watching tracers behind my hands in front of me. Feeling as if I'd drank a barrel of wine, I brought my palms to my eyes, trying to clear my eyesight. The world fell black around me, encompassed in so much shadow, the dark sands leached away the starlight, leaving nothing but a black mass as I fell to the ocean floor. I remembered to swim, only to forget again as my mind began to race, my life flashing before my eyes as foreign magic swept me away.

Standing on the starboard bow, I looked up to see my father holding my mother by the wrists as he snarled in her face. She glanced over to me and flashed a vicious smile. She was fine. All was well. Just a silly game my parents played from time to time. I went back to singing a beautiful melody as the sun burned my naked toes.

The memory faded away as another began to take form. I shook my head, demanding my mind to take control, but it didn't work.

"It's only a loaf of bread, my girl. Walk up, distract with one hand as you swipe with the other. A magic trick, Lyra. Pretend you are a magician."

"Okay, Momma." Nerves rattling in my bones, I did as I was told, flawlessly tucking the loaf of bread into my pouch before the tall lady at the market knew it was gone. I met eyes with a girl who must have been my age, hiding in the shade around a corner. She used her small wings to fan herself as she watched me. I lifted the flap of my pouch to give her the bread. I knew we didn't need it. The task was only practice. A lesson.

"No, Lyra," my mother said, pulling my hand away, her sharp nails digging into

my skin. "We reward ourselves for success by keeping our treasures. We never give them away."

"Yes, Momma."

The face of that girl had stayed with me, as did the steep lesson from my mother. I groaned, wishing the memories would stop, but they continued as I crawled along the seafloor, never once forgetting my mission.

My cheek burned bright red with the sting of the slap my father had just given me.

"I don't care how you do it. Just see it done. By tomorrow."

I turned away, refusing to let the fiery tears be seen by a male that did not deserve the power they would give him. My mother had just mysteriously died and he was taking it extremely hard, staying up all hours of the night just to read her journals, as if he only wished to hear her voice again. He'd tasked me with a job that always took the two of us. I'd have to go without a lookout this time, which made it all the more dangerous, stealing from one of the queen's favorite advisors.

I pushed my hands along the black grains of sands, letting them bury inches deep as I crawled in what I hoped was the right direction. I'd nearly forgotten about that job. It was the first time I had to use my song to escape after being caught. I'd succeeded, but only just.

"I can't even look at a female right now," the commander grumbled. "I don't want to be alone forever, but I don't want to go through the shit you and Fen do either."

Oh, gods. Not this. Anything but these memories. "Please make it stop." I was swept away again.

"Stop." He pulled away reluctantly, resting his forehead on mine. "Sorry. I'm sorry."

"It's one night, not a lifetime."

If only I'd known then what he would become. "I know this is you, sea witch. I'm begging you. I can't see him like this. I can't live through these memories, knowing how it ended."

"But has it ended?" the smoky voice echoed through my mind.

The warmth of tears hidden by the sea fell down my cheeks as my emotions exhausted every part of my body.

Standing in the kitchens of Morwena's castle, I watched Leora hustling around, throwing dishes together in disarray as she looked back to the door several times. She burned her hand and dropped three dishes before Kai walked in.

"Where is she?" he asked, fuming.

"She did not come, my lord."

He dropped the parcels he'd been holding on the table and began picking up the pieces of glass from the floor. "Please don't call me that. Just Kai, okay? Show me what to do and I'll do it."

"But it's not your job. You've no need to work in the kitchens." Her light dimmed with her sad words.

"We're a team. If one person can't pull their weight, it's not your job to suffer for it. I don't mind helping."

"She is not used to work. She will do better next time."

"Those are kind words for a selfish female that does not deserve them."

The vision faded away, replaced by another that wasn't my own. The sea witch's magic was stronger than I could resist.

Leora stood on the island alone. I was supposed to go with her, but I didn't want my father to reveal his relationship with me. Surrounded by Morwena's slimy advisors, they lashed out at her as she shivered, holding a crate of food she'd spent so much time preparing for them.

"Why should you be free, lesser? When we are stuck on this gods forsaken island with nothing but each other for company."

Leora opened her mouth to answer, but another advisor kicked the crate from her hands, causing her to yelp in surprise.

"Free us, or we will rip you to pieces and no one will ever find you."

She moved slowly toward the gate. She needed only three more steps backward to be out of reach, but instead, another came in and pinned her to the ground, lifting a fist high above her as his face turned red with anger.

A scream that shook the world came from outside the gate as a giant tentacle reached inside and swept Leora away from the menacing crowd. The gate slammed shut.

The memory faded far quicker than my guilt. Which seemed to be the theme of these recollections.

"What makes you worthy of my presence, siren?" a voice asked.

"Nothing. Absolutely nothing."

Dim light finally glowed in the distance and, though I anticipated another haunting memory, the fog over my mind lifted with the darkness. I'd entered the sea witch's lair and judging by her death glare, she was not happy to see me.

I swam forward, keeping a respectable distance as I tried not to eye the walls lined with skeletons. I had no idea how to introduce myself, having just entered her hideaway without an invitation. A cool calm settled over me as I showed a confidence I didn't feel. "My name is Lyra, and I've come to ask for a spell. I'd like to bring my mate back from the Ether."

Her hair was dark as the sands around her. The glowing lair gave a hint to the tentacles below her heavy body. She threw her head back and laughed, the deep sound echoing off the cavern walls. "Just a little spell. Why Lyra? I can see your brown aura. You're selfish and guarded. But something is missing. Where is your blue?"

"I don't understand."

Her eyes swept over me once more as she studied the waters around me. "You are a siren, are you not?"

"Half."

"Born with a song though, yes?"

Warning bells rose like a sudden storm. Revealing my vulnerability would make me easy prey. Lying would get me killed. "Yes." I dropped my head. "It was stolen."

"Ask for that instead. A song is a much lower cost than a life. Especially for a creature with such a selfish nature."

"I am flawed and even though those memories were meant to break me and show me how horrible I am, it didn't work. I know my heart and can see how far I've come. Every one of those moments molded me into the person I am now. I have regrets, but I don't want to live in those choices. I am better than that. And I think my mate, though I shattered him, still believed in me. I'll do anything. Pay whatever price. Just please help me bring him back. I don't want my song anymore. Only him."

Her mouth twisted into a sly smirk. "Would you trade places with him? Give your own life for his?"

"If that's what it took to make this right, I would." My heart pounded in my ears until they were nearly aching, and my anxious nerves vibrated below my skin. This was it. The cost was my life. Talea had warned me. "I would be with my mother. Maybe that's enough."

"Do you not wish to bring her back instead?"

I imagined who she would be without the torment of my father looming over her. To give her the life she deserved, instead of the life she'd lived. Was her life any more or less valuable than Kai's? I tumbled her words over and over in my mind before answering.

"I am selfish. I would still choose my mate. The male that loved me even when I didn't deserve it. Even as I deceived him and lied to him."

The sea witch slithered forward, her round appendages carrying her through the water as her face, beautiful and haunting, moved into the light. She studied me with amethyst eyes as she tapped her fingertips together, deciding if I was worthy enough for my request. "All magic comes at a cost. This would require a great deal of magic. What have you brought to wield such power?"

"You could have my ship. In payment."

She tsked, shaking her head. "You misunderstand, girl. A magical item is needed for such a task. One with great power within. If you've brought nothing, I cannot help you. As simple as it sounds, you can't trade your life for his."

"What about this?" I lifted Vexyr's key from around my neck and held it out to her. "Surely this has great power."

She chuckled. "You do not understand the magnitude of great power, Lyra. I need something greater than a glorified hairpin."

I pulled back, feeling defeat swarm around my severed soul. I pictured myself old and wrinkled with gray hair, still waiting to be with him. I couldn't live an eternity without him. I'd sooner face The Mists than that fate.

"I could find something. Steal an item of your choosing. Please." I fell to the ocean floor before her, begging without shame. The grains of sand burned below my scales.

"Now that's an idea," she all but sang as I lifted my head to meet her eyes. "There is something you could retrieve for me."

"Name it. Anything."

All movement in the sea stilled and she loomed over me, squinting her eyes. "That confident, are you?"

"That desperate."

"Perfect." She drew the word out until it settled in the still water. "There is a stone buried deep within a prized treasure. It glows with the power of the sun but is protected by a fearsome beast. You must retrieve the stone without waking the beast and bring it back to me. The Sunstone will be unmistakable. You must return within three days' time. Do we have a deal?"

"Yes. Where do I go?"

She held out her hand, palm up. "Your hand, siren."

I didn't breathe as I placed my hand in hers. She turned it over, pressing a nail so hard into my palm it broke the skin. "With this blood, a deal is struck. Retrieve the stone and return within three days and I will bring your mate back to this land. It will be his choice to stay or to return to the Ether."

The world swayed around me as the drop of blood floated intact, lingering in the water between us. She captured it with a vial and turned away.

"Try not to die. Oh, and don't touch anything else. Tempting as it may be, thief."

Without warning, the world fell out from under me. My stomach rolled as many times as my body as I traveled through oblivion, wondering if I'd just made a deal with a demon and not a witch. Blinding light struck me, and while my eyes adjusted, I waved my tail in a panic, trying to gain control of my tumbling body.

As the world came into view, I found myself deep below the ocean, surrounded by the greatest treasure known to fae. Which meant only one thing. I'd be stealing from the Kraken.

CHAPTER 39

Blinding light shot through the piled treasure in beams coming from somewhere within the trove. I could only guess it was the Sunstone. In awe, I slowly rotated, eyeing the overflowing chests stacked so high they created towering walls in a perfect circle. The brightness of the stone gave each jewel a thousand features, each coin and brick of gold unrivaled dimension. It was no wonder so many seafolk spent their lives seeking this euphoria. I thought of my father. Though it was impressive, was this treasure worth more than my mother's life? More than my freedom? To float within these waters while danger lurked so close by?

Finding the Kraken's treasure was one thing, taking a single item would be an entirely different story. I lifted my hand and studied the sea glass ring on my finger. The light from the Sunstone gave it more intricate depth than I'd ever seen. Had I any sense of self-preservation, I might have stopped to ask the sea-witch what she meant to do with the stone after I'd retrieved it. Surely, something so powerful had a much bigger fate than fulfilling my greatest wish.

The entire ceiling, completely black as though I were swimming beneath a mountain, shifted above me, causing the water to roll so strongly it sent me tumbling. I looked up and my mouth went dry as I realized I was not in a cove but nestled under the fearsome body of the Kraken itself. His form went on forever. There was not a speck of sky or ocean surface above. Only the beast of legends and lore. A monster so large, the hydra was dwarfed in comparison.

Unable to see his bulbous head or the end of any of his eight gray tentacles, I closed my eyes, trying not to cringe at the suckers above me that opened and closed in turn as the beast slumbered. I didn't want to know how the sea witch had known it slept.

I swam as carefully as possible, noting all movement within the water. For so many reasons, my life was on the line. It stood to reason the Sunstone was not buried. If it were, its light would be dimmed, if not smothered.

They said there used to be a god that ruled the sea, but the Kraken defeated him long ago. Now, only seven gods ruled the world, which was why the sea had become an untamed entity, living and breathing and dealing death. The sound of water gurgling caused me to pause. To study the pattern of bubbles as I held still, a statue, until once again the water grew silent. My eyes raked over the glistening seafloor, made solely of piles of coin and the occasional skeleton. He'd hoarded everything from silver shields to golden statues, some erect, some laid over.

Slow as a sea slug, I swam through the enormous trove, avoiding touching a single piece as I went, fearing something magical would alarm the Kraken. A chest full of pearls caught my eye. Not because of the sheer size of them, but the humming that came from within. As if a muffled siren's song was buried far below. For a moment, I thought it might be mine. Something familiar lingered just under my skin, but even if it were something that would replace it, that wasn't what I'd come for.

Following the opposite direction to my shadow lying on the ground, I knew I was getting closer. My eyes burned as though I stared directly into the center of the sun. The source of light came from just ahead. Shielding my eyes as I weaved through the towering piles of coin, drowned and useless, I finally spotted the Sunstone. I was unable to look directly at it. I'd have to blindly swipe it, which would make me a giant fucking beacon, before somehow managing to sneak away. All the while, having absolutely no idea where I was in the ocean. Even then, I only had three days to find my way back to the sea witch.

I closed my eyes and thought of Kai. I pictured him beside me, leaning his shoulder into me as he grinned, wiggling his eyebrows as he waited for me to take the stone. There was a calmness that spread over me, and I had to believe it was him, truly there with me as I reached forward and attempted to swipe the stone.

I grabbed a clear box the stone was locked in.

A horrifying screech burst my eardrums and the water began to spin, jerking me into a circle, as a massive whirlpool was created by the tentacles of the Kraken. Losing control of every muscle in my body, I could do nothing but hold the massive box under my arm as I was whipped through the water like seaweed in a storm.

Tumbling this way and that, I couldn't orient myself without the use of my hands. I couldn't let go of the box either. Unable to look into the gleaming Sunstone, I used every muscle in my tail to remain upright as the Kraken moved above me, scattering his precious treasure. There were no holes to unlock with my nails. This box was locked with magic.

I didn't have a chance of survival. The beast was more than a thousand times my size. I felt blood pouring from my nose as I tumbled. Although I tried like hell to whip my tail against the pull of the water, it sucked me further and further into the eye of the whirlpool. Beating his tentacles against the water, I had only moments before he'd smash me. It would only take one time. One strike and I'd be nothing more than salt to the sea.

Only then did I remember the key around my neck. Opening the box would at least give me leverage to balance myself. Spinning out of control, I lifted the long necklace and shoved the key into the box, feeling the case dissolve around my fingers until the Sunstone began to fall. I waved my hand blindly, trying to catch it, but as my body tumbled, the Kraken moved again, and in a sudden jerk of the water, the stone was gone.

I rubbed my fingers over the sea glass ring on my finger. "I'm so sorry, my love. I've failed you twice."

With no other choice, I turned. No longer trying to swim against the current, I swam with it. My head throbbed, my body ached and my heart was broken. It felt as if admitting defeat meant losing him twice. At least this way, I'd die too. Maybe that was always the way it was supposed to happen.

The light from the sun above dimmed as a single tentacle rose above me. I squeezed my eyes shut, terrified of the pain that would follow, and swam like hell.

I nearly made it. But 'nearly' didn't save a soul. The tentacle crashed down on the fan of my tail and I screamed as the pain of a thousand knives shot through my body, sinking to the sand with a tail that would likely never move again.

My body was pulled into the eye of the whirlpool and I crashed into the ocean floor just in time for another tentacle to come down on top of me. The claw at the tip sliced into my abdomen as the water claimed me, and the entire world faded away to nothing.

I thought I'd see him. That when I died, he would be there to greet me; to finally tell me how he felt. To tell him 'I'm sorry.' The words he was owed. But he didn't, because every encounter I'd had with him since his death was not real. Desperate dreams of longing and heartache had caused my mind to imagine the things he'd say. The way he'd touch me and soothe my aching soul.

He didn't come. As I stood on fae legs in a pitch-black expanse of nothingness, I knew the truth of it all. He would never forgive me. He'd told me he never wanted to see me again, and he'd meant it. Wren was wrong. I fell to my knees as hot, angry tears burned down my face. I hated me. All of me. I was as everyone said. Selfish and hateful. Deserving of nothing but the seeds I'd sewn. Stealing from fae with nearly nothing, only for sport. Betraying the one fae in my life who'd never lied to me.

I think I felt another sliver of my soul rip away as I dug further into my own self-loathing. I'm not sure how I expected anyone to love me when I couldn't love myself. Couldn't forgive myself.

"Is this it, then? I'm to spend eternity alone, unable to see my hand in front of my face?"

My voice didn't even echo along the unseen walls. Nothing answered. I moved back to my feet, unscathed in this nothingness, and began to walk.

Grabbing fists full of my hair, I screamed into the abyss, wishing I could just burn the world down. I shouted until my voice was raw, until every tear I had fell to the bleakness. Short, stinted breaths wracked my body as my throat restricted. Full panic set in. The Kraken had killed me, and I'd spend eternity alone, left with only the memories of the vile person I'd been.

I fell to the floor, curling into the fetal position as I clasped Kai's ring to my chest and regretted the day I was born.

CHAPTER 40

I jerked awake. Pain at the sudden movement caused me to hiss. Wiping white sand from my eyes, I peeled them open, a tiny trickle of sunlight falling upon me. I hadn't died, but I felt like I'd been chewed up and halfway digested before being spat out. Moving more slowly than I had in my life, I lifted my aching body from the ground and wracked my memory as I tried to place the island I'd somehow washed up on.

Having no idea how long it had taken to heal, I ran my hands along my abdomen, a red-hot welt had replaced the wound I thought would kill me. Shifting my tail, I winced as immense pain shot through my body. The swelling on my palm was still there, reminding me of my bargain with the sea witch. I'd promised to return and so I would, even if it was empty-handed.

I thought I'd never swim again, but as I inched into the water, focusing only on fanning my injured tail, relief swam through me as it complied. Reluctantly, and not without severe pain, but I could swim.

I'd never missed Leora's cooking as much as I did now, fully drained and having had no sustenance for so long. I captured a fish and ate him slowly. Though not my preference, firegill was full of nutrients and would have to do.

Creeping through the water once more, I swam back toward the Cliffs of Mor, knowing definitively what I would bargain for. What I should have asked for in the first place. I was a fool to think I could bring Kai back. To think for a single moment that he would ever forgive me. That black room had shown me more than enough. On the doorstep of my own death, I'd been alone. Not even my mother came to be with me. I was not worthy of love. I wasn't even sure why the sea had spared my life.

Though I slithered, aching and sore, and contemplating all of my life decisions, I finally made it back to the witch's black, sandy cliffs. The same memories haunted me as I passed through her magical mind games, but still, I pushed on, beyond the fogginess of my mind, across the replay of my most recent failure, consumed by all the bad things I'd ever done.

I wasn't sure who was more surprised I'd made it, but the sea witch's face was lit with anticipation.

She held her hand out, shaking with eagerness. "The Sunstone, siren. Where is it?"

"I failed. And nearly died. I'm not even sure I didn't, for a little bit. But somehow I've made it back."

She huffed. "Why would you bother returning without my treasure?"

"Because a deal is a deal and I said I'd return in three days." My shoulders sank as the defeat weight heavily upon them.

"It's been nearly a week. That ship has sailed."

"I'm sorry. I've returned to ask for something different. Something smaller."

"Get out." She backed away from me and sank upon a large chair made of driftwood and coral.

"No. Please." I threw myself to the ground once more before her, crawling forward as the last tendril of my dignity faded away. "I cannot go on like this. You don't understand."

"You have a nerve asking anything of me when you failed the only task I gave you. What is it you wish for this time? The moon? The stars? The Sea Court's rule?"

"I wish for you to take away all of my memories. My mate died on a battlefield and clearly my fate is not as kind. I'm not strong enough to live without him. I've tried. I cannot do it."

Her face twisted into something like horror. "You would take away your entire life of memories?"

I nodded, fighting back the tears. "There's nothing there worth celebrating, anyway."

"And what would your payment be for such a spell? You have nothing more than you had before."

I looked down to the sea glass ring upon my finger. The one I'd kept hidden the last time she asked for payment. A sharp lump grew in my throat, and I swallowed heavily as I slipped it off, pushing away the memory of the night he gave it to me as he promised me a life of unmeasured happiness. I couldn't think of him anymore. I couldn't suffer through the memories. I dropped the tiny trinket into her hand as my voice broke. "I know it isn't much, but it's all I have."

Tears fell easily down my cheeks, and I'd never been so grateful for the camouflage of water. I'd broken my own heart with this choice, and I deserved the pain. Moving off the ground, I rubbed my chest. Pain rippled through me, though from a broken heart, or damaged body, I wasn't sure.

"You are an absolute fool, and so is Kaitalen for giving this ring to you. I suppose a twist of fate would be just the stroke of luck it promises."

I blinked away the tears. "I don't understand. I never told you his name."

"This ring belongs to me, siren. A long time ago, a wild boy saved my life. It holds a life debt inside, bringing luck to the owner until the debt can be repaid. Had he been wearing this, he might not have died that day. It's probably the only reason you didn't die from waking the Kraken."

My eyes grew wide as I stared at the ring I'd dismissed as sentimental. "How did I not feel that amount of power? And in sea glass, no less."

She lifted her chin high into the air. "If I had wanted you to know it was powerful, I would have made it so. A witch's power is different than yours. It's conjured. Spelled."

I swiped at my tears. "So, you're saying because I had his lucky ring, I'm doubly responsible for his death?"

Tilting her head, she looked at me as if I was the most ridiculous person alive. "I'm saying I can bring him back, you stupid girl. Move away."

I blinked a thousand times, trying to process her words. "You can… but I thought…"

My jaw refused to form any more words as it dropped. Feeling like I needed to sit before I passed out, I sank to the sands of her lair.

Shifting to the side of the room, she lifted the ring to peer through it, then mumbled several words as she placed the ring upon a sleek stone work bench in front of her. Thumbing through an ancient book, she turned to me and winked before pulling a tiny skull from a shelf overhead. The sea witch chanted a lovely melody, though it caused the pressure in the cove to rise so high, I thought my head would explode from the density of it. She blew a string of bubbles over the skull and it crumbled in her fingers. Sprinkling the debris atop the ring, her singing grew louder and more foreign; the words so powerful it felt as if the ocean stilled. As if all the world paused and time itself bowed before the witch stealing a soul from the God of Death with more ease than I'd ever stolen anything.

And then he was there. Every inch of him perfectly intact, including his beautiful cerulean merfae tail. With his back to me, he looked only at the witch as she spoke to him.

"You *are* a hero. Even if you are a little annoying."

Looking up and to the side, he cleared his throat, but I could not see his face. "I saved you," he whispered.

I moved back a little further, fighting the urge to rush forward and throw my arms around him. The last time I'd seen him, he said he never wanted to see me again. I doubted much had changed.

"A life for a life, Kaitalen. My debt is paid. But it is your choice. Do you wish to stay in the Ether, living an eternity of peace?" Her eyes moved, fixing on where I cowered. "Or do you wish to be returned to this world, to live with your mate?"

Only then did he turn. Only then did he realize I'd been waiting behind him.

My ears rang as his beautiful eyes raked down my body, catching on the welt at my stomach, the scratches on my tail. Embarrassed, I ran my fingers through my tangled hair. How I must have looked…

He swam forward until he was a breath away. "Where the sea meets the sky, that's where you'll find me."

Every bone in my body buckled beneath those words. I couldn't hold back the tears as he reached for me. "I'm so sorry, Kai. For all of it. I wish I could take it back. I'm sorry."

"It doesn't matter. None of it matters. We're together now. You, me, and the creepy sea lady."

"Very much not my name," the sea witch snorted.

I laughed through my tears and hugged him again. "I can't believe you're here."

"I promised I'd always find you." He brushed a thumb over my cheek, and it left a trace of heat. Pressing my lips to his, I melted into him, letting him consume me just as thoroughly as he had haunted me. My tongue grazed his and a growl left his throat as he held me firmly.

"Uhm, you can't do that here," the sea witch said from behind us.

Kai turned to her, keeping my hand locked in his. "In case it wasn't obvious, I want to stay."

The ring sitting on the table cracked audibly and the sea witch retrieved it. She cupped in her hands while she closed her eyes and muttered into the gaps between her fingers. A faint whisper of light appeared, then faded away.

"Here." She flipped the ring through the water and Kai caught it.

"Why would you give this back to me?"

"You managed to get yourself killed as soon as you didn't have it anymore. I have no desire to repeat this disaster. The life debt is paid, but what's a little bit of luck between old friends."

"Aw. You big ol' softy." He dropped my hand to hold his out, waiting for the sea witch to take the hug he offered.

Instead, she smirked, snapping her fingers. The world went pitch black around us and I swore I heard her call him annoying as we found ourselves in our fae forms, standing in the hull of my ship, anchored just off the shore of the Flame Court. If there were even courts anymore.

"My lady?"

I couldn't take my eyes off my mate. "Binsin, I'm going to need you to find somewhere else to hang out for a few days."

"Aye," he said with a lightness to his voice. "I think I can handle that. Scuffling and a splash, and he was gone.

Kai stormed toward me, taking my face into his hands as he kissed me, laughed, and then kissed me again. Soft at first and then deeper as something feral within our shared soul called to one another.

For a moment, the world stopped. The air stilled, the spray of water halted; not a breath was heard, as a feeling that was certainly ancient magic melted over us, mending what was severed. Whole once more, our soul sang its own song. The only one I'd ever need. Beautiful melodies filled the world as I studied eyes as pure as the ocean, devouring me.

Just as quickly as the world had stopped, it began again. I reached to move the curls from his eyes, but hesitated at the last second, unsure of everything.

Moving faster than ever, Kai's apt hands ripped the clothes from my body and then his own. His tongue left a searing path from just below my ear, over my collarbone, and down to my exposed breasts. He fell to his knees, continuing to move down as he removed the rest of my leathers, bearing me to the world. I couldn't have cared less. I'd missed this, missed him.

I moved to my own knees, wrapping my arms around him, halting his frantic pace as I slowly kissed him, pushing my hands through his unruly hair. Hot tears stung my eyes, and he froze, pulling away.

"I'm sorry. I can't help the need for you, Lyra."

I shook my head. "It isn't that. I just… you died. I wished on every star in the sky and prayed to every god that I could have this back if only one time. Now that it's happening, I don't ever want it to stop. One time will never be enough."

He took a long, deep breath. "Do you know what happened while I was… gone?"

I shook my head, swiping away the tears now falling freely. Knee to knee, he pulled me to his chest and held me. I listened to his heartbeat as a flash of his mangled body on the battlefield entered my mind. "Were you afraid?"

He chuckled. "Terrified. I lingered in this place. I never went to the Ether. Instead, I sat in a black room alone and watched my life play through my mind. I could feel someone watching me. As if Nealla, the God of Death, was waiting for me to step forward. To agree to leave you behind and come with her. But I didn't. I knew the only direction I wanted to go was backward. I knew, more than anything else in the world, I wanted to come back.

"So, I thought of you. Of the life we could have had. The mistakes I made. That last day, there was a moment standing on top of the hill just before the battle. I knew I could die and it put everything into perspective. My only fear in the world, was not the army we faced; it was never holding you in my arms again. I didn't care why you lied. I knew you loved me. Even then, I knew it was real. The minute I left, I wanted to come back. To tell you how I really felt. But it was too late."

He moved a hand to my waist, circling the welt from the Kraken with his thumb as his lips found mine again. So gentle and slow, he began. A tease of his tongue as his hands moved higher. Until he caressed my breasts in his hand, kneading as he pinched my nipple, sending a rush of desire straight to my thighs. He laid me across the deck, the heat from the sun warming the planks to an almost unbearable degree, and my back arched against the warmth.

"You are everything." He slid his fingers across my throat, brushing the hollow before he leaned in and kissed every inch his fingers had traveled.

"I need you to know that when it came down to it, I was going to swim away," I said. "They captured me in a net. I dropped the charm, hoping they couldn't get on the island without it. I'm so sorry. I should have come to you."

"I would have moved the world for you. If that's what you'd needed, it would have been done. I love you. I loved you then. I would have destroyed them all, just to bring you peace. I forgive you, Lyra. We'll move forward together." He brought his forehead to mind, teasing filling his eyes. "Did we learn our lesson?"

I smirked, still lying flat on our ship. "I don't know. I might need to be punished."

He tsked. "Maybe later."

Hooking his arms around my legs, he spread me wide open and pressed his mouth to my clit. I moaned in sheer pleasure as I felt the throbbing begin immediately. That tender spot grew more and more sensitive as his tongue stroked back and forth. Sliding two fingers down my wetness, he locked his eyes with mine as he slipped them inside of me, causing another arch of my back in answer.

"Tell me what you want, Vixen. Tell me what makes you feel good."

"That." I panted, as he pressed his mouth back over me, working his tongue in unison with his fingers. "I want that until you hear me scream. And then I want every inch of you as slow as you can bear it. I want to feel you pulsing inside of me."

I knew he could barely handle the words and the sounds I made, but when the climax rose, and my scream was only a breath away. He stopped.

"Kai," I groaned.

He smiled down at me. "I want to go together, my love. Everywhere you go, I want to go with you. I've missed you so, so much."

He slid his naked body up mine until the slick tip of his shaft rested against my opening. I lifted my hips and he slammed forward, taking me right back to the peak. Pure bliss racked my body as he pulled out and slammed himself back into me, finding a slow but hard pace. Face strained, he leaned down and bit my neck, the sensation painful until it melted into sheer bliss.

Higher and higher we climbed until his thrusts were no longer slow, and my whimpering turned to something wild and unrestrained. He lifted my hips, ramming forward as a guttural sound left him and that was it. I clenched, riding waves of euphoria as he spilled his seed into me, breath ragged and corded muscles straining.

He leaned down, kissing the bite mark gently, then moved to my lips. "Okay?" he whispered against them.

I shifted, feeling him grow hard again while still inside me. "Utterly perfect."

"Yes, my siren. You are."

EPILOGUE

KAITALEN

"I take no responsibility for this," Lyra said from beside me as I held her hand.

"That's fine. I'll blame Doris."

She giggled and it was the most beautiful sound in the world. "You're lucky that hydra loves you."

"Everyone loves me. I'm lovable."

"Okay," she said, shaking her head as she looked over the great expanse of ocean.

We stood on the cliffs I'd leaped from as a child to save a little girl. Never in a million years could I have guessed that choice would lead me to this moment, but though I'd walked through death, I'd do it all again, just to be here.

I'd lied to Lyra. Death was not just an empty black room, but something far more haunting as I lived through all the moments of my own life, the judgment of each decision weighing me down. I couldn't protect myself from my memories. It started like reading a book, turning each page of my past, reliving each moment. Standing before my mother when she loved me, playing sword fights with Fen and Greeve, racing through the streets of Halemi chasing females, and then everything changed. Morphed into something to fear. Each memory twisted into something horrific and terrifying. The God of Death wanted me to leave the doorstep of the Ether. She believed her game of torment would push me forward to officially leave my life behind. Instead, I endured it, believing in my mate, even when she didn't believe in herself. Refusing to believe the world was done with me.

Her beautiful hair caught in the wind, threading across her lashes. The spray of the ocean waves crashing into the cliffs, soaking us as we watched the point where the sky met the sea. Our spot, far in the distance.

I pulled her to me, stroking her light hair back into place as I leaned down and kissed her again. Something I'd never tire of doing. "Don't worry, I'll take all the credit for this pure stroke of genius."

"But a bedsheet?"

I tugged her hand, beginning our journey toward the castle. "Trust me."

She laughed, following. The trail back was similar, but different. As if the world held more vibrant colors, as if the warmth of the sun seeped a little further into my skin. The genuine smile on my face held and we sank into the deep red sand as we walked. Bumping her hip with mine, Lyra dropped my hand and raced away, looking over her shoulder as she giggled. I chased her, finding more bliss in that simple moment than I'd known in my whole life. I caught her easily, wrapping my hands around her from behind and swinging her around as I growled in her ear.

She squirmed in my arms until I put her down and we stopped to kiss again. I didn't care if we never made it to the castle, so lost in appreciating each moment. I contemplated laying her down on the sand, intertwining my fingers with hers as I took her slow and steady. I would never get enough of her.

She'd hurt me, but she could hurt me a thousand times over and I think I'd still come crawling back. Because every bad moment with her was worth a million good moments alone. I hadn't understood it with Fen and Greeve. Why they'd let themselves suffer the complications of having a mate. Until I'd found my own and realized there was no choice. It was worth it. All of it.

We entered the castle through the back, creeping into the kitchen. I stood, my heart aching, as I watched Loti mixing something in her favorite wooden bowl. Tight silver curls swaying as she worked. I'd forgotten how much I loved her until I'd spent time recollecting how she'd looked over us all since we were kids. She was our family.

I cleared my throat, hoping not to startle her. Lyra took a step back and Loti stiffened, turning slowly as if she knew who she'd see when she turned. As if she remembered every tiny sound the children of her heart made. The bowl in her arms crashed to the floor as her eyes filled with tears. The tip of my nose tingled, threatening to expose my own swelling heart as I crossed the kitchen in three giant strides, swept her up, and swung her around like I'd done a million times.

She held me tight, burying her face in the crook of my neck as she wept. "My boy," she whispered. "My sweet boy."

I set her down gently, but she held on for dear life. "What time is lunch?" I muttered into her ear.

She finally pulled away, laughing so hard she snorted. "It really is you." Straightening her apron, she looked around me to see Lyra standing there. She held her arms open and waited for her to step into them. "You brought my boy back. I don't know how you've managed it, but thank you."

Though I could feel the hesitation through our bond, she hugged Loti anyway, and as we left the kitchens, Loti promised the biggest lunch of my life. She knew the direct path to my heart, and I loved her for it.

"Can you do your sneaky siren thing and find me a bedsheet?"

"Are you sure this is what you want to do?" Lyra narrowed her eyes at me, which only boosted my confidence.

"It's going to be the greatest moment of my life." I beamed.

In no time at all, she returned, a massive white bedsheet in her arms. "I think I'll wait here. Let you get caught up."

"Are you sure? You should come."

She reached forward and patted my shoulder. "I'm sure. Have your moment. I'll be here when you're done."

I shrugged and threw the sheet over my head. "I can't see."

"Yes. That's generally what happens when covering your eyes." She moved in front of me and ripped at the fabric with her sharp nails until two small holes appeared. "Better?"

"Perfect."

I wound through the halls of the castle I'd grown up in. Loti had told me there was a presentation in the great hall and that's where I'd find them. When I rounded the corner and found them all there, Fen, Greeve, Ara, Wren, Rhogan, Temir, Nadra, a small blond boy, and a few others, I leaned against the doorframe and watched through the holes of the sheet, as they stared up at an object cloaked in a long crimson fabric, shoulder to shoulder.

There was a time when I thought I'd never see them again. Each of their faces had flashed through my mind as I'd lain beneath the talons of the harpies that killed me. My heart ached then just as it did now, staring at the backs of my family.

The older fae holding the small boy's hand stepped forward and yanked the fabric away, revealing a larger-than-life statue made of glass. Wren's wail filled the room as she took in my carved face. Stunned, I pulled the sheet from my head and inched forward for a better view. Sniffles from Ara wrenched my heart.

"He was always the best of us." Fen's voice broke, and even though I couldn't see his face, I could hear the sorrow laced within his words.

I noted the conch shell at my feet and the sword in my hand. Though I'd hidden a lot of my doubt and frustration from my family, they had still known me so well. Even in the details.

"So, this is what you do all day now? Stand around and stare at me?"

Gasping, they turned. Wren was in my arms before I even saw her running. "Kai? Is it really you?"

"It's really me, baby bird."

She moved away and Fen was next. He faltered for a moment,

blinking rapidly before he punched me as hard as he could in the shoulder. "We have got to stop sacrificing ourselves for each other. I suppose now I owe you a life debt."

I wiggled my brows as I rubbed the pain away. "That did work out well for me last time."

Ara shoved him aside and leaped into my arms. "I fucking missed you."

"There's that dirty mouth." I laughed, swinging her around. "I missed you too."

Setting her down, she stepped to the side as Greeve moved in for a quick hug. His eyes were darker and heavier than I'd seen and then I realized Gaea wasn't here and there was a second cloaked statue.

"How?" he asked. "Just tell me how."

I glanced at Fen, recognizing the shadow of death lingering above him. Not to strike him down, but something like a mark, showing me that we'd both been there and somehow come back. I couldn't look at my friend and tell him I didn't know, but I also couldn't promise him something he'd spend his life chasing. I pulled away, searching my mind for something to say, but nothing felt right.

"Someday," he said in answer. "I'll find a way."

"I'll help you, brother. Whatever it takes."

He nodded. We stood shoulder to shoulder as the fae from before whipped the second piece of fabric from Gaea's memorial. A small cry came from the boy at Greeve's other side and he lifted him up, stepping closer as they studied her likeness and cried together. My brother reached forward, laying his hand on hers as he stroked the small ring on her finger. Only then did I see a golden band on his own.

We stood there for a very long time. Eventually, Lyra joined us, taking my hand as we slowly crowded in toward Greeve. Until we were all surrounding him in one giant hug as he fell to his knees and wept with the boy in his arms. As every what-if and question of what could have been lingered above him. His heartache was nearly unbearable to witness. Ara was the first to pull away, shielding her face as she swept out of the room.

Hours later, we gathered for lunch, which was every bit the feast Loti had promised. Though our hearts were heavy, they were also lifted. My presence was bittersweet. I was surprised to find how close Lyra had become to Wren and Rhogan, who had lost a wing in the battle. They joked and even tossed food at each other and something in the way she nestled right into my family flooded me with pride.

Fen stood, clanging his fork against his wine glass as he gathered everyone's attention. "A toast," he said, lifting his glass. I moved to push my chair out, assuming he meant me, but froze as he said, "To Lyra. Who brought my brother back from the Ether by sheer stubbornness and incredible luck. Thank you, siren."

Wren snorted and nudged me as I fell back into my chair. "It's not all about you," she whispered.

I lifted my glass toward my mate, who blushed but returned the gesture. Turning to Wren, I clinked her glass. "I mean… I didn't see your statue in there."

She giggled. "The room wasn't big enough. Thank goodness it didn't have to hold your ego too."

I shoved a slice of bread slathered with yellow jam into my mouth and smiled. "Good thing it wasn't one of those naked statues. Might not have fit."

Mid chew I gasped, leaping from my seat, effectively lodging the bread into my throat. I began choking and Fen flew around the room, beating me on the back as if that was going to help me swallow. Eventually, I worked the bite down.

"Guess we're even now." He grinned, socking me one more time.

I nearly lost my train of thought until I remembered the most important thing I'd ever learned. "Did you guys know sharks have two penises?"

THE END

ACKNOWLEDGMENTS

To the readers first, thank you so much for pushing through this story. It definitely had one of those book-throwing moments when you just can't find it in you to go on. When you're so mad at what happened to a beloved character, it seems nothing else matters.

But this story was never about Kai. As much as we love him and his silly jokes (because everyone needs a pirate hat, right?) it just wasn't. This story was about a survivor. Someone that thought she was strong enough to take on anything. And then we watched her fail. And fail again. Until there was nothing left. Because that's where heroines are born from. The ashes of their failures.

And I know people are going to feel some kind of way about resurrecting someone that died. But for each of you that hates when that happens, there are three more begging for this story to be written. And so, it was.

I may never #bringherback but also, I might. And if I do, it'll be the most amazing story I've ever written. Gaea was a hard loss, on me as the writer and on the readers. But her story is incredible. Kidnapped at a young age, she was raised in a castle full of people that hated her, just like they did Temir. Only she didn't handle it the same way. She became destructive and an escapist and many toxic things that made her one of the most relatable characters ever. And Greeve? Poor Greeve, may live buried in his namesake for the rest of his long life, but I bet if you asked him if he'd rather forget it ever happened, if *he* could have those memories taken, he'd take your life before you finished that sentence. He has but one regret, that he couldn't save her.

To my daughters… Stop growing. Don't leave me. Boys are stupid.

To Dustin… This is the year we both chase our dreams, my love. We have crazy, wild plans, but look how far we've come. We have only the world left to conquer. I'll go with you.

To Darby and Claire… My dream team… I think about all the things I want to say to you. To place into this book for eternity, and nothing compares to what's in my heart. Thank you for dragging me, kicking and screaming, through the very last page of a trillion edits on this book. Darby, you know this one's for you. The story that was never going to be written. I hope I've done him justice. That you close this book one final time with a deep sigh, satisfied through the very end. Tides and Ruin was a year of hard work, but there wasn't a day when you weren't there beside me and I'll never find the worlds to thank you both for that. Be it one breast or two, scratchy sheets, or tears underwater, you remained steadfast in your faith in me. I love you both.

To Taire… You have been here for me before anyone else. When I had no idea what I wanted, only that I needed you as a cover artist. And that desire has never faded. All of my future plans start with what the covers will be. Like you, I'm a visual person, which is why I put so much time into the aesthetic of my books. But you read them. Even when you didn't have to. And you were one of the first to read this story. And you loved it all, right when I needed that pick me up. I am so honored to have you on my team. I couldn't imagine a step of this journey without you and your kind soul. Thank you.

To Nichole… my writing buddy, my friend, my lover of all things spiritual… I just love you. Where would I be without you on this journey. Every word of this book was written in tandem with yours. The hours and hours we spent sprinting just created this unique bond between us and I'm forever grateful for you. You pushed me when I needed it, shoved me when I needed it. Gave me a big old dose of reality when I needed it and did it with absolutely no grace. Because as much as I love you, you're also a dick.

To Jess… My biggest cheerleader, one of my oldest friends and my constant. Without you, I wouldn't be able to keep writing these books. You're never lacking for a compliment and everyone just needs one of those kind of people in their corner. We're still learning the ropes together, but it's always easier knowing I have you in my corner.

To Karley… oh my Karley… My sweet alpha reader that sent me a completely nude, sobbing picture of herself after chapter twenty-five… the answer is still no. But I love that you never forget to ask… just in case. The world is a better place because you're in it.

To Chloe…Thank you for reading this book when it was hard to find time to read and devouring it as thoroughly as it needed. I'm so grateful for your feedback, but more so for the friendship that bloomed because of it.

To my street team… I'll never be able to thank you all for everything you've done for my entire Fae Rising series, from the women that have been with me from day one, to our new crew… you all inspire me daily. You are moms, and wives, and influencers, and women that make time to help build people up. You waited so patiently to read this book, knowing I was coming in hard just to break your hearts. And you let me. And then you took the time to shout about this book from the rooftops. You've recruited friends, you've recruited strangers, you've never backed down when something needed done. I've always credited my street team for the success of this series and I stand by that. You are the reasons my dreams come true. Thank you. I couldn't have hand crafted a better team than this one.

And finally… to my Mick. This was the acknowledgement I didn't want to write. I didn't want to cry through it. Yet here I am… a glutton for punishment as I credit the kind heart of an old dog. I didn't want to love you when we first brought you home. You were so clumsy and you knocked over the baby all the time. You ripped up brand new carpet and ate expensive sunglasses. But somehow, you stole my heart anyway. An old soul buried within the heart of a boxer. As I struggled through this story, you struggled through the last days of your life. You loved me harder than I deserved and there will never be another like you. I'll see you there, buddy! You were the BEST boy.

ABOUT THE AUTHOR

Tides and Ruin is Miranda Lyn's fourth novel. She grew up smack dab in the middle of the United States with nothing to do but dream up stories of fantastical creatures and powerful heroines. Now married with three children of her own, an idea sparked a buried passion within her to follow a dream and teach her children that anything is possible if you're willing to work hard for it. Be sure to check out her social media!

Instagram: https://www.instagram.com/authormirandalyn/

Facebook: https://www.facebook.com/authormirandalyn/

Twitter: https://twitter.com/AuthorMirandaL

Check out our website for extras, character art, and exclusive content. www.faerising.com

Also, click here to sign up for the mailing list and get access to more exclusive content and giveaways!

https://www.faerising.com/subscribe

www.ingramcontent.com/pod-product-compliance
Lightning Source LLC
Chambersburg PA
CBHW020246030826
48979CB00030B/2632/J